CW00971961

The Circles of Archimedes

PADRAIC FALLON

The Circles of Archimedes

LINTOTT PRESS
Manchester and Glasgow

First published in 2009 by
Lintott Press
Manchester and Glasgow

ISBN 978 1 84777 104 9

Printed and bound in England by SRP Ltd, Exeter

For Nancy – and Conor

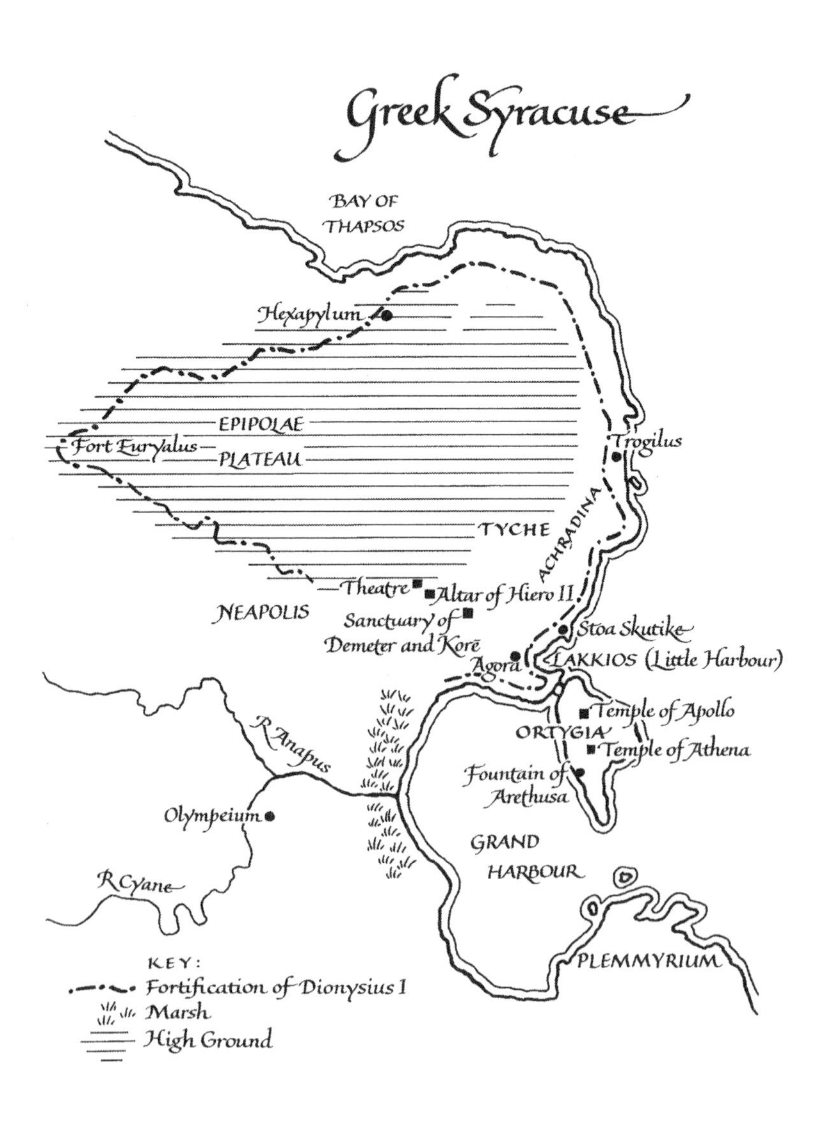
Greek Syracuse
BAY OF
THAPSOS
Hexapylum
EPIPOLAE
Fort Euryalus
PLATEAU
Trogilus
ACHRADINA
TYCHE
Theatre
Altar of Hiero II
NEAPOLIS
Sanctuary of
Demeter and Korē
Stoa Skutike
Agora
LAKKIOS (Little Harbour)
Temple of Apollo
ORTYGIA
Temple of Athena
R Anapus
Fountain of
Arethusa
Olympeium
GRAND
HARBOUR
R Cyane
PLEMMYRIUM
KEY:
Fortification of Dionysius I
Marsh
High Ground

Preface

I once imagined a dreamy man who fell asleep on a sunny autumn day on the side of Silbury Hill and woke with a solution to the oldest mathematical mystery of all, the secret of *pi*, the elusive proportion in every circle. It was probably inspired by my first sight of the hill and of the stone circles in the great henge of Avebury which lies nearby. My imagination was certainly prompted by descriptions of how serious modern mathematicians devoted their lives (many still do) to finding such a solution, more than two millennia after Archimedes of Syracuse had discovered a close approximation to it.

In time these led me to the circle itself and what it symbolised to the Stone Age peoples, its importance to the Babylonian astronomers who first divided it and the mathematicians of Ancient Greece who tried to square it. I read of the perfectly circular cosmos that the Ancient Greeks saw, of its importance as an ideal to Plato, and later yet I read of the significance to the psychologists Jung and Neumann of the circular images that are common in different religions and cultures everywhere. It occurred to me then that perhaps Archimedes saw something more fundamental than a circle of geometry in his wax tablets before a Roman soldier killed him.

The full moon was the earliest circle that the ancients saw, a round full of vitality and light that waned, then vanished each month before it reappeared as a silver bow and grew into a circle once more. It has proved to be the earliest calendar, its cycle carved on bone by Stone Age man. The Moon Goddess, the symbol of the universal Great Goddess herself, was probably the first deity, bringer of life and death, rain and health and fertility, a universal image across civilisations in different geographies that is particularly well described in Jules Cashford's works. The moon must have been the first object in the heavens that the earliest scientific astronomers studied as they gazed at the night sky over the Euphrates, perched on the ziggurats of Babylon where religion and astronomy fused and the spherical dome above was divided by them into a circle of 360 degrees. When the Greeks introduced geometry into astronomy, the moon at its full, with its mythical implications to them, probably inspired the concept of the perfect circle and the spherical cosmos that Euclid and the philosophers assumed. To square that circle became a legendary challenge to the Greeks, a challenge that found its way into their drama. The infinite mystery of what the Greek mathematicians found when they failed has intrigued their successors down the ages.

The genius who found a practical way through this great intellectual challenge of antiquity, yet left the circle with its mystery intact, was someone who swam in the stream of Greek learning and philosophy as it continued to flow after the death of Alexander the Great and the succession of his generals, when knowledge was prized and the search for truth and learning was generally uninhibited by religion or persecution. It was an era that would not recur. The book burners did not yet exist, nor did the society that frowned on Darwin. The Greek philosophers who gathered at the Library of Alexandria were probably the last truly free people on earth, devoid of guilt at being born into the human race, unaware of any conflict between truth and religion. I saw them as adventurous Mediterranean people in an Orphic tradition, seeking the beauty of truth.

The figure of Archimedes, through a kind of natural selection, shone out to me as an outstanding example of the type. I chose him as the hero initially because of his approach to measuring the area of the circle, then I began to glimpse the genius in him, the essential freshness that scholars such as Reviel Netz see in his work, the intellectual discipline that demanded a proof for every proposition he wrote, even as I welcomed the opportunity his presence in the work gave me to explore his world. Little is known for certain of him beyond his works and a few bare facts, so I began to imagine him, to try to gather his bones, as it were, and to put flesh on them. At some point in the process he seemed to breathe and live again, to think once more, to speak to me. I began to see his surroundings, his household, his father the astronomer

AEGATES ISLANDS
Phorbantia
Hiera
Aegusa
Motya
Lilybaeum
Drepanum
Segesta
Panormus
Cephaloedium
Mylae
Pt Pelorus
Messana (Zancle)
R. Asines (Acesines)
Tauromenium
Naxos
Mt Aetna
Selinus
Mt. Cronium
Enna
Catane
IONIAN SEA
Heraclea Minoa
R. Himera
Morgantina
Akragas
Leontinoi
Mt. Ecnomus
Megara Hyblaea
R. Anapus
R. Gelas
Gela
Syracuse
Pt Plemmyrium
R. Helorus
Hellenistic Sicily
Camarina
Helorus
Pt Pachynus

whose personality seemed to emerge naturally as I wrote, the customs and civilisation of the Hellenistic era, and the old Greek city of Syracuse with its temples and its theatre. I speculated on the influences on him as a man of his times, on his work and on his personality and spirit, and developed a great affection for the Archimedes of my imagination as he acquired a persona that seemed in keeping with the tone of the letters of his that we have. These prefaced his works that survived, and suggested to me a generous, sometimes mischievous man, humorous, spiritual, energetic and positive, someone who demonstrated that the Heroic tradition of the Greeks lived still as he defended his city against the Romans, a true Greek philosopher with a restless intellectual curiosity that was never in conflict with the psychic communion he felt with the goddess Artemis, the protectress of Syracuse, the Goddess of the Full Moon. Above all, the character who appeared so vividly to me was an intensely human person whose curiosity refused to die with him, who saw an objective reality that he described so carefully in his work, a man whose shade survived to speak through his goddess to someone in the present era.

The ancients, of course, often shared their gods, or absorbed them from other cultures and renamed them. Aengus of the Birds has been described as the Apollo of the Old Irish. Brigid or Bridget was clearly a female deity in the tradition of the universal Great Goddess, as were Isis, Artemis and the Virgin Mary, among many others. Seth was an aboriginal god of Upper Egypt who became a paradigm for Satan. The pantheon of the Greeks easily became that of the Romans, when Zeus became Jupiter and Artemis, Diana. The goddess that the Stone Age peoples worshipped at Avebury and Newgrange and the other Stone Age sites as the Goddess of the Moon was probably interchangeable with the goddess to whom the Minoan Cretans offered at Knossos, with Isis of Egypt, with Artemis and Athene, and with Gaia, the virgin mother of the first Olympians. The Great Goddess, as Graves wrote and as Marija Gimbutas proved in her research into the artefacts of the Stone Age, was a universal image among early mankind, a protean deity who was the Earth itself, the bearer of the womb of life, an image that survives in the collective unconscious to this day. Because of the particular association of Greek

Syracuse with its protector goddess, it seemed very credible to me that Archimedes saw her as Artemis of the silver bow.

It seemed natural, too, that the man to whom the shade of Archimedes would speak would be someone most likely to enter into a communion with him. I chose a figure drawn loosely from the myth of Aengus the god, who would take the labour Archimedes set him as seriously as he would take the people he encountered in his own life. These last, like Aengus, were also loosely taken from myth, and I drew them to show what I see – however reluctantly – as the unchanging character of human nature since man first stood, as capable of selfless love or brutal acts now as he was in the beginning. Anyone who finds it incredible, for instance, that in the twenty-first century a person may be effectively held captive for a long period by a relative with a terrible purpose need look no further than the daily news.

Through it all, something else seemed clear to me, and that was what the ancients sometimes saw, why some of the myths they built and the visions of Creation of which they sang seem remarkably close to what the physicists see today, and why the collective memory of all life may carry the image of its ultimate origin in the first fire festival, the moment of Creation.

Acknowledgements

I owe a great debt to Michael Schmidt of Lintott Press for appointing Helen Tookey as the editor of this work. Helen edited the book with a definite yet light touch, and she is not responsible for my deliberate distortions of Hellenistic history. The tomb of Alexander probably did not rest in Alexandria until Ptolemy IV (Philopator) moved the body from Memphis in 215 BC. I have placed it there earlier, in the time of Ptolemy II (Philadelphus), Pharaoh of Egypt during the earlier lifetime of Archimedes. I did so because its legendary magnificence and ugliness seemed to sum up the culture of the Greek Pharaohs. Neither do I have any grounds to suggest that Archimedes was the first Greek to discover how the priests of the Nile forecast the height of the annual inundation so accurately. I jump a century or so for convenience when I write of the degrees of an arc or an angle, as the Greeks did not adopt the degree as a measurement from the Babylonians until the second century BC. The rest of the book is generally built around facts as far as I could establish them, but where they were lacking I made assumptions or used my imagination, reminding myself that I was writing a novel, not a history. This freed me to send Archimedes to Eleusis and Thermopylae, and to elaborate on the Roman attack on Syracuse. Archimedes may have met the poet Callimachus at Alexandria if one takes the estimated dates for both as fact, but there is no evidence that he did. Neither do we have proof that the mathematician even went to Alexandria, but we do know that he corresponded on a friendly basis with Eratosthenes who became Librarian, and with Dositheus, making it probable that he visited or studied there. Perhaps it was while he was at the Library that he developed an interest in military catapults, a possibility suggested by Serafina Cuomo. Similarly I have assumed, as the mathematical historians seem to have done, that he was later than Euclid, perhaps by a generation or two.

The champion of this book until his death was my brother Conor, whose wife Nancy read an early draft before she predeceased him. Conor encouraged me throughout, from the first draft to the one that lay by his bed when he died. He saw the book's many flaws, too, and pointed them out to the last, encouraging me to cut this and expand that, to build an aura around the characters to lift them above the ordinary, and to strengthen the thread throughout the work. I did not tell him that I built the personality of Aengus around him.

Jane Miller helped me with research nearer to home, and encouraged me with her customary good humour to write the best book I could.

My wife Gillian came with me to see what remains of Greek Syracuse, to the remains of the walls of Dionysius I, the Altar of Hiero, the Fountain of Arethusa, the Theatre, the temple of Athene (now the cathedral of Syracuse) and of Apollo, the wonderful Museum of Paolo Orsi, and the Fort of Euryalus, where the wildflowers flourished on the morning we went there. We boated up the Ciane river to see the papyrus that legend says was planted by Archimedes, and around the harbours and the shoreline of Ortygia. The notes she took found their way into the book, and the patience and loyalty she showed enabled me to write it.

My thanks go to all of these, and my apologies to anyone I have unintentionally omitted.

Bibliography

Alsop, Joseph, *From the Silent Earth*, Harper & Row, 1962

Angel, Heather, and Pat Wolseley, *The Family Water Naturalist*, Michael Joseph, 1982

Archimedes, *Works*, ed. T. L. Heath, Dover, 1912

Aristotle, *Metaphysics*, Penguin, 2004

Arnold, Dieter, Lanny Bell, Ragnhild Bjerre Finnestad, Gerhard Haeny and Byron E. Shafer, *The Temples of Ancient Egypt*, Cornell University Press, 1997

Bagnall, Nigel, *The Punic Wars 264–146 BC*, Osprey, 2002

Baring, Anne, and Jules Cashford, *The Myth of the Goddess*, Penguin, 1993

Barton, Tamsin, *Ancient Astrology*, Routledge, 1994

Bastian, Hartmut, *And Then Came Man*, Viking, 1964

Bayley, Harold, *The Lost Language of Symbolism*, Volumes I and II, Ernest Benn, 1996

Beckmann, Peter, *A History of Pi*, St Martin's, 1971

Belozerskaya, Marina, and Kenneth Lapatin, *Ancient Greece*, British Museum Press, 2004

Berlinski, David, *Infinite Ascent*, Phoenix, 2006

Boyer, Carl B., *A History of Mathematics*, Princeton University Press, 1968

Braudel, Fernand, *The Mediterranean and the Mediterranean World*, Volume I, University of California Press, 1996

Browning, Robert (ed.), *The Greek World*, Thames & Hudson, 1985

Buck, Philo M., Jr, *The Golden Thread*, Macmillan, 1931

Burckhardt, Jacob, *History of Greek Culture*, Constable, 1963

Callimachus, *Aetia, Iambi, Hecale and Other Fragments*, ed. and trans. C. A. Trypanis, Harvard University Press, 1968

Campbell, Duncan B., *Greek and Roman Artillery 399 BC–AD 363*, Osprey, 2003

Campbell, Joseph, *Myths to Live By*, Paladin, 1985

— *The Inner Reaches of Outer Space*, New World Library, 2002

Cashford, Jules, *The Moon – Myth and Image*, Octopus, 2003

Casson, Lionel, *Travel in the Ancient World*, Johns Hopkins University Press, 1974

Caven, Brian, *The Punic Wars*, Weidenfeld & Nicolson, 1980

Chandler, John, *Wiltshire: A History of its Landscape and People*, Volume I, Hobnob Press, 2001
Chugg, Andrew Michael, *The Lost Tomb of Alexander the Great*, Periplus, 2004
Collignon, Maxime, *A Manual of Greek Archaeology*, Cassell & Company, 1886
Cotterill, H. B., *Ancient Greece*, George G. Harrap, 1913
Crawford, O. G. S., *The Eye Goddess*, Phoenix House, 1957
Cuomo, S., *Pappus of Alexandria and the Mathematics of Late Antiquity*, Cambridge University Press, 2000
— *Ancient Mathematics*, Routledge, 2001
Curtis, Neil, *The Ridgeway*, Aurum Press, 1989
Dames, Michael, *The Avebury Cycle*, Thames & Hudson, 1996
Dijksterhuis, E. J., *Archimedes*, Princeton University Press, 1987
Diodorus Siculus, *Library of History* Books XIX.66–XX, trans. Russel M. Geer, Loeb Classical Library, 1954
Ducat, Jean, *Spartan Education*, trans. Emma Stafford, P. J. Shaw and Anton Powell, Classical Press of Wales, 2006
Durando, Furio, *Greece: Splendours of an Ancient Civilization*, Thames & Hudson, 1997
Dutta, Shomit (ed.), *Greek Tragedy*, Penguin, 2004
El Mahdy, Christine, *The Pyramid Builder*, Headline, 2003
Evans, James, *The History and Practice of Ancient Astronomy*, Oxford University Press, 1998
Evslin, Bernard, *Gods, Demigods and Demons*, I. B. Taurus, 2006
Fletcher, Joann, *The Egyptian Book of Living and Dying*, Thorsons, 2002
Flower, Derek Adie, *The Shore of Wisdom*, Pharos, 1999
Frayn, Michael, *The Human Touch*, Faber & Faber, 2006
Freeman, Charles, *Egypt, Greece and Rome*, Oxford University Press, 1999
Gardiner, E. Norman, *Athletics of the Ancient World*, Ares, 1930
Gardner Wilkinson, J., *The Ancient Egyptians: Their Life and Customs*, Volume I, Senate, 1994
Gimbutas, Marija, *The Language of the Goddess*, Thames & Hudson, 1989
Goddio, Franck, *Alexandria: The Submerged Royal Quarters*, Periplus Ltd, 1998
Goldstein, Rebecca, *Incompleteness: The Proof and Paradox of Kurt Gödel*, W. W. Norton, 2005
Grattan-Guinness, Ivor, *The Rainbow of Mathematics*, Harper Collins, 1997
Graves, Robert, *The White Goddess*, Faber & Faber, 1948
— *The Greek Myths*, Folio Society, 1996
Green, Peter, *Alexander the Great and the Hellenistic Age*, Weidenfeld &

Nicolson, 2007
Greenidge, A. H. J., *Roman Public Life*, Macmillan, 1901
Gregory, Andrew, *Eureka! The Birth of Science*, Icon, 2001
Hamilton, Edward, *The River-side Naturalist*, Sampson Low, Marston, Searle & Rivington, 1890
Hansen, Mogens Herman, *Polis: An Introduction to the Ancient Greek City State*, Oxford University Press, 2006
Hardy, G. H., *A Mathematician's Apology*, Canto, 1992
Harris, W. V., and Giovanni Raffini (eds.), *Ancient Alexandria between Egypt and Greece*, Brill Academic, 2004
Harrison, Miranda, *Ancient Egypt and the Afterlife*, Scala, 2002
Harwit, Martin, *Cosmic Discovery: The Search, Scope and Heritage of Astronomy*, Harvester, 1981
Heath, Robin, *Sun, Moon, Earth*, Wooden Books, 2001
Heath, Sir Thomas, *Aristarchus of Samos*, Oxford University Press, 1913
Heer, Friedrich, *The Intellectual History of Europe*, Volumes I and II, Doubleday Anchor, 1968
Herodotus, *The Histories*, Penguin, 2004
Hobson, E. W., *Squaring the Circle*, Merchant, 2007
Hornblower, Simon, and Antony Spawforth (eds.), *The Oxford Classical Dictionary*, Third Revised Edition, Oxford University Press, 2003
Richard Humble, *Warfare in the Ancient World*, Cassell, 1980
Jannelli, Lorena, and Fausto Longo, *The Greeks in Sicily*, Arsenale Editrice, 2004
Jenkins, G. K., *Ancient Greek Coins*, Barrie & Jenkins, 1972
Journal of Hellenic Studies, Volume 114, *The Unity of Callimachus' Hymn to Artemis*, 1994
Judge, Harry (ed.), *The Oxford Illustrated Encyclopaedia: World History from Earliest Times to 1800*, Guild, 1988
Jung, C. G., *Man and his Symbols*, Dell, 1964
— *Dreams*, trans. R. F. C. Hull, Routledge, 2002
Keller, Werner, *The Etruscans*, Bookclub Associates, 1975
Kingsley, Peter, *In the Dark Places of Wisdom*, Element Books, 1999
Kinzl, Konrad H. (ed.), *A Companion to the Classical Greek World*, Blackwell, 2006
Koestler, Arthur, *The Act of Creation*, Hutchinson, 1969
Larson, Jennifer, *Ancient Greek Cults*, Routledge, 2007
Lawrence, A. W., *Greek Architecture*, ed. Nikolaus Pevsner and Judy Nairn, Penguin, 1957
Lefkowitz, Mary, *Greek Gods, Human Lives*, Yale University Press, 2003
Levy, G. Rachel, *The Gate of Horn*, Faber, 1948
— *Plato in Sicily*, Faber & Faber, 1956

— *The Phoenix' Nest*, Rider & Company, 1961
Lincoln, Frances, *The Garden of Greek Verse*, 2000
Lousley, J. E., *Wildflowers of Chalk and Limestone*, Collins New Naturalist Series, Bloomsbury, 1990
Lunn, Sir Henry, *Aegean Civilizations*, Epworth Press, 1929
Macleod, Roy (ed.), *The Library of Alexandria*, I. B. Taurus, 2004
Margulis, Lynn, and Dorion Sagan, *What is Life?*, Weidenfeld & Nicolson, 1995
Marshall, Peter, *Europe's Lost Civilization*, Headline, 2004
McKenzie, A. E. E., *Hydrostatics and Mechanics*, Cambridge University Press, 1941
McLynn, Frank, *Carl Gustav Jung*, St Martin's Press, 1996
Messineo, G., and E. Borgia, *Ancient Sicily*, Getty, 2006
Monod, Jacques, *Chance and Necessity*, Collins, 1971
Moore, Bob, and Maxine Moore, *Dictionary of Latin and Greek Origins*, Barnes & Noble, 1997
Morrison, J. S., *Greek and Roman Oared Warships 399 BC–30 BC*, Oxbow, 1996
Murray, Margaret A., *The Splendour that was Egypt*, Sidgwick & Jackson, 1961
Nataf, André, *Dictionary of the Occult*, Wordsworth Editions, 1994
Netz, Reviel, *The Shaping of Deduction in Greek Mathematics*, Cambridge University Press, 1999
— *The Transformation of Mathematics in the Early Mediterranean World*, Cambridge University Press, 2004
— and William Noel, *The Archimedes Codex*, Weidenfeld & Nicolson, 2007
Neumann, Erich, *The Great Mother*, trans. Ralph Manheim, Routledge & Kegan Paul, 1955
— *The Origins and History of Consciousness*, H. Karnac, 1989
Norwich, John Julius, *The Middle Sea*, Vintage, 2007
O'Leary, De Lacy, *Arabic Thought and its Place in History*, Routledge & Kegan Paul, 1968
Oakes, Lorna, and Lucia Galilin, *Ancient Egypt*, Anness, 2002
Orrieux, Claude, and Pauline Schmitt Pantel, *A History of Ancient Greece*, Blackwell, 1999
Plutarch, *Greek Lives*, trans. Robin Waterfield, Oxford University Press, 1998
Powell, Anton, and Stephen Hodkinson (eds.), *Sparta Beyond the Mirage*, Classical Press of Wales, 2002
Quennell, Marjorie, and C. H. B. Quennell (eds.), *Everyday Things in Ancient Greece*, revised by Kathleen Freeman, Batsford, 1968
Ridpath, Ian, *Astronomy*, Dorling Kindersley, 2006

Russell, Bertrand, *Wisdom of the West*, ed. Paul Foulkes, Macdonald, 1959
Sagan, Carl, and Ann Druyan, *Shadows of Forgotten Ancestors*, Random House, 1992
Samivel, *The Glory of Greece*, Thames & Hudson, 1962
Schmidt, Michael, *The First Poets*, Vintage, 2005
Schofield, Louise, *The Mycenaeans*, British Museum Press, 2007
Service, Alastair, and Jean Bradbery, *Megaliths and their Mysteries*, Weidenfeld & Nicolson, 1979
Shaw, Ian, and Paul Nicholson, *The Dictionary of Ancient Egypt*, Harry N. Abrams, 1995
Singer, Charles, *A Short History of Science to the 19th Century*, Dover, 1997
Spawforth, Tony, *The Complete Greek Temples*, Thames & Hudson, 2006
Stobart, J. C., *The Glory that was Greece*, Sidgwick & Jackson, 1949
Talbert, Richard J. A. (ed.), *Atlas of Classical History*, Routledge, 1988
Tarn, W. W., *Hellenistic Civilization*, Edward Arnold & Co., 1927
Thiel, Rudolf, *And There Was Light*, trans. Richard and Clara Winston, André Deutsch, 1958
Vitruvius, *The Ten Books on Architecture*, trans. Morris Hicky Morgan, Dover, 1960
Warde Fowler, W., *The City-State of the Greeks and Romans*, Macmillan, 1908
Warre Cornish, F. (ed.), *A Concise Dictionary of Greek and Roman Antiquities*, John Murray, 1898
Watterson, Barbara, *Gods of Ancient Egypt*, Batsford, 1984
Watts, Ken, *The Marlborough Downs*, Ex Libris Press, 2003
Wendl, Herbert, *Out of Noah's Ark*, Weidenfeld & Nicolson, 1956
Young, M. J. L., J. D. Latham and R. B. Serjeant (eds.), *Religion, Learning and Science in the 'Abbasid Period*, Cambridge University Press, 1990

The Circles of Archimedes

εἴπε, θέη, σὺ μὲν ἄμμιν, ἐγὼ δ' ἑτέροισιν ἀείσω.

Speak, Goddess, you to me, and I will sing it to others.

Callimachus, *Hymn to Artemis*

Narrative

The wind had danced at the top of the compass since a raw dawn, backing north-west for part of the morning before it shifted again as a tall man in his thirties, brow furrowed, came down the path past Silbury Hill, making for Swallowhead Springs. The airstream, born in Arctic cold, drove sleet or rain over the conical hill and ruffled the muddy circle of groundwater at its base.

An old raven flew above the man, almost stationary in the gusts before it turned on its wingtip to cross West Kennett Barrow, while a roebuck, deep in cover, watched the lone figure from the higher ground.

Aengus had left his cottage by the River Kennet early that morning, tramping upstream past woodlands and pasture, following canal towpath and railway line until they turned away from him. He took a bus for part of the way and walked the rest.

Avebury was almost deserted when he arrived. Heavy nimbostratus dropped rain, then sleet, then thin snow, then rain once more as he walked among the megaliths, tall sarsen stones that formed the circles created by a prehistoric people. He sheltered behind one of these to read his map, the wind flapping its edges. A lull followed after a time, as if nature had changed its mind. Wind dropped and rain stopped. A window of watery light appeared in the lower sky, to reveal briefly a pale landscape of rolling downland topped with beech stands.

He folded his map as he studied the wide stone circles, walking down Beckhampton Avenue to stand between the weeping stones known as Adam and Eve. Here he turned to scan the valley where the people of the Stone Age had built and worshipped, as if he sought contact of some kind. It was his second visit to the site. His first had been several weeks before.

The Wiltshire landscape was still foreign to him some months after he had begun to work nearby, but the open skies called to him. Handsome villages with thatch, flint-and-brick, plain voices with a hint of West Country burr, rolling downland and the long ridgeway with its sense of age and mystery, the abundant wildlife and flora, barrows and standing stones combined to capture him. He still missed coastal waters, the calls of gulls and gannets and waders, but grew to like the chalkstream country where the porous stone filtered impurities from groundwater before releasing it into the underground aquifers that fed the streams and rivers. The annual miracle of the rivers' fly life would spring from the chalk-stream beds in late spring and early summer, when the flow would buoy the white and yellow water-lilies and ruffle the water-crowfoot swaying gently in the depths, and the water would be as clear as that from a tap, but rich in aquatic insect larvae that fed trout and grayling.

That season seemed very distant on this day when Wiltshire wore its wet winter coat of brown and watered green. He spent much of it at Avebury and at Silbury Hill. The light would fade before long, the wind was dropping, slipping back into the west, the rain intermittent but growing heavier. It was that time of year, he thought as he left, when the end of winter and the beginning of spring seemed indistinguishable, when one could so quickly disguise itself as the other. Yet he had already seen the robins in the hedgerows contest their territories and begin to pair, and a song thrush seeking a mate had sung passionately above his head for several hours while he worked in a clearing in the brisk wind, the cock bird hunching anxiously on a branch above the snowdrops as it ran through an astonishingly broad repertoire that imitated the calls of the blackbird and the nightingale.

When he neared his cottage by the riverbank, an hour or more after leaving Avebury, he saw that lights burned dimly in Seth's gloomy house, almost hidden by a grove of evergreens on the opposite side of the main road. He gazed at it for a time while a buzzard-hawk flew slowly along a hedgerow beyond the house to flush the dunnocks in the last of the light. The rain became constant. He crossed the main road and took the woodland paths to his home, where he removed coat and cap, towelled himself dry, kindled a log fire, washed, and cooked supper.

When he had eaten, he sat at the plain deal table in his kitchen, alone in the whitewashed cottage except for his books, conscious of the brimming river that flowed past his porch, but remembering the voice that had woken him from a deep sleep on a moonlit, very still, frosty night some weeks before. The memory returned and the voice rang clearly still, the voice of a ghost.

The Greek

I am the shade of Arkhimedes of Syracuse, son of Pheidias. I was a mathematician when I lived.

I come to you to speak of unfinished work, of a discovery to do with the cosmos that is lost, of the paths that led to it, and of the mystery of my death. These are the strands of my life that I gave to the Fates to spin.

I died from the spear of a Roman soldier, yet he did not kill me. I unlocked the door to the geometry of the cosmos, though the secret did not live. I pursued the beauty of mathematical proportions, but found it, very late, in imperfection.

I am far from the fields of peace and sleep, far from where the terrible dog waits at the gates in the gloom. My shade, spurred by the light of Artemis, is uneasy and troubled.

Stranger, I have a labour for you. The moon sinks, but I will return. Farewell.

The Book of Aengus

I heard the voice only once, some weeks ago, but its firm timbre still resonates in my memory, a musical voice, like a song of the Mediterranean. It woke me from a deep sleep, and as it spoke I felt a presence in the room. The voice wasn't unfriendly, but seemed full of power and purpose, a revenant force. It stopped abruptly, leaving a silence broken only by the sounds of the river and the bark of a dog fox.

I won't speak of this to anyone. Silence is natural to me, as I live alone and see few people, but this journal will be my mute witness, my account of anything this shade says if it returns. I'll add whatever occurs to me, but it may be a short book. If the voice speaks of mathematics, of some lost or forgotten theorem, it'll quickly lose me. My mind will close, and the spirit, or whatever it is, will lose patience and move on.

I begin where I think it began. It may have been a coincidence, but earlier on the same day I had what was, in hindsight, a disturbing experience. I went to Avebury, for the first time, a casual visitor, interested to see its stone circles. I knew Dowth and Newgrange from my childhood in Ireland, and Skara Brae from my time in Scotland. The day was grey and brisk. It was a Saturday, but the cold had kept the visitors at home.

As I wandered through Avebury I felt only content with the solitude. There was nothing to alarm me, no man or god or spirit among the standing stones to disturb my thoughts. I spent about two hours there with a map of the site, then walked to Silbury Hill. I saw its girth as I approached, but was surprised how tall it appeared from ground level when I was close to it. It was forbidden to climb it, so I walked around the base, reflecting on the people who had built it, the largest manmade prehistoric hill in Europe, at roughly the same time that the Egyptians built the Great Pyramid, two and a half thousand years before Christ. I was absorbed in these thoughts until – and this is hard to explain, even to myself – I sensed a presence and felt my hair stand on end. I had a conviction that the Hill itself was suddenly alive in some way, reaching out to me, drawing me to it. The sensation vanished as abruptly as it had arrived and I felt alone again. I was suddenly conscious of a change in the wind, feeling slightly foolish and a little shaken, yet I was more curious than afraid. I'd read of such feelings, and knew of the Hill's association with the Great Goddess of the ancients, but I hadn't experienced such a sensation before.

When I went home I convinced myself I'd imagined it. It was a fine night by then, windless and quiet, with the moon lighting my bedroom and a hard frost settling outside – a hoar frost, as the willow branches were heavy and ghostly white. I probably fell asleep soon after my head hit the pillow. That's all I remember before I heard the voice speak to me, urgently at first, then more gently.

Could it have been a dream? I don't think it was, because I remember that I was conscious that I was conscious. I was conscious of my breathing, of how cold it was, of hearing the fox bark, even of glancing at my watch in the moonlight to try to see the time. Above all, I remember the conviction of the voice, how it rose and fell, yet how powerfully it rang.

He hasn't returned, so I went back to Avebury today for my second visit to the site, perhaps seeking reassurance, perhaps from curiosity. I experienced nothing except a sense of the ordinary. When I went on to Silbury Hill, part of me expected a recurrence of whatever phenomenon it was I felt on my first visit, but I found only an unresponsive stillness. It seemed a different place.

I sum up as best I can. The ghost-voice of the greatest scientist of the ancient world has spoken in the night of the fields of peace, which must be the Elysian Fields of the ancient Greeks. This wandering soul is not in Hades, where Cerberus was the great dog that guarded the gates, nor, presumably, in Tartarus, their deepest hell. Instead it has found me here, to talk of unfinished work, of the goddess Artemis, and of a mystery of his death.

In the last few weeks I've read or reread some of the histories of his time, the Hellenistic period of the Greek world that began with Alexander the Great over three centuries before Christ. Some of these, like the works of Plutarch, were written two or more centuries after the death of the mathematician and may therefore be unreliable, but they describe how the genius of Syracuse, the greatest scientist of antiquity and an old man by then, died in around 212 BC when a soldier of Marcellus, one of the two consuls of the Roman Republic, killed him with a spear when the legions took the Greek city-state of Syracuse, richest in Sicily, after a siege that was a great turning point in history. He was said to have been studying a diagram with circles when he was killed, but there are different accounts of his death.

The voice spoke of a discovery to do with the cosmos, the small, ordered universe of the Greeks. The scholars say that the work of his that comes down to us is of original genius, of discoveries in mechanics, the invention of hydrostatics, the law of the lever, the measurement of the area of a circle and a scientific calculation of *pi*, which I remember as the ratio between the diameter and the circumference of a circle. They write of his pioneering mathematics of the time, on cones, spheres and cylinders. His work on spirals, containing a warm attribution to his friend Conon of Samos, solved two of the three legendary problems in Greek geometry.

His reputation in the West seemed to sink with him into the darkness of European history until the Renaissance, when the Humanists were attracted by his mechanical works. The books he wrote were lost or destroyed, perhaps at the sack of Syracuse, or by the book-burners at Alexandria, but copies of most of the works were removed to the East, to Byzantium or perhaps to Baghdad, from where those that survived made their way back as copies, or copies of copies, to the West many centuries later, translated into Latin or Arabic. These were as available as the works of Plato and Aristotle were to Western scholars by the time of the Renaissance, yet they continued to be neglected until Galileo read them and saw his genius. Those of his works that have reached us, as Boyer says, have done so by a slender thread, but they've allowed modern scientists to marvel at the originality of an imagination that was the first to introduce mathematics into physics. The most recent discovery of his work is a palimpsest now known as the *Archimedes Codex*, which the scholars have used to advance by several jumps what the world knew of him.

All of his works that we have were supplied with short proofs, terse but elegant, drawings of angles and chords and circles and polygons and conic sections, with scrupulous, generous tributes to other scientists who'd worked on the same problems. He used the rich Doric dialect of Classical Greek, with its different stresses and shades of meaning, to the fullest in the letters that prefaced them, suggesting that he knew his literature as well as his mathematics. He's said to have written one mechanical book on making spheres, which is lost. Yet he doesn't seem to have discovered a great secret of the cosmos. Those we accept today as great achievements had to wait for Galileo, Copernicus, Kepler and Newton in a different, relatively modern age.

The closest I find on the subject is an exercise in large numbers, *Psammites*, or *Sand Reckoner*, where, frustrated by the limitations of the Greek numbering system that was based on their alphabet, he used an assumption about the size of the cosmos to exhibit the power of a revolutionary – I don't think that is too strong a word – system of numbers he invented, roughly eighteen hundred years before Newton and Leibniz. It was a calculus of the infinite, capable of measuring the entire universe.

Narrative

The house of Seth stood back from the main road, surrounded by the great estate where Aengus worked. It was almost hidden by spindly evergreens, a brooding place in a dell the sun seldom reached. Peeling paintwork and unpointed brick combined to send a simple message to the passerby, to keep out.

It had once been the dwelling of a small farm, and even then was viewed as an unlucky house, the site of successive family disputes and untimely deaths. Over time the property had been split, when the land was bought by the neighbouring estate. The house had been sold separately, together with a shed in a broken concrete yard overgrown with weeds. It was fenced off from the foot of a gently sloping hill that was topped by a handsome wood of oak and sycamore and ash.

Its air of passive misfortune and neglect had changed into something actively sinister when Seth had rented the place a few years before, probably because of the stories that circulated of the tenant's brooding nature and his past. The postman visited infrequently to deliver the household bills to the post-box by the gate. He had little to tell his friends other than that two women lived there with Seth. One was a tall figure in her forties, with striking green eyes, a mane of wild black hair with flecks of grey, and the bearing of a gypsy queen. The second was a hauntingly beautiful girl whom the others treated as a servant, probably a little touched in the head, said the locals, who rarely glimpsed her but thought her mad to share Seth's roof. The tall woman owned a great dog that strained at its leash when the postman called, its teeth bared as it threw itself at him. She was said to be Seth's mistress, the girl a relative of some kind.

That was as much as the neighbourhood knew, so rumour expanded to fill the vacant space. The man was said to have faced murder charges twice and been acquitted on both occasions for lack of evidence, a witness to the first becoming the victim in the second. The neighbours took the charges as fact, ignoring the silence of the local police who called on the man from time to time to question him. Many of the murders associated with him – generally in big towns or cities within easy reach – had been particularly gruesome, punishment killings of a kind that were spoken of in whispers. As the talk grew looser, to include satanic rituals, seances and dark rites, so the house's threatening aspect grew, as if it, and not just its tenant, menaced all around it.

Aengus had heard this talk soon after he had had arrived to live and work on the estate. On his walks he studied the house through a gap in the evergreens from a distance, drawn by its blank, alien stare and the mysteries within. It reminded him of the deserted dwellings in the lonely Ireland of his boyhood, isolated places said to be haunted by one former occupant or another, yet none of those seemed to have had such an air of malignance or repellence.

The estate was divided almost evenly by a trunk road noted for its generous width and for the speed of its traffic. It was more than five thousand acres of woodland, water meadows and pasture, with over thirty dwellings that ranged in size from the owner's Queen Anne house to the semi-derelict cottage that had been empty for four years before Aengus arrived. The estate owner lived abroad. He shot pheasant and partridge here five or six times a year, and fished the beautiful stretch of the Kennet occasionally. His agent, an upright, organising man in his later years who ensured that his owner's interests were well served, ran the estate in his absence.

The River Kennet flowed through the estate from west to east, absorbing tributaries or carriers joining from the water meadows. Some of the carriers were nearly as wide in places as the mother stream, others short and narrow, scarcely more than drains. Narrow stands of willow and alder followed the course of the river. In the shallow water near the banks in summer common reeds, flag irises, watercress, forget-me-not and bur-reed flourished, while meadowsweet, angelica, brooklime and water-parsnip grew on the banks, shaded by willows and alder and hawthorn bushes. Southern marsh-orchids, marsh valerian and lesser spearwort flourished in the wetter water meadows, and the drier ground hosted red campion and the common poppy. The wooded, marshy areas between carriers and river, filled with rotting vegetation and fallen trees colonised by Buckler-ferns, were almost impenetrable except to wildlife. Coot and moorhen flourished in the reed beds, as safe as they could be from predators from ground and air, sharing the wetland wilderness with duck and swans and water voles. Enough herons survived to reassure conservationists. Aengus knew of at least two otter holts, and left them undisturbed while the keepers concentrated on trapping mink. In all, there were five miles of trout angling, for which members of the fishery paid the estate an annual fee to fish it six days a week in the season that ran from late April to the end of September. Herds of shorthorn cattle pastured in the water meadows, fenced from the river to keep them from ruining the banks. Aengus mowed these banks to keep them clear for the anglers, and trimmed branches from willow and alder to leave enough foliage, weed and common reeds to keep the trout shaded and cool.

Downstream from his cottage the river entered a dense wood, flowed out into open meadows again, and retreated once more into a further wood. There were several wooden bridges and one of stone. Part of his job was to maintain these. There was work throughout the year, particularly in spring when the growth of vegetation resumed and vermin numbers multiplied. River-keepers and gamekeepers worked in harness on the agent's instructions. Jays, magpies, rabbits and foxes were shot by the keepers. Mink were trapped as they entered artificial log tunnels that hid steel traps, roe deer and muntjac culled by the men using rifles from the towers placed on the edges of the woodland. Grey squirrels were trapped and knocked on the head and their drays destroyed in a constant effort to keep the numbers down. The numbers of raptor birds, by one means or another, not all of them legal, were reduced that gamebirds and fish and songbirds might flourish. The keepers' task was to tip the balance of nature in favour of game and farm animals.

The cottage of Aengus was the smallest on the estate, once a dilapidated, nineteenth-century labourer's dwelling, adjoining another that was occasionally used as an estate workshop, and an open shed that the barn-swallows returned to in spring. The buildings stood beside a grove of crack willow, screened from general view, beside the junction of a carrier with the main river.

He had renovated the cottage soon after moving there, enjoying the work, repairing doors and sash windows, rewiring, painting the walls white, building bookshelves, ripping out the original lintel that had rotted and replacing it with one he cut from an old oak beam. He staunched the leaking of the roof by replacing the slates and repointing the crooked chimneys, and began work on the garden, removing the rubbish of years, bringing trailers of topsoil from elsewhere on the estate in preparation for the coming of spring.

When a van carrying his books from his last home arrived, he felt more settled, a log fire drawing in the hearth that he had restored, his long body relaxed in a worn armchair, a stack of books beside him, a pleasant tiredness causing his eyelids to droop, the ticking of an old tin clock a pleasant companion after a day in rain and wind. He was settling gradually into this new life, temporary though he knew it would probably be, and was exploring the surrounding area when his peace was disturbed by a voice in the night. He was to hear this voice again some weeks later, only days after he had written of its first visit in his journal.

The Greek

I return to find a raven by your door, and to see you alert, as though you wait for me.

My life was a circle, Stranger, a moving point that curved on an arc from my youth to my death, from my youth when I set out to capture the irrationality of the circle, to my death when the cosmos lay before me in the wax.

I will speak of mathematics to you only in passing, and I will be as plain and clear as I can when I do, on the assumption that your interest in life thus far has lain elsewhere. Certain parts that concern the use of geometry will be laid before you at the beginning of what I have to tell you, because they are central to my life, but you need not shrink from them, or turn away. They are simple rudiments. It is what flows from them, from the abstract to the physical, that I hope will interest you, and encourage you to involve yourself.

I will tell you all that might matter to you of my life for my purpose here, and such histories as you need to keep your attention, and perhaps I can add a little more here and there if you are kind enough to listen, and if we have time. As to the last, I think we will have enough. The poet Kallimakhos might be disappointed in me, and say I was born in the age of the short poem that was written to be read rather than sung, but the oral tradition of Hellas continued to flourish in my lifetime, particularly among the Greeks of Sicily. To be candid with you, we liked to talk, unlike the Spartans our cousins, and I have always had a weakness for the epic.

I begin with my interest in the mathematics of the circle because you cannot begin to know the truths of the cosmos until you understand its geometry. To the Greeks, the circle, the most fundamental shape of all, lay at the centre of this.

One of the truths of mathematics is that you cannot square a circle, a short way of saying that you cannot calculate its area exactly. We use the term *to square* because mathematicians like to reduce the area of an object to a square as it is the simple, basic unit of proportion in geometry, one whose measurements can be calculated perfectly, and that is why a mathematician seeks *to square* the area of any object, to reduce it to a square, or a sum of squares, an exact figure. To square any figure that is contained by straight lines, regardless of how it may appear, was simplicity itself to us.

A great achievement of earlier Greek mathematicians was to calculate the area of an object that is contained by a series of curves, something that once seemed impossible. If I had a wax tablet or a papyrus roll I could prove to you in a few moments that Greek geometers learned to square a number of such curvilinear figures – as we call them – to allow their proportions to be calculated exactly, using only a ruler and compass and the imagination of the geometer. A circle, however, is an exception. It cannot be squared. Its *idea* or its essence is the perfect shape to some of the philosophers who view it as the motion of the cosmos itself, but we can never calculate it exactly. We can square the lune, but not the circle.

The explanation lies in its very essence. We cannot square it because its essential, inner proportion, the relationship of the diameter to the circumference, is irrational, without a common factor that would reduce its proportion to a ratio. The relationship is the same, a constant, for every circle that exists, yet it is not a whole number. It is one we called an *incommensurable*, and the Pythagorean brotherhood called an *irrational* number, as it cannot carry a ratio. There are many such irrational numbers or proportions whose nature intrigued the philosophers and touched the poets. We learned to master most of these, yet a mathematician might devote his life to finding an exact value for the relationship between the circumference and diameter of a circle and go to his grave without an answer.

Early mathematicians knew little more than that the length of its circumference was more than three times the straight line that passed through its centre. That was dissatisfying to the Greeks, a challenge to those who saw its importance, who, like me, were determined to calculate its area and so unlock the proportions of every circular object, circle, cylinder, cone, sphere, earth, and even, one day, the cosmos. Many tried and many failed, and so the circle kept its secret, as it would always do.

I accepted that, of course, yet I saw the concealed proportion in the full moon over Syracuse when I was a boy, the symbol to me of the Goddess herself. I saw it in the orchestra of the theatre. Later I saw it in the wax of my tablets or in the rolls when I worked.

Philosophers need terrible, wrenching jolts from time to time to be forced beyond our imagination. Perhaps then we may find something that, if we are lucky, lights the mind for an instant. The proportions of the circle sent me to a higher plane, to find a hidden great truth.

The Book of Aengus

It wasn't a dream. It was the same musical voice, with the same ringing delivery. He has returned, to speak of the circle and of *pi*. I search my feelings, knowing I should be angry or awestruck to be the object of a revelation of some kind. Instead I feel a sense of the familiar, as if an old friend had come to visit. This feeling is mixed with relief that he hasn't come to me to talk of mathematics except, as he says, in passing. Soon he may move on to what brought him here, but in the meantime I can keep up, with the help of a growing library, as he tells me of the purest intellectual challenge of the ancient world.

You can square the lune, but you cannot square the circle. I'd forgotten what a lune was, if I ever knew, but looked it up to find it's a figure entirely bounded by curves, like a crescent moon. An earlier Greek mathematician calculated its area, and his proof is the oldest to survive.

He hasn't come to speak of mathematics, as he says, but of the enigma of the circle and of its importance to the cosmos, the ordered unity of earth, moon, sun, planets and stars that the Greeks saw as a compact, circular whole, reassuringly small, so ordered that it took its name from it. He sees it *in the wax*, almost certainly referring to a diagram he has drawn on a clay tablet with a wax face.

I've since scanned the more popular works of the ancient Greek philosophers and found that the greatest of them believed that the circle in its essence was perfection. To Plato and Aristotle it was the motion of the cosmos itself, where sun and moon and the five known planets revolved within invisible spheres in perfectly circular orbits around the sphere of earth, with man at its centre.

I know enough, from the basic maths books I've bought and read in the past few weeks, to write that the circle's key dimension, the number we now call *pi*, is inexpressible as a finite series of numbers, or as a fraction, and is one of only two numbers that mathematicians call transcendental, aloof from all others, irreducible to a decimal place in our modern notation and inexpressible as an algebraic equation. It seems an endless series of digits that might reach around our universe and back without telling us anything of value or result. It has intrigued the men of numbers since antiquity, and does so still. A mathematician might go to his grave without the answer, he says, and many have.

I search the histories and find that the ancient Greek equivalent of our adjective *irrational*, used so frequently by us to mean *unreasonable*, meant something different, something more specific, to the mathematicians of ancient Greece. A closer rendering might be *inexpressible*. In the lexicon of ancient Greek philosophy, of which mathematics was part, such numbers that could not carry a ratio – where there are no factors common to both – were better known by the fourth century BC as *incommensurables*. The most quoted example of one such seems to have been the relationship between the diagonal of a square and its side. Divide one by the other and you will not find a ratio, just a broken series rather than a whole number, which meant little in the ancient world as it lacked the decimal system. Incommensurables intrigued the philosophers like Plato, while Aristotle, in *Metaphysics*, said nothing would surprise a geometer more than if the diagonal of a square proved to be commensurable with the side. One Hellenistic philosopher even saw divinity in these irrational proportions.

I've heard that when modern mathematicians see any number, they instinctively seek its character, its properties, and slip into an intuitive gear where the immediate questions that arise are whether the number is a prime, or a square, or a cube root, or one that could be reduced to a fraction or a ratio, and so on. If it starts as a fraction and is then reduced to decimals, would it result in an endless series of zeros, satisfyingly exact, very definite, totally contained? If it's irrational, might it be reduced through algebra to a simple equation, even if it's infinite in arithmetic?

The maths books state there are many such irrationals or incommensurables, but that *pi* holds a special place among them. The diagonal of a square, to use Aristotle's example again, has since been reduced to a simple equation in algebra even though it's an irrational number in arithmetic. *Pi* cannot be so reduced, and is therefore transcendental. To a code breaker, seeking some form of repetition or concealed meaning, it would be uncrackable. Gifted modern mathematicians, convinced that if they computed the number to billions of places they would find a meaning of some kind, a pattern of repeating digits perhaps, or possibly the abrupt appearance of a logical sequence that would grant immortality to its finder, or even – against all known evidence – a series of zeros that would show *pi* to be finite, have thus far at least failed to find that it contains anything except a relentless stream of random numbers. No pattern appears. If this stream of digits conceals a mystery, *pi* has yet to release it, yet its proportion seems to be the basic key to measuring the universe and its motion. Much of science could do little without it. Kepler used it for his Third Law, Heisenberg for his Uncertainty Principle, Einstein for General Relativity, Euler for his Identity Formula, and so through physics, mathematics, engineering, astronomy, and genetics where it sits in the double helix of life. The great Indian mathematician Srinivasa Ramanujan, once a starving Madras clerk – an original genius with a startling insight into number – left mathematicians the basis for an algorithm used to calculate it to within an atom's breadth of its true value. Solutions to such complex problems, he said, sometimes came to him in dreams, just as a goddess had appeared to his mother.

Narrative

The woods swayed in the wind as the men worked on the fallen tree. The sycamore had toppled in a gale the night before. It blocked the riverbank near the eastern boundary of the estate, close to an oak where a green woodpecker had wintered. The workmen had taken the Mule – the little vehicle the estate used to negotiate the riverside paths – as far as the tree. Bill Worthy, the under-riverkeeper, had driven tractor and trailer to the edge of the wood and left them there, as the riverbank was not wide enough to take their passage. Aengus and Sid the keeper, an older, short, neat man with a face shaped like a sharp spade, were cutting the tree into uniform lengths with chainsaws, watched eagerly by the blue tits and nuthatches awaiting the resulting spoil from the rotten stump. Bill, a plump young man who wore a bright anorak, lived on junk food and suffered from flatulence and spots, watched the other workers vacantly, swaying slightly to the music from his headphones. Sid, his mood black, snapped at him to help. The youth, idly fingering his pimples, did not hear. Aengus tapped him on the shoulder and motioned at Sid, whose face was working into a fury. Bill saw the keeper's face and dropped his music player in fright. He picked it up and ran clumsily to the Mule, started the engine and drove it back and forth to the trailer where he unloaded the logs. He looked warily at Sid when the chainsaw stopped.

The keeper had straightened suddenly. He looked down the bank. "Seth!" he said.

Aengus saw a figure on the path near the wood.

"Is that the man they say is a murderer?" he asked.

"Bad lot," said Sid shortly. Aengus noticed the keeper was sweating.

Sid placed the chainsaw on the ground and stood on the bank. A hush seemed to fall. All looked toward the approaching figure.

Juggernaut, thought Aengus while the figure approached, an unstoppable force, as the Christian missionaries in India had slandered the great celestial car of Krishna, something that crushed all in its path like a steamroller, without mercy or remorse.

This figure seemed to the watchers to walk on air, trampling all beneath it with disdain, as though nothing mortal could oppose it or stand in its way because it had inhuman powers and was used to abusing them.

As it came closer the three men saw, as through a haze, what seemed to be a barrel of a man. The head was heavy, majestic in a sense, topped by thin, reddish hair, with narrowed eyes and thick, cruel lips, yet it had a strangely intelligent look. Eyes like a reptile's flicked once at them at them as the figure drew near, as if daring them to interfere, but otherwise it ignored them.

"Mornin'," said Sid, gathering his courage. "You know there's no right of way 'ere."

The figure continued on its path, walking between the three men as if they did not exist, and rounded the bend in the river.

The Greek

The stars tonight have an unfamiliar northern look, yet the sight recalls my childhood with a sharpness that is close to pain.

Tonight, let us begin there. When I was very young I learned the works of Eukleid and before I entered my ninth year I knew every definition, postulate and theorem as well as I knew Homer.

I had a lucky childhood. Syracuse had only recently escaped destruction by its old enemy, Carthage, but then our city entered a long span of peace, and of immense prosperity. Much of my early education was conducted in darkness on the roof of our house, and my earliest memories are of learning the names of the bright stars and of the constellations because my father studied the sky every night and filled my infant mind with myth. I knew how the Muses took the lyre of Orpheus after his death and placed it in the heavens as the constellation Lyra. I heard how Orion, the mighty hunter who hung high in the winter sky, forever pursued the Pleiades, the seven sisters who attended Artemis, with Sirius at his heels. I knew the legend of Kassiopeia the queen, of the Twins, how the Archer was placed in the sky by the centaur to guide Jason to Kolkhis, and of the labours of Herakles. I knew the work of Hesiod, too, and the time of year as the sun entered the sign of the Ram, when day and night were equal and Pheidias sang to me:

When Zeus has finished sixty wintry days
After the turning of the Sun, then the star
Arcturus leaves the holy stream of Ocean
And first rises brilliant in the twilight.

As I heard Pheidias I began to suspect that this love of myth had set him on the road to his life as an astronomer. The heavens were his work, but the night sky of the constellations was his book of heroes.

I was the child who viewed these constellations as wise friends who looked down kindly but distantly on the man and the boy who, in turn, gazed up at them. They seemed unreachable beings who knew the answers to the mystery of why the planets at night sometimes inexplicably wandered around the path across the sky that the sun rode by day. These were the secrets that my father attempted to unlock, and many times during my childhood I offered to the queen in her chair as she chased the Bears across the northern sky, asking her to whisper her secrets to my father in return. Sometimes I believed that she did, and he did not hear.

He taught me my histories of Syracuse, too, of our fighting tyrants who made Carthage tremble, Gelo the victor of Himera, his brother Hiero I of whom Xenophon wrote, Dionysios I who knew Plato, Timoleon of Korinth who saved the city, and the terrible Agathokles, a potter by trade, who slew his own people as casually as his enemies, and called himself king of all Sicily. I learned also the histories of Hellas itself. We were of the same blood as the Spartans, we Syracusans, being a Dorian people, as they were, and so we gloried in the tales of the heroes' death of Leonidas and the Three Hundred at Thermopylai when Xerxes and his Persians crossed the Hellespont from Asia into Greece. I learned how Sparta, when the Persians fled Greece and Athens over the next eighty years grew powerful and greedy, sent its best general to Syracuse to save us from the Athenians in the war of the Peloponnesos, and how their navy went on to defeat them at Aigospotami. Although all of this took place long before we lived, the deeds of Leonidas and Lysander rang in our household, more loudly even than the conquests of Alexander the Great. Distant though we were in Sicily from the mainland of Hellas, we were sadly aware that the glory of Sparta had long passed.

Our lives were quiet, the household comprising only father, son, and slaves. Each dawn the pedagogue my father had bought, a boy only slightly older than I, took me to the gymnasium and later to the gymnastic master. The schoolmaster, a man much respected for his ability to flog boys in a manner they could not forget, told us that his task was to beat childishness from us and teach us the work of the great poets so that each of us might develop a noble character. He did so with energy, using an oxtail strap we called the Stinger to encourage us until we learned our letters and great passages of the poets so well we could declaim them in our sleep. At this point in our lives, a knowledge of literature was held to be superior to any other learning. Herodotus the logographer was ignored. Practical mathematics, including astronomy, was considered to be beneath us, lacking a noble character, banausic, knowledge suitable only for trade, but music stemmed from the Muses themselves, and so the harp master's task was to teach us to play the lyre and to sing in the chorals that were part of the religious festivals of the city.

I describe Pheidias to you. He was a big man, taller than many, a traditional Dorian, stern when he needed to be, devoted to work, family and *polis*, kind almost all of the time, rarely emotional unless he spoke to me of my mother, whose character he said I had inherited, or of his own father the sculptor who had cut in stone a celebrated likeness of Artemis, and from whom he had inherited a love of proportions. My mother had died when I was very young, and Pheidias did not remarry. His knowledge was such that while he had the reputation of being a dreamer, he was also reputed to be the wisest man in Sicily, and the Tyrant frequently proclaimed him to be so, although Pheidias did not seek Hiero's favour, preferring to offer advice only when asked to do so by his relative. His dedication was such that each morning he rested only for a few hours, then resumed his work, filling his tablets with observations. Before the day ended at sunset and a new one began, he would summarise the results on rolls that he stored carefully alongside those of the copied works of the Babylonians, whose most recent astronomical work he admired above all for its accuracy.

I see his sensitive head as though he were with me still, muttering as he took an angle through the twin *dioptrai* he had designed himself, noting the time of night by glancing at the eastern horizon to see which constellation was rising, turning to me to repeat it. I scarcely knew then what his purpose was, but later I realised that he was measuring movement in the heavens.

I remember those moments so clearly when, in the quiet of the night, he would tell me of the different observations that had once puzzled astronomers, such as those of the Great Bear, which did not sink below the disc of the earth when viewed from Syracuse, but did so in Egypt.

That question had been answered long before us, legend said by the Pythagorean brotherhood who said that the earth is a sphere. You had only to observe the shadow of the earth on the face of the moon during even a partial lunar eclipse to believe them, said Pheidias, who spoke sometimes also of the hypothesis of Anaximander the Ionian philosopher of old, that the sun possessed a much greater mass than was believed, and was therefore very distant from us.

To a young mind this last was almost impossible to imagine until one night my father told me of Parmenides, the philosopher who sang in his poem that all was not as it seemed in the cosmos, a statement that Pheidias had made his own. There were two views of the world around us, he believed, the one that you thought you saw, and the one that was.

So spoke Pheidias in the pursuit of the great unfinished work of his life. He studied the course of Ares, devoting every moment he could to discovering why the red planet would travel backwards for a time, then abruptly appear to fly towards us. Those were the periods when he concentrated most, the moments when I dared not interrupt him as he looked through his sighting tube, found the planet, and clamped the instrument before noting the change from the last angle of observation.

At the time I feared he lacked ambition, but later I realised that he had a wider, grander purpose of which he did not speak, even to me then. If the movement of one of the planets could be explained, then so might that of the others, and in time the motion of the entire cosmos might be known and proven, for the first time, by direct observation.

The clever Babylonians knew of the wandering bodies in the heavens long before Greece as we knew it existed. They viewed the night sky as a great roof made of black jasper on which the god Mardokhaios wrote the future, and devoted themselves to deciphering each movement of the god's moving hand in the heavens so they might foretell events below. Every movement of sun, moon and planets through the constellations was ominous to them because it came from the hand of the god, and every movement of such heavenly writing was therefore recorded and charted in parallel with events on earth, such as the dates of the births and deaths of their kings, the harvests, famines and floods, plagues, good fortune and bad. Earlier in their history they had invented writing, and to describe in detail in an encyclopaedia the portents they saw in the heavens, said Pheidias, they developed a form of lettering that resembled the constellations themselves.

The Babylonians predicted eclipses of the sun and moon too, Pheidias said, for the same divine purpose. They continued to do so in our time when they were ruled by the Greek Seleukids, a dynasty descended from one of Alexander's generals. They did so with increasing accuracy, but they lacked the curiosity of the Greek philosophers, who, from Thales onwards, opened their minds to seek and offer an explanation for the phenomena in the cosmos, including its composition and its motion. Plato in his search for Truth as Goodness saw the heavens as a series of transparent concentric shells turning on a great axle (the outer wall of the shells forming the circular path of each body) with a singing Siren sitting on each shell and the three Fates spinning the shells in circles, which to Plato was the best of motions. That, said Pheidias, did not explain the strange, retrograde movements of the planets at times, nor why the Fates involved themselves, but it was an intelligent hypothesis by a great philosopher who later recognised its obvious inaccuracy and encouraged his pupil, the gifted Eudoxos of Knidos, of whom the poet Aratos sang and who brought geometry into astronomy and discovered the arithmetic of proportions, to refine his idea, to construct a plan of the cosmos with yet more transparent shells, some of them with different axes, all revolving in circles, some sharing in the movement of their neighbours, the combination explaining the wandering movement of the planets. Again it was a worthy attempt, said Pheidias, but it contradicted his own observations, and those of the Babylonians. Aristotle took the hypothesis further, imagining a circular cosmos that seemed at first to accommodate the movement of the planets, and took its power from an Unmoved Mover. Subsequent astronomers produced subsequent refinements, but Aristotle's cosmos, based as it was on the work of Eudoxos, remained largely untouched when it came down to us. The earth, said Aristotle, was a sphere at the centre of the cosmos, and had assumed its shape because the heaviest objects naturally moved towards the centre. His explanation, said Pheidias with his typical generosity, was worthy of a great mind that had left us with such a mighty inheritance, but perhaps the broad, open-minded stream of our philosophy had sometimes dwelled a little too plentifully on theories and ideas, and not sufficiently on proof. That statement seemed to me a profound one, and impressed me deeply. Later I was to remember that even the great Eukleid did not rely on observation when he stated that the earth lay at the middle of the cosmos, basing his proof on the common assumption that the heavens were spherical.

Yet we were the lucky ones, Pheidias told me, to have such ideas come down to us from the pure spirit of inquiry into the nature of things, into the relationships between the ordered and the rational, on the one hand, and what was visible or evident to us on the other. We were the inheritors of the ideas of the wise men who asked how the cosmos came to be as it was, of Thales who inquired of what it was made, of Anaximander who said that matter is continually in strife, hot against cold, wet against dry, of the Pythagoreans who saw musical harmony in the heavens, a mathematical proportion in the tuned string of the lyre, and *arithmos* or number in everything, of Herakleitos who fused the hypotheses of the last two to declare that the real world is a balance of opposing forces like a strung bow and that there is a universal formula, or *logos*, to explain the underlying principle of all, of Empedokles who gave us the roots of things as the four elements, fire, air, earth and water, said that light takes time to travel, and that the beam of the moon is a reflection of the sun, of Anaxagoras who said the stars were made of hot rock, that the gods were the source of all motion, and that the sun was larger than the Peloponnesos. Pheidias took me through them all, or most of them, through the Eleatics who believed in the potential of unending divisibility of matter and the Atomists who did not, through the Stoics, who disdained riches, said that Good was the foremost virtue and told us that all happens for a purpose in a manner already decided, and so through the Sophists, who sold mere opinion to the innocent as a wineseller peddles drink, and on to shoeless Sokrates himself who engaged in dialogue about Virtue with anyone he met and said that Evil, by definition, results only from ignorance, that to reach the Good we must have knowledge and therefore knowledge is Good, a teaching that runs through the heart of Greek philosophy, descending as it does from

Orpheus. He took me through the thoughts of the wise men in the order that I quote to you tonight so I might remember them, and frequently returned to those he said had the greatest intellects of all, to Plato and his geometrical view of the cosmos, and to Aristotle who laid down how knowledge should be organised and said that rational contemplation was the best of all activities. This last statement was the guiding principle of Pheidias.

Stranger, all of this did not happen at once, but over the years as my young mind absorbed it, slowly at first as we viewed the night sky through Pheidias' sighting tubes, or reclined on our couches to eat, but then knowledge lodged in me at an increasing rate as my curiosity grew, and when Pheidias came to talk of the mathematicians, of how they selected a shape in geometry and set about the proof of a proposition concerning such a figure, I sat up, a wide-eyed boy in the isolation of the darkness. I heard how they rejected any method of physical measurement of objects and said that the solution to every geometrical problem must come only from the mind of the mathematician. I learned of Menaikhnos who cut cones into geometric slices in his imagination, of Eudoxos and his theory of proportions, of Hippokrates who squared the lune and left us his book of *Elements*, and of the three great challenges in geometry. When Pheidias one bright morning loaned me his own rolls of Eukleid, copied as they had been by the delicate hand of an Alexandrian scribe, I was ready to learn every proposition. Here, said my father, were the rigorous proofs of the best mathematical philosophers, the *Elements* compiled by the great man himself. If I understood and accepted the basis of this work, with its definitions, postulates and axioms, I might one day solve the most complex theorems.

I copied those rolls of Eukleid myself, Stranger, every diagram and every proposition, from the *protasis* or enunciation, through the *ekthesis* or the setting out of the problem and so by logical stages to the *sumperasma*, the conclusion where the mathematician might look back on his work and say: *which it was required to prove*. It was hard for me in the short periods between my return from the gymnasium or from games at the *Palaistra*, and such times as my father permitted me to join him in his nightly planet watch, but I finished it at last, often beginning my work before the sun lit the *exedra* of the house. I saw the deduction in each line of proof and the integral beauty of the diagrams as I worked, and I came to know each proposition as a friend.

Such, Stranger, was my late childhood and early boyhood, when I spent as many hours after darkness as he permitted sitting beside Pheidias, bound to silence unless he spoke to me, listening to the nocturnal sounds from the harbour as we sat or knelt at our places on the open space at the top of the house, grateful for the cooling breezes that swept away the stench of rotting fish and human waste in the hot summers.

I saw the geometry of Eukleid in the night sky as the northern stars revolved and the moon rose, ascended like a queen across the sky, and sank. We joined in the silence of the heavens as the moving constellations rotated, and the blaze of silvery light when the sky was clear and Artemis had departed. In the silence I allowed my young imagination to roam and invented constellations of my own, fitting new shapes to the bright stars, seeing scattered silvery faces that smiled or grimaced at me. Sometimes I studied the face of a woman I imagined as my mother. I saw the great shaggy head of Zeus himself, disguised as a bull as he pursued the princess Europa, and the beautiful features of Artemis that shone from the face of the moon when it was full. I saw bears, and horses, and fleets of triremes sailing between the stars in a race they could not win. In the waning moon I saw clearly the figures of the *Moirai*, the three Fates. When cloud covered the yellow sickle I believed they had drawn a cloak over them to sleep.

So the years of childhood passed, a childhood unlike that of other Greek boys. My voice was breaking when Pheidias told me to put my geometry to use. I was to make my own observations of the moon.

I waited for the silver bow to appear in the west as the sun set, saw it travel through the constellations, measured the angles of its ascent and descent, saluting it as it plucked itself free from the hills and turned the sea to silver on its transit, to beam its light on the temples and white stone houses and narrow streets of Syracuse. I observed in which constellation it rose when it was at its highest in the sky, measured the arc of the angle it travelled each day, and counted the nights between one full moon and the next. I estimated the two places every lunar month where the moon, on its ascent and descent, cut the daytime path of the sun, which astronomers called the ecliptic. I saw how its apparent size and its speed across the heavens seemed to change as the month went on, which puzzled me even then. I filled the wax with diagrams showing its movement, noting how it travelled against the background of the fixed stars by one span of its diameter on average every hour, and through each constellation every two or three days.

The full moon seemed a perfect circle, intense with meaning to an impressionable boy, an image that has remained with me since. That is how it began.

The Book of Aengus

When the Greek left I lay awake, restless, while in my mind I built a picture of him and his surroundings when he was in his prime, drawing on what I've read and from my imagination.

I see a noble head with a high brow and a long, sharp nose, a full head of greying hair and a longish, untrimmed beard. He strides quickly, a tallish, very spare man with thin, bare arms swinging, wearing a white *chiton* or long linen garment, and dusty leather sandals. He hurries through the dirty, untidy, impossibly narrow streets of Syracuse, glancing over the tiled roof-tops at the blue of the Ionian Sea, passing houses built from the greyish-white, cut limestone of Sicily. He reaches the shade of the *stoa* at the side of the *agora*, the heart of the city.

The Syracusans are descended from the original adventurers from Corinth who sailed on sea lanes favoured by current and wind five centuries before, after consulting the Pythoness, the Oracle of Delphi at the sanctuary of Apollo on the mainland of Greece. The settlements became city states known as *apoikia*, the *separated*, as they left their mother cities, the *metropoleis*, behind them. They were independent, but kept their ties with the land they called *Hellas*, and considered themselves as Greek as a Spartan.

The hungry Greek adventurers founded city-states in Sicily and on the mainland of Italy, colonies collectively known as *Megara Hellas* or *Magna Graecia* – Greater Greece – killing or enslaving the local tribes of Sikels and Sikans and Etruscans, bringing their dialects and cultures from the mother cities, evolving them as time went on. The indigenous Sicilians, slaves at first, probably fused their blood with that of the Sicilian Greeks to create a sturdy, enterprising race known as the Sikeliots. The culture remained Greek, with a local flavour. Some of these daughter city-states, Syracuse included, annexed or founded other *apoikia*. They laid out their cities on mathematical lines like a grid, with the *agora*, or open market space, at or near the centre, to create what the Greeks called a *polis*, an independent state comprising a city and the integral surrounding or neighbouring area of countryside called a *chora*, which was essential as it fed the city.

The *polis* was the basis of civilisation throughout the Greek world, Aristotle's ideal state where culture and nature fused and where the frontier with the neighbouring state could be seen from the *acropolis*, the citadel usually built on the highest point of the city. There seem to have been around fifteen hundred of these *poleis* at one time across the vast area of the known world where Greek would be spoken as a first or a common language for a further seven hundred years or so after Archimedes' death. Until the Roman conquests the Greeks seem to have been good at defending themselves and thwarting the imperial ambitions of others, perhaps because for long periods the two great *poleis* of Athens and Sparta maintained an uneasy balance of power with minor empires of their own, yet even when Alexander towards the end of the fourth century BC conquered most of the Greek world, and great tracts of Asia and North Africa –and even into the early period of Roman rule – the *poleis* were generally left to function as they had, with their peculiar sense of intimacy and identity.

The *prytaneion* building, with its sacred flame to Hestia, served as the communal hearth, the religious centre of the city, while the *thesaurus*, the state treasury, was generally nearby. Syracuse probably also had its assembly – an *ekklesia* – and a *boulé* – a citizens' city council – although the buildings, like much of the Greek city, have since disappeared. The powers of these gatherings rose and dropped under different kings, tyrants, democracies, and *strategoi* – military rulers – but they would have been valuable barometers of political opinion, as were the conversations in the *stoae*, the roofed colonnades or porticoes that served as meeting places and sheltered markets.

The citizens of Syracuse are Dorian Greeks, proud of their

descent, like the Spartans, from Hercules the god, and over the centuries they've created the richest city-state in the Mediterranean. It's strategically situated on the sea lanes of the Ionian Sea at the eastern edge of Sicily, has four distinct quarters and is going though a building boom that compares in scale with that begun under the tyrant Gelo over 250 years before. The original city, the island or peninsula of Ortygia that is bounded by the Grand Harbour to the west and the Ionian Sea to the east, is only a hundred acres in area and is the most densely populated. At one time, under the ferocious and very successful tyrant Dionysius I, it was an almost impregnable royal fortress, but successive civil wars have levelled the walls to the ground and urban development has created newer buildings in its place. The Fountain of Arethusa lies among them, fed by an underground spring of fresh water that flows almost miraculously beneath the Grand Harbour, from one side of it to the other. The underground stream is the eternal home of the river god Alpheios who searches, maddened by love and desire, for Arethusa the nymph whom Artemis, to protect her from her pursuer, has turned into a fountain. The people of Ortygia believe they hear the god cry out to Arethusa at night, and they have the image of the nymph near to hand as they see her head, circled by dolphins, on the faces of the beautiful silver coins of Syracuse.

Across the causeway, to the north, is the city quarter of Achradina, named for its wild-pear trees, running from south-west to north-east to finish at the sea walls to the north of the city's second harbour, the little port of Lakkios that doesn't offer the magnificent shelter of the first. The *agora*, far grander than the original market place in Ortygia, probably lies either in Achradina, or near the Theatre in Neapolis.

Further north and west, in the *chora*, looms the triangular limestone plateau of Epipolae, on relatively high ground, at the foot of the Hyblaeon hills. Between it and Achradina lie the other city quarters, Tyche to the eastern or seaward side, and Neapolis, the most recent addition to the city and where the building boom is most apparent, to the west, below the slopes of Epipolae. Most of the religious processions and the festival honouring Dionysus the god, the *Dionysia* to which all Greeks are invited, are held at Neapolis.

In the ensuing ages Syracuse could be viewed as a lower rung in the ladder of European history, a city-state that would be united in subjection with the rest of Sicily when Archimedes would die and the city fall. The island would become Rome's first province with its own governor. Rome would rule Sicily from Syracuse for six hundred years and would be followed by Vandals, Ostrogoths, the Byzantines under Belisarius, the Saracens, Normans, Germans bearing the banner of the Holy Roman Empire, the French Angevins, Spain, the Kingdom of Naples, the Two Sicilies and finally Garibaldi's united Italy. The blood of the Dorian Greeks of Syracuse is therefore much thinned, if it survives at all, and the city, once very rich, is a mere tourist attraction in the poor south of Italy, on an island more celebrated for the mafia than for its contribution to pure knowledge.

The work of Archimedes flourishes when Greek civilisation, already old, has passed through the greatest cultural epoch in the history of man and has entered the Hellenistic Age that began when Alexander the Great of Macedonia conquered the Persian empire of the Achaemenids and continues under the descendants of his Macedonian generals who rule much of the territories he conquered. This Hellenistic era – like all periods of history, a creation of its logographers – spans the three centuries or so from Alexander through the Roman conquest of many of the lands he invaded and won, when Greek culture and language were exported to Asia and North Africa. It may not seem as romantic a period as the fifth-century BC Athens of Pericles – few are, at least in the imagination – but it has a distinct, modern culture with a flavour of the exotic from the vast, conquered territories of Asia and Africa where Greek is spoken as the common language, and a restless energy that matches anything in history. Much of that energy goes into fighting other Greeks, perhaps due to an ingrained tradition of belligerence, rivalry and hero worship, and perhaps because the underlying economic philosophy of the Greek rulers seems to hold that the way to become richer quickly is to conquer another state and enjoy its riches for as long as possible, probably the principal motive that spurred Alexander to invade Persia. As a result war seems always present in a bewildering series of conflicts as the Greek *poleis* and kingdoms fight and quarrel and temporarily ally with each other.

It's 250 years since the death of the Spartan king Leonidas at Thermopylae, when Athens and Sparta united to repulse the Persians, and around 160 since the Peloponnesian wars ended in victory for Sparta over Athens, which has long ceased to be a great power. Athens' influence as a centre of learning and philosophy, while still important, continues to decline. Sparta, once the more dominant power in Greece and never a centre of learning or philosophy, is almost spent. Power in the Greek world has moved to the Macedonians, once despised as a hairy people on the outer edges of the Hellenic world, viewed as barely Greek, relatively uncivilised, yet a people who were to embrace Greek thinking and culture at an astonishing pace under Alexander's father, Philip. The descendants of Alexander's generals control the lands that Alexander conquered. Much of the old mainland Hellas bends its knee to the Antigonids of Macedonia, while the Seleucids rule Mesopotamia, Syria, Palestine, and parts of Asia Minor, and Ptolemy the sister-lover owns Egypt, the greatest prize of all.

Homer, Hesiod, Pindar, Socrates, Aeschylus, Sophocles, Euripides, Herodotus, Xenophon, Plato, Demosthenes and Aristotle were among the most creative geniuses of the astonishing cultural eras of the past, but their work is very much alive at the time of Archimedes, as it is played and read and studied and discussed at the Academy and the Lyceum at Athens, at the Attalids' new Library at Pergamum in Asia Minor and probably most intensively of all at the Great Library of Alexandria-in-Egypt, as literature and philosophy continue to flourish and new ideas emerge.

The greatest threat to the future of this civilisation has arrived as the young Roman republic, victorious over its enemies on the Italian mainland, seeks to expand beyond that, into the Mediterranean basin, and encounters an enemy that's shockingly powerful and tactically superior in many ways, the empire of Carthage, traditional enemy of the Greeks in Sicily who controlled much of the east and south of the island. The First Punic War between Rome and Carthage has continued for eleven years, and will last for a further twelve. Much of the fighting is in Sicily, partly because Rome fears a Carthaginian invasion of the Italian mainland from the island, across the narrow Straits of Messina. To prevent it, the Romans have taken the fighting to the

Carthaginian cities in the north and west of the island, a comforting distance from Syracuse which is allied to Rome. One of the richest of these cities, Panormus – today's Palermo – has recently fallen to the Romans, so denying Carthage one of the island's natural harbours.

The mathematician is greeted respectfully by acquaintances in similar costume, white being the distinguishing colour of the dress of the privileged class in a world split into rich and poor, *hoi plousioi* and *hoi polloi.* They're friends who share that unique sense of community peculiar to the *polis*, perhaps a closeness impossible today. He joins them, and takes a *kylix* of heavily diluted white wine and a little dried fish from a young slave who carries an *oinochoe* of wine and a beaker of water and who salutes him respectfully. It's early summer, as the Greeks generally called spring, but the sun nears its zenith and he's glad of the *stoa*'s shade.

Some of the men talk excitedly of rumours that a great Roman fleet has been wrecked a few days before in a storm off Libya, perhaps with the loss of all two hundred quinqueremes, while others speak of the arrival of a ship that morning from Piraeus with news of the end of the Second Syrian War between Ptolemy II Philadelphus, Pharaoh of Egypt, and Antiochus II, and with it suggestions that the Seleucid ruler would soon repudiate his queen Laodice and wed Pharaoh's daughter Berenice. Elsewhere in the group there is praise for the skill of the discus-thrower who is favoured for the Pythian games, of the charms of a certain *hetaera* who plays the *cythara* like a nymph, and of the race in honour of the goddess Artemis to be held on the following evening. His neighbour is still offended at the performance of a drama staged during the recent *Dionysia*, the festival which has put on a revival of a work by the city's own Epicharmus who had turned comedy into an art form centuries before. The performance was an insult, almost an impiety, not only to the gods, to whom of course all performances are dedicated, and to Demeter the goddess in particular whose theatre it is, but also to a Syracusan audience of fifteen thousand of the most sophisticated theatre-goers who congratulate themselves on being the most sophisticated critics in Sicily. It was a disgrace to have a protagonist whose timing and diction were so poor, whose voice cracked and quavered as it carried beyond the orchestra of the theatre that the generous

Tyrant recently had rebuilt at great expense, a theatre famed throughout the Greek world for its echo chamber (a whisper from the *skene* would carry clearly to the highest members of the audience, helped by the breeze from the sea), and for the fact that Aeschylus' *The Persians* was first played there. The ruler of Syracuse, the benevolent Tyrant Hiero II, at the rumoured instigation of his son Gelo to whom Archimedes would dedicate his most revolutionary known work, has recently enlarged the *theatron*, or auditorium, which some persist still in calling the *koilon*, to 67 tiers of seats, and introduced a new *aeorema*, a crane that flies the actor to the *skene* like a god from a machine in half the time it took its obsolete predecessor. More controversially, the rebuilding has also introduced a *logeion*, a raised platform above the *skene* or stage that allows actors to stand and be seen while they watch the performance, which many of the more traditional critics in the *stoa* this day view as an innovation better suited to the Ionians.

The voices are loud as they ring from the old stone walls of the *stoa*, in the typical daily arguments of leisured Greeks everywhere in the civilised world, in *agorae* such as this from Syracuse to Epidaurus and Corinth and Athens and Alexandria-in-Egypt, across to the very borders of Bactria, modern Afghanistan, everyone talking at once, heated voices in a quarrel here and there by the squat Doric columns, while lowered voices at the edges of the group murmur of the political ambitions of the Tyrant's two daughters and his scheming son-in-law, Andranadorus. A wandering troupe of Phrygian dancers with accompanying lyre players and flautists walk past, grimacing at those who do not reward them with a coin.

The mind of the geometer is elsewhere. This morning he's been working on the problems of finding both the volume and the surface area of a sphere, something no mathematician had been able to achieve. Even if he were inclined to share his thoughts, it's very unlikely that he would be able to do so with anyone in the *stoa*. He's almost certainly the only mathematician there, probably the only one of the slightest note in Syracuse at the time. Some scholars argue that the number of pure mathematicians in the entire Greek world at the time could probably have been counted in tens – little more than a hundred at most – with the largest collection then in Alexandria, where it might have reached double figures. Yet this

Greek world is a busy, trading network, and the ships that make Syracuse rich carry his letters, book after book of rolled papyrus, each with its diagrams that form an integral part of each proposition, the short, almost brusque texts set out in a manner that scholars believe originated from the Greek oral tradition.

Mathematicians in other *poleis*, particularly the great polymath Eratosthenes who has become Librarian of Alexandria, are his correspondents with whom he shares his proofs in a world where structured institutions of learning, with set lectures, qualifications and examinations, don't exist. Greek mathematicians may feel they are in a minority among philosophers in general, but they don't feel isolated in a world where they're part of the broad stream of philosophy, the search for truth, a roof that shelters everything from magic and mysticism to what today we call science. Most routes are viewed as legitimate paths to enlightenment in a society that has opened four centuries before to ideas of almost any kind, where they flourish side by side with religion and myth. Philosophy was a respected occupation for members of the leisured classes by the time of Plato, who died sixty years or so before Archimedes was born. The mathematician of Syracuse, if he pauses to consider his life in the abstract, probably feels comfortable with the philosophies of Socrates and Plato where knowledge and the Good are inseparable, and especially comfortable in the discipline of Euclid and the mathematicians who believe that a theorem isn't a theorem without a proof.

The buzz of conversation goes on around him while he thinks. Subconsciously he's aware that every dialect of Greek is spoken in the *agora* this morning: the Ionic-Attic of the Athenians and the eastern Aegean, the Aeolic of the Lesbians and Boeotians, the *koine* or common language that's a version of Attic Greek and is spoken everywhere in the Hellenistic world, and the musical local version, Siculo-Doric, the vernacular of the men in the *stoa*. Syracuse is the great entrepot centre of the region and has earned its recent era of prosperity through trade under the clever governance of Hiero, who served under the mercurial King Pyrrhus of the empty victory and who would keep the peace for half a century, an astonishing gift to the Syracusans who traditionally fought with everyone, including one another. Hiero is said to be the illegitimate son of a nobleman and one of his women slaves and is related to Archimedes, presumably on his father's side, as the mathematician clearly belongs to the leisured class. The Tyrant would co-rule with his son Gelo for the latter part of his life, and he would live long enough to survive his son, to die at the age of 90.

There are sailors in short, dirty tunics and rough sandals assembled in noisy groups – some of them already drunk, in spite of the hour – from across the Greek world, many of whom use the *koine* because of the differences in dialects: Ionians from Asia Minor, Cyprians, rough Macedonians, Rhodians, Euboeans, Corinthians, sly Cretans. There are others from Sicily itself – Seluntinians, Catanians, Leontinians – and more from beyond it, Egyptian merchants from the kingdom of the Ptolemies, and darker-skinned Africans from the vast land mass across the straits to the south-west of the island. Musicians play under the hot sun out in the open area of the *agora*, perhaps near the great sun dial of Dionysius, wandering in file among the slaves carrying the morning's marketing, and a ragged Thracian plays the *syrinx* – the pipes of Pan – oblivious to the growing morning heat. Unaccompanied women of the lower class bargain loudly with the stallholders for fish and vegetables and olive oil, their shrill voices adding to the clamour of the *agora*, while slaves market for the wealthier households. The moneychangers, known as the tablemen or *trapezites*, compete loudly for the sailors' custom, weighing the coins, testing their metal by scratching their surfaces with a touchstone of black jasper, cheating the more gullible. On the near side of the *agora* a troupe of *phylakes*, clownish mummers, extracts threats from the porters carrying baskets of fresh fish from the harbour, and laughter from the citizens. Throughout this our Greek nods absent-mindedly in reply to his friends, his mind clearly on other matters. They're used to this and don't expect more.

Presently he salutes them, places a few coins in the hands of the attending slave, tucks the lower part of his *chiton* into his *zone* or belt for ease of walking, and returns to his house to work, passing the gymnasium, crossing the two main streets of the city until he reaches the quieter area where he lives. His house is plain and pleasant, the typical *oikos* of the modest Greek of the wealthier class, enclosed behind walls for shade. One of the rooms probably contains two or three couches on one of which he reclines to eat and, later, to sleep. Beside them are several three-legged tables on which the food is placed. He doesn't mention who his womenfolk are, but if they joined him from the *gynaikeion* – the women's quarters – at mealtimes they'd have sat on chairs or stools, as couches are reserved for men. The Greek world is a masculine society where the *kyrios* of the household legally owns not only the slaves, whose condition is universal and generally unquestioned, but also his wife and daughters, who appear only on family occasions or, if in public to visit a friend or relative, accompanied by a slave.

If a man wishes to entertain his friends to a *symposion*, or banquet, he may employ a number of *hetaerae*, trained courtesans who play the *cythara* and wear the classical *peplos*. Perhaps there will be a handsome young man or two as well, depending on his friends' tastes, as homosexuality is an accepted part of Greek life. The entertainers will sing, recite, and frequently physically couple with the guests, according to their wishes, while the female members of the family remain in their quarters.

There's little sign of any form of hedonism in the house of Archimedes, however. The main room has few decorations apart from several shelves with particularly fine black-figure vases, and a lyre that hangs on a wall. The house has three rooms on the ground floor, including the *thalamos* of the master, which is crammed with mechanical instruments including a model of an endless-screw device with a crank, wax tablets in neat piles, and papyrus rolls stored on shelves. The rooms interconnect – privacy is foreign to the Greeks – and finally open into a courtyard with a well and a little altar to Hestia that is occasionally used for sacrifices. There are flowering creepers on the external walls, upstairs quarters for any women of the family, a kitchen where the smoke from the fire escapes through a vent in the roof, slave quarters, shade for the porter at the door, and the *exedra*, which has several meanings in Classical Greek but seems in this case to have been an open courtyard with a little grove of olive trees at one end that shades the stone seat where he works. It serves as the study of the greatest scientist of antiquity.

At the end, sheltered by the outer wall of the dwelling, is a very steep set of stone steps. A towering clay vat, a *krater*, so tall that a ladder stands beside it, is at its top. Water spurts from a narrow spout at the bottom of the vat and glides through an intricate series of slim clay gutters that connect a number of pots, before flowing on to drive a delicate bronze paddlewheel that rotates an engraved dial once a day through a system of gears. The dial carries the signs of the Babylonian zodiac and passes through an arrow that marks the horizon dividing earth from sky, indicating which constellation is rising and which setting, even in daylight when they are invisible. On the flat lid of the vat is a mechanism of balanced weights connected to an articulated lever that drops with the water level to strike a bell when it's time for a slave to refill the *krater* to its brim. This is his *klepsydra*, the water thief, stealer of time, his own creation of which he's shamefully proud. Close by it is a horizontal, plane sun-dial of bronze, a *gnomon* or shadow clock, adjusted for the clime of Syracuse, with a chiselled shape on its surface that resembles the outline of a bat and a triangular wedge that divides each day and night into twelve hours, daylight hours that are correspondingly long in summer and short in winter, the two main seasons of the Greeks.

He sits at a stone bench, takes a wax tablet and draws a diagram on its face with a sharpened reed. The hours pass as he works without a pause in the most precise dialect of all, the language of mathematics. When the sun begins to sink and the Greek day formally ends he's already transferring his proposition to a roll of papyrus, which he fills rapidly, without punctuation between the words, dipping his stylus in a pot of black ink, writing in majuscule letters throughout until the proposition is complete.

Narrative

Aengus finished the entries in his journal, slept for a few hours, then strode down a woodland path before daybreak. The rawness had gone from the wind. A waning moon, low in the sky to the west, cast a silvery light on the bare trees.

He remembered that the vernal equinox would occur within weeks, and halted to look at the sky. The Bears danced around a wisp of cloud to the north-west and fading Cassiopeia hung on an unseen thread from a branch of an old oak in a clearing. Venus was sinking to the south-east, taking part of the night with it.

The stillness of the wood filled him with a sudden, unreasonable excitement, a conviction that the earth had paused in its daily revolution to greet him before the Bears turned it on its axle and brought forth the day. As the feeling grew, so did a strange confidence that a magical event would overtake him that morning. He shook his head quickly, fearing that reality would intrude, yet the conviction remained.

He looked again at the darker night sky and saw the Lyre almost directly above him, Hercules close by, and thought how strange the stillness was as he waited for the birds to call and for the scuffles in the undergrowth as the night animals finished their hunt. Having stood for a few moments, savouring the unusual quiet, he went on.

The eastern sky was lightening as he walked around a bend in the wood, a right of way through the estate, half-expecting to see a roe deer or a badger in the clearing. Instead he saw the slight figure of a young woman directly in front of him, surprised in the dawning light like a startled nymph, her arms filled with crocuses and snowdrops.

The rising light caught her white face and shone on her dark hair, stressing the paleness of the face and the great eyes shadowed by high cheekbones that were covered with skin like white marble, perhaps drawn by sadness or sorrow. She was a slim, willowy figure, her beauty strangely enhanced by her shabby outdoor garb, a virgin mistress of the woods. He stepped closer, and saw pride and defiance in her stance.

He thought that he dreamed still, and that his dream was too beautiful to last. Soon he would awake, he knew, to the realities of the world, to the noise and smells of civilisation, to anxiety and uncertainty and the sound of traffic. These came into his mind in that order, for a reason that later he could not fathom, as he continued to stare at the vision who seemed to him Artemis, Deirdre of the Sorrows, and the Virgin, a trinity in one.

Then he saw, as if in slow motion, the vision melt into the wood and heard a light footfall on leaves and twigs. "Wait!" he called urgently, surfacing from his daze, "Wait, whoever you are!"

The tempo of the footfalls increased, the sound gradually fading. He stooped to pick up the flowers she had dropped and held them as the sun came up and the lonely song thrush began to sing once more.

We were the measure of our own proportions. We were born into a natural and rational order that was based on the ideal form of the Greek body placed at full stretch within a circle, with the navel at the centre. We took our standard measurements of length from the proportions of that ideal man in a circle, beginning with the smallest, the *daktylos* or the breadth of a finger, and so on up through the width of a palm and a handspan to a *stadion*, six hundred times the length of the human foot. Thus the measure of the ideal Greek was in every temple, in every theatre, in every stadium. All were the measures of man, Stranger, and I tell you this to bring you inside the Greek mind so you might understand our love of symmetry and proportion.

When you look at a temple you may see the beauty of the whole. Look through that beauty and you will see the proportions of the ideal human body in strict mathematical ratios to one another. In many ways, that is even more beautiful because you may see the simple geometry of every part that makes the whole, circle, square, rectangle, triangle, perpendicular. Every column, every capital, each *ekhinos* and *abakos*, the *triglyphs* and *meitopes*, *pronaos* and *opisthodomos*, all are cut in stone to the measure of the Greek in the circle, and all are in ratio to each other, as in the harmony of a musical scale. The height of each temple must agree with the length, the length with the breadth, and every ratio with the whole, balanced like a lever in equilibrium. The same discipline is in a theatre, built in exact proportions around the circle of the orchestra, the symbol of the ancient circle dance around the altar of Dionysos the god.

It was a joy later to me as a mathematician to discover other proportions that seemed to fall into place naturally, without a struggle, as the parts of a temple or a theatre did. I think of how the surface area of a sphere proves to be exactly four times the area of its greatest circle, and I remember how I reminded Eratosthenes of this when he measured the circumference of the earth. I think of the satisfying truth of many mathematical and mechanical relationships, that two weights balance at distances that are reciprocally proportional to their magnitudes, that the lost weight of a body that is immersed in water is equal to the weight of the liquid displaced, and so on. All of these are rational. They carry an outer beauty, like the lune of Hippokrates, yet they have an inner proportion that is satisfying exact.

The circle was very different. Of course it was the symbol of many things, perfection, proportion, the cosmos itself, and so on, and in my boyhood fantasies, as I said, I saw within it the face of the Goddess in the moon. Yet no geometer had calculated it, none could tell the area of the shape that itself contained the measure of man. That seemed the greatest irony of all, the challenge that constantly loomed at me.

I thought deeply about this as a young man, and during my travels, as I will tell you, the image of the Goddess in the circle of the full moon was a reminder of it, but it was not until I was in my twenty-second year, following my return to Syracuse, that I settled my mind to find a solution.

I had accepted as a given, as I said, that to square the circle was impossible, but I began to ponder whether a proportion could be discovered that would be so close to the truth that the remainder would not matter.

That, Stranger, became my labour, the first of many.

One early morning, while my father still slept, I went to work. Over the weeks that followed I constructed hypotheses that failed, time after time, seeing an infinite magnitude in every calculation, a magnitude that seemed to run away from me as I tried to capture it. These approaches failed, but geometers are used to failure. I would try again.

I sought a new approach as, once more, I rose early one day. To clear my head I went out through Akhradina and Neapolis, to the *khora* and the spring of Alpheios where a cult of an earlier age had erected a shrine to Artemis Potamia. There I looked into the clear water and saw infinity once more. I walked up to the defences of Dionysios, walls that were falling slowly to ruin, and sat on a fallen stone block. The day was pleasant, the view stretched out to sea beyond the harbour, and I found it easier to think. I was used to dealing with irrational or incommensurable numbers, as they had been known to Greek mathematicians for more than tens of Olympiads. The Babylonians and the Egyptians knew them, too, while Plato and Aristotle discussed them in philosophical arguments. The brotherhood of Pythagoras were said to have discovered, to their dismay, that irrational numbers lay within the right-angled triangle, as indeed they do. This particular incommensurable I knew by instinct to be fundamentally different from all others, enclosing a mystery of its own. It required a different approach, a method I had not tried before. I searched for one on that beautiful morning.

The air on the plateau was filled with the pleasant hum of insects among the flowers that grew like a mist around the walls. I looked at the old defences of the city, and I saw a picture in my head of a proposition from Eukleid in which he estimated the volume of certain solids within greater and lesser limits, an image that had lived in me in the depths of my mind. It came to me then that the way to trap an incommensurable number such as this was to imprison it between walls.

Narrative

Aengus saw his vision of the lady of the woodland again the next day. He drove the tractor and trailer loaded with logs into one of the farmyards by the main road and recognised her as she entered the house of Seth. That was all he glimpsed of her before he turned into the farmyard, his mind suddenly in turmoil.

A voice called from a shed doorway. "Over here! You're late!"

He mind cleared and he saw Sid and Bill staring at him. "Sorry," he said. "I was held up." He turned the tractor, backed the trailer to the shed, and stepped down.

While they unloaded the logs, he turned to Sid. "Doesn't that man Seth live over there?"

The keeper grunted irritably. "Why?"

He persisted. "Does he have a wife?"

"A woman called Kate lives with him. I dunno any more. Let's get on."

Curiosity won. "What does she look like?"

Sid looked angry, but answered: "Big woman, strong, face like a gypsy, with a big dog, a fierce bugger of a dog."

Aengus exhaled slowly. "Does anyone else live there with them?"

"Yes. A younger woman. They say she's his sister. Treats her like dirt. Stay away from them."

"What's the sister called?"
"I dunno. Now let's get on."
"I think she's called Bridget," said Bill Worthy.

The Greek

I seem to remember every moment of that morning, how I returned to the house to find my father breakfasting, how I was torn between hunger and an eagerness to begin work. Hunger and respect won, and while we ate in companionable silence I found Pheidias studying my expression, as though he sensed an eagerness or excitement that had been lacking in me during the last few days.

Eventually he nodded, and rose to write his notes. I sat at my usual place close to him in the shade of the morning, thinking, holding my eagerness in check. After a time I took a compass and inscribed a circle in my tablet, looking absently at the circumference while a breeze from the sea countered the growing heat. I thought of how the Egyptians drew a circle on the ground with rope and peg, and measured it by stretching a papyrus rope across the diameter and around its circumference to give them a rough approximation of the circle's dimension. I, in contrast, in the tradition of Greek mathematicians, would calculate its proportions solely in my mind, without leaving my seat, by enclosing the circumference of the circle between two figures I would construct with ruler and compass. Their sides would be of straight lines, so it would be simple to calculate their proportions.

I could not be exact, but I would be as close as I wished. I would draw these two figures – regular polygons, as the geometer calls these figures with equal sides and angles – so they would grip this circle by its circumference, one from the inside and one from the outside, so tightly that they would be indistinguishable to the faulty human eye from the circle itself. Then I would calculate the length of the sides of each polygon. That, as I said, would be simple, as its sides were of straight lines.

I began inside the circle, drawing a figure of six equal sides within it so that its vertices touched the circle's circumference. Doubling the number of sides of this hexagon produced a figure of twelve sides, a dodekagon. The circle began to fill as I doubled the number of sides once more. I added as many sides as I wished, loading the inner circumference of the circle with as many straight lines as it would bear, until the sides grew so short that the later polygons began to resemble the circle itself. I did not halt until the final polygon had 96 sides. I could have continued indefinitely, but that was enough for my purpose.

I paused and gazed at the figure in the tablet. The polygon seemed to fill the entire area of the circle, exhausting all space within, although I knew it to be slightly smaller, that it had to be so, as its outer limit was confined by the circle's circumference. I glanced at my father, still deep in his work, then continued.

I let the figure stand in the wax while I began work again on a fresh tablet, calculating the sum of the lengths of the polygon's sides – simple to do, as they were composed of straight lines – and divided the result by the length of the diameter, the line that I drew through the centre of the circle. The result of the division produced a ratio that made my inner self sing. The first part of the work was complete. I had the inner wall.

It was time to build the outer, a second polygon, again of 96 sides, immediately around the circle so that the sides again touched the circumference, but *outside* it. Once more I calculated the sum of the sides, and the polygon's diameter, then divided the one by the other, holding my breath in anticipation then releasing it audibly as I arrived at a perfect ratio that was a little greater than the first.

I paused then as the breeze rustled the olive trees, and reminded myself that I had trapped the incommensurable, that it lay within the two ratios or limits. Between the two, the inner or lower, and the outer or higher, lay the answer, as it was a given that it could not be less than the first or greater than the second. The two limits served as geometrical walls to contain the number that was the measure I sought. The mean of the two gave a figure that was close enough to the truth to calculate the area of any circle and unlock the door to the mathematics of every curvilinear object in the cosmos.

The circle had kept its secret. It could not be squared, but its area could be calculated to an accuracy that was as close as I wished. So I calculated it, and when I finished I set out to prove that I was wrong.

The three men seemed to drink an unlimited amount the next evening until the pub closed. Sid's mood grew darker as the alcohol flowed, his eyes flickering from one companion to the other at first, as if seeking a challenge, then dulling as the evening aged. He spoke little, shoulders slumped. There was an urgency about his drinking that spoke of a lack of inner content, a restlessness disturbing to Aengus who eyed him warily, wondering whether the keeper was ashamed of his failure to confront the figure of Seth. He thought once more of the reptilian eyes, like those of a Nile crocodile stalking a drinking buffalo, and of the haze of menace that surrounded the great head as it swam past them.

Aengus was careful not to upset the countryman who had been kind to him, even to the point that he avoided reminding the others of the correct pronunciation of his name. Sid had called him Angus when they met, and Angus he remained as far as everyone on the estate was concerned.

Bill, however, seemed oblivious to the keeper's mood. Several times Sid stirred or looked away in irritation and anger, and after a time Aengus judged it time to leave. Without a word Sid turned and walked outside to where Bill Worthy, waving a cigarette and smiling vacuously, very drunk, danced to the music in his earphones before he tripped on the laces of his trainers and fell sprawling, his jeans muddied. Sid stared at him in disgust, then began to sober as the cold wind began to work.

"Townie bugger!" Aengus heard him mutter, but could not decide whether Sid referred to Bill or the landlord, a newcomer with a face like a ferret.

"Let's get him home," said Sid in a clear voice, and lifted Bill in a fireman's lift, without a stagger.

"You've done this before," said Aengus, surprised at the keeper's steely strength.

"More than once," said Sid, breathing easily. "He can't hold it." Bill began to snore. "Walk behind. Tell me if he's going to be sick."

A half-moon lit their way as they arrived at the young man's cottage and delivered him to his girlfriend, a teenaged, dyed blonde dressed in her sleeping garb of an outsize pink tee-shirt and men's boxer shorts, who looked accusingly at the two as they lowered Bill on his bed. "He'll get it in the mornin'," said Sid, then seemed to remember abruptly what awaited him at home, a wife who was much larger than he, with the reputation of a termagant. "You're lucky you ain't got no wife, Angus," he said, with more than a trace of envy as he arrived at his back door.

The wind had died when Aengus left him and set off for his own cottage on the other side of the wood, walking upstream by the river, the moon a ruffled yellow shape in the watery mirror. He heard the night birds calling, and the yelp of a vixen. A sudden crashing from the wood betrayed a roe deer or muntjac disturbed.

He sat on a fallen tree by the riverbank to clear his head. "*Tiri, tiri, tiri,*" came from the tall reeds by the water's edge, then "*tier, tier, tier, zach, zach, zach.*" Aengus sat like a statue, ear cocked. It was a reed warbler, he decided when it called again, a bird that liked a still night. Its nest would be halfway up the reeds in front of him, sheltered from the spring gales.

Another animal crashed through the undergrowth as he made his way to his cottage a few minutes later. Muntjac or roe deer? He heard a snuffle. Muntjac, he decided. Sid hated them.

He saw a flash of white by his cottage door and stopped, confused by memories of a different night-time visitor. Then he collected himself, sober suddenly, and stepped behind a hawthorn bush. The moon had slipped behind a cloud and the air was stiller, bringing the murmur of the current to his ears. A tawny owl called. Another answered from deep in the wood.

He saw a faint glimmer of white once more, this time only a few feet away. Crouching, he waited for the moon to emerge. When it did he saw clearly the face of the young woman he had surprised in the wood at dawn.

He waited, and saw her turn as if to walk back along the path from his cottage.

"Are you real?" he called, choosing his words on impulse.

The figure stood still, then turned and the moonlight caught it again.

It spoke: "Yes," in a quiet voice that betrayed little fear. "I didn't mean to disturb you."

"You don't disturb me," he said. "Come inside."

He unlatched his door and switched on the light, seeing her

close at hand for the first time. She had strikingly large eyes whose pupils were of dark blue, like a deep sea in sunlight. They looked at him then, looked straight into his before they looked down, the light catching the shadow cast by her high cheekbones. Glossy dark hair hung to her shoulders.

He pushed a chair forward. She turned her face, and he saw again his image of her at dawn in the woodland clearing. "It's late. I must get back."

"Were you coming to see me?"

For a moment he thought she would not speak, then she answered, her voice firmer: "Yes."

He waited.

After a pause she said in a low voice: "I'm sorry I ran away that morning. I thought you were someone else."

"How did you know I lived here?"

"I saw you working on the estate. Kate knew who you were."

"How does she know?" He remembered Sid's description of the tall woman with the face of a gypsy.

"She seems to know everything," the girl responded slowly, letting her gaze wander around the plain kitchen. "I haven't seen so many books for a long time," she said wonderingly. Her voice was musical, pleasing, with the suggestion of an education that did not fit with her being related to Seth.

She picked up an open volume of poems on his table and read aloud, in a vibrant tone that startled him:

O Moon! Old boughs lisp forth a holier din
The while they feel thine airy fellowship.
Thou dost bless everywhere, with silver lip
Kissing dead things to life.

She put down the book. For a moment her eyes had sparkled. "This is Keats, isn't it?"

"It is," Aengus replied. "*Endymion.*"

She looked away, her energy fading. "I read it once," her voice low, "but I've forgotten the story."

"It's about a shepherd-boy whom the goddess of the moon is in love with," he replied, studying her face once more.

She looked around the room, eyes still in shadow. Her head

sank. "Your name is Aengus, isn't it?"
"And yours is Bridget."
She sat up straight, then said: "How do you know?"
"I asked," he said.
"I suppose they said to avoid us," she said.
"Yes, they did."
She was silent, evidently reflecting.
He broke the silence. "I like the name Bridget. It resonates of spring, the turning of the year."
She said, as if in a trance: "The spring that does not come, the year that will never turn. Winter. Perpetual winter."
She did not move. He waited, wondering if she were deranged.
She raised her head and said in a stranger voice, as though still in a trance: "Aengus. Aengus and his song. Silver apples of the moon, golden apples of the sun. Wandering Aengus. Aengus of the Birds."
"Are you a wanderer, too?" she asked after a long pause. Her voice seemed more normal.
"I suppose I am."
"And you live alone." It was a statement, not a question, with a slight suggestion of envy. That made two people in one evening who envied him, Aengus thought.
"Yes. I'm divorced."
"What was she like?" It was interesting, he thought, how few matters could arouse any woman's curiosity more than another woman. He was oddly pleased to see that she was not different, though the question pained him.
He hesitated, unwilling to speak ill of someone who had been so central to his life, yet reminded of failure and unhappiness. The girl saw the hesitation, and rose. "I must go."
She stepped into the darkness, refusing his offer to walk with her. He stood in the doorway long after she had left, cleft by different feelings. Desire for sleep left him. He sat at his table and took up his journal, recording all that the Greek had told him, his mind whirling.

The Book of Aengus

Even I could follow him as he approached the circle, determined to grip its perimeter within his mathematical walls until he controlled it from inside and outside, easily accepting the rigid discipline inherited from the earlier Greek mathematicians, that all problems in geometry must be solved in the mind, shunning any method of physical measurement, to describe an abstract but objective reality that carried a beauty of its own. Only ruler and compass could be used, a ruler to draw a line – not to measure something – and a compass to describe any figure with a curve. These were used to create the diagrams that were an essential part of every proposition, so integral to each that a proposition could not stand without them.

Thus Archimedes gave us his book *On the Measurement of a Circle* and with it a figure for *pi*, a number that left the circle with its innermost secret yet yielded a solution the world would use for the next two thousand years. It was one of the daring feats of mathematics, the historians say, creating a platform for the great men of the modern era. The method he used gave us what mathematicians call the Doctrine of Limits, essential to the calculus of Newton and Leibniz and the mathematics of today.

I set out to prove that I was wrong. This seems to have been the fabled Greek technique of proof by double contradiction. If his calculations showed that one magnitude was greater than another, he set out to prove that it was smaller, looking for a contradiction. If they showed that it was smaller, he set out to prove that it was greater, again seeking a contradiction. Some proofs worked on contradiction alone. It was part of the so-called indirect proof of the Greeks. The scholars say Archimedes was a master of it.

Almost two millennia later – from Galileo onwards, when the work of Archimedes re-entered the mainstream of science – the mathematicians were to look at his method and to be astonished by how modern it seemed, how original and ingenious, and now, centuries after Galileo, they say how close the mathematician of Syracuse was to the calculus in his approach to calculating the measurement of a curved object. Today's scholars speak of how he was prepared to use an infinite number of sides of his polygons to search for a number until he was as close to it as he wished to be, evidence that Archimedes understood the concept of infinity and taught himself to deal with it. *I could have continued indefinitely…*

The histories of mathematics I have ploughed through are full of the great names – Galileo, Descartes, Euler, Gauss, Laplace, Lagrange, Leibniz, Newton, Hamilton and many more – who inherited his work and built on it to uncover abstract truths, most of them beyond my grasp but, as I read of the more modern age, the twentieth-century mathematical logician Kurt Gödel, close friend of Einstein, looms from the histories as a radical heir of Archimedes. It was Gödel who looked through and beyond mathematics to see a philosophical truth, and was genius enough to invent his own mathematical language to prove his hypothesis, as Archimedes did. Gödel, a tortured mind, shook his world when he proved that any system of arithmetic a mathematician might use contains true statements than cannot be proven, that every such system is incomplete as a result, and that an objective reality therefore exists that lies beyond the ability of arithmetic to deal with, a truth known as *Incompleteness.*

I look at the maths books, at the diagram Archimedes drew when he built his walls inside and outside the circle, I remember how he viewed the face of Artemis in the moon, and a series of images, unconnected with mathematics, gather in my brain, images I saw in the East and Middle East, images I see in every Christian church, images common to anyone who looks for them. I hear again the voices of a Lamaist monk in Tibet, a pandit in India, a mullah in Iran, all earnestly explaining to me what these images mean, the image Jung writes of as a *mandala.* Archimedes the geometer may see a circle with its polygons, but I wonder if the spiritual Greek man also sees an inner image, built through his imagination when he was a boy observing the moon, a circular symbol etched deeply in the unconscious, a symbol that Jung says occurs everywhere, in all religions and cultures.

Perhaps he'll speak again of this, but for the present it's enough to know that the circle was frequently a sacred shape, in history and prehistory, and the psychologists say it was present at the dawn of human awareness. Erich Neumann, who had been a pupil of Jung, said the circle is a symbol of original perfection that is there at the beginning of the evolution of human consciousness. It manifested itself in physical form throughout history in many forms.

One of them, Cashford relates, was through the measurement of time, a fundamental signal of early human awareness. Later in the last century, a few years after Neumann's death, the anthropologists discovered from Palaeolithic artefacts that man from the early ages marked on bone the passage of the moon to measure time. The symbol of original perfection that Neumann posited before the anthropologists' discovery, the circle, had been proven to have a physical existence from the earliest times, and its image was that of the moon.

Throughout the eras that followed the importance of the circle continued to assert itself, through the henges and the great stone circles such as those at Avebury and Stonehenge, both places of worship and solar calendars, where the male sun symbolically entered the female earth. There the Stone Age people worshipped the universal Earth Mother or Great Goddess whose symbol was the moon. They probably did so, too, at Silbury Hill, the largest prehistoric mound in Europe made by man, built of perfect concentric circles four and a half thousand years ago. The circle or sphere is a symbol of the Self, said Jung, and it expresses the totality of the psyche in all its aspects, including the relationship between man and the whole of nature. I have the passage in front of me: *Whether the symbol of the circle appears in primitive sun worship or modern religion, in myths or dreams, in the* mandalas *drawn by Tibetan monks, in the ground plans of cities, or in the spherical concepts of early astronomers, it always points to the single most vital aspect of life – its ultimate wholeness.*

...*Or in the spherical concepts of early astronomers*, wrote Jung. That's the phrase I remembered, the one that jolted my memory. It could as easily have read: *Or in the circular constructs of early mathematicians...*

The evidence shows that the importance of the circle as a sacred image continued throughout the Stone Age, through the Bronze and Iron Ages and beyond to become, in its ideal, abstract form, part of Greek philosophy. Archimedes spoke earlier of how the circle of the orchestra in a theatre, where the chorus stood, originated in Dionysian dithyrambic dances. It may have done, but we know the tradition to be much older. Standing stones or menhirs were representations of the Great Goddess or Earth Mother, and the ancients danced around them in a circle. Hence Artemis was sometimes known as the *Stony One*. The tradition of this sacred ring dance probably goes back to Upper Palaeolithic times – some time between ten thousand and forty thousand years ago – and there are ceramic remains from the fifth millennium BC showing naked women joining arms in a dance around a circle, perhaps the forerunner of the dances to which he refers.

Many of the early Christian churches seem to have been built on the sites of stone circles, probably to exorcise their power and to replace it with another. I know of a churchyard in Wales built on the site of a sacred circle where the megaliths of the Stone Age people remain today in the outer wall. The early Christian church leaders destroyed most of these pagan stone circles during daylight, but the myth persisted, as though the Goddess watched while her followers faithfully rebuilt her symbol in the darkness.

Narrative

Aengus watched the house of Seth when daylight went, hoping to glimpse the girl, then wandered the woods on a wild night, heedless of the gale that sought the older, weaker trees and blew them over to join the masses of rotting wood and vegetation a few yards from the riverbank. A torn sky showed a gibbous moon riding imperiously through the broken cloud, and a barn owl, dipping occasionally with furling wings, hunted like a ghost across the water meadows.

A dog fox barked from the other side of the railway line. He crossed it into the adjoining estate and heard the fox bark again, its tone supplicating. He made a noise like a vixen and moved closer.

He found it in a thicket and shone his torch on its face, twisted in a snarl of agony. He shone his torch on its hindquarters and found the problem, a steel trap that held the fox's left hind leg. The fox whimpered and licked his hand.

Aengus shook his head. The keepers on the estate where he worked shot their foxes, shunning the illegal traps evidently favoured by the keepers here. The fox whimpered again, his eyes shining with a desire to live. "Let's see what we can do," Aengus murmured to him, and prised apart the terrible jaws of the device, noting with relief that they had not closed completely because a light branch had evidently caught in the trap earlier without triggering it. The fox whirled and began to lick its leg. Then it stood, motionless, eyes fixed on the man before it turned and walked away. After a few yards it halted and turned its head to look again at the man. Aengus obeyed and followed.

The fox took him through the woodland paths and into an open meadow where a down of hares sat motionless in a rough circle, heads uplifted to the moon.

He felt an abrupt chill as he watched, wondering what would happen next. It left him in a moment as he saw the hares scatter, a female plainly in oestrus among them, using her forepaws to bat away the males easily as they chased her through the grasses, bodies on springs in the moonlight. He sought the pathfinder fox, but it had vanished into the wood.

The Greek

Tonight I will tell you why I have come to you.

I jump forward in time to the final days of Greek Syracuse, Stranger, when the city had lain under siege from the Romans for almost three years and the citizens quarrelled among themselves.

The new rulers of Syracuse, duplicitous barbarians, had forgotten all that had been learned when I had conducted its defence after the consul Marcellus attacked us by sea and land. Nor did they ask my help, refusing any advice I offered.

The Tyrant Hiero and his son Gelo, who had ruled together for many years, had generally consulted the wishes of the citizens at meetings in the public buildings, but the new rulers had suspended meetings because they were afraid to face the people. The politics of Syracuse was in paralysis, *stasis*, without a leader, a strong man, even such as the terrible Agathokles or Dionysios the Tyrant himself.

I, an old man by then and alone, watched the heavens at night while the Romans waited for the opportunity to enter the city and sack it. I saw the stars circle the northern roof of the cosmos and the moon come up from the sea, and knew I had little time to finish the greatest work of my life, one with the powers of the Lyre of Orpheus.

Throughout the siege, I lived simply, forbidden to take part in the defence of the city. My wants were few, bread, oil from my olive trees, some fish, fruit, and a *kylix* of water mixed with a little wine which the slave brought to me during daylight while I worked. Syracuse was cut off from the outside world by the Roman soldiers on land and by the picket ships at sea. Occasional letters from Eratosthenes at Alexandria reached me through the smugglers, but they became rarer as the siege continued and the Romans tightened their grip. Although grown used to my own companionship, I felt strangely alone. I slept little, and spent the nights on the roof of the house.

On the final day of my life, Syracuse was betrayed and the Roman soldiers finally entered the inner city. They came into my house, sweeping aside the porter and slaves. One, an uncivilised barbarian, came to me and shouted to me to stand.

I said: – *Do not touch my work*, but he thrust his spear through my chest.

The Romans are a backward people. They do not see the wonder that we do in free thought. They see only straight lines, not curves. They regard life, from birth to death, as linear. They think in squares, not circles. They see an object only for its use. They cannot sneeze without fearing what it portends. Mathematics as we know it is nothing to them, as I was.

So much for them. We come to the mystery of my death.

The protector of our city state was the Goddess Artemis, yet it was while Syracuse celebrated her festival that the Romans first entered the city.

Go to the Goddess, Stranger. Seek her presence at the next festival to her, because it was the Goddess who killed me.

The Book of Aengus

The scholars conjecture that Archimedes often communicated elliptically. I am a living witness to that, and try to unravel what I can. He says the goddess Artemis killed him after the sacred festival to her, almost in the same breath as he speaks of the Roman soldier who murdered him.

Artemis was the Goddess of the Moon, the huntress, mistress of nature, shooting her arrows of silver light. She controlled the tides, this beautiful daughter of Zeus and twin sister of the sun god Apollo, and she was the protector of the cities she loved, jealous of their devotion to her. Syracuse was one of them.

As with all Greek deities, her influence and importance

changed over the ages, particularly when the power of the male god overtook that of a goddess, sun over moon. Her myth is among the oldest in the Olympic pantheon, much older than that of Aphrodite, Goddess of Love. Graves says she recalls the *Lady of the Wild Things*, the nymph-goddess of the archaic totem societies of Crete, who probably elected one of the handsomest young men as a stag-king to serve as her consort for a fixed period and tore him ritualistically to pieces at the end of the reign, giving him a head start before loosing her hounds. Actaeon, whom Artemis turned into a stag after he'd seen her bathing in a sacred spring, was probably originally a sacred king of an ancient stag cult.

Greek myth is interwoven with references to her, principally as the huntress, but also as patroness of childbirth and healing, and as the White Goddess, from the colour that her priestesses painted their faces. She was frequently represented carrying a silver bow, the emblem of the new moon, sometimes with bow and quiver in a splendid chariot pulled by two white harts. The early Christian church tried to absorb her myth by making her a saint. It called her St Artemidos, a distant vision from the wilful girl-child to whom the Hellenistic poet Callimachus sang in his hymn.

We know that the moon was universally worshipped in most ancient societies, much more so than the sun. It was the provider of life itself, raingiver, healer, the essential fertility symbol, a shining symbol of the Great Goddess or Earth Mother. To the Greeks the moon was also the home of the three *Moirai* or Fates, Clotho, Lachesis and Atropos, who spun and measured the life-line of Greek man and in time decided when to cut it. The Goddess of the Moon, often viewed as the Great Goddess herself, had power over all, not only in Greek society, but in most others, a universal image to mankind. For a period of Greek mythology, Artemis was the most powerful deity in the entire pantheon, more so than Zeus her father, and more so than her brother Apollo.

In time she was joined as Goddess of the Moon by two others. Selene would become the goddess of the waxing moon, while Hecate, viewed as the dark one who in later times was seen as a witch, became goddess of the waning lunar image, responsible for the moon's fall into darkness until Selene returned. Artemis, however, retained her central power as goddess of the full moon. Other goddesses in Greek mythology, including Athene, Demeter and Aphrodite, were also interchangeable as the Great Goddess, but Artemis and her female consorts comprised the Triple Goddess of the Greeks, the Great Goddess in one.

They were an early trinity, part of a tradition of a female threesome that resurfaced as the three Marys present at the death of Christ, and even found its way into *Macbeth*. Trinities were common to the Greeks – there were three Fates, three Furies, and Cerberus the dog had three heads. This particular trinity was a symbol to the Greeks of the successor to the primordial Great Goddess, the Earth Mother herself who was symbolised by the moon. The Great Goddess was universal in different ancient civilisations, and survives as an important archetype in the human psyche.

There were festivals to Artemis everywhere in the Greek world, particularly in the cities of which she was patron and protector. Pindar wrote of one at Syracuse where she was honoured as *Artemis Potamia* and *Soteria* every spring. At one time an Artemision, a temple to Artemis, stood alongside the temple of Athene at Syracuse, and across the square the archaeologists have discovered an early sanctuary, an *oikos* as they call it, to the goddess. They have also disinterred, in the same square, an eighth-century BC pottery cup for ladling wine, called an *oinochoe*, on which Artemis is portrayed as *Potnia Theron*. That title refers to her manifestation as nature goddess, but perhaps it had a broader meaning, a cosmic implication of some kind.

The most remarkable of the temples to Artemis was at Ephesus, rebuilt during the time of Alexander the Great by his architect Deinocrates. It was massive, though not beautiful, probably the most celebrated temple in the history of Greece, one of the seven wonders of the world, built to house the most powerful goddess of all.

His words echo once more. He was murdered by a Roman soldier, yet he was killed by Artemis the Goddess, the maker of time, the bringer of death, and a shining light. I, a mortal born two millennia and more after he died, am charged with finding an answer or answers to a series of elliptical questions, including those surrounding his death, by seeking her presence in some way. I must go to the next festival to her, he says, viewing me with more powers than I have, and implying that in some sense she is nearby.

It's late, and the wind is rising, soughing through the willows, but I'm no longer alone.

Narrative

A raven flew over the canal a week later, watching a tall man hike wearily along the towpath from Kintbury. Aengus had returned from a day trip to London.

He had been to Lincoln's Inn Fields to see his solicitor, the only person from his previous life who knew where to find him, the only friend he had kept. Simon had news of his former wife. She wanted money.

"She must know I don't have any." The feeling of inadequacy returned. He saw her as she was when they met, not beautiful in a classical sense, but perfectly formed for an age that liked its women skinny. She had been as slim as a stick, tiny-boned, small-breasted, blonde hair cut like an urchin, a tiny nose with a hint of freckles, the tinkling laugh that was peculiar to her, that drew men. He tried to visualise her from the lawyer's description, to see her as she had become, an addict entering premature middle age whose friends had deserted her, yesterday's woman, today's derelict, tomorrow's lonely crone if she survived that long, which she probably would not.

He shook his head and concentrated. "I have a little money saved. I'll send it to you. Give her that."

"You don't owe her anything."

"Give it to her anyway. Tell her that's all I have. If she asks – which she won't – tell her I'm well, and that I've met someone else."

"Is that true?"

"I hope so."

The raven flew above the towpath, watching the tall figure stride along, gliding occasionally towards the woods, seeking carrion. Aengus went straight to the cottage and changed to his work overalls, then joined the keepers who were unloading tanks of stocked trout from a lorry. "Get hold of that there tank, Angus," instructed Sid with scarcely a glance at the new arrival. "We've got to get 'em into the shed overnight, leave 'em quiet, then we'll put 'em in the river tomorrow."

They placed the tanks in the shed, water brimming over the sides. The trout lay low, at the bottom of the tanks, almost invisible.

The agent arrived, his back like a ramrod, an immaculate man in tweeds and Hunter boots. "Did you men see or hear anything strange last night?"

Sid lifted his cap and scratched his head. "Can't say I did," he said after a pause. "You, Bill? You, Angus?"

Each shook his head.

"Someone was prowling around the estate. The description matches that man Seth."

Aengus saw her when he passed the bend in the river near his cottage. She sat on a rough chair by his front porch. She stood when she saw him approach and came in a hurry to meet him, urgency in her step, wearing a simple dress, no makeup, flat shoes.

"I'm glad you came," he said. "I passed your house earlier."

"I know," she said, her voice very tense. "I saw you."

He was surprised. "Why didn't you come out?"

"Seth was there," she said, then looked around with a searching eye. A robin hopped from the porch rail, alarmed. Automatically, Aengus looked, too, then turned his head to her.

"Are you afraid he's following you?"

"Yes, always. He'd kill if he saw me with you."

She saw his shock. "You mustn't come near the house. I came to tell you that."

Anger took hold. "Why don't you leave him? Go to the police. Tell them he threatens you. I can stop him harming you."

"I can't. It would be madness." Her voice was flat, definite, warning him off.

He waited until his anger cooled, then said: "Come inside for a moment."

She looked back along the path, then stepped inside when he had unlocked the door.

"Will you be more careful?" she asked, a mute appeal in her eyes.

"You say he'd kill," he said. "Do you mean that?"

"Yes. It's his nature." She looked earnestly at him, her gaze level with his.

"You mean he'd kill us both?"

She was silent. Her hands were clasping and unclasping.

"You came for help," he said. "What can I do?"

She looked away, then faced him. "I would come to you for help if I could, but nothing can help me."

"They say Seth is your brother. Why would he harm you?"

"He's my half-brother." She looked down, hair covering her face.

"Why would he harm you?"

The wind was rising, the branches of the big willow slapping the cottage roof. The windows rattled. She was silent.

He tried a different approach. "What about Kate?"

The question surprised her. "Kate?"

"Yes, Kate. What is she to you?"

"She is a friend – sometimes."

"What is she to Seth?"

"He thinks she's his whore." The word shocked him strangely, particularly as she did not give it emphasis.

"Isn't she?"

"No. She's not a whore."

"What is she, then?"

She paused, then said: "She's from a different world. He doesn't understand that."

He stood and looked at her, noting the curve of her cheekbones and the whiteness of her skin. The willow branch whipped the roof once more and the windows rattled again, but he did not hear them, searching her eyes where he found sanity and honesty and a desperate courage that suppressed any temptation to ask for help. He saw pride in her steady gaze, too, a refusal to surrender to an instinct that would bring an appeal from a weaker spirit, and he resolved not to question her again.

The Book of Aengus

I began this journal to record the visits of the Greek, but a different mystery fills me with an emotion that I believed died long ago. It grips me in a way I can't put in words except to write that judgment, reasoning, sanity, balance, all seem to be overwhelmed by this sensation that overcomes me when I remember her look. I saw pride there, of course, an infinite pride, but it haunts me to believe that for an instant I also saw hope. That pains me most because I can think of nothing I can do to help. I know little of her, yet I sense her goodness, that she speaks the truth. Such a young face should be full of laughter and compassion and love. Instead it seems strained with grief and an unbearable tension that she cannot release.

I feel guilty as I force myself to turn to my thoughts of the Greek.

At least I'm beginning to know him, to catch his changes of tone, the inflections and the pauses and the emphases, as though they rose and fell from the echo chamber of the theatre at Syracuse. On his last visit I heard him speak, like a singing head, of the power of the lyre of Orpheus, as though it were a symbol of a cosmic force.

The Greeks called him *Famous Orpheus*, this poet, hero, Argonaut, sacrificial victim, the son of the Muse of epic poetry, this mythical youth who told the Greeks to seek truth and beauty. The ancients sang of how the music of his lyre put a spell on opponents, clearing the way to steer Jason and the *Argo* through safely to their destiny, and viewed him as a hero rather than a god. A few nights ago Archimedes spoke of him in connection with the power of his own last work. The cult of Orpheus saw the lyre, with its seven strings, creating an overpowering harmony of its own, a civilising power, preventing wanton destruction through the truth and beauty of its music. Apollo is said to have presented him with the first lyre, which would accompany the poems he wrote and sang, to give lyric poetry to the world. His music not only entranced, but moved rocks and trees to listen to it, so his lyre was a symbol of power as well as of beauty to a people who viewed music as their gift from the Muses, something utterly central to their lives.

The Orphics had an important additional symbol, the *Omphalos*, which they viewed as the Egg of Creation, the cosmogonic egg, the source of the cosmos itself, original spontaneous life. This was usually represented as an ovoid stone, as in a temple at Delphi where it was viewed as the navel or centre of the earth, the centre of gravity of a circle, and of the cosmos. The calendar points of the universe flowed from there.

Examine the essence of the cult of Orphism and we see it not as a discrete religion as we would recognise it today but as a cult or movement that swept through Greece on a hot breath of change to reform some of the more violent beliefs and Dionysiac rituals of the time. Its imagery was shocking, yet uplifting. Orpheus, husband of the lost Eurydice, was torn to pieces by the Maenads – frenzied Bacchanalian women followers of Dionysus – and his head thrown in the river. The head sang throughout its journey and continued to do so when it came to rest at Lesbos, to become an oracular competitor to the Pythoness at Delphi until Apollo bade it to be silent. The writings named after him were the *Orphic Hymns* or *Rhapsodies*, and became so influential that Orphism is viewed, in addition to its other properties, as a body of literature. The hymns told, among other things, of *ecstasis*, or ecstasy, stepping out of the physical body for the true nature of a man's soul to be revealed. His journey to Hades to visit the dead, or to rescue Eurydice (which some of the mythologists view as a later addition), seem part of a divine tradition that would both predate and survive him. Zoroaster, Osiris, Horus, Adonis, Hercules, Hermes, Baldur, Quetzalcoatl, Dionysus and Christ all descended into the underworld to be with the dead and rose again on the third day, the period that symbolised that part of the month when the moon retreated into darkness. When the Hymns of Orpheus sang of rebirth and purification, his teaching appealed to the higher nature of the Greeks who saw it as a call to seek truth and beauty, a call that probably inspired the birth of Western philosophy.

This is where the influence of Orpheus becomes very interesting in historical – rather than purely mythical – terms, as it seems to have been in the sixth century BC in the town of Miletus, on the eastern edge of the Greek world called Ionia, or what is now the western coast of Turkey, around the time that Orpheus made his first known appearances in the writings of the lyric poets Ibycus and Pindar, that the mind of man began to wander, to speculate, to think freely about his surroundings, to travel outside the body to ask questions about the physics of the cosmos or the order of matter, and to offer the first scientific explanations for them, crude though they appear at first glance.

A search for knowledge about the physical nature of things, then of perceived human qualities such as virtue and goodness, unconnected with the gods, began, possibly because of the civilising influence that had entered Greece and brought a spirit of inquiry with it. Religion and tradition were not rejected or cast aside in any sense, and this intellectual activity was initially confined to a very few, but the first Western philosopher that we know of seems to have appeared as the name of Orpheus entered the poetry of the Greeks. Thales and his Ionian philosopher successors asked whether the primary material of which the world was made was water or air or something else, questions that we might not think of as sophisticated, but the unspoken questions underlying the spoken had a more fundamental, intelligent motive. They asked how the cosmos originated, and speculated whether it was made of a single form of matter, accepting the obvious complexity of the universe yet wondering whether its essence was simple, as Einstein and the atomic men did and as the physicists do today. They sought a single principle for the physical matter that they saw in such diversity around them, and they made statements that their successors criticised, implicitly or explicitly, to answer with statements of their own, statements as revolutionary in thought as that of Heraclitus of Ephesus, a generation after the Ionians: *This ordered world no god or man has made, but it always was and is and will be, ever living fire, kindled in measures and going out in measures*, where the use of the word *measure* implies an ordered, regular world.

Such were the products of the first purely intellectual thinking of Western man who made statements that today we would regard as sweeping and without proof – as their successors Aristotle and Plato would do – but for the first time they lacked a divine explanation or material purpose. They were offered as physical explanations to the questions of the physical world, with only the authority of the intellect behind them, as the imagination of man separated the natural from the supernatural and so began to accept a concept of nature. Lightning need not be a bolt from Zeus. It might be explained instead as the energy of matter, even if the Greeks would not have put it in such words.

These were the intellectual ancestors of the great philosophical schools of Athens, of Socrates and Plato and Aristotle, of the Stoics and the Epicureans, their probing sometimes supplied in the form of a dialogue into which the unwary fell (What is Goodness? Can it be taught? If so, who shall teach it?), and they were in turn the intellectual ancestors of the Greek mathematicians who asked questions of themselves, answered them from their own minds, used a consistent system of logic, supplied proofs that have survived the stresses of modern investigation, but seem not to have forgotten the original mythical figure who began it all. When he speaks of the Lyre of Orpheus, therefore, Archimedes hints in his typical fashion at an insight into something of great power or meaning, something of cosmic significance, perhaps something that flowed from the image of the circle, something more important to him than his death, something that has brought him here. He is the philosopher, in the finest tradition of the Greeks, searching for truth.

Narrative

Strangely, the person he began to brood on as the key to unlock Bridget's mystery was Kate. He thought of her after Bridget had left. He considered Seth and the invisible power that bound the girl to him, but his mind shifted with a will of its own each time he thought of the others, to the tall dark woman who seemed more of a queen than a whore.

He saw her a few days later, saw her leash her dog and leave the house. Once he followed her for part of the way until he heard the deep rumble of the animal as it sensed his presence, hidden though he was from sight and scent.

He could not explain this sudden fixation of his, even to himself, and when he reluctantly brought it to the light of reason his only defence was that Kate might impart something to him that the others would not, that if any side of this triangle were neutral it would be she. Yet he did not trust this surface reasoning, knowing within himself that he yielded increasingly to a darker curiosity, a search for a memory of some kind forcing itself up from the unconscious that his protective shield sought to suppress.

The brooding appearance of the house of Seth grew more pronounced as he spied on it, but the appearance of Kate at its door was more deeply disturbing. He felt his spirits sing when he saw Bridget and a chill on his spine when he saw Seth, but his equilibrium left him when he saw Kate walking with her purposeful step and in his mind he saw a terrible blackness that he could not fathom, as if the light had left the world and nature was stilled for ever in perpetual winter.

The Greek

Where the poet sees beauty, Stranger, I see order. I see natural laws, like that of the buoyancy of a ship, or a lever in balance, and I know that they, and every other natural law in the cosmos that makes up its order, can not only be explained through mathematics, but that they are *best* described through mathematics.

Begin your journey into knowledge with the postulate that mathematics, being the only accurate language that exists, will describe the physical things whose proportions may seem irrational or imperfect but are natural and so can be described, and remember that your relationship with the gods is on a different, personal plane where it should remain. Such was mine with the Goddess, Stranger, and such is the mystery of my death.

To me this sense of the order of the cosmos begins with Homer, yet I did not see it at first, although I knew him by rote. As a boy I saw only the heroism and the battles, the profound issues of life and death and the moods of the gods. I saw the poet presiding over a stadium of human emotions at Troy, the great fissure between Agamemnon and Akhilles, the rage of Akhilles over the death of Patroklos, the treachery of the likeable Paris, the tragedy of Polyxena and so on.

I saw all this and never ceased to be attracted by it, yet it was Pheidias the astronomer who saw what lay beneath, that the poet portrayed gods and humans who behaved in an orderly way, that it was not only the Greeks, Trojans and gods behaving intelligibly, but the whole cosmos of heavens and earth, of the human and the divine. Whatever the philosophers spoke of, he said, we owed our view of order to the poet.

Many pursued explanations for this order. None did so with more dedication than Pheidias, and none admired that dedication more than I. When manhood neared I told him that I felt he wished me to be an astronomer, to carry on his work. There was a long silence while he continued to take his angle. I held my breath. Slowly, he turned his head to me and told me that this was not his wish.

I would not make a good astronomer, he said, because I demanded a proof to everything. Most astronomers were prepared to go to their deaths without one. I would not, in his judgment, grow used to such uncertainty. I protested, but he signalled me to be silent. I had a surplus of intuition and a shortage of patience, he went on. Time might cure the last, but the approach I took to the questions he set for me was that of a philosopher who was more interested in the propositions of Eukleid than in the movements of the planets. I should consider one day going to a great centre of learning that would open my mind further. I thought of Alexandria-in-Egypt, the greatest centre of knowledge in the world, and my pulse quickened.

Our lives continued for a time as they had, until one day, by chance, I fell in with two members of a secret brotherhood in a street near the *agora*. They wore the sign of the pentagram around their necks, and were from Gela in the south of the island. They were intent on making the pilgrimage to Eleusis, without an obol between them, having been sent ashore from a ship because they could not pay their passage to Peiraias. I took them home where my father, kind man, opened his house to them, although, starving as they were, they would take only vegetables and goats' milk. For several days, until we found a ship for them, they told us as much of the brotherhood as they were allowed to divulge, and of how its founder the mystic had made the same pilgrimage long before, to be initiated in the rites of the two goddesses that brought forth Dionysos the god as the divine child. Most of the time, however, they talked of triangular and friendly numbers with the same reverence they showed their founder, filling my head with the essence of their arithmetic. They filled me also with the desire to make the pilgrimage, and so become a *mystes*.

The Book of Aengus

The mystic he refers to must be Pythagoras of Samos, who sang of *metempsychosis* or the transmigration of souls, follower of Orpheus, mystic, showman and lyre-player, a man who may have existed only in legend.

We know nothing of him that could be put to a proof, yet his myth took its place in Greek philosophy and his cult survived through a secret brotherhood which became so powerful at times that it ruled entire city-states. He left nothing in writing that survives, copied or otherwise, and his myth might have dissipated after his death but for Plato, who sought a cosmos of rational harmony to incorporate into his own beliefs and saw it in Pythagoreanism, a great web spun of number divinity, cosmology, Orphic teaching, and genuine mathematics. The notion that Pythagoras himself was a great mathematician has been annihilated, yet this mythical man with the golden thigh seems to generate as much literature as Aristotle or Plato.

Everything in the cosmos is a number, said Pythagoras, and ten is the number of the cosmos, whose sacred symbol is the mystic's perfect triangle, the *tetractus*, created from ten pebbles. Logic seems elusive here, magic to be nearby, yet the vision of a universe that's best explained through mathematics has proven to be true.

The Greek

The raven watches your house tonight, Stranger. I felt it sense my presence. We called it *korax* for its call, and had the great Alexander listened to the ravens of Babylon he might have lived.

You have set a trap for me. I see a rough cut of a pentagram, the sign of the Pythagorean brotherhood, by your side. It holds the most pleasing of all the natural proportions, the Cut, but that is not why you have it by you. It is because you wish to know if I became a brother.

I did not. For a time – a very short time – the cult attracted me because of the secrets of mathematics it seemed to possess, yet I soon felt that mathematics and mysticism did not mix well because they confused objectivity with subjectivity. To me, mathematics describes a reality that exists beyond us, without us, independent of us. There is nothing mystical in it. The purpose of the mathematician is to discover truths that are already there, to describe them, and to prove them through the use of a consistent logic. Numbers exist without us. The laws of geometry exist without us. We did not create them. We deduced them, just as we deduced mechanical laws. They were already there, as I say, waiting to be discovered, as is everything in the cosmos. If something exists without us, it is natural, by definition. If we wonder at the existence of a proportion like the Cut (strange or godlike though it may appear at first) we should not ask whether such proportions are natural – they are – but instead we should ask what they may say about the essence of nature that they may describe.

Plato had made Pythagoras live again, but mysticism among Greek philosophers began to fade when Aristotle created one of the greatest advances of all, the method by which knowledge is organised. That cut a new path for the great Eukleid, among others. The influence of Pythagoras began to wane, but I remember something the brothers said, mystic though it seems. It has to do with his teaching that odd numbers were male, even ones female. He saw a number whose factors add up to the number itself as perfect, and therefore divine. Six is the first of these, as a child will tell you that its factors are one, two, and three. To Pythagoras it was also the number of Creation, and he taught that the cube, a solid with six faces, held the secrets of the earth. The brothers I met were manic in their secrecy and kept my questions hanging in the air, but I suspect that to the Pythagoreans the number, like the Knot of Gordium, concealed a name, a female name, perhaps that of a goddess.

The Book of Aengus

I'm ashamed that I used such a trick, yet he sensed my motive the instant he saw my pentagram. I drew what I thought was a good likeness of it on my third attempt, taking care to join the five points of my star so that each intersecting line divided the next unequally in two, in such proportions, as the textbooks state, that the shorter section has the same ratio to the longer as the longer has to the line as a whole, but I failed to impress him. So much for my drawing.

He calls the proportion that such a division of a line produces the most pleasing of all, possibly because it is the only one such proportion in mathematics, where the smaller length and greater govern each other while both govern the whole. The Greeks called it the Cut, Leonardo knew it as the Golden Section, others as the Golden Mean, and anyone with too much time on their hands might spend a lifetime reading of the meanings that cults have given this natural ratio over the ages, from Pythagoras to the alchemists. The Babylonians and Egyptians apparently knew of it long before any of these, as the section, or something very close to it, occurs in the Great Pyramid of Cheops at Giza. The mystique surrounding it continued down the centuries, into the Renaissance where the painter/mathematician Piero della Francesca was said to have used it in his work, as was Leonardo.

If they did, so much the better, because it expresses something about nature. The Greeks could not reduce it to a number because they did not have a zero or our decimal notation system to do so, but, much later, the Italian mathematician Fibonacci found that the section also naturally expresses itself in arithmetic. This shows nature working in numbers, as the Fibonacci sequence commonly occurs in chemistry, animals and plants, in several of the Platonic solids, and in Mendel's laws of heredity, just as *pi* occurs in a circle, without a divine purpose, unless, of course, you see Nature as divine.

Narrative

The moon waned over the Kennet, the spring gales brought rain, the birds left pasture and the more exposed woodland to shelter in the hedgerows and the Greek did not visit. The girl did not return to his cottage, though he glimpsed her several times near Seth's house. He had returned many times to the clearing where he had first seen her, but she had either abandoned her walks or chosen a different area.

The notion that she avoided him, that perhaps she was disappointed in him, brought a sharp, inexplicable pain. He began to brood about his past, thinking of the Greek's childhood and comparing it with his own. His, too, had been solitary, his upbringing leaving him largely unaware of the differences between him and other children. As a young boy, the only child of an Irish academic and an Icelandic mother, both lecturers at a Scottish university, it seemed natural to him that a hare in a mountain meadow did not bolt from its form when he approached, or that a freshly ploughed field dotted with curlews was not disturbed when he walked the headlands. The corncrake, shyest of rails, spoke to him with its rasping call from a few feet away after a meadow had been cut, its crest showing above the end of a windrow as it studied him curiously, head to one side. The birds of hedge and wood unhesitatingly took food from his hand. All of this seemed normal to a boy without siblings and with few companions of his own age. It surprised him at first when others saw the animals' acceptance of him as a gift of some kind, something unnatural, when it seemed to him to be the most natural thing in the world.

With only his parents' friends for company in the long summer holidays with his father's bachelor uncle in the West of Ireland, the animals became companions of a kind. At night he would escape through the open front door of the house when his parents slept, to watch the boar badger making the rounds of his boundary in the moonlight, fully aware the animal was aware of his presence, hungry for the handful of apples placed downwind by the solitary child. He watched the foxes on their nocturnal hunt, listening to the roosting birds as they gave their alarm calls, hearing the squeals of a captive rabbit with a mixture of sympathy and resignation.

He was not yet in his teens when his parents died in a car crash. His father's uncle, the only surviving relative on the paternal side, took charge. Aengus would go to boarding school and spend holidays with his relative.

The confines of school were like a prison until he encountered subjects that interested him, but the holidays were especially welcome. In winter he haunted a nearby estuary, watching the migrants land from their long flights over water, or the woodcock flight in under a full moon. As the seasons turned he found that his knowledge grew, and so did the consciousness that his own life was part of a natural cycle as old as life itself.

In his final year at school his great-uncle died. He was a very solitary young man when he went to university, to find it a less painful process because of the freedom it brought and because of the greater mental stimulus, yet he found himself frequently apart from his fellow students, out of sympathy with their moods and aspirations, preferring his books and the rugby field. He had had few girlfriends by the time he married.

He had great success he had not expected in a career in

London, drifting for what he thought would be a short time into a financial institution that called the world its market. There he had discovered, almost by chance, that he had a gift for financial alchemy, and that the clients of the bank trusted him. A rival institution snatched him away and it was several years later, at the height of his earning power, with bonuses larger than his ambition, such as it was, that he met a girl like a blonde waif, became infatuated with her, and married her soon after.

The Book of Aengus

Concealing the name of a divinity seems to have been relatively common, possibly because it added to the mystique of the god. Ancient civilisations were adept at it, hiding the identity of Dionysus at Gordium, the old capital of Phrygia in Asia Minor, where the name of the fertility god had been concealed for centuries within a knot that Alexander finally sliced open with a stroke of his sword. The Pythagoreans were naturally secretive in any case, obsessed with their perfect and friendly numbers and what they symbolised, yet it was then the dawn of arithmetic in the West, and number magic where numbers were interchangeable with letters of the different alphabets became a cult in itself, concealing their meanings to all but the initiated.

Magic squares first appeared in China five hundred years before Pythagoras, and gradually made their way into the West, where they would flourish among the Greeks and the Hebrews. The followers of Kabbalah were to create a magic square that would conceal the name of Yahweh, while in relatively modern times the number of the Beast in *Revelation* would be gnawed like a bone throughout the Reformation, the Catholics seeking to prove that its trinity of sixes was a cryptogram for Martin Luther, the Protestants maintaining that it clearly identified the Pope. Newton, who described the universal laws of gravity, laboured fruitlessly to discover the age of the universe for the last thirty years of his life, relying solely on the Bible, while Napier, the discoverer of logarithms, worked long and seriously on a mathematical proposition that he hoped would prove the Pope to be the Antichrist.

Coincidence or not, six continued to be a holy number through Judaic and into Christian times, seemingly changing gender in the process. Six was the number of Creation to Pythagoras. In the Old Testament man was created on the sixth day of the creation of the earth, possibly signalling a common Babylonian origin. It was a perfect number to Pythagoras. It was also perfect to St Augustine, creator of much Christian doctrine, because of its biblical implications. The common link between them is that they both symbolise the origin of the cosmos. The distinction is that one has female associations, the other male.

Greek philosophers generally did not believe in an Act of Creation as such. Plato assumed Chaos instead, and saw a craftsman god who fashioned it into order. Aristotle believed the world and man had always existed. Anaximander saw that man in his present form could not have survived Chaos, and surmised that he developed from a fish who had.

Perhaps the divinity whose name the Pythagoreans concealed as a number was Demeter, Goddess of the Earth, perhaps it was Artemis, Mistress of Nature, or even Gaia, the earliest Great Goddess or Earth Mother of the Greeks, ancestress of the Olympian gods and of the Titans, the first virgin goddess to give birth and who rose from primordial Chaos. We cannot know, but it seems to touch a particular sensitivity or curiosity in the Greek.

We do know that the earliest divinities were female earth goddesses, just as we know that the oldest civilisations in Europe were matriarchal. Early Minoan pottery in Crete, for example, depicts only women bearing arms. The scholar Marija Gimbutas spent a lifetime studying the artefacts of Palaeolithic and Neolithic times in Europe and found nothing in the Palaeolithic age at least to show an awareness of a Great Father or of any male figure that was the object of worship. The Life Giver and the Death Wielder were one entity, a Great Goddess, Gimbutas says, and this figure symbolised regeneration and renewal and controlled the fertility of Life itself, because She was its source. That is probably the oldest myth, part of our human psyche, touching us now as it touched the Greek.

Narrative

Greece had drawn Aengus after his marriage had failed, as had Egypt, Mesopotamia, India and Pakistan. He had tidied his affairs for a few months in London, giving his wife everything her lawyers demanded, keeping only a few unquoted investments which the accountants and lawyers valued at nothing, concealing a sneer as they looked at the list, eyes fastening eagerly on the valuations of the marital home, his bank balance, and quoted investments. He worked at the bank for a few months more at the request of its clients, saved as much as he could and then left and set off, for seven years, travelling, working where he could, living the simplest of lives, his books the heaviest of his physical burdens, sending constant demands to the London bookshops as he tried to satisfy his need for knowledge of all kinds, history, philosophy, archaeology, psychology, anthropology, poetry, mythology. He did not know why this hunger, like an addiction, suddenly seemed to possess him, but it began to fill his mind to the exclusion of almost all else as he travelled.

He read Xenophon near the site of the old Persian capital of Susa, Goethe and Schiller where Babylon had stood, and Jung under the light of an oil-lamp in a tent in the foothills of the Himalayas, hearing the distant roar of a tiger as it warned the junglefolk away from its kill. Darwin and Thesiger were his companions along the Euphrates, Flinders Petrie up the Nile, Plato and Aristotle and the *Vedas* across the more arid parts of Pakistan, Vitruvius, Plutarch, Polybius, Thucydides and Herodotus in Greece and Heer in the villages of southern India, in no particular order as the mood took him or as the books caught up with him.

Once he fell very ill and felt close to death in Iran when a Muslim cleric took him to his house and nursed him back to health, praying by his side and giving him a copy of the Qur'an when he recovered, telling him earnestly in sign language that his life had been saved by the Prophet's intervention. His patient was comforted by the flowing lines of Arabic, and as soon as he could he acquired an unauthorised English version and a history of the life of the Prophet and read them on the banks of a salt lake near Q'om. He followed them with tomes on the Islamic philosophers and their open acceptance of Greek, Persian and Indian thinking, and from that time he read everything he could find on religions and their philosophies, re-reading Frazer's *Golden Bough* and the works of Eliade and Campbell. In Mumbai he sheltered from the monsoon in the tin shanty of a pandit who fed him, lectured him on the three-in-one god, taught him a little Sanskrit and a great deal about Hindu philosophy and the *Vedas*. Aengus taught him Darwin in return, watching the small man fire up a clever argument against this point or that, seeing through the intelligent eyes the brain of the Brahmin searching for flaws while the rain drummed urgently on the roof, all humanity teemed by on the street a few feet away and a cow rolled its eyes at him from the open doorway.

Throughout his travels he avoided the tourist trails and contact with his own tribe, lodging with villagers or sleeping in the open with his bag of books beside him, acquiring the reputation of an eccentric in some places, that of a mystic in others. He grew very thin, almost emaciated, but vastly more confident and questioning, and it was in that frame of mind that he decided to return and to take up his life again.

The Book of Aengus

Last night when the Greek didn't visit I dreamed of Pythagoras, a dream so real I could almost touch him. Perhaps I did so because of what Archimedes has said, or because I was reading Burkert's tome on the mystic when I fell asleep.

In my dream I saw a face with the staring eyes of a fanatic, strong jaw, olive skin, thick lips, beard of black with a little grey, a big head with long, dark, curling locks resting on his shoulders, staring at the waves breaking on the rocks on which he sat at Crotona in southern Italy, brooding.

He saw me then, and seemed to look straight through me. After a time he rose and began to draw on the sand. I saw appear the three shapes in geometry from which the five regular solids later named after Plato are made, the solids where every one has equal edges, every face is a perfect polygon, and every point is the same distance from the centre, each a mathematical sculpture so perfect it is empty of art, each a symbol of the five natural elements to the Greeks, the stuffs of which the cosmos of Aristotle was made. The five are the only regular solids it is possible to construct that can be inscribed in a sphere, and a sphere, a circle in its third dimension, is the shape and motion of the cosmos to Plato and Aristotle and even, for a while, to Kepler in the seventeenth century. Insert the elemental figures into the sphere and you have the cosmos itself, complete in all respects, orderly, proportional in every way, mathematical perfection.

He begins with a point in the sand, a point from which all direction can flow. He draws a line from the point. The line is the radius of a circle, and lies there while the compass rotates about the point. A circle, the perfect shape of two dimensions, is created.

He begins on the next shape. He creates a point, then another, joins them with a line segment, then creates another point equidistant from the others, joins each with further line segments and so creates an equilateral triangle.

He moves on to the third, joining four points, each equidistant from the last and the next, to create a square. Using these three shapes he can create all five regular solids, symbols of the five elements.

The first, the tetrahedron or pyramid, is formed when he takes the equilateral triangle and creates a fourth point, at a distance that is equal from the other three, and joins the points. It now has four vertices and four faces, each an equilateral triangle. It represents fire.

The second is the octahedron, constructed in the same way but with six points and eight equilateral triangles. It represents air.

The third is the cube, with eight vertices and six square faces. It is the earth.

The fourth is the icosahedron, with twenty equilateral triangles, which is water. The last is the dodecahedron, with twelve five-sided faces, the ultimate regular solid. It represents the aether, the quintessential element of which the heavens are made.

The five together, which would become known as the Platonic Solids, are the shapes of the cosmos, symbols of the five elements of which heavens and earth are made, all fitting within the sphere of the universe as the Pythagorean brotherhood conceived it, reflecting their belief that reality at its most profound is mathematical. As I looked at this sacred construct I realised fully the Greek love of proportion, of rationality, of the order of mysteries of the world they believed they had found, and I knew that Pythagoras displayed them to me as a magician would produce a rabbit from a hat, that he'd taken the shapes from elsewhere, that they weren't his, that whoever had conceived them it was not he.

As the dream began to fade I saw the mystic pick up a lyre and begin to play, glancing in my direction from time to time, but I couldn't hear the music. Instead I sensed a rippling power spreading outward as each string was plucked, sending waves of light and energy into space, as though the lyre itself were a powerful, living thing, at one with its master, an Orphic to his fingertips. I knew then that this was the power he had over his followers, the power to entrance Plato, the power to build a myth that proved to be empty, a blank tablet, yet enchanting those poets who saw his mysticism in themselves.

Narrative

Memory continued to flood him on the dark nights when the Greek did not visit. He stirred uneasily as he remembered how the confidence he had rebuilt on his travels had left him on the strath of a river in Scotland where he had worked as a seasonal ghilly. On his return from his foreign travels, unable as yet to face a return to the society he had left, he had avoided the cities and struck for the north. He had not halted until he reached the Hebrides and Orkneys, taking the ferries from isle to isle, then back to the mainland where he found work in the open, sometimes at a salmon hatchery in late autumn, sometimes as a river watcher patrolling for poachers, sometimes as a stand-in when a ghilly fell ill.

His first home of any kind since he had left on his travels was a netsman's cottage, abandoned when the riparian owners had agreed to quit netting the estuary as salmon numbers fell. He had rented it for a titular sum, repaired it and sat at the window at night with the sea to his right, the estuary directly below, the cries of the oystercatchers and sandpipers floating up to him on the rare days of calm. Winter gales had buffeted doors and windows and formed orchestras and ghostly choirs in the chimneys, but inside it was snug, warm away from the draughts, peaceful. He grew a beard, hiding in his anonymity. His store of books from the London shops rose at a gluttonous pace. Spring tides and north-westerlies covered windows with salt, but the worse the weather grew the more inner peace he found. He could be almost anonymous here, and he was, greeting the villagers and the visiting anglers with a quiet courtesy, evading the curiosity attached to a single stranger who lived apart. He planned to stay until the urge to move on took him.

When spring hesitantly arrived, the call to work came from a fishing lodge up the strath and he joined the other ghillies, sometimes fishing the river with a fifteen-foot fly rod when asked by the owners to keep the catch at a respectable level if there was a vacancy in a tenancy for a week, acquiring the efficiency of movement and deftness of the other ghillies, rolling out the fly with a minimum of effort, the rod doing the work. He learned to read a river at different water levels, instinct dictating to him where a salmon would lie, often fishing late into the evenings on the townspeople's beat where fresh, peaty water from the hill met the salt of the flooding tide.

The lodges were fully tenanted in summer as the peak of the season approached. The six beats of the river were rotated daily, tenants from different lodges fishing each in turn over six days, Sunday a day of rest for the salmon.

Aengus set off from the lodge on a hot Monday morning when the river was low, the fishing pointless, most of the pools empty apart from the top where the salmon were red and bored. He drove the tenants up the strath, pulled in at a passing place on the single-track road to allow an approaching car to go by, and saw the woman who had been his wife.

She sat in the front of the other vehicle, and for a moment he hoped that he would pass unnoticed. Her head was turned towards a man in the rear seats, her blonde head sideways to him, her hair cut short as he remembered it. Then she threw back the head that he had tried to forget and laughed as she had laughed at his innocence, her pearly teeth visible against a perfectly formed upper lip and as she turned to discover why the car had halted she glanced at the bearded ghilly in the other vehicle and he saw that she knew him. Her smile slipped and she stared, and then Aengus was past, his brain spinning and his heart thumping with despair.

He drove up the strath, despair turning to anger. The peculiar tinkle of her laugh came back to him vividly as he stepped from the car to guide his tenants to the pools they would fish. A hen-harrier chased its prey on the opposite hill. The sun shone from a sky of light blue and a soft breeze came from Klibreck as he realised that he must move on once more.

He did so a few days later, shaving his beard, packing a few things, then wandering south by bus and train until he reached England, working a week here or there to feed himself. After a few months, hungry and broke, he stopped outside a Berkshire cottage near a handsome chalkstream and asked the riverkeeper for work.

The Book of Aengus

The Greek is still absent. I haven't seen Bridget for days. Even the lonely song thrush has ceased his song. Perhaps he has found a mate at last. I'm idle, frustrated, reading without concentrating, jotting notes here and there, for some reason reflecting on what the Greek said about the beauty of his temples, their inner symmetry, and how the measure of man was in their every proportion. That was true of Doric buildings, but the Ionians took their measures from the ideal woman to build their more delicate temples and public buildings, adding spiral volutes to the capitals, a feminine touch.

Some of the finest Doric temples stood near him in Sicily, and one, in Syracuse, in particular had an interesting fate. This temple of Athena at Ortygia, the Athenaeon, stood at the highest point of the island, the *acropolis*, and hosted a very large sculpture of Athena that could be seen at sea. Later, the Roman governor Verres looted the painted tablets from the *cella* – the most sacred part of the temple, where the goddess was housed – in the first century BC, and was successfully prosecuted by Cicero who, as quaestor in Sicily, also claimed to have found the gravestone of Archimedes with its sphere inscribed by a cylinder and to have restored it. If he did, as Boyer says drily, this was the only contribution Rome made to mathematics. The Christians later converted the temple into the cathedral church, the Duomo sull' Ortygia, building a crude wall between the squat Doric columns to enclose the peristyle. Virgin and saints today stand on their plinths within, and Mary the Virgin, in the tradition of Athene, looks out across the Grand Harbour.

He talks of these temples as an example of the Greek love of mathematical proportions, the inner beauty of exact and rigidly applied rules of ratios that was the soul of the buildings, as beautiful a concept as the temples themselves.

They let their natural creativity loose when it came to decorating them, yet kept the harmony. Greek temples were polychromatic, decorated with bright – sometimes harsh – colours, strong reds and blues, or softer blues and yellows, yet each was balanced against the other to create a whole, very different to today's popular image of white marble which was not used widely until the opening of the rich quarry at Pentelikon allowed the Athenians to build the finest classical buildings in history. The temples in most Doric city-states were generally of limestone or sandstone.

He doesn't say so, but the early Greek architecture of the Archaic period owed much to the Pharaohs. The Egyptians built wonderful temples, lavishly yet painstakingly decorated, to Re and Amun and Ptah, although rarely with the perfection of the Greeks. A further significant difference between the two was their respective sizes. Egyptian temples were necessarily large because they contained the worshippers, while the Greeks' were smaller because they housed only the gods. The references say he probably studied at the Library of Alexandria, so he knew Egypt, and must have known the obsession of the Egyptians with an unchanging system over the centuries of proportions in pyramids and their temples and in the figures that decorated them that were painted from the same rigid grid, using architecture on a scale that makes Greek buildings puny in comparison.

The majority of temples in Greece were Doric, after the Dorian invaders of Greece in the twelfth century BC. The Dorians were the fabled Herakleidae, sons of mighty Herakles, or Hercules as it was anglicised, who became a god, as many heroes did. They were from the north, possibly from the Danube basin. Probably an earthquake weakened or partly destroyed the Mycenaean civilisation that preceded them and which was among the most sophisticated in the world, perhaps second only to the Minoan of Crete, but Greece seems to have fallen into a dark age that lasted for centuries after the invasion, and there is little evidence to record how the Mycenaean civilisation was absorbed.

The more refined temples, such as the Parthenon, contained a product of Greek genius. The architects saw that a tall, rigidly proportioned column appeared to the faulty human eye to narrow in the middle. They compensated for this apparent concavity by the use of *entasis*, allowing the shaft to swell (*entasis* literally means *stretching*) gradually, then to taper away once more, using strict proportions to reach what we might term an imperfect perfection. In Ictinus' Parthenon, for example, where 34-foot columns supported the building, the maximum convexity of these shafts reached a mere three-quarters of an inch. The columns of drummed and fluted stone also inclined inwards, again to correct an optical illusion, an inclination so slight that, hypothetically speaking, the vertical axes of the columns wouldn't have met until they were well over a mile above the surface of the earth. For the same reason the architects gave a horizontal convex inclination to the centre of a set of wide steps leading up to the temple.

I look at the notes I made on Greek cosmology after he talked of Ares, the red planet which we call Mars, the study of whose path became the life's work of his father. In the open spirit of Greek philosophy the early astronomers looked at the passage of the sun across the sky and at what they saw in the heavens by night and drew up a series of explanations. Some of them believed divine forces to be at work, but these thoughts were offered as explanations of the force needed to make the cosmos rotate, not as some form of religious doctrine. Other philosophers were free to question such assumptions, and did.

The movements of sun and moon and the constellations of stars that revolved in the northern sky – the circumpolar stars – led many of them to say that the earth was the central point of a spherical cosmos, with the heavenly bodies rotating around it in a circle. These theories could not account accurately for the fact that the sun set in a different position each day, ranging from north of west to south of west, but they seemed broadly sensible to astronomers who could not know that the sun's settings were the consequence of our planet's annual movement along a curving path oblique to the equator, a slant that is responsible for the seasons. They could not explain why different stars appeared before dawn or after sunset as the year progressed, although they knew what time of year they would appear and built star calendars – *parapegmata* – that were probably copied from those of the Babylonians and were the only accurate guides to the changing year that the Greeks possessed – and the only ones they could agree upon, as every *polis* seemed to have a different calendar, every one of them inferior to the Egyptians'.

The movement of the planets was probably the biggest challenge to their conviction that the earth was the centre of the universe. Philosophers saw these bodies go into retrogression from time to time, noted that they deviated within the belt of the zodiac to either side of the ecliptic, the path the sun follows against the stars, and did their best to describe their motions in a pattern that would show their paths to be predictable, ordered. The cosmos of Eudoxus showed two of his spheres describing a motion so like a horse fetter that the Greeks called it the *hippopede*. Nearly four hundred years after the death of Archimedes the astronomer Ptolemy of Alexandria, author of the *Suntaxis* – or *Almagest*, as the Arab translators who saved it for posterity called it – built a description in which he introduced the *epicycle*, giving the planets a complex set of looping movements which they do not have but which was seemingly accurate from the point of view of an observer viewing the heavens from the earth. This was therefore accepted as the correct version of the visible universe until the seventeenth century, when Kepler, almost reluctantly, discovered the truth.

Archimedes talked of how the Greeks pursued knowledge with open minds, but he has yet to speak of why the most sophisticated astronomers appear to have ignored or dismissed the hypotheses of Aristarchus, the Alexandrian scientist who said that the earth revolved around the sun. Aristarchus wasn't much earlier than Archimedes, and we know that Archimedes knew of his work and even criticised a slight mathematical error in it, as he wrote about it in *Psammites*, or *Sand Reckoner*, the work of Archimedes that appeals most to me because it was the first work in history to show the power of number.

The theories of Aristarchus may have been repressed because it was central to Greek thinking and philosophy that the earth was the centre of all things, but that seems unlikely, given how open-minded philosophy was in general. The Stoic Cleanthes called for Aristarchus to be charged with impiety, but there seems to be little evidence that this was taken seriously. It seems more probable, given how tolerant the Greeks were to ideas, that the theory was dismissed rather than repressed, that it sank because it would have raised more questions than it answered. They knew nothing of gravity or the earth's atmosphere. Without telescopes, they saw the cosmos as a small place, a reassuringly compact system which revolved around them, neatly, in that ideal of motions, the circle. To Plato and Aristotle, to the Stoics and to most in the broad stream of philosophy the earth was at the centre of the cosmos, with man at the centre of the earth, but all of this was based on reason rather than on systematised belief or dogma, part of the broad search for truth. Christian theology seems to have absorbed the same central theory and evolved it into doctrine, perhaps because the theologians reasoned that it was God's law that man, as a divine creation, must be at the centre of all, below heaven.

Narrative

It was some time since he had seen the fox and the hares under the moon, but he found the fox again one night, seemingly in perfect health. It waited for him outside his cottage, so Aengus went back inside and foraged in his kitchen. The fox licked his hand as he fed it meat and an apple, then led him to the high ground on the estate where it squatted, head pointing to the west, in the direction of Avebury and Silbury Hill. He watched it for an hour against the dim skyline, seeing its head lift expectantly from time to time. A new moon like a silver bow hung above a wrack of cloud, then disappeared behind it. He shone his torch a few minutes later. The fox had given up its wait and moved off.

Restless, drawn by the emotion that increasingly gripped him, he went to spy on Seth's house, moving as close to it as he dared. The lights shone on the crumbling yard and he heard voices from within, the low rumble of Seth's, the shrill replies of Kate and an occasional growl from the dog. The lights went out, and all was quiet once more. At home, he lit the fire, late though it was, took up his journal and began to write as he waited.

The Book of Aengus

All's quiet. The owls don't call. Perhaps they haven't begun their hunt. The logs weren't dry enough, crackling and spitting until I added parts of the old lintel. Now I've a blaze while I await him. I welcome it. It was cold by that ugly house, but the moon is new and I think the fox has gone to guide him here. I feel certain he'll come, and I've read while I waited. I scribble what I've learned.

Eratosthenes was his friend, a mathematician not many years junior to him, his pupil in a sense, to whom he dedicated at least one of his works. He was one of the great scientists of antiquity, the first to measure accurately the circumference of the earth.

There is a reference by Archimedes in a letter to Eratosthenes – by then almost certainly the Librarian at Alexandria – which describes, in passing, Sicily as the Thrinacian Isle, so called because the island is shaped like a crude triangle. I have the puzzle he sent to Eratosthenes about the cattle of Apollo:

If thou are diligent and wise, O Stranger, compute the number of cattle of the sun who once upon a time grazed on the fields of the Thrinacian isle of Sicily…

These were divided into four herds of different colours, with bulls among them in set proportion:

Understand, Stranger, that the white bulls were equal to a half and a third of the black together with the whole of the yellow, while the black were equal to a fourth part of the dappled…

…and so on, creating the forerunner of what modern mathematicians call a Pell equation, a tortuous problem for Eratosthenes' students at Alexandria, born from a Sicilian myth which went back at least to Homer:

Thou shalt ascend the isle triangular,
Where many oxen of the Sun are fed…

In the *Odyssey*, some of the crew of Odysseus, shipwrecked on the coast of Sicily and starving, slaughter a few of the cattle of Apollo and are drowned when Zeus, in revenge, sends a thunderbolt.

I saw once a piece of pottery – I think it was a plate – in the Louvre that shows Apollo's cattle under the sun. Curiously, on a bare branch above it is shown a silhouette of a hare, which the ancients viewed as a child of the moon.

I hear his voice.

See us in the morning sun on the road to Thermopylai, Stranger, glimpsing the high peaks of Parnassos, the place of the Muses, as they sailed through the high cloud. We were in the heartland of Hellas, my father and I, and I had grown to manhood.

I had completed the rites of an *ephebe* months before, proud of my short hair and newly grown beard, and I was due to make the pilgrimage to Eleusis to be initiated into the mysteries of the Two Goddesses, for which a mystagogue had prepared me. Pheidias, prone to spring pleasant surprises, had decided that we would go first to Thermopylai, where, long ago, the Spartans lost a battle but turned a war. There, in respect to tradition, I would renew my vows, but in truth I sensed he wanted me to see it, as he had visited it once before my birth. We would take ship to Korinth, then walk through Boeotia and Phokis into Lokris. On the return from Thermopylai we would part at Athens, he to sail to Syracuse, I to join the procession on the Sacred Way.

Perhaps we went to Korinth because it lay on our road to Thermopylai, perhaps because it was our mother city. Pheidias did not say, and I accompanied him very willingly on this, my first visit to the mainland. I had no reason then to expect that the law of the lever would begin its gestation at Korinth, or that the future defence of Syracuse against the barbarians of the Roman republic would suggest itself at the pass where Leonidas fell. Perhaps both ideas were to be connected by the Fates.

The wind was fair for much of the way from Syracuse to Korinth, but a storm from the west forced us to shelter behind Kephallonia for two days. When the weather calmed the ship left the island behind and sailed east to enter the gulf from where we saw the mountains of the Peloponnesos, land of the Spartans and Argives, look down upon us. At Korinth we offered to Poseidon for a safe voyage and stayed for a few days, admiring the handsome temples in the city from whence our ancestors had sailed to found Syracuse. We saw also the *diolkos* of Periander, of which I will speak later.

We took the road across the isthmus to Megara, walking, or hiring a cart when the road permitted, with four armed slaves as bodyguards who attended to the pack animals, halting for shade and rest when the sun was high. Pheidias wore a *petasos* I had not seen before, with a brim that seemed broad enough to shelter his entire body at noon. He was unusually talkative, as though the planets had released him. He had the rolls of Herodotus dealing with the Persian wars to hand and consulted them daily, grunting when he reached a particular passage that he said had been inspired by an Athenian with little sympathy for Sparta.

It seemed strange to lie in the shade by the path through this pleasant land, or to sleep on a cool night within a few days' walk of Delphi, and have Herodotus remind us of the peril that had threatened Greece almost fifty Olympiads before my birth. To me it seemed very long before, far distant from the pleasant passes where we rested, and without relevance to our own time. Pheidias shook his head when I spoke of this. There were always wars, he said, but there was no longer Sparta, almost a broken spear by our time, to fight our battles. The pity, said Pheidias, was that Alexander had conquered the east and left the west in the control of the barbarians. The Makedonian genius had died when he was too young, and the Ptolemies, Seleukids and Antigonids feasted on the territories he had conquered and did not rest unless they fought one another for more, leaving nothing in our time to unite Greece. For the first time since the Persians were defeated, all Hellas lay with its throat exposed to whoever had the sharpest sword. Tiny Syracuse had been the greatest force in the west at one time, but our situation had become little better than that of a pebble on an anvil, reduced to such a perilous state that our Tyrant had to choose between Carthage, our enemy since Syracuse began (this Pheidias knew only too well, as he had defended Syracuse against it), and Rome, another barbarian state whose citizens claimed descent from the defeated of Troy. We must hope, he said, that neither would overcome the other, because surely the victor would swallow us.

We were approaching Plataia where the Greeks, led by Leonidas' nephew Pausanias, had won the final battle against the Persians, when Pheidias remarked how strange it was that while Syracusans and Spartans were Dorians, the two *poleis* were so different. Consider, he went on, how Syracuse overthrew its tyrants at a whim, yet Sparta had kept a double kingship – a dyarchy – since the Dorians had arrived, a stability unknown to the rest of the Greek world, kings such as Leonidas who were of the very blood of Herakles, descendants of the god, and who led the state into battle while the ruling council of Ephors governed it. Consider again, he said as we stopped to rest in the shade from the noonday sun and the insects hummed from the olive groves, how the Spartans despised gold, lived to fight, and did not need walls because none dared to attack them, while the Syracusans preferred to trade, built walls to hide behind and hired mercenaries to do their fighting. If the mothers of the Spartans who had survived a lost battle wept for shame (in public at least) that their sons had left the field still carrying their shields, the mothers of such Syracusans would have anxiously inquired instead as to what booty they had brought with them.

Such, he reminded me, to our shame, had been the attitude of Syracuse at the time of the Persian threat. When the ambassadors came from Sparta and Athens to ask the Tyrant Gelo (who by then was lord of all Sicily, having beaten Carthage at the battle of Himera on the same day that Leonidas fell) to send ships and men to Greece, his eventual response was to send a ship full of treasure to wait off Delphi. If Xerxes defeated the Greeks, the treasure would be given to him, together with earth and water from Syracuse as a sign that Gelo bent his knee to the Persian king. If the Greeks won, the ship was to bring the treasure home to Syracuse, which it eventually did when the Persians were routed. That, said Pheidias drily, was the empty contribution of Syracuse to Greece in its peril.

A hero, above everything, calls like a Siren to the hearts of the Greeks, but a hero without subtlety and cunning repelled Pheidias, so the character of Leonidas was of intense interest to him. As Homer mocked the gods for their behaviour and lifted the reputation of cunning Odysseus above them, so Pheidias with a similar lack of reverence cut the character of the young Spartan king into pieces and placed the parts together again, examining each in turn before deciding whether the whole represented a true Greek hero. The examples that appealed most to him were the brave but clever, those unafraid to use the sword but who preferred to outwit an enemy with cunning and guile. If a tale of a hero was to include a fight, it must do so in a manner that would induce everyone to respect not only his bravery, but his intelligence. Bravery and the willingness to be killed in a great cause were the qualities of all heroes for whom the audiences wept at the theatres, but those of whom the poets should sing were the powerful dead who combined all the qualities of greatness. Given a choice between Odysseus and Akhilles, Pheidias chose Odysseus.

In that manner, Herodotus in hand, he studied Leonidas, through his actions the attitude of the Spartans to death, and the final piece of evidence he seized upon to reach his judgment on the leader of the Three Hundred was the fate of Aristodemos, one of only two Spartans who had not died at Thermopylai (the other, Pantites, sent by Leonidas to ask help from Thessaly, had hanged himself – a woman's death – when he returned too late to take part). Aristodemos did not fight at Thermopylai because he was almost blinded by a sickness of the eyes and therefore Leonidas sent him home before the battle. Perhaps one or both men deliberately delayed their return to Thermopylai. In any case, when Plataia came, Aristodemos, recovered but filled with angry shame, threw himself at the Persians like a wolf anxious to die. He slaughtered the men of Xerxes until they ran from his fighting madness. He was killed, yet the Spartans would not honour his bravery because they did not respect his wish to die.

That produced two conclusions to Pheidias. The first was immediately evident, that Leonidas would not allow one of the Three Hundred to die needlessly, even if he were shamed when sent home to Sparta. The second, and more profound, was that the sense of duty of each fighting Spartan did not allow him to seek his own death, as his death did not belong to him, but to the men by his side and the state of Sparta.

I asked: If Leonidas truly owned these values, why did he not fight his way clear and escape with his remaining men when he realised they faced certain death if they remained?

Pheidias: He knew from the beginning that Thermopylai was ultimately indefensible, that the Persians could not be stopped for more than a few days unless reinforcements came up, but he knew also that his death and that of the Three Hundred would serve Sparta better than his escape. The Ephors would be shamed into throwing Sparta fully into the fight with the Persians, and all Greece would determine to avenge him, as it did when news came that Xerxes mutilated the body of Leonidas, possibly because the Spartans killed two of Xerxes' brothers in the battle. At the end, Leonidas obeyed the holy ritual of the Spartan kings, and chose to die to remind the Ephors of what it meant to be a Spartan.

So Pheidias talked as we walked or took the carts into Attika and on to Boeotia, disdaining the many inns along the way that he said were full of uneducated whores and lice. We slept like the Spartans in our *himations* on the rocky ground, with our swords close by and a bag of staters and owls between us. I secretly missed the comforts of Syracuse and worried about snakes and the mountain bears. Pheidias slept like the mountain itself. Eventually I did the same, only to dream of the terrible moment when Xerxes and his Persians, having sent his fleet to stand off the shore in support, invaded Greece with the largest force the world had seen, so great that it took a week to cross the floating bridge of seven hundred ships the Persian king placed across the Hellespont from Asia into Europe. I awoke while it was still dark, sweating, the vision still fresh of a great army stepping off a swaying platform on to the sacred soil of Greece.

I told Pheidias of my dream a few days later as Mount Parnassos came in sight. What saved Greece then, he said as we walked, was the ancient custom of suspending hostilities between Greeks for the Games or the pilgrimages to Eleusis and Delphi. He recalled the confusion and fear throughout Greece as Xerxes killed the Ionians or medised them, the fear and the desire to repay old slights that led other Greek states to enter the war on the Persian side and induced Greek to fight Greek. It was only the spirit of the annual holy truce, in his view, that allowed Sparta and Athens and the others to meet in council, and even though all Greece realised that freedom was in terrible peril, they could not agree how to save it, just as the new Greek powers of our own day would not agree to fight as one, even if the soldiers of Carthage or Rome invaded the mainland and defaced every temple.

The spirit of the holy truce had not worked at once. While the Persians advanced, he pointed out, the Ephors of Sparta wished to conduct only a defence at the Peloponnesos and build a wall across the isthmus of Korinth, abandoning the rest of Greece, but the Athenians, led by Themistokles who combined high strategy with low corruption, reminded them that Athens was above that point, while Sparta was below it. Even then the response of the Ephors lacked genuine commitment. They and their allies from below the isthmus sent only a token force to Thermopylai, an army of three thousand soldiers from the Peloponnesos that included three hundred Spartan *hoplites*, the bodyguard of Leonidas. The rest of the Greek army – Thebans, Thespians and Phokaians – probably numbered the same. In all, the Greeks were fewer than seven thousand. Thermopylai, the gate between northern and middle Greece, was such a narrow pass between a high cliff and the sea that it slowed a flood of soldiers to a trickle, but a force of that size could not hold it for long, and the Ephors must have known that Thessaly had flanked the defences there in an earlier war.

We reached Thermopylai at last, and sheltered from the thunderstorms that enveloped the mountains. I caught the sombre mood of the pass as we crossed the little river Phoenix, named after the redness of the stream bed, at the western approach to the pass, then climbed along the cliff by the sea to look down on the west gate of Thermopylai. Lightning flashed near us as we walked carefully along a dangerous, lengthy slope to a towering cliff, above the hot springs that gave the place its name. Around these springs, in the rain, we saw deposits of sulphur, a blanket of white on the sullen landscape, surrounded by great rocks and mountain brush. This was the middle gate of Thermopylai, where the passage of the pass was at its narrowest, and in an instant we could see the value in drawing the biggest army the world had seen into a narrow defile where it could be stopped by a tiny, disciplined force. I was not surprised to hear Pheidias remark that it was where Leonidas drew up his men to meet the Persians.

It grew very dark suddenly then, as the heavy clouds descended. Bolts of lightning were hurled into the ground along the bottom of the cliff as we went further into the pass. We sheltered beneath it and there in the lightning flashes I saw the ruins of a wall on top of a mound, dwarfed by the rock above, with a valley below it. I was pointing to it when I saw that Pheidias wept.

I turned away at the sight, paralysed in the rain, embarrassed at such weakness. Then the truth came to me. It was behind this wall that the Spartans took their last stand.

The Phokian allies built it at the command of Leonidas. When it was finished the Spartan king sent the Phokaians to guard the Pass of Anopaia, which we climbed with great effort when the storm abated to see where the Persian Hydarnes and his Immortals turned the defences of the Greeks. This was of the narrowest. A wagon could pass through the middle gate of Thermopylai, but we found, with great physical effort, that only one man at a time could go through the Pass of Anopaia, along a high valley dense with forest, negotiating between great rocks on both sides, until he arrives at the point on a cliff above the middle gate. There the ravine descends abruptly to the mouth of the Anopos river. Down that ravine on the third day of the battle, as the Phokaians fled, went the men of Hydarnes, guided, it was said, by a Greek traitor, and down that ravine fifty Olympiads later, pursued by lightning, went the astronomer Pheidias of Syracuse and his son, wet to the skin.

The storm passed. The slaves lit a fire to dry our clothes as we stood in the sun in the place where Xerxes had reached the pass and waited for his army to come up. This, said Pheidias, must be the place from where he ordered the Spartans to surrender their weapons, to which they replied, as they combed their long hair and donned their red cloaks and bronze armour, that they preferred to keep them.

Heads bowed, we returned to the wall where two days later Leonidas had led his men to take their last stand when he knew the battle was lost. Hydarnes had cleared the pass. The Spartan flautist had played the song of Kastor, and the remaining hoplites of the Three Hundred had sung the paean of death. On that ground I took my vows, and that is where Pheidias told me that poets and philosophers might also be heroes.

The Book of Aengus

A Greek mathematician in the Hellenistic age is still imbued with the Heroic spirit of an earlier time, with the paradigms of Ulysses and Achilles, the stuff of Homer, and I wonder whether Pheidias took him there to remind him that that spirit did not have to die with Leonidas. It is the tactics of the Spartans that appeal to the analytical brain, and I think it is the *diolkos* of Periander, where ships were carried across the Isthmus of Corinth on great wagons pulled by horses and oxen, that appeals to the mechanic whose system of pulleys and blocks would later dazzle the Tyrant of Syracuse as they were used to heave a heavy ship across a beach.

I was puzzled about the bag of owls until I remembered that the coins of Athens were struck with the image of an owl, symbol of the city, and realised I'd listened to ancient slang for the currency that was accepted throughout Greece. The stater was a coin in general use in the Greek world, including the Macedonia of Alexander. Perhaps travellers in mainland Greece then carried both. A *chlamys* was a form of long cloak.

The voice of Archimedes in the night tells of the heroism of Leonidas and his bronze men in the same tone that he uses to speak of the mathematical poems called theorems, the sonnets of geometry. If he brought a wax tablet to Thermopylae, it probably left with a diagram of the battle on it.

Now he makes his pilgrimage, as so many great men did before him, to the town near Athens where he will be initiated in the sacred rites and therefore become a *mystes*, a title that carried respect everywhere in the Greek world. We do not know everything of the Eleusinian Mysteries, but we know they were then already very old, that they were essentially fertility rites, that they were held during a waning moon as the year began to die and that Demeter, Goddess of the Earth, was reunited with her daughter Kore who reluctantly ruled the underworld with her consort Hades during winter and returned in spring to symbolise the earth's rebirth.

It stems from what is probably one of the oldest of the known myths, drawn from the more ancient civilisations, and it has a particular resonance in Sicily, one of the places Demeter is said to have lived. Hades, king of the underworld, surfaces through a chasm in the earth of his making, kidnaps beautiful Kore, daughter of the Goddess of the Earth, as she gathers flowers in a meadow, and takes her down into the darkness to be with the dead. Demeter, filled with anguish at the loss of her daughter, searches everywhere, fails to find her, settles in Eleusis which becomes sacred to her, then abandons her duty as Earth Goddess/mother. No crop will grow. Famine strikes the earth, which is condemned to perpetual winter. Zeus intervenes to order the girl's return. The Fates decree she may do so if she has not eaten while in Hades. The cunning god of the underworld offers her his fruit, pomegranate, the food of the dead, as the serpent offered the apple to Adam and Eve. Kore accepts and eats. Zeus at length pronounces judgment: Kore would spend a third of the year in the underworld, and for the remainder would be united with her mother, who would bring rebirth to the earth each year when her daughter returned. The festival at Eleusis would celebrate her return as the end of winter, and the arrival of a divine child, the god Dionysus, as a rebirth of life. The myth is recalled in a Homeric hymn where Demeter

...sits aloof in her fragrant temple, dwelling in the rocky hold of Eleusis

until her daughter is restored to her. Thus began the annual procession along the Sacred Way from Athens to Eleusis and back that would be made annually for a thousand years and which would initiate the pilgrims into her mysteries, the secrets of the earth and of its rebirth.

It was the most important annual pilgrimage of the Greeks, restricted to the pure of body, forbidden to those who did not speak their language. At the centre of the mysteries lay the belief of the Greeks, in common with most ancient cultures, that divine intervention was necessary, or at least desirable, to ensure that spring would arrive and the earth be reborn, just as Plato and Aristotle would rely on divine forces to make the cosmos revolve. Such phenomena did not necessarily happen of themselves, so each year Kore must be restored to her mother, Goddess of the Earth itself, while Dionysus the god, the symbol of fertility and the most popular deity of the Greeks, must be present as the divine child at the ceremonies that would initiate the pilgrims into the secrets of the earth and so admit them into Elysium in the after-life.

The content of the rites at Eleusis was closely guarded, but the scholars write of the two goddesses being present in some way, of strange forms and dazzling lights springing from the darkness, of the statue of Iachus, as the Dionysus child was known, appearing, crowned with myrtle and bearing a torch, and of a voice calling from the background: "The Great Goddess has borne a sacred child," a signal that fertility and earth had been united, that spring would come again.

Mother and daughter goddesses dominate the ceremony, a sign of the age of the rites that stemmed from an era when female deities dominated religion. The ceremonies themselves probably pre-dated those of Eleusis, as Dionysus, a god worshipped at least as early as the time of the Mycenaean civilisation in Crete, would become the most popular figure – though not to the exclusion of others such as Zeus and Apollo – in Greek religion.

I went last night to spy on the house where she lives and saw Kate standing in a field with her dog, looking at the moon. For a moment I saw her as a withered crone, a dark witch, or a hell-hag. When I looked again she was back to the Kate I recognised. Then she turned her head and I felt she knew that I watched her.

The Greek

I saw you with the pathfinder tonight, Stranger. Trust him. He and the bird are of a kind.

I will tell you all I can, of the exhilaration I felt when the cry went up – *To the Sea, Mystai!* – and thousands of young men and women from everywhere in the Greek world, each carrying a little sacrificial pig that cost three drachmae apiece, ran into the ocean to be ritually cleansed, how the air was full of shouts and squeals, of the solemn call of the sacred herald echoing from the Painted Stoa in Athens on the previous day inviting us to participate in the ceremonies, and of the noise of the crowd of initiates as we processed from the Pompeion, joining the *hierophantes* and an escort of chosen *ephebes* who guarded the sacred objects brought from Eleusis for the procession. They held the statue of the divine child aloft to us as we cried *Iakh' o Iakhe! Iakh' o Iakhe!* So our pilgrimage began.

It is a little like a dream to me now, that journey to Eleusis, but I remember vividly still the Sacred Way, a wider thoroughfare than I had seen, with clefts cut in stone along its length to allow chariots and wagons to pass at speed. It stretched ahead of us as we marched, leaving a great cloud of dust behind us, through the pass between Mount Poikolon and Aigaleos, the air warm despite the lateness of the year. We reached the shrine of Pythian Apollo, chanting hymns to Demeter as we went, and the great blue bay of Eleusis appeared to our left, lit by the late morning sun, a haze hanging over the horizon as we walked in a great jostling procession. I can taste the dust and hear the voices still, and feel the welcome coolness of the water as we took lustration in the Rheitoi river, sacred to Demeter and Kore, where we waited in turn for the ceremony of the *krokosis* as saffron ribbons were tied to our right hands and left legs.

There were pilgrims from everywhere in the Greek world anxious to participate in the Mysteries of Eleusis, taking advantage of the holy truce that was proclaimed in every *polis*. The truce lasted for 55 days each year, which was as well, for there were wars everywhere, but on that road to Eleusis on the nineteenth day of the month of Boedromion all animosity was suspended and Greeks were brothers and sisters again, the lowest born mingling freely with the highest.

That peace was tested when we reached the river Kephisos. There the low-born citizens of Athens jeered and threw stones at us, singling out the initiates from the nobler Athenian families, but we bowed our heads as we crossed the river. We knew that the stoning was part of the ceremonies. We were there to be humbled.

The women danced at Eleusis that night before a day of fasting for all initiates. Then the ceremonies began.

I draw a cloak over them, yet I can tell you that there were things performed, said, and shown in the Eleutherion to initiate us in the mysteries of life, and it was while these secrets were being revealed that a great *katharsis* came over me. I was purified, as the other initiates were, but there was an additional gift from the Goddess that I am convinced was reserved for me. Stranger, in the middle of the revelations of the Mysteries I heard a voice telling me that I was destined for great work, that I must devote the remainder of my life to using the gifts I had been given at birth, but that I must avoid the sin of *hubris* at all cost. If I failed in this I would lose these gifts.

A wave of enthusiasm entered me. It was followed by a terrible reaction as the *katharsis* took hold of my body. I felt my limbs lose their strength. My eyes seemed to leave their sockets. My face contorted as the frenzy grew stronger. When I began to recover I thought that my actions would have been apparent to the other initiates, but when my sight returned I saw nothing on their faces except a rapt attention to the revelations of the Mysteries.

I stumbled from the building when they ended and leant against a column in the *peristasis*, sweating like an animal, feeling weaker than I had felt until then. Throughout the final night in the Anaktoron I continued in a daze that seemed to last through the libations for the dead on the following day. I felt weakened still on the ninth day when we retrod the Sacred Way to Athens to hear the ruling assembly at the Eleusinion warn us against impiety. The pilgrimage was finished and the sensation of stupor receded, to be followed by one of joy when I realised that I, Arkhimedes of Syracuse, could justly say: I fasted for a goddess, I drank the *kykeon*, I have been to Eleusis, I became a *mystes*.

The Book of Aengus

He speaks of a wave of enthusiasm entering his body during the rites at Eleusis. Etymologically this means that the god entered the worshipper, who believed that he became one with the deity. That would seem to agree with the Greek's account, as would the scholars' belief that the initiates were given a hallucinogenic drink – the *kykeon* –before they entered the building. Most of the initiates would therefore have been in some form of trance when the Goddess spoke to him, and would not have noticed.

I think of the early Christian Latin Masses in the darkness of the catacombs of Rome, and of their similarities to the rites of Eleusis, their enthusiastic fundamentalism, the sacrifice of the Eucharist, the consubstantiation of the bread and wine with the flesh and blood of the Saviour, the enthusiasm of the partakers when they received Communion, believing that the body of the god fused with theirs. Many aspects of Christianity seem remarkably similar to the much older myth of Dionysus. They include the bringing forth of the divine child, the symbol of the vine, rebirth or resurrection (Dionysus was reborn from the thigh of Zeus), a journey to the Underworld, the miracle of the wine (Pausanias describes how the priests of Dionysus placed pots of water inside a shrine and how, overnight, the water turned to wine), and the association with the mother image. The symbol of Dionysus, the son of Zeus whom the Romans called Bacchus, was the vine. It would also become the symbol of Christ, who would tell his followers: "I am the vine, you are the branches."

The central importance of the female goddesses waned in different religions, but such a fundamental myth would not be denied, and it would recur in Christianity. Mary, one of a long line of virgin mothers that stretched from Gaia, the mother of the first Olympians, was born, as her name implies, from the sea in the manner of other Great Goddesses. Her images were frequently depicted with the halo of the full moon, circle-symbol of the Goddess, behind her head. She could be viewed as a continuation of the myth of the earth mother or Great Goddess, the *Magna Mater*, whose gentle son was the new sun god, a reborn Apollo, fathered from the distant heavens, and she grew more important as the myth of the ancient Goddess inexorably resurfaced, this time within Christianity, probably in response to a deep psychic need of mankind. The Reformation reduced her status in some countries from the mother of the god to the mother of the man, but in Catholic countries her influence was to approach that of her son, even to eclipse it. Christianity seemed to change as it reached northern Europe, absorbing the more sombre beliefs of the region and losing the sunnier, pagan influences of the Mediterranean peoples. Milton believed that by the seventeenth century Christianity had abrogated Mosaic law, the Old Testament rock of the religion at its earliest stage. Perhaps the Reformation essentially rejected the southern roots and colourful rites of a Christian church that had over the centuries reabsorbed much of the old paganism of the Greeks and Egyptians, with its emphasis on the mother figure, and renounced it in favour of a strict interpretation of the written word, a strongly masculine religion with its emphasis on the Word of the Bible, a symbolic victory of the sun over the moon.

Early Christianity appealed to the universal instincts of man but needed also to appeal to his intelligence, so it swallowed parts of Platonism to give it the philosophical authority it lacked, as later, through St Thomas Aquinas, it would embrace much of the teachings of Aristotle to create Scholasticism, the church's intellectual counter to the knowledge revolution that would sweep into Europe with Islam. It was not, however – in spite of the more liberal mediaeval Christian bishops who encouraged the pursuit of knowledge at some of the monasteries – a religion that encouraged the attainment of knowledge in the Socratic tradition, which said that man sinned only because he lacked knowledge, and therefore Knowledge was Good. Christian ethics must be, by its very nature, subordinate to Christian doctrine, and the Christian religion valued a pure heart above an inquiring mind.

It is a goddess with a very long tradition that I am ordered to seek, whose early likeness was not that of beautiful Artemis, or slender, graceful Demeter, or the Athene of Phidias with her aegis, images that could only be created by the Greeks, the lovers of beauty who sculptured their myths to their own ideals. The images of the great goddess of the Stone Age settlements, the figure that was worshipped by the peoples of Avebury and Stonehenge and Skara Brae and Dowth, are deliberately exaggerated, emphatically fertile like the Venus of Willendorf (an early example, carved from limestone thirty thousand years ago), seemingly basic, uncouth, agricultural, of an earlier age, but she is the archetypal goddess all the same, whether as a corn dolly or as a grossly pregnant pottery figure with a gaping vulva, a goddess who was worshipped by a people at the circles of Avebury and Stonehenge more than two thousand years before Archimedes drew his circles in his tablets at Syracuse.

I feel an absurd elation in my spirits tonight. From habit I went to the clearing where we met, and found her there, an image of tragic beauty alone in a grove, waiting for me. We stayed together for an hour, careful not to be seen, listening to the birds, sometimes talking about everything except ourselves, and when she left her head was high.

The Greek

Something disturbs the birds on your riverbank tonight. The raven is restless.

Syracusans were born with sea legs, children of saltwater and sun, a maritime people like most Greeks. The big ships generally called at the port, from Alexandria and Peiraias to the east and Massalia to the west, filled with grain and linen and pots, great beamy vessels that did not need to hug the shore but met the heavy waters of the Sicilian and Ionian seas with ease, riding all but the big storms without running for shelter. On one of these vessels I sailed from Syracuse to Egypt.

My immediate destiny had been settled since I had returned home from Eleusis. I was to study at Alexandria. Once that was decided we found a ship for me that was expected to call at the Grand Harbour within days. That left us little time to think of parting. We offered to Poseidon for a safe voyage, went to the *agora* for me to say farewell to his friends, and I went on board. The slaves stowed my boxes in the little cabin, and I went back on deck. Pheidias said little as we parted, but stood on the harbour wall at Syracuse as the sailors cast off the ropes and loosed the brailing of the sails. He still stood there until my eyes misted and I could see no more.

The winds were favourable at first, and the Hyblaion Hills above Epipolai began to recede as the ship met the choppy waves of the Sicilian Sea. Sudden squalls brought rain, but I stayed on deck, catching occasional glimpses of the island of my birth through the wind and rain, until the sun fell. Next morning Sicily had vanished over the horizon.

We saw land at times during the earlier parts of the voyage, then the *kybernetes* turned the ship's beak to the south-east. The winds were variable, sometimes blowing hard in our faces, sometimes flukey. They dropped to nothing when we reached the Sea of Krete. The voyage became tedious. We lay for days on a windless sea, the heat oppressive. A fight broke out among two of the sailors, both of them drunk, which the *kybernetes* settled by taking the tiller handle, striking them with it until they became insensible.

The wind returned in force then, as if by an order from Aiolos, and the ship lifted her bows to the short swells, the masts and yards tense once more as the sails filled. Soon, helped by Zephyros, the kind wind from the west, the ship lifted its wings and sped. The following day we saw a land to the north, which the sailors told me was the fabled island of Krete.

I stood by the prow to gaze at it, the birthplace of mighty Zeus, a mystical patch in a sea of pure blue. Clouds hung from its mountain tops, and gradually Mount Ida itself, sacred to all Greeks, appeared, its summit above the clouds. That was a sight that endured in my memory. The sun was setting in the ship's wake, casting its light on the distant mountain, placing the eastern flanks in shadow. I could imagine the young god growing up on its heights, tutored by the Idaian Daktyls.

We saw several sails on the following day after we passed Krete, all of them seemingly peaceable, while the steersman, long experienced in such voyages, kept the ship's head pointing south and east while the sun grew hotter, judging our direction each night by the stars, by the sun during daylight.

The wind stayed fair, and within days it shifted into the north-west. We had caught the Etesian wind that would bring us down close to the coast of Africa. Soon we would be where the waters of the River Aigyptos mingled with the sea, at the end of a journey that began in the darknesses of the great land to the south.

We could smell the land during the night, a hot, fetid smell from the delta, as the wind shifted and a night breeze blew from the shore. This was my first scent of Africa, an unknown land of scorching heat and floods, and animals that I had never seen. As we worked closer to the land next morning the scent grew stronger and we could spy the land of Egypt. I can see it now, a distant flatness, shimmering with heat, so different from mountainous Sicily.

The sailors pointed to the town of Pelusion on the eastern shore, at the outermost mouth of the river. We altered course to the west and eventually entered the delta through the Canobic Mouth, the wind favourable. If it held we would reach Alexandria on the following day.

It did, and on that sultry night, as the ship swung at anchor in the delta with the sails brailed up, we saw a beacon shine. That was the Pharos light, the beam from the great lighthouse of Alexandria, the tallest building in the world. On a clear night its beam could carry for three hundred stadiums, a full ten parasangs. At the top was a cupola supported by eight columns. Inside that there was said to be a fire of resinous wood reflecting off a series of convex plates of polished bronze, but that was guarded by Pharaoh's men. None could enter without his permission.

The next morning we saw it through the early mist on the delta, a pillar of white marble on top of a great stout building, built by Sostratus of Knidus and dedicated to the Dioskuri, twin guardians of the sea. It stood on the island of Pharos, at the entrance to the twin harbours of Alexandria, connected to the mainland by the Heptastadion, a mole seven stadiums long, dividing the harbour in two as at Syracuse and Sinope.

The sun came up and around us lay a sandy coast, with the early morning mist clearing from the shimmering waters as we approached. The lighthouse grew taller until gradually we saw its full immensity.

I stood in the bows of the ship with the other passengers, and soon heard that the Great Harbour lay to the east or city side of the island of Pharos, sheltered by the western horn of the Heptastadion and the island, on the one hand, and on the other the eastern horn, formed by a causeway that extended from Lokhias on the opposite side. I was told that Lokhias sheltered the Royal Harbour and the Gate of the Moon, while inland from the Royal Harbour, to the east of the island of Antirrhodos, lay the Royal Quarters, whose southern perimeter ended at the widest street in the Greek world, the Meson Pedion, which ran through the city as straight as a rod, all the way from the western gate of the city to the Canobic Gate in the east. We would enter the harbour through the narrow passage between the horns, almost directly beneath the lighthouse where the white spray showed as the short waves dashed against the rocks. To the west, beyond the Heptastadion, we could see the second harbour, a man-made haven called Eunostos, near the old quarter of Rhakotis, where a small town had stood when Alexander decided to build his city. The harbours seemed to be full of vessels of all types, trading vessels from everywhere in the Hellenic world and many other ships from barbarian countries, some of them with strange designs and rigs that I had never seen before, small boats rowing from ship to ship, everywhere a medley of different dialects and languages.

The waters here contained dangerous reefs and shoals and the wind was freshening, so we entered the Grand Harbour slowly, under foresail alone, passing one of Pharaoh's warships, a monstrous ten, as it put to sea, the buildings and temples of the city gradually rearing above our heads as we neared the harbour wall. Soon we stepped ashore in the first Greek city in Africa.

The Book of Aengus

He calls it Greek, but it might better be described as Ptolemaic, or Macedonian Greek fused with Egyptian, a new hybrid culture that promotes Greek literature and science and at the same time embraces the civilisation and religion of the old kingdoms of the Pharaohs.

Greek or not, I marvel at its history and the opportunism of Ptolemy who created it. Alexander dies unexpectedly in 323 BC and Ptolemy, one of his generals, hardened in battle, boyhood friend (perhaps even the bastard half-brother) of the great conqueror, seizes Egypt where he will eventually become Pharaoh, a king who is also a god, and take an Egyptian name that makes him beloved of Amun and the chosen of Re, gods probably unknown to him when he was a boy in uncouth Macedonia, when Egypt, with its rich and ancient civilisation, must have been as distant to him as the moon. Ptolemy's new kingdom becomes the wealthiest economy on the planet, he builds a monumental city on the Mediterranean that is the wonder of its time, lives in a splendour beyond his dreams, founds a dynasty that will last until Cleopatra's death three hundred years or so later, and owns the biggest collection of books in the world. He even invents a new god for his subjects, a composite of Osiris and Apis to be worshipped as Serapis, and houses him in a new temple, the Serapeum, that would become a secondary part of the Museum. That can hardly have been what the young Ptolemy expected when he was Alexander's boyhood playmate in Macedonia – perhaps tutored by Aristotle – yet that was his destiny. Search through history for such a story of opportunism and dynastic creation. I know of few to match it.

Ultimately, Ptolemy owes the opportunity to Alexander's father, Philip, who seized power from his ward, the rightful king of Macedon. Philip created a corps of the finest mounted troops in history and he invented the phalanx, destroying the Greek armies, in which Demosthenes, his most eloquent and bitter opponent, fought as a lowly *hoplite* and took his own life when Athens lost. When Philip was murdered he left behind his plan, inspired by Xenophon's *Anabasis*, to invade Persia, and a son who more than fulfilled that plan.

The historians tell us that the Hellenistic world became more Greek than ever under Alexander, that Homer rang in his ears when he went into battle, and that he saw himself as a reincarnation of Achilles. Ptolemy is not the military genius that Alexander was, but the Greek poet's works are also close by him as he sets out to create a dynasty that enriches the world of knowledge.

This new dynasty is known as the Lagids, after his father, and General Ptolemy becomes Pharaoh, without a drop of Egyptian blood pumping from his heart, to be known as Ptolemy I Soter

(Saviour) after he frees Rhodes in one of his many wars. He obeys the sacred wishes of Alexander to construct a great city as its new capital and, within it, a library.

When Alexander died he had already taken Egypt from the Persians and been named Pharaoh in 331 BC – the first Greek to be so called – at Memphis, the ancient capital. He then sailed north down the Nile towards the delta and, in a vision, saw a great city at the mouth and ordered his architect Deinocrates to build it on the geometrical Greek grid, *agora* at its centre, wide streets at right-angles to one another, the port to be built first and the new city to be named after himself. He took his armies to the East without seeing the first stone laid and never returned, but he intended it to be a healthy place. The chessboard plan of Alexandria, approved by him before he left, is angled in such a way that the Etesian winds blow unobstructed through the streets to the Lake of Mareotis, the city's inland border, moderating the climate in summer and reducing the risk of malaria, the scourge of the Greeks. Mareotis carries the Nile traffic from the rest of Egypt and a constant supply of fresh water to the city. Summer, a common season for diseases, is comparatively healthy at Alexandria, as the Nile waters flood the swamps of the lake. It seems to have been healthier than Babylon, where Alexander died, so the scholars conjecture, from cerebral malaria.

The Lagids live like eastern despots and sometimes marry their sisters in the pharaonic custom, yet write Greek poetry and use every means to create a centre of Greek civilisation. Religions and gods merge and change. Amun-Ra becomes Zeus Ammon. Cybele, the Great Goddess of the Orient, creeps in from the east like a shining new moon to rival her fellow moon goddess, Isis.

So Ptolemy I Soter, the tough Macedonian general, and his son Ptolemy Philadelphus who succeeds him and marries his own sister, build the great city and its lighthouse, one of the seven wonders of the ancient world. To make it emphatically unique Soter lifts the body of Alexander, an inestimably great prize to the Macedonians, when his fellow generals are not looking and takes it to Egypt where it would be entombed as a shrine, and to make it complete he follows the instructions of Alexander that a *biblion*, or repository of books, be added to his plans. Here we have a departure, as none of the great Greek cities, including Athens, had a public library. Instead Alexander probably took the tradition from Mesopotamia, where writing had been invented at the city of Uruk on the river Euphrates more than three thousand years before, and where the practice of housing writing tablets under one roof began, thus preserving, among others, the epic of *Gilgamesh*. Since Alexander's conquests the collected written knowledge of the Babylonians (as the successive civilisations and kingdoms of Mesopotamia, the lands of the Akkadians and the Sumerians, were called), and of the Egyptians, has been available to the Greeks, to be translated and distributed at will, particularly to those at the Library. The astronomical observations of these Babylonians of the moving bodies in the night sky, viewed by them as the heavenly writing of the god Marduk (*Mardokhaios* to the Greeks) and described in cuneiform writing whose characters sometimes resembled constellations of stars, are particularly prized by Greek astronomers like Pheidias. It is an age of enlightenment and great technological progress, actively encouraged and financed by the rulers of Egypt. By Hellenistic times books had become a prized source of knowledge, rolled on wooden dowels and wrapped in linen to protect them, scarcer than gold, made of papyrus or of parchment or animal skin, delicate, flimsy scrolls, some of them *palimpsests* where the original writing on skin has been effaced and replaced by another.

In common with Greek academic tradition the library does not have a structured system of examinations, nor does it confer degrees or qualifications. Students either seek out teachers or study alone, many of them working from rolls of papyri or parchment that are housed in the buildings. These are said to shelter four hundred thousand books, parchments or rolls, although some scholars quote seven hundred thousand. Soter was the patron of a former tyrant of Athens, an exile called Demetrius of Phaleron who saw himself as a philosopher-king and was effectively the first Librarian. It may have been Demetrius who commissioned seventy Jewish rabbis to translate the Pentateuch, the first five books of the Old Testament, into Attic Greek, a version that would become known as the Septuagint.

Legend has it that every ship that called at Alexandria was forced to hand over such books as it had aboard, making up the so-called ships' libraries. The first Ptolemies desired every book that existed, and Galen says one wrote a letter to every tyrant and sovereign asking to borrow theirs, sent them a deposit of fifteen talents that he subsequently forfeited without a twinge, took the original texts of Aeschylus, Euripides and Sophocles on loan from Athens, had them copied, sent the copies back and kept the originals.

The Library would survive for perhaps as long as six centuries, although that and much of its history is unclear. Even its exact site is not known for certain, although the archaeologists seem to be getting close. Julius Caesar is said to have burned it by accident when he fought Cleopatra's brother, but probably only part was destroyed then. Later, Theophilus, Christian patriarch of Alexandria and reviled by some as the patron saint of arsonists, is said to have ordered it to be burned because of the pagan knowledge it contained. Arab invaders are said to have finally destroyed it on the orders of Caliph Omar, but some of the scholars say that is unlikely, and that the last books – perhaps many of Archimedes' and Aristotle's works among them – had ceased to exist by the end of the sixth century AD.

Ptolemy Soter and his successors are enlightened men, cultural imperialists with a desire to make the city the centre of knowledge of the civilised world so they might enjoy the reflected glory. They are very aware that the Egyptian priests are their civil servants whom they need to keep the kingdom stable, and so, pragmatists that they are, they honour the old Egyptian gods and the religious rituals of the river. Egyptian society continues much as it had when Soter eventually assumes the title of Pharaoh, after much fighting with Alexander's other generals which seems to have continued afterwards with scarcely a pause. A Graeco-Macedonian upper class arises, probably inter-marrying with the wealthier Egyptian families, possibly also with the Jews who form the largest ethnic group in the city. The kingdom seems to flourish as never before, with new roads, canals, better organisation of grain farming and distribution, and the added impetus of the benefits from the greatest trading port the world has seen, a bridge between Greece and Africa and Asia. Gradually Soter shares his rule with his son, who succeeds him as Ptolemy Philadelphus, the sister-lover, in 285 BC, soon after the birth of Archimedes. They build a Temple to the Muses, probably immediately to the west of the Royal Quarter, which is directed by a priest called an *epistates*. This is the Mouseion, from which we derive the word *museum*. As a religious shrine, it is therefore given the same status as Plato's Academy and Aristotle's Lyceum at Athens.

The Great Library, presided over by a scholar-librarian personally appointed by Pharaoh, lies near the Museum. The two buildings, together with those that follow, form the centre of world knowledge. This centre attracts two of the great poets of the time, Apollonius of Rhodes and Callimachus (Kallimakhos in its Greek form) of Cyrene, the rivals of Hellenistic literature, and Soter appoints Zenodotus of Ephesus, the grammarian, as the first official Librarian. He's succeeded by Apollonius who writes *Argonautica* to revive the epic and who's almost certainly the Librarian when Archimedes arrives. Apollonius will be in turn succeeded by Eratosthenes, Archimedes' junior and close friend to whom he'll send the riddle of Apollo's cattle. Eratosthenes is the scientist who would create a catalogue of 44 constellations and a list of 475 stars, together with a mythical explanation of each constellation, invent a system for discovering prime numbers, and calculate the circumference of the earth at twenty-five thousand miles.

It's already the cradle of intellectual greatness, as Euclid has worked and perhaps died here, and it's the centre of literature, of medicine, geography, philosophy, astronomy, mathematics, and mechanics. Aristarchus has estimated the relative distances and sizes of the moon and the sun, and hypothesised that the earth revolved around the sun, but many of Alexandria's best days lie ahead as Archimedes steps from his ship. Hipparchus of Rhodes, born about twenty years after our Greek, would become one of the greatest astronomers of antiquity, to discover the wobble of the earth's axis that would be known as the precession of the equinoxes, compile the first trigonometric table, and predict a solar eclipse, using data collected by the Babylonians centuries before. The works of his successor, Ptolemy the astronomer, would be accepted until Copernicus.

Soon we may hear more at first hand, but the list is long, making Alexandria the greatest single centre of learning of the ancient world, a place of creative focus and study and mechanical invention for much of its existence, and not simply the greatest repository of books. Among its great scientists would be

Herophilus, arguably the first anatomist, and Galen, the founder of modern medicine as a body of work. The principle of hydraulics would be born in the Library, as Hero of Alexandria would produce inventions using pneumatics and hydraulics nearly two millennia ahead of their time, including an automaton that would use compressed air to sound a trumpet, the first working steam engine, and a robot that would pour libations, drink, and sing.

The Greek

I knew some of the great cities of Greece, but Athens or Korinth did not prepare me for Alexandria. When we walked from the ship to the Posidion to thank the god for a safe voyage, I looked about me, at the buildings and the crowds. For a moment my courage failed me and I wished I had not come. Looking back, I realise I had a fever.

Everything seemed out of proportion, vast, new, tall, strangely clean. The Greeks are a trading people, but I had not expected to see so many merchants. We are a sea race, but all the sailors of the world seemed to be in this great port, next to the pedlars, the soldiers, porters, carters, clerks, scribes, horoscope sellers, beggars. The city was packed with people from every barbarian nation and Greek *polis*. Every alleyway around the harbour was a busy market, the sidestreets filled with wagons bringing cargoes back and forth from the ships in the port, the drivers yelling at one another to stand clear.

These streets teemed with warehouses and shops – winesellers with tall amphorae standing by the doorways, food shops smelling of all the spices of the orient, open sacks displaying their wares to the marketers. Some of the people were dressed in the simple *khitons* of the Greek, some with colourful *himations*, many others in the bright dress typical of the orient.

Even when I recovered and grew to know the city, all seemed magnified. If I would draw the character of Alexandria and this Egypt of the Lagids I would sum all in one building, that which housed the tomb of Alexander the Great, a shocking, vast structure whose architect seemed to have been influenced simultaneously by the ziggurat of Babylon, the Pyramid of Kheops, and the tomb of King Mausolus at Halikarnassos, combining all these styles into one building that soared above Alexandria. It lay behind high walls in a sacred *temenos* at the centre of the city, near the Royal Palaces and the two great streets that intersected at the Royal Quarter. It swarmed with guards, hand-picked men of Greek blood only. In a crypt of white marble, sunk into the ground for coolness and far removed from the sunlight, lay the body of Alexander, wrapped in bandages soaked with honey and herbs, in a golden sarcophagus decorated with the scenes of his greatest battles.

This was a building like none other I have seen, magnificent in its ugliness, yet the Sanctuary of Pan nearby, constructed on the summit of the tallest hill in the world made by man, the Gymnasion with its monstrous *propylae* that stretched more than the length of a stadium to the Canobic Way, the Serapeion, the Mouseion itself and the Library each attempted to rival it, to impress all who came there with the majesty and richness of the Greek Pharaohs.

My sharpest memory after I left the temple was of the noise, noise everywhere, greetings, imprecations, the rattle of cart wheels, the cry of a slave being beaten or the yell of a petty thief who had been seized. Pharaoh's guards seemed always watchful and vigilant, appearing from nowhere if men gathered in numbers. Syracuse was not a silent city, nor a small one, but the sheer scale and noise of Alexandria overwhelmed me.

I shrank from the noise, the crowds, and the overpowering size of everything. I felt ill, whether from the great heat, or a sense of being crushed by the crowds, I knew not, but I shook with a fever. My legs were weak, unable to carry my weight. My vision dimmed. My mouth was dry. All about me I saw a sea of unsympathetic faces. I sat or collapsed on to a wall near a fish market. My slave, who had been with us all my life, ran up and down the market in panic, wailing, convinced that I was dying. At that moment I hated Alexandria.

He brought water, and I revived a little, enough to send him to find the directions to our lodgings in the Brukheion quarter where the Greeks lived. He returned, urging me to follow him. We forced our way through the crowds, or he did while I followed him into a quieter, more open quarter. When we reached the lodgings I collapsed on a couch.

I slept then, Stranger, and when I awoke a young man with pleasant features stood by me, anxiously asking after my health. Could I not eat something, he asked? I thanked him, but said I had a fever instead of an appetite.

– *Do not worry*, he said, – *this city affects new arrivals in that way after a long voyage.*

I asked him his name.

– *I am Konon of Samos*, he said.

He knew my name and birthplace, having questioned my slave. He told me that he, too, had come to Alexandria to learn, and lived in the same lodgings as I. – *We will be friends*, he said, and so we would be for the rest of his life, Stranger. When he died before he had reached his time I knew him to be one of the greatest mathematicians in the Greek world.

He left me, telling me to sleep, offering to escort me to the Library next morning and introduce me. I accepted, my spirits beginning to revive as my fever abated. I drank the water the slave brought, ate a little bread dipped in wine, and slept soundly again. When Konon returned next morning I had washed and breakfasted and unrolled my notes of introduction from my father and from Hiero, *Strategos* of Syracuse, who was not yet Tyrant then.

We walked through the clean, wide streets that were shaded by great trees. It was cooler then and quieter, a pleasing contrast to the harbour quarter. Soon I saw the squat building of the Museum loom before us. A crowd stood near it, close to a great altar, with a hierophant in his robes shouting something at the people. Konon explained that the city prepared for a great festival, a particularly splendid one where many sacred bulls would be sacrificed by order of Pharaoh whose soldiers had won a battle, he had forgotten against whom – possibly the Antigonids, he thought, or perhaps it was the Seleukids. The Egypt of the Lagids was constantly at war, but as war was the natural order in the Greek world it did not affect the work in the Library. Most of the learned men there, he said with a light laugh, cared little whether Egypt was at war or peace as long as they were not disturbed in their work.

As he spoke thus, we entered the Library of Alexandria.

It is the peculiar, subdued sound I remember, Stranger, a strange, continuous murmuring that echoed from the great soaring roof of the building, like the humming of a myriad of bees on a summer's day, that and the smell of oil lamps, suspended from the roof. I looked tentatively about me while my eyes grew used to the gloom and saw a high, narrow chamber, contrasting in light and shadow. In the lighter parts I could make out the shapes of men, hunched over rows of high desks.

No voice was raised. None called a greeting. When men passed one another on the Library floor they rarely acknowledged the other apart from an occasional lifted arm in salutation. Here and there a few conversed, but always in low tones, as though they were in a friendly conspiracy together and must be on their guard from outsiders. These conversations, a muted roar, were the source of the noise.

Most stood at carved desks under the oil lamps, reading the rolls of papyri and parchments while the covers of the rolls littered the floor. Many wrote notes on fresh papyrus, which I found later was astonishingly plentiful and therefore cheap in Alexandria. Pharaoh wished it to be so in the interests of learning, and as Egypt controlled the world supply, he could afford it, just as he could afford not to sell it to other centres of knowledge, particularly to the Attalids of Pergamon who, rumour spoke, planned to build a rival library.

The mien of these learned men in general was that of a deep concentration, their narrowed eyes squinting at the rolls as they scanned the work of other men of knowledge before them, some gathering up a roll in disgust and signalling silently to the attendants to remove it and to bring the next. Others, like a hunter spying a deer, fastened on a passage or a set of figures written by a Babylonian astronomer or a Greek poet many Olympiads before.

There seemed to be scores of these learned men standing at the raised desks, some muttering to themselves, while others crossed the floor hurriedly in the shadows, their arms full of bound rolls. At the outer areas of the floor there were many long, sloping tables with scholars standing at them, some of them murmuring or whispering as they appeared to compare notes.

Konon caught my arm and pointed at the walls and there I saw the sight that had made the Library of Alexandria so renowned. The walls contained countless rows of large niches and in these were shelves of rolls and clay tablets reaching to the top of each niche, myriads of rolls, the largest single collection of knowledge in the world, all of it under one roof.

At the centre of the wide floor stood a raised table where stood a grave individual with a white beard, a prominent nose and a high forehead, a learned man of such obvious importance that I gestured towards him with a questioning look. He, whispered Konon, was the Librarian, one of the most respected men in all of Alexandria, the confidant of Pharaoh himself. He was said to be working on a great revival of the epic. To him also fell the task of persuading the wisest men in the world to come to Egypt and to do their greatest work there. A queue of attendants waited on him.

None seemed to notice us as we walked respectfully towards him. Here and there as we went Konon pointed out some of the wise men, a Homeric scholar to whom Pharaoh had personally entrusted the task of producing a favoured version of the *Iliad*, an Egyptian astronomer whose Greek name resonated with the scholars of the civilised world and with whom my father corresponded, a geometer whose work on conics even I had known of in distant Syracuse, a geographer engaged on mapping the known world, a wise man of medicine, a renowned Peripatetic and so on. I felt very insignificant.

We waited in line to give honour to the Librarian who seemed harassed and irritable as he wrote on one roll of papyrus after another, handing each to the attendants for despatch before putting stylus to the next. At length our turn came and I presented to him my introductions. He unrolled them quickly, read the greetings, then said kindly that he hoped I would bring good to the Library. Speak rarely, like a Spartan, he said, and listen always to the wise men, as an earlier generation of young mathematicians listened to the great Eukleid in this very place. Some of them were still there, passing on what they knew. Learn from them, he said.

There were many diversions for young men like I and Konon, he advised, in a city so large that it offered every form of temptation known to man, but if I wished to honour my father – an astronomer of great distinction whose work was most respected by his colleagues here in Alexandria, he remarked kindly, much to my joy – for the kindness he had given in sending me here, I would avoid them. This was a different land, he said, full of strange gods and dark cults and mysteries.

He dismissed us as the line of men who sought his attention grew longer. The harassed look returned. Konon whispered as we left that it was common knowledge that Pharaoh put great demands on him, inquiring frequently as to what books the Library had acquired, and whence, what work had been produced, and how weak he thought the tragedy recently presented in the god-king's private theatre, written in honour of Pharaoh's queen Arsinoe who had died not long before. So Pharaoh thundered: What was the purpose of having so many books if works of great genius did not flow from such a body of knowledge? Where was the next Aiskhylos or Euripides to come from, if not from Alexandria, Ptolemy Philadelphus was said to have asked the Librarian in a rage, shaking on his throne. At this the poor Librarian is said to have replied in a voice of sorrowful respect that there could only be one Aiskhylos and only one Euripides and, for that matter, only one Sophokles. Pharaoh had rebuked him savagely, saying there was only one Librarian at Alexandria at present, but he could be replaced by another. What would he say to the appointment of Kallimakhos of Kyrene, long his rival as a poet? The Librarian had bitten his lip but bowed his head and told the god-king that if it was his pleasure to remove him he would accept at once whatever destiny Pharaoh wished for him, whether death or exile. Pharaoh, much attached to the Librarian and ill-disposed towards Kallimakhos, had calmed, inclined his divine head and said that he had merely jested.

Pharaoh Philadelphus was very sensitive about his queen, as she had been his sister. Konon told me this in a whisper, looking around him to ensure he was not overheard. He had directly involved her in affairs of state and had conferred divine honours upon her before she died. A few months before my arrival a man called Sotades of Maroneia had written a satire on this. One night he was taken from his home and drowned in the harbour. The poets of Alexandria subsequently sang openly only of Pharaoh's wisdom and virtues.

When we left the great room I assumed I had seen the entire Library, but Konon told me I had only viewed where the books were kept. The *stoae* and chambers adjoining the great building were where the wise men read and worked at leisure. We walked through some of these, then he took me to see several other buildings almost as large, all of them seemingly built recently, to the Doric tradition but of a style so heavy and monumental that it seemed peculiarly Ptolemaic. We passed chambers where skilled artisans in metal, wood and stone worked to the directions of men waving rolls of diagrams. In one, under the watchful eye of a dishevelled man who was plainly using his pulse as a time-keeper, men were pouring water into a descending line of large stone pots which emptied into those below them, which I assumed to be a water clock or *klepsydra*. In another, artisans with rasps and files worked on series of tiny metal wheels, patiently cutting notches in the circumferences so that each wheel would engage the next, work so fine and delicate that I was dazed with admiration. From a chamber further on steam poured in a scalding, choking vapour, and we saw a fire burning under a closed cauldron of some kind from which a series of pipes extended, the entire structure hissing and shaking like a Sicilian mountain with an angry chthonic god beneath.

The last chamber we glanced into was one where work was taking place that was of special importance to Pharaoh. It was large, on a scale several times greater than the others, swarming with artisans building machines of war. That was all we saw before the guards sent us away. Evidently the Library of Alexandria was not simply a place of learning for the sake of pure knowledge.

We emerged into the sunlight of the morning to pass a *stoa* at the side of the Library and at that moment I felt that I was back in the *agora* at Syracuse. It was full of men who had evidently struggled to suppress their rhetoric until they were outside the Library. They then gave full vent to it in typically Greek fashion, loudly, with many gesticulations, screeching like fish-sellers, either using their own dialects or the *koine*, leaving me to reflect that while wisdom rests easily in silence, as the Librarian had advised, silence is not always the companion of wisdom.

Stranger, as the weeks and months passed I settled into the life of Alexandria. I took my place in one of the *stoae*, next to Konon, and began my study of the measurement of curvilinear figures. My life assumed a regularity that suited me for a time. I rose early, breakfasted lightly and went to the Library, generally with Konon at my side. I studied the work of the Babylonians and the Egyptian priests from the papyri or the palimpsests. I went to the outer *stoae* to hear the wise men argue. In short, for a time I was a diligent, attentive scholar, and I wish I could tell you so that I continued to be so.

It would be easy to blame Konon who loved a *symposion* to excess and the *hetairai* of Rhakotis, beautiful as they were, even more. At first we behaved as two young men of abundant vitality in the houses of the quarter, visiting them occasionally, but as time went on we seemed to forget the Library completely during our visits to these Egyptian nymphs who sought to please, and I confess to you that I was sometimes the first to suggest that to spend time at Rhakotis was preferable to the study of an ancient Egyptian papyrus roll dealing with the squaring of the circle. You may be surprised at this, but you should remember that I was young and, for the first time in my life, free from the kind but persistent supervision of my father. My companion was in much the same situation.

You should also know that I favoured one of these nymphs in particular and was wildly jealous of anyone else who might visit her, a passion that lasted for some months. She demanded much in return for her promise of constancy. In my madness I humoured her. I grew ashamed of the number of times I wrote to Pheidias begging for money and of the number of times he obliged without question. Looking back, I am sure he detected every falsehood I sent him and hoped that wisdom would gradually overtake desire. Perhaps that took longer than he expected, as the tone of his letters gradually became more questioning, but the madness began to leave me one evening when I entered the house at Rhakotis without warning, to surprise her in the arms of another, a spindly geographer from Krete whom I had seen leaving the house on other occasions, avoiding my gaze as he passed. I saw also that night that she did not paint her face for the Kretan as she did for me, and that she had not been entirely truthful about her age – certainly she looked much older without her customary wig and the kohl that circled her eyes when I visited. Perhaps I had been more generous than the Kretan. Nevertheless I chased him through the streets of Rhakotis, still blind with rage and jealousy, caught him and threw him down, beating his head on the ground while his shouts drew a crowd that began to stone us. I was forced to run before them, almost weeping with rage, and escaped into the city where I met Konon and told to him the events of the evening. If I expected a sympathetic response, I was to be disappointed, as he laughed all the way through the Brukheion. The following day I waited, determination growing, and when evening arrived I set forth for Rhakotis, resolved to punish her for her unfaithfulness by dismissing her. When I arrived at the house they told me she had unexpectedly left that morning, in haste to visit her family in Upper Egypt. I returned to our lodgings, miserable and feeling sorry for myself. Next day there came a further letter from Pheidias, reminding me more firmly of my purpose in Alexandria. By then I was in debt to the moneylenders. Konon, in the meantime, had spent every drachma his father sent him, and was in the same plight. We conferred, reminding ourselves that the moneymen could not pursue us into the Library, as it was a sacred *temenos*, a sanctuary. We returned to our studies at last, much chastened, and after a time of avoiding our pursuers by hiding in the Library, fasting, and severe privation we repaid our debts. We were, once more, free to explore Alexandria, but our paths seldom took us to Rhakotis.

The city was a strange one to us because it was so ordered. In reality it was a series of five areas which were known by the first letters of our alphabet. We lived in Beta, to the north of the city, where the Museum and the palaces were. The Greek part was the richest and most important as it administered the law of the land and housed the *ekklesia*, the city's council which, of course, answered to Ptolemy's governor.

The Greeks were not the only rich in Alexandria, nor was the division between the citizens as strict as the ruling class suggested. We wandered through the quarter of the wealthier Egyptians, mainly merchants who traded in grain and papyrus and cargoes from everywhere in the world. Their great houses, many of them richly painted, seemed more akin to temples than dwellings, ornamented with *propylae* and obelisks, the entrances between high towers, with long panelled walls and shaded gardens that were often connected by canal to the lake of Mareotis, so that their gardens might be watered. Some of these houses contained tamed animals from the wilderness to the south, and the first lion I saw outside of its cage roamed at the end of a long chain in the garden of a rich Alexandrian merchant. It was a sentry that only a brave robber would pass. Tamed monkeys were common. When the time of the date harvest arrived we saw many that had been trained to run to the topmost branches, pluck the fruit, descend, then place it in a flat basket of wickerwork at the foot of the tree, before re-ascending to repeat the operation. That was not their only use. One evening, as we returned from our walk, we witnessed rows of monkeys acting as torch bearers after a feast.

In another quarter to the north-east – a prosperous one, but plainer – lived a hardy people, most of whom spoke the old Hebraic language, who were of the same race as the Phoenicians but of a different tribe and language. They were the most numerous of the population of Alexandria, which then numbered fifty myriads – even more numerous than the Greeks or the Egyptians themselves, though they were few at the Library. They were hardy and honest and much given to quarrels, particularly in the interpretation of their religion, and at their insistence Pharaoh had allowed them to pass their own laws. They admitted of no goddess and of only one god. At one time in the distant past they had been enslaved by earlier Pharaohs and put to the building of the pyramids before their escape, an event that was central to their holy book. They appeared to have little interest in mathematics or literature, but were clever merchants, dealing in precious stones, metals and silks. They prayed much to their unseen god and when they were not praying they were trading overland, mainly with the Phoenicians but also with more distant lands. Pharaoh, it seemed, welcomed them for the taxes they paid.

The quarter of the Greeks was where we lived, as I said, and the richer part was unlike that of the Greece we knew. It was full of great houses of a splendour foreign to me. Here, side by side with the wealthy Greek merchants, Pharaoh's generals and lawmakers dwelt, iron-fisted men mainly of Makedonian descent who answered to the god-king for the safety of his land. They were feared by most, but particularly by the Egyptians who had endured Persian rule before Alexander arrived, yet might still think of their own days of empire.

If the people of Syracuse loved their games and festivals and theatre, the Alexandrians loved them more. We went sometimes to the hippodrome to the east of the city walls, beyond the Canobic Gate, to watch the chariot races at which the Alexandrians – Greeks and Egyptians alike – became inflamed with fervour for their champions. The theatre, which lay by the Maeander water-garden near the Royal Harbour, attracted the best of actors from throughout the Greek world, while the games in the vast stadium on the shores of the lake near the Serapeion – a stadium that held at least four times the numbers of spectators held by that of Syracuse – were of the standards of the Olympic and the Pythian. Nothing was too great for Alexandria.

Our furtive return to the library was remarked upon, with glee here, cynicism there, and by a gentle rebuke from the Librarian who had been disappointed by our absence. Shamed of face, I threw myself into my work and became so absorbed in it that months passed before I seemed to lift my head. When I did I was to be reminded of the goddess who protected my city, the goddess I had neglected in the heat of my passions. It came from an unexpected direction.

All at the Library knew of Kallimakhos of Kyrene, the high-born poet, rival of the Librarian. Some disliked him, yet most admired him, some for his high birth, some for his wit, others for his brilliance, and all for his learning that combined with his energy. All recognised his ungainly, squat figure as he wandered through the *stoae*, but I had not met him. We knew that his moods and passions seemed to depend on whether the particular youth he pursued at the time returned his love or spurned it. Later he told me that he wrote best when he was in hopeful pursuit, as he phrased it, but that a dangerous mood overtook him when a handsome boy turned away from him. He lost control of himself then and his words frequently grew bitter, his tongue dipped in poison. The same tongue had almost brought about his exile or even death when he attacked the revival of the epic and, by implication, the present Librarian, by crying out intemperately when Pharaoh was present: *Mega biblion, mega kakon.* Pharaoh did not agree that a big book was a bad thing. On the contrary, he had urged Apollonios to write one. In the *stoae* it was whispered that Kallimakhos had narrowly escaped the fate of Sotades, though his *Pinakes* was a catalogue to every roll in the Library, his epigrams known in every city.

Sometimes he gave a discourse on a fresh poem he had made. Usually this took place at a remote *stoa* at the end of the Museum, where the audience divided between his followers and that of the Librarian. In truth we went there expecting a fight when rumour flew through the Library that he was to speak. As we approached the *stoa* we heard a few hesitant shouts of support. They were quickly drowned by the opposition, as the Librarian was known to be a favourite of Pharaoh.

We arrived to find the poet calmly confronting his critics, waiting for the noise to fall. Gradually, it sank to silence.

Kallimakhos began quietly, taking time to prepare his voice, to speak of a hymn he had made to Artemis. Jeering began once more. He waited until it grew quiet again. His voice lost its ugly rasp, rising as his tongue loosened, telling us of how he chose, after the usual beginning to a hymn, to proceed in two steps, the first when the goddess is a small child. The numbers of the audience increased as the scholars pressed forward to hear him abruptly change his voice, like an actor, lifting it to imitate a pampered girl-child attempting to reach up to and pull the beard of mighty Zeus her father as she demanded one gift after another, eternal virginity the first, more names than her brother Apollo, another. She wished for a silver bow of her very own, a little curved bow, with slender arrows – No, the child decided abruptly, changing her mind, the Cyclopes would surely make those for her.

I heard then the little girl, through the poet's voice, press her father for the gift of sixty Oceanids and twenty nymphs of her own from the river of Amnisos in Krete as her escort. She also wished, she said, to be Light Bringer.

She had asked for eternal virginity in the same wilful tone, and for permission to wear a short *khiton* to her knee for the hunt, for the carrying of the torches she would light directly from a bolt of Zeus, then the swift hounds she would need, each sentence seeming to begin with *dos*, the word used by every child in Greece who is indulged too much and so demands more. He paused then, and his audience waited, unsure of what would follow.

Without warning, the tone of the poet changed as the girl-child dropped her wilfulness, to become dutiful. She offered to protect any city that Zeus might name. A fresh murmur went up as we heard this, struck by the sudden change of tone of the girl-child, hitherto interested only in her world of the hunt and of the mountains and groves. In that pause she stepped on the path to becoming a goddess, a full member of the pantheon of Olympus, prepared to protect a city, all selfishness gone.

Kallimakhos paused again, and a great hush came over the audience. No-one jeered him then, but all lifted their heads as the deep voice of mighty Zeus spoke, like one that echoed and rang from the stone of the theatre at Syracuse, a low rumble of thunder infused with love for the child-goddess. We heard this voice promise her thirty citadels with towers to be built to exalt her alone, and to call her own. There would be more that would be shared with other gods, but each would have a grove and an altar dedicated to Artemis.

The tone changed again and every word seemed to dance in the air as the poet-scholar indulged us in his role of poet-actor, developing the life of the goddess, taking us to where the monstrous Cyclopes, rough as the cliffs of Ossa, with single eyes glaring like an ox-hide shield, were hammering out a trough of iron for Poseidon's horses (such a massive thing, Stranger, that the resonance of the hammers caused Aetna in Sicily to cry out in pain, Italy to scream and Corsica to roar). Throughout this the little child, fearless unlike her frightened nymphs, confronts the giants and asks them to build her a Kretan bow as she, being twin sister to Apollo, is also child of Leto, who is very special to the Cyclopes.

I feel the tremor still as I felt it then when he reminded us of the significance of her silver bow, of the reputation of the goddess who would use that bow to protect her cities but who would be completely unforgiving to those who transgressed. He told us how she took the weapon the Cyclopes made for her, and fired four arrows. She aimed the first two at trees in the distance, the third at a wild beast, and the fourth at a city where the rulers had betrayed her trust.

The poet moved on to the second part, the fulfilment of the goddess, after which the two long parts of the poem fused to be one, as the goddess was one, yet we sensed a climax approaching as the tone changed abruptly once more. Kallimakhos switched to the first person as he asked the goddess directly (calling her *Potnia*, Mistress) for her personal protection and for the gift of song to be in his care forever, and we began to sense that he communicated directly with her, that the poem was in reality her gift to him, as we saw, through the metres the poet sang that seemed to linger in the air, the Amnisian nymphs encircle her in a dance on Olympus. All listened in solemn silence to the terrible warnings in the final verse to honour this goddess, not to shun her yearly dance, vie with her in archery, or compromise her modesty, whatever else we did in our lives.

– *All hail, Goddess*, he ended, and be gracious to his song.

– *All hail*, we murmured in return.

He left while the *stoa* was still in tumult, halting here and there to greet those who saluted him. I, strongly affected, was among them. I told him that the goddess was the protector of my city.

– *Then tell your city not to betray her trust*, he said, and left.

Narrative

Aengus walked a great distance that day, feeling his head clear from the sharp air, his strides lengthening as he crossed Aldbourne Chase, past Snap and the Ogbournes and on to the Ridgeway, up to Barbury and south to Fyfield Down where, late in the afternoon, he remembered his sandwiches. He ate them in the shelter of an elder bush and of Long Tom, a friendly monolith that gazed sightlessly across to where Four Mile Clump topped the horizon. Here, while a woodpecker yaffled at him from a spinney, Aengus read some lines of a pocketbook of Greek verse that contained Cory's translation of Callimachus' epigram on the death of his friend Heraclitus of Halicarnassus:

I wept, as I remembered, how often you and I
Had tired the sun with talking and sent him down the sky.

The sun was long down when he took up his journal, and it was later still when he heard a familiar voice.

The Greek

A few days later Konon and I climbed the hill to the Sanctuary of Pan, and on the way back to the Brukheion we talked of the mathematics of the Egyptians. The Library contained many original papyri on banausic mathematics, some of them relating to the building of the later pyramids and temples, some demotic but most of them hieratic, written by the priests. I searched these papyri for anything to do with the measurement of the circle and other curvilinear figures, but found nothing that was not known and already copied. The search itself, however, demonstrated a great truth, that the mathematics of Egypt was the mathematics of the river. To the Egyptians, and particularly to Pharaoh, it was the mathematics of life and death, the mathematics of Pharaoh's rule itself.

I saw why they had become good astronomers, why they had a calendar that was so accurate it shamed the Greeks, why Pharaoh respected the religion of the Egyptians, and why the priests were held in such awe. The existence of the river dominated all, and the priests were the guardian of its secrets. Yet I could not see how they knew in advance how high the annual flood would be, a piece of priceless information that the peasants believed the priests were told each year by the god Osiris.

Stars or moon or sun would not tell them this. Neither could their mathematics. In any case they were poor at arithmetic. They were more advanced in geometry, but for only one reason. They used it to advance the wealth of Pharaoh.

You see, Stranger, Pharaoh personally owned Egypt – all of it but a few cities – because Alexander had taken it by the spear. Land, by Greek custom, belongs to the conqueror, and land in Egypt is either worth a great amount or nothing at all. It rarely rains in the kingdom of Pharaoh, and without water the kingdom would be a desert, worthless. Everyone in Egypt lived close by the Aigyptos for that reason. Pharaoh's greatest possession, the one that paid for every splendid extravagance, every pyramid and temple he built, every war, lay at the mercy of the flood that came from deepest Africa every year. With the river to irrigate it, Egypt is a granary, the richest kingdom in the world. Without it, it would be the poorest. All of Egypt, said Herodotus, is the gift of the river, and the religion of Egypt, its festivals and rituals, flows with it.

That is one reason why the priests were so powerful. They knew enough geometry to measure each piece of land on the flood plain, many of which changed shape during the inundation. The peasants who worked the land paid taxes to Pharaoh, the amounts based on the size of each farm, so the priests stretched their ropes each year and took their measurements, and each year Pharaoh's treasury took its share, while according to rumour some of the priests took more than theirs.

The priests needed to know when the flood would arrive, and that is why they had become astronomers. A long line of predecessors had studied the heavens from the dawn of their history and observed that the flood always began soon after the star Sirius, absent or invisible during the winter, reappeared in the east.

They observed that the first heliacal risings of the star each year were separated by a period that lasted 365 days, and they had secretly established a solar calendar of twelve months, each with thirty days, to the total of which they added five feast days to make a year, a much better calendar than any Greek state possessed. They were far ahead of us in this, yet they had developed it some two and a half thousand years before my arrival in Alexandria. They knew almost to the day when the flood would begin and, to maintain the support of Pharaoh and hold the common people in awe of them, they kept their method a secret when they announced the due day. They were clever, these priests. That is probably why they survived successive conquests of Egypt.

There remained the secret that I wished to pierce. Their books showed that they were remarkably accurate during the earlier stages of the flood at forecasting the height of the waters at their peak, as I said. How they did so was a mystery.

Their predictions, I saw, were rarely totally accurate, but they were generally close, sometimes very close. Such prophecies, I thought, were beyond price to Egypt. I read descriptions of the methods they claimed to use, most of them to do with signs from the gods or conjunctions of the stars. I read Herodotus and his wonderfully detailed description of the river and its people, but did not find an explanation. My curiosity grew as I sensed that the priests concealed something. As Konon and I returned from the Sanctuary of Pan that day I told him that I felt a growing desire to see this kingdom for myself. If the explanation for the prophecies of the priests did not lie in Alexandria, perhaps it lay along the river itself.

Konon seized on the idea with all his enthusiasm, which I must tell you was considerable, and when he was excited the tempo of his speech quickened. We would make an expedition of it, he said.

We would plan it from beginning to end, copying the best maps from the Library and such histories as we could find. We would need a guide, an experienced guide, a guide who knew the river as well as he, Konon, knew Samos and I, Syracuse. We would need food, provisions, tents and, of course, a boat, a boat large enough to hold our supplies for five or six weeks, and a reliable, safe crew. We had never seen a pyramid, but he burned with zeal to view one. We were in need of a change after months of studying, he said, and deserved such a change, for had we not done well, and would our fathers not wish us to see such things while we had the opportunity, an opportunity that might never again befall us? So he reasoned, and I agreed, though with a twinge of remorse as I remembered how I had lied to Pheidias. We would travel to Heliopolis together and, if the wind was fair and there was still time before the flood, we would go on to Memphis.

We left several weeks later from the harbour below the Gate of the Sun on Lake Mareotis, the centre for the river traffic, in a long flat-bottomed boat with our slaves, a crew of four Egyptians, a cook, and a guide who was the son of a Makedonian father and an Egyptian mother. In this strange craft with sails of papyrus we passed the splendid pleasure fleet of Pharaoh, bright with gaudy awnings, and set a course to take us into the delta.

The shallow waters by the banks were rich with orchids and anemones, the weather in the delta was hot but not too hot as yet, the wind fair, filling the sail and rustling gently in the date palms on the shores, and soon the guide, eager to impress us, began to point out the sights. He showed us the ibis, the sacred bird of Thoth, which he said was frequently mummified and buried with the Pharaohs. We saw the falcon, sacred to Pharaoh as the guardian of the god-king, and many vultures, kites, cranes and herons. On the low skyline we saw the herdsmen, worshippers of Hathor, grazing their cattle whose bellows carried easily across the water. The guide said the cow was sacred and must not be killed, a crime punishable by death.

Lake and river were busy with boats carrying cargo downriver to Alexandria and south to Upper Egypt, the prevailing upstream breeze helping us stem the current with ease. Many stretches teemed with fishing boats, some with nets and some in flimsy crafts of papyrus, fishing with twin-pronged spears. We saw them hauling their nets as we passed, and bought their catch from them which our cook spitted on a fire at the camp, to the surprise of our guide, who told us that in Egypt fish was the staple of the poor. The priests were forbidden to eat it. In Syracuse, I told him, it was the staple of everyone.

As we sailed to the south, out of the delta, the cattle pastures gave way to low plains which later would fill with waving corn. We saw low houses with rush palliasses on the roofs, and the guide explained that the peasants slept there, using all available space in their unstable dwellings to store grain, dried fish, and river water. Their lives were hard. Pharaoh told them what to grow each year, forbade them to leave their villages, forced them to cultivate such land as he chose for them, to maintain the dykes and canals, and could dispossess them at a whim.

We passed elaborate systems of dykes and canals as we sailed, the gentle wind at our backs, and sometimes saw heavily armed men on horseback – Pharaoh's cavalry – inspecting them. The guide said it was a great crime to damage the dykes. The farmers prepared for the flood, repairing dykes and strengthening them by boat, light craft made from bundles of papyrus, lashed together in the shape of a crescent. We went ashore to look at the dykes and canals and saw how they were built to allow water to flow to the furthest areas at high levels of inundation, then to be trapped when the gates were closed as the flood receded. The river was very low, and the farmers were using buckets suspended on crude levers to lift water, pour it into small tanks on the backs of the beasts of burden and transport it to the fields. It was near one of the dykes that we saw a crocodile, asleep in the shade above the muddy bank. Its length seemed to be three times my height, yet the Egyptians feared the river horses more for their temper. Parts of the river teemed with both creatures. Strange to say, they had made gods of each, just as they worshipped cats and bound their dead bodies in bandages.

Our guide told us that the inundation generally began at the beginning of summer, soon after the solstice, which was a time of great rituals on the river as all Egyptians offered devoutly for a good flood. There followed a gradual rise in the levels over several weeks. The water turned from clear to red and turbid in appearance as it brought down deposits from the unknown interior of Africa. It then became green and was unwholesome to drink. The people of the delta provided for this by laying up in jars the red water which they drank until the river turned red once more, at which Konon remarked that the Egyptians were probably the only people to measure the age of water as others do that of wine.

The kind breeze took us further upriver against a gentle current, so gentle that we found it difficult to believe that all around us would be inundated before long. The guide, who liked to impress us, told us that the farmers here hoped for a flood of around fourteen cubits at the peak. Then it would cover the surrounding plains, until the farmhouses stood out like islands in an archipelago, and when it receded late in the season it would leave layers of black silt on the land, alluvial deposits that produced the most fertile of crops. There were cults to whom this silt was sacred.

If the flood was weak, and stopped at a height of eight cubits or below, the plains would bake in the sun and the people would starve. If the flood were too great, up to sixteen cubits, the water would sweep away the crops and still the people would starve, many losing their houses to the river. As a result every household in Egypt that could afford one seemed to have its own granary, raised high on cut stones and separated from the house in case of fire. The granaries of the wealthy were sometimes of several levels, and probably housed several years of supply.

Some villages flooded easily. The guide had seen the farmers dragging the goats they used to tread the grain, and their other livestock into their boats in a desperate attempt to salvage what they could. Even their houses would disappear in a great flood – disappear for ever because they were built of mud bricks which dissolved into the river from whence they came.

As the rains that flooded the river annually were many parasangs to the south, in a mountain wilderness where few had been, the farmers could not know whether their crops would fail or thrive. They relied on the prophecies of their priests, as I said.

We did not tell the guide why we wished to visit a temple, merely that we wished to do so to converse with the priests, as Herodotus had. He hesitated, warning us to be careful not to offend them in any way. We gave him our assurance that we had no wish to show anything but respect for the Gods of Egypt, just as Pharaoh honoured them. After a time he put one of the men ashore, speaking to him in a low voice, glancing over his shoulder as he did so. Konon shrugged and smiled at him.

On the following day we were bidden through the gates of a small cult temple close to the river. We were received by the priests, who looked on our bearded faces with wonder. The guide told us later they shaved all bodily hair every second day and washed twice daily and nightly, applying malachite to their faces to protect them from the sun. They wore only linen robes and shoes of papyrus. All else was forbidden. They welcomed us formally, answering our questions through the guide. We ate dried beef and bread baked from sacred corn, and drank barley-wine, a welcome change from our usual diet. They conversed with us, but they did not share our food. It was forbidden to eat with foreigners, who were deemed unclean. When we had eaten they showed us much of the temple, though not the innermost part where stood the statue of the god, and close to a wall I saw a well with stone steps down to it. A priest stood on the steps, writing something on a tablet. We walked on, though not before I had seen marks cut on the side of the well. We had found the explanation behind their prophecies.

We saw other wells as we went upriver, of different styles but built for the same purpose. In the temples close to the river, concealed within the walls, the priests sank a wooden beam in a well with the depth gradations marked by them, or built a culvert that ran from the riverbank into a well situated inside the temple walls in which depth markings were placed. We saw these in other temples we visited and guessed that the priests kept careful records each year. They had clearly learned over the ages that different daily rises in the water levels portended different levels of inundation. They relied on these records to predict the level of the flood, and such was their experience and attention to their records that their prophecies were usually very accurate.

We had found what we sought, and lazed at our camp one evening, listening to the wild cats hunting in the undergrowth, watching the sun set on the river and the flat country beyond it, the date palms stirring with the night breeze, when an idea came to me. Konon was speaking to me of the geometry of spirals, but

I heard him only at a distance. My mind was racing as I thought of the peasants working the lever and bucket machine. Someone had lit a beacon on a nearby hill, and I watched it idly, wondering what it signalled. I went to sleep to the sounds of the night birds and the frogs and when Konon and I took to our boat again next morning the idea that had come to me early in the day was as clear as the morning light.

As we sailed upriver I took blank papyrus and began to draw. In my mind I saw a mechanical device, an endless screw, that would force water up a pipe.

It took shape as I drew, Konon, who loved spirals, throwing suggestions at me. First I designed a cross-section of a cylinder. Inside it I placed a spindle with a spiral helix, the upward angle of the spiral carefully balanced. It would need to fit very tightly to prevent leakage, yet be free to rotate. At the top end of the spindle, outside the cylinder, I drew a crank, a simple handle to be turned in a circle. Insert the cylinder bottom in the river, wind the crank, and the waters of the Aigyptos would flow uphill to the fields, a maximum of use coming from a minimum of force. So began a fascination with mechanics.

Narrative

Aengus stood on the swampy ground of the marsh by the little river Dun, ten miles to the west of his cottage, eyes following the overgrown cuts in the earth that betrayed the water meadow – not any water meadow, but the sophisticated floated water meadow system that the Berkshire meadsmen of the seventeenth century had perfected. A breeze from the west that bent the common reeds behind him promised rain, and the gathering cloud mass approaching from downstream supported the promise. Duck, coot and moorhen quarrelled in the reedbeds, unconcerned by his presence.

He stopped where the meadsmen three centuries before had opened the sluices on the riverbank, usually in April, diverting the river into the drowner channels to soak the meadow ridges, the overflow running into a drain that flowed back into the river. When he pictured this happening – the Berkshire men in their smocks opening the sluices, stepping back as the Dun changed course – he saw how the system had acquired its name. The meadow ridges would have appeared to float as the drowners filled. "Probably not that different from the farms on the Nile," he muttered. This system had died slowly, when the dependence on the sweet hay of the water meadows declined in favour of turnips and swedes.

The Book of Aengus

In 1839 Francis Petitt Smith built the first screw propeller to be installed on a ship, a steamer called *Archimedes*.

Every schoolboy knows of Archimedes' Screw. Brunel saw that it would drive a ship more powerfully and efficiently than a paddle-wheel, and proved it in spectacular fashion when he installed a screw in one boat, a paddle-wheel in another, placed an identical engine and boiler in each, put the boats stern to stern, and made each pull its hardest, an aquatic tug o' war. The screw boat won, and Brunel went on to build his great iron ships. The aeroplane propeller works on the same principle. So do the machines that lift grain into tall silos.

Brunel had built the *Great Western* to use paddle-wheels, and was preparing to use them again to build the *Great Britain* when the *Archimedes* steamed into Bristol. The engineer visited her and delayed building his ship for months while he studied the principles of screw propulsion. When he opted for the screw he had to adapt his engines – designed by his father – which he did by creating an enormous chain drive. The ship was one of the wonders of the industrial age, and became the first screw-driven iron ship to cross the Atlantic. Eventually the screw killed the paddle, a change inspired by the sight of peasants lifting water from the Nile more than two millennia ago. Archimedes' account of his invention also kills Plutarch's contention, almost certainly inspired by Plato's contempt for technological progress, that the Greek saw mechanics as unworthy, beneath him.

A cubit was the length of a man's forearm, so a rise of sixteen cubits would have been one of around twenty-five feet, or even more. That places the annual levels of the Nile in perspective.

The life-giving powers of the Aegyptus, as he calls the Nile, draw him as does the pantheon of the Egyptians from which originated, says Herodotus, most of the Greek deities, particularly Dionysus.

I cannot think straight today. It is raining hard, the sky is heavy with water, and we have finished work early as a result. I have only my books for company. The river is coloured and filled with branches and debris. I watched her house for a while in the rain, and saw no-one except Kate with her great dog. Perhaps she will return to the woods tomorrow.

The Greek

The fire at our camp warmed us one evening against the cool air after dark on the river, while the guide told us that we would soon come to where the Aigyptos split in two as it flowed into the delta. A short distance from there lay the ancient city the Greeks called Heliopolis, a centre of sun worship, once one of the largest in the kingdom, behind only Memphis and Thebes. It had been a great centre of astronomy and of bull-worship. The bulls, viewed as manifestations of the sun god Re, were buried in a sacred *nekropolis* when they died.

We had spent much of our journey confined to the boat and therefore said we would like to see it. The guide shrugged and said it contained nothing of interest except a vast temple of the sun, many other temples falling into ruins, and the pillars – which we took to mean obelisks – for which it was famous, and from which the city took its Egyptian name.

The city had not recovered from a great pestilence of a few years before. Much of the remaining population had fled to Alexandria.

– *Take us there,* said Konon.

– *There is nothing to see*, said the guide, – *just temples and pillars.*

– *Take us there,* said Konon again.

The guide looked afraid.

– *It will be very hot tomorrow*, he said. – *The floods will come before long. We must turn soon and go downriver. I do not want you to drown, to meet your* ka *so soon. You wished to see the pyramids. There is little time.*

– *Nothing will drown Arkhimedes of Syracuse*, said Konon, with the smile of a daemon. – *The Fates have a different plan for him.*

The guide looked more afraid.

– *The people say the priests of the city have great powers from the god Re*, the guide said at last. – *I, of course, do not worry about such things, but the crew will be frightened.*

– *They need not come with us*, said Konon.

– *There may be danger*, said the guide.

– *By Apollo!* Konon laughed. – *I think it is you who are afraid.*

We sailed upriver, the guide growing more restless as we went, until we reached the place where we set our camp, near the mouth of a turbid canal that connected the river to the city. The canal gave off a miasma that smelled of putrefaction, like an open *nekropolis*. Swarms of biting insects filled the air. The guide talked in low tones to the crew. None slept well that night except Konon. He was always cheerful.

Before dawn next day we rose, eager to leave that place, and were walking up the canal bank as the sun rose over Egypt, lighting the wide river behind us. We saw nothing in the fields, neither people nor farm animals. Soon it grew very hot, without a hint of wind. There was an uneasy stillness, as though the gods had stopped breathing. Again the guide attempted to dissuade us from our visit. Again Konon laughed at him.

We saw the tips of the obelisks of the city as we walked through the outer parts that appeared abandoned and desolate. We drew close and saw several decaying temples with long walls made of mud brick, baked from the deposits of the river, and a great altar, a rounded block of alabaster surrounded by stone blocks in the shape of a hieroglyph. One of these solar temples was very large, with the thickest walls I had seen, guarding an obelisk that soared to an impossible height. The Egyptians knew how to build. We saw a priest, bent with age or sickness, in front of the temple *propylae*, near what had plainly been an *agora* of some kind, a market of sorts with a few people buying fruit and fish.

We came into the centre, the guide chattering nervously behind us, and came into an open space. The obelisk stood before us, piercing the sky. A stone pyramidion was set on top of it. The morning sun reflected on it and it flashed. I caught the gleam of shining metal set into the stone. All three of us gazed at it, unaware that someone had joined us.

He wore the dress of a priest of the lowest rank, a torn uniform, but clean. He waved at the obelisk and said something in a voice like a creaking hinge. His face was green with smeared malachite. Most of his teeth were missing. Spittle drooled from his lips. He looked very old, and sick. The guide backed away, pulling us with him.

– *What does he say?* Konon demanded.

– *O! He is old and demented. Let us leave! Please! Remember there was a pestilence here! They say Seth cursed the city.*

– *What does he say?* Konon demanded once more, standing his ground in the dusty square.

– *It does not make sense,* said the guide, eyeing the priest, who drew close once more.

– *Tell us what he says,* Konon ordered.

– *I will tell you what he says, and you can decide what he means,* said the guide.

– *Well?*

– *He says the god is in the stone,* said the guide, gesturing at the obelisk.

We looked once more. The sun caught the shining metal.

The priest spoke once more, a long stream of words that seemed to repeat themselves. Even Konon was repelled, and when the guide urged us once more to leave he did not resist. As we left that terrible place and its air of death and desolation the priest's voice rose to a howl.

We walked down the canal bank towards camp and river with relief as Konon asked:

– *What did he say as we left?*

– *He shouted the same words over again,* said the guide, clearly anxious to be away from there.

– *Yes, O wise one,* said Konon sarcastically. – *But what did he say?*

– *He said the Sun is our father.*

Narrative

The perpetual winter that the appearance of Kate suggested to him in his darker moments was slowly surrendering to spring, after several consecutive days of glorious sunshine that brought sleepy dormice and hedgehogs from their hibernation for a few hours. Aengus saw the countryside subtly springing to life, the willows and alders a filigree of green, riverbanks and woods beginning to sound with birdsong. The bare chalk-country hedgerows of privet and travellers' joy, spindle tree and dogwood had begun to fill imperceptibly with sprouting buds and young leaf, and the chaffinches postured in their sexual displays and chased one another through the alders. The days were noticeably warmer, although the nights still brought frost. Soon lady's-smock, among the earliest of the riverside plants, would appear, spreading its four petals of pure white or gentle heliotrope. It would be followed by the marsh marigold with its glossy, kidney-shaped leaves from which single flowers like a buttercup, a magnet to insect life, would display from March to May.

Aengus, walking the riverbank in the mornings, saw that the river water crowfoot in the chalky bottom was gradually losing its drab winter hue and had begun to assume an olive colour. In summer a separate species, the common water crowfoot, most at home in backwaters and ditches, would respond to the rise in temperatures with a splendid display of white and yellow flowers opening to the sun, to nod gently above the current, while in the deeper waters the white water-lily would float its big leaves and produce the largest flowers of the British natives, the glory of the chalkstream.

The trout that had survived the fishermen and the ensuing winter emerged from the inertia that had gripped them and began to feed on caddis pupae and nymphs. Coots and moorhens squabbled in the reeds, watchful for hungry stoats and weasels.

The keepers knew that the neighbourhood rang with rumours of a figure stalking through the woods at dead of night, sometimes with a fox or a deer at his heels. The farm people hung, fascinated, on the tales of the cowman who swore he had seen a tall figure fording the shallowest part of the river in the moonlight. The figure, the cowman asserted, was that of a man, but with the head of a stag. Another farm worker said he had seen the man at dawn, striding down the path between the woods when a flock of dunnocks appeared to gather about him, then disappeared as abruptly as they had arrived. Sid the keeper, setting his mink traps at dawn, was convinced he had seen a fox follow this figure like a faithful dog, but said nothing to anyone, not even to his prurient wife.

The Greek

We disembarked at Memphis, a great crowded city that seemed full of cheating guides who competed to show us the pyramids. We had seen them in the distance from our boat as they shimmered in the hot sun, and began to sense their mass when the guide told us that they were still some parasangs distant. Slowly, as we sailed south, they grew larger.

We saw their volumes then, and saw them even more clearly when we left Memphis and walked to them, the day clear and hot, the pyramids seeming to sway in the heat. We trod dusty tracks past farms with goats and donkeys, the farmers watching us carefully, fearful, said the guide, that we were tax collectors.

Eventually, already weary of our guide who cursed those who sought our custom, we drew close to the enormous mass of the pyramid they call after Kheops, each side facing one of the four points of the earth.

I walked around the base, and suddenly I felt very alone, convinced that I was the first person in the world living then to see this pyramid as it was, in the abstract. I sensed a great energy emanating from its very mass, as if that mass could pull me to it and envelop me in an invisible force. I felt that I knew it, that I had seen it before, not in the physical sense, but as a form that surfaced from the depths of the psyche to confront me with a truth that had a peculiar familiarity. My body ceased to exist as I sank into the timelessness of what the pyramid represented, and the words of Herakleitos came to me clearly as the sun rose majestically above the apex high above and the shadow of the structure on the hot earth shortened to a distorted triangle that twisted and shrugged in the warm air. For a moment the top of the pyramid seemed to be on fire, the flames drifting lazily across a pure blue sky.

I closed my eyes against the sudden glare and waited for the others to join me, opening them once more as the mistiness passed and reality returned with the heat of the morning.

Narrative

The keepers saw the change in him, how each day Aengus quit promptly when the hour to finish arrived, went to his cottage to wash, then left the estate on foot, impervious to hints or veiled questions. He was rarely seen at weekends, although Bill Worthy thought he had glimpsed him entering the belt of trees that sheltered the house of Seth. Later the same day he had spied a tall man walking the woodland paths with a girl with a willowy figure.

"He's seeing that girl," he told Sid.

"I know," said Sid shortly. "Bad lot. I told him. What more can a chap do?"

The Greek

The pyramid was a book, a book of ancient geometry in which the Egyptian mathematicians of old buried their knowledge, knowing it would surface in a later age. I, who searched the library of Alexandria for evidence of abstract learning, I, who found nothing except the work of rope-stretchers and the greedy agents of Pharaoh, I was among those who dismissed them as backward, and only when I saw the Great Pyramid did I see the significance of their work.

I saw what we owed these ancients, and I remembered that our geometry sprang from our astronomy. The foundations of this came to us from Egypt and Babylon, and the basis of Egyptian astronomy was the obelisk.

Konon and I saw many of them as we travelled through Lower Egypt. Some were heavily decorated with hieroglyphics in honour of the Pharaohs, a god such as Horus, or the deity that most captured my imagination, Anubis of the jackal-head. We looked at the writing which the guide pretended to translate for us, although it was clear that he lied, that he did not understand a symbol. We saw only one recurring glyph that we came to recognise.

The shape of the obelisks was viewed by many as suggestive of male fertility and therefore of the sun, but it seemed to us that the older ones in particular were gnomons, or shadow clocks using early geometry.

At their simplest they would be used to fix the meridian between north and south, as the priests methodically observed the sun's shadow cast by the gnomon on the ground when the shadow was at its shortest at midday. The early Egyptian astronomers marked this by stretching a rope of twisted papyrus along the arc created by the shadow as the sun moved across the sky. These astronomers recognised a year as the time elapsed when the shadow cast by the sun was at its shortest, at the summer solstice.

Once they had fixed the meridian as a line running from north to south they were able to select a point in the heavens that gave them the corresponding line of direction at night. When the Egyptians were building their pyramids they knew that the sun's shadow at midday pointed towards the place in the heavens where the same stars were visible throughout the year, the point around which the stars revolved. They knew through observation that a bright star in the constellation of Draco revolved in a tight circle around this point. Its light gave them the ability to find the meridian, and therefore all general directions, at night. This unchanging point of light was chosen by the Egyptians as the North Star.

I have heard that the pyramid of Kheops was built with such perfection that when Sirius, the sacred star that brought annual life to Egypt, transited the meridian, the light from the star was at a right angle to the south face of the Great Pyramid and shone directly down a shaft they had designed into the very centre of the pyramid. It lit the head of the dead Pharaoh.

The Book of Aengus

He felt its mass draw him, and was awed by it what it represented to him. The pyramid was the symbol of fire to the Greeks, the first of the Platonic solids, hence perhaps his impression that he saw flames at its apex. The symbol was not confined to the Greeks. To the Brahmins it expressed Siva, the god of fire. To the Buddhists of Japan the element of fire was a pyramid.

I have read of the theory that the Pyramid of Cheops was aligned with Sirius. Bayley, a respected authority on ancient symbolism, says that *Sirius* is a corruption of *Osiris*, which is very credible, as the shine of the star was the light of the god that would bring rebirth. It seems probable that Pharaoh (the title may originate from *Phrah*, or the *sun*) was deemed to be responsible for the rebirth of the river each year. The pyramid tomb was the site where Pharaoh himself would be reborn, while the solar barque, as the great ship placed by the Pyramid of Cheops came to be known, was his symbolic transport into the afterlife. Rebirth of both Pharaoh and river were probably central to the building of every pyramid.

The Pyramid of Cheops, the largest on the plain of Giza, was built during the same era as Avebury, around 2500 BC, with the last stone at Avebury erected five hundred years later. The timing is a coincidence, yet we have two completely distinct civilisations building great projects at roughly the same time, as if inspired by some common instinct or a collective need, just as we have different mythic images of the Great Goddess appearing at the same time in geographies as far apart as Asia, Europe and Mayan America.

Both civilisations used a form of mathematics based on astronomy. Both used a meridian line to calculate the solstices and equinoxes. Both probably used the same star in Draco to fix their celestial north, as the Pole Star was not then in that position.

The glyph he talks of is probably the *ankh*, a common sign on Egyptian temples, tombs and houses. It symbolised life or health, and formed the second part of Tutankhamun's name (the last part was in reverence to the god Amun). The early Egyptian Christians adopted the ankh as their cross, the *crux insata*, or Coptic crucifix, which was clever of them, and remarkably economical. When they turned the old temples to the Egyptian gods into Christian churches they could leave the ankh glyphs on the walls, and did so. Perhaps they were direct descendants of the priests of the Pharaohs. Anubis, the god with the jackal's head, conducted the dead through the wilderness into the afterlife, and had the wiliness of a fox, his European counterpart. That makes me pause.

Archimedes dismissed the mathematicians of Egypt as rope-stretchers when he first arrived at Alexandria, but then he saw that the builders of the Old Kingdom had inquiring minds of their own. They did not leave any papyri behind that survived to persuade us otherwise. Instead they left a pyramid as their book, set in stone and containing all they knew.

The Stone Age peoples of Britain and Ireland and other parts of Europe did not leave us with a book of the dead, or a trace of writing, not a tablet which a Ventris could have deciphered, not a hieroglyph for a Champollion, no Linear A or B for an Evans to hang his reputation upon, and lose it, not a hidden city for a

Schliemann to unearth, not a name or a hieroglyph cut into stone, yet they left us their stone circles and their henges. They left us Avebury, and Silbury Hill, which is a conical, carefully constructed manmade hill built upon a series of perfect, concentric circles. *Sil*, Bayley says, means *fire*, or the *Light of God*.

The hill was not a burial place or barrow, as first thought. There is an elaborate and well-constructed theory that it symbolises the womb of the Great Goddess, and that the surrounds, including the little Kennet, complete her body, set in the classic reclining position of the fertility goddess, a place for the Stone Age people to worship, particularly at the fire festivals.

The Greek

The Library welcomed us back and my days merged into the next as I plunged into the propositions of the Greek mathematicians before Eukleid and after, determined to master every proposition before I could begin to originate my own. While I studied the works of Demokritus of Abdera I engaged Konon in what I thought to be the Sokratic manner. Remember that I was young:

Arkhimedes (confidently): Let there be a cone, and let it be cut parallel to the base, giving us two circular surface sections. Are they equal in area?

Konon: Do you wish them to be?

Arkhimedes (exasperated): That is not an answer.

Konon: If they are equal that would mean the cone is a cylinder, which is absurd.

Arkhimedes: Ah! So they are not!

Konon: If you tell me so, but if they are not the cone would have an infinite series of indentations. That would make it irregular, which is absurd.

Arkhimedes (triumphantly): So what is your answer?

Konon: It is one you must arrive at by yourself. I am going to my couch.

I had better luck at the *stoa*, where many joined the discussions that merged into the warm, luminous evenings of Alexandria, evenings of conversations with poets, philosophers, geographers, historians. Kallimakhos, though older than Konon or I, joined us after a time, finding the company convivial, and seldom left without extracting a few drachmae from Konon or from me to fund his nightly entertainments. Late though he might revel, however, we knew he would be at work again before daybreak. The amount of work he produced was prodigious. So the weeks and months passed in a growing closeness and friendship, though the discussions grew heated at times, and sometimes continued at a *symposion* where they grew more heated still.

One evening as the wine flowed freely Konon inflamed Kallimakhos with long extracts from some epic or other while the poet, drunk on unwatered Mareotic wine, his eyes as red as a Spartan's *khlamys*, denounced us as a pair of *tekhnes*, banausic sign writers, little better than pyramid guides. Did we not realise that the epic, magnificent though it was of its time, belonged to the past, as did the era of the great Athenian tragedians, which lasted for fewer than twenty Olympiads? Did we not see that verse must move on from the oral tradition, to be read rather than recited in the new age of reading, its style to belong to our time when there was a gymnasium in every city, where anyone might learn his letters? So he moved to his views of the Librarian, who had unwisely shown his unfinished epic to someone indiscreet enough to whisper of its content to one person at a time, until it reached Kallimakhos, who seized his chance. Was the sole fate of Jason to be the hero with whom every handsome woman in the Aegean wished to copulate, he asked? Was that the only purpose fit for a Greek hero, to bull a woman on every island between Hellas and the Troad? It seemed so, from what he had heard of the Librarian's work. He ranted until it became our turn once more. We wasted our time trying to square the circle and duplicate the cube, he said, his words slowing until he slumped on his couch, his eyes closed. Soon he began to snore. Yet within a short candle he was up, face bleary but tongue loosened, setting a different course to despair about the Greek wish to destroy ourselves, and how this destruction would come about through the emasculation of the traditional city-state. The temperament of the Greeks, he said in a voice that did not invite contradiction, was unsuited to living anywhere other than in a *polis*, where the citizens were homogeneous and the language the same, unlike these artificial kingdoms of the Ptolemies and Seleukids that could not compare with Athens or Sparta. After a time even he tired of his own rhetoric. There was a short silence while he looked blearily into his undiluted wine, muttered that it needed good conversation more than water, drank another *kylix* in a gulp, gathered his robe, borrowed a few drachmae from his neighbour, and left.

We emerged some time later, and found him waiting for us as we walked towards the Brukheion, past the darkened mass of the tomb of Alexander. The beam of the lighthouse played on the waters of the harbour, then seemed to blink. Kallimakhos must have drunk several skinfuls that evening, yet his voice, while unusually subdued, was clear. The Pharos light profiled his nose and beard and he halted, swaying slightly, his eyes in shadow.

He threw an arm wide to bar our paths, raised the other sharply to point to the lighthouse, and loosely intoned:

Thus base-born Pharaoh remembers Troy's end,
Speaks each night to Upper Egypt,
Into the darkest parts he rules,
And dreams he is a god.

He stared at our faces: – *O, the Mathematikoi! Do you not know how he uses the God of Fire?*

Narrative

He saw the police car outside Seth's house next morning. The estate rang with talk of violent death and mutilation in a nearby town, with the name of Seth spoken in a whisper.

He looked in vain for Bridget, and that night he watched the house from the edge of the nearby wood. When the lights went out he returned to his cottage, anticipating the midnight visit.

The Greek

I studied the work of Demokritus at the Library when Konon came to me carrying a roll.

– *I have it,* he said in an undertone.

I looked at the title: *Agamemnon*, the first play of three of the *Oresteia* of Aiskhylos.

– *I saw it during the Dionysia at Syracuse,* I told him. Silently, he pointed to the beginning. I remembered it, and saw again the lone watchman who stood at night for ten years on the roof of the Royal Palace at Argos, bleary-eyed, looking for the distant beacon's light that would tell him that Troy had fallen and that victorious King Agamemnon, leading Polyxena, daughter of Priam, would soon return home to adulterous Klytemnestra, who would murder him in his bath, an obscenity to make the audience cry and groan aloud. I remembered, too, how the news reached Greece, so much faster than the swiftest courier.

– *The Greeks lit a beacon on the highest ground near Troy on the night it fell*, I said, realisation dawning. – *All the way from the Troad and Asian Mount Ida, across the Aegean to Lemnos, and so to Mount Athos on the mainland and down into the Peloponnesos, a series of beacons carried news of the victory at the speed of light. That was what the watchman saw.*

Konon looked carefully around us, and paraphrased in a low tone: – *So Pharaoh speaks at night to the distant parts of his kingdom, using the God of Fire.* He paused: – *The lighthouse is also his signal station.*

Konon returned the roll and we left the Library, seeking a safer place to talk. In the shade of the Museum wall, he said: – *I have heard whispers of such secret work by the* Tekhnes *at the Library, also on* katapeltes *and other war engines.* He looked around to make very sure we were alone: – *I have also heard that the medical men conduct experiments on prisoners – live prisoners.*

I shuddered at that. I had heard of this, too, more than once, but said – *It is likely the* Tekhnes *built the signalling system, too, perhaps using shuttered beacons with coloured lights. It probably controls all Egypt.*

– *We must be careful*, Konon replied. – *Kallimakhos talks too much.*

We avoided the poet's favourite *stoa*, our usual places in the Library, and the symposia. We saw him rarely for a time and heard that he worked on a fresh poem. The Library was full of suspicion and whispers that Pharaoh's men listened and watched everywhere, but while Kallimakhos remained free our fears lessened. The danger of a night-time visit from Pharaoh's agents became more remote, and we breathed freely.

I was persuaded by Kallimakhos on one point. While I was privileged to live and study in the greatest city in the greatest kingdom in the world, by temperament I, as a Greek, did not feel free in a land where there was not the commonalty of the city state. I could not spend my life there, even though Alexandria possessed all that for which a Greek might wish. It had its theatres, its games, its religious festivals, even a new god for those who needed one. Yet it was not Greek. A new civilisation that was foreign to me had grown up in the kingdom of the Ptolemies. On the surface, the culture was Greek, yet it was not Greek. It was Greek in form, but not in its psyche.

When I looked at the full moon over Egypt, I saw again the Goddess in the shining circle and began to wish that I viewed it from Syracuse. I heard my father's voice in the night, as you hear mine, and I longed to see him again. I saw the dusty, narrow streets of the old city and scented the cold, resinous air that blew down from the mountains in the Sicilian spring. Syracuse called me home.

The Book of Aengus

He prompts me to read Jung again, of his theories of the archetypes and of his analyses of dreams. I wonder what the psychologist might have made of the relationship of Archimedes with the Goddess, of the spiritual communion he feels with her.

Jung saw consciousness as the product of the unconscious, but the smallest fraction of its size. At the conscious level he would see a Dorian Greek, descendant of a race of conquerors, distant cousin to the Spartans, living in a privileged fashion in a Hellenistic civilisation where the Stoics were so influential but the Olympians continued to flourish, as human as the rest of us, as his life in Alexandria suggests, a believer, like Aristotle, that the city state was the pinnacle of civilisation, that the boundary of the state should be visible from the *acropolis*, and that all who lived outside this were less fortunate, so a mild xenophobe; a lover of Homer in the tradition of all educated Greeks, and in a sense an heir to the Heroic tradition, knows his tragedies, and is a friend to Callimachus who brings verse into the modern Hellenistic age with his short, elegiac poems that were to influence Ovid and Propertius, frugal and disciplined like his fellow Dorians, the Spartans, probably the best educated scientist in the world, with a strong inheritance from his father the astronomer, absolutely disciplined in his work, yet with a free mind, a man who delights to discover proportion in all things, whether temples or conic ratios, probably a little irritable at times, especially when he grew older; yet a man of a generous nature, as shown by his desire to share discoveries with colleagues and followers. Jung would see a scientist, not unlike himself in some ways, with an intense intellectual curiosity to know more.

Probe beneath the conscious, into the deepest well below. The Greek was a *mystes* and received what he regarded as a divine calling at Eleusis, an epiphany that he took with him to Egypt where he learned much, including the myths of the old kingdoms, and had several profound experiences of his own, some of which at least he has related to me, so we can describe him as a highly spiritual man. In his unconscious the Goddess is both a primordial memory – a classic Jungian archetype – and numinous, an active, symbolically visible presence. The full moon transiting over Egypt is a monthly reminder of her. *I saw again the Goddess in the shining circle*, he says. The simple interpretation I had, when Archimedes first described the circular construct he drew to calculate *pi* and place it within two geometrical walls, seems close enough. The Greek has built an image in his dreams or imagination and expressed it scientifically through his geometry. It retains its secret but yields the solution the mathematician seeks. In practical terms, he has squared his circle, but its spiritual mystery, its seeming imperfection, its ultimate unknowability, remains to haunt him because it continually questions him. We don't know its precise meaning to him, but the circular image contains goddess and cosmos. Jung studied such images closely for much of his life, concluded that they were the archetype of a dream circle, recurring in the unconscious of man everywhere, and saw these *mandalas* in every culture dating back to the Palaeolithic, a psychic centre of the personality, distinct from the ego, that he imported as an important symbol into his psychology.

It is one of the oldest religious symbols of humanity, an image that persisted in the unconscious from the earliest times. There seems to be endless literature on it, illustrated over the centuries. It is repeated in Hinduism, Buddhism, Lamaism, and in Islam which forbids images of Allah: a crescent moon represents the religion itself, while the circular dome of the mosque is the heavens, the universe. The literature of the alchemists teems with similar drawings and pictures, the Masonic tradition has a circle representing the universe of God and Eternity, while the Babylonians, who divided the circle into 360 degrees – and so created the angle – drew the twelve zones of influence through which moon, sun and planets passed, to give us the horoscope. It's widespread across Christian imagery with its holy figures crowned with the sacred circle of the halo, symbol of sun or moon, the Celtic cross and the rose window, the wedding ring symbolising union and eternity in one. It is something of this nature that the Greek sees, a simple image but a fundamental one. Perhaps the answer to the question it asked of him came to him before he died. Perhaps it left more that he could not answer.

The Greek

I wake you, but I will not be long.

Two years more passed and my time in Alexandria was coming to a close. I had decided on the broad nature of my work. I had learned all that I could at the Library to equip me for it. I also had found that I worked best when I was on my own, away from others, even Konon. That surprised me at first, until I reasoned that enough stimulation would come from corresponding with others, but ideas must come from the inner self.

The timing of my departure was influenced by a letter from Pheidias. It contained little news as such – more observations of Ares, a remarkable shooting light in the heavens, a walk through Neapolis to the river Anapos early in summer, an unexpected visit from the Tyrant who had inquired after me – but it caused me to lift my head and remember the evenings in Syracuse when Hesperus rose in the dusk and Pheidias went to his viewing place on the roof.

I heard the echo of his voice from my childhood as he told me of Homer and the heroes, of the Spartans, of perfidious Alkibiades, how the Syracusans had defeated the Athenians in the Grand Harbour, of brave General Xenophon among the Persians. I longed to see him again.

I went home, Stranger, to be reunited with my father. I took leave of Konon and Kallimakhos and my other friends and boarded ship, my boxes laden with rolls and mechanical devices. Friends came to the quayside to say goodbye. To my surprise the

Librarian of Alexandria was among them as I stepped on board, the sails were unbrailed, the ropes were cast off, and the ship moved away from the wall, the lighthouse towering above me for the last time, the sailors calling to each other as the sails were sheeted home. So I left Alexandria.

Narrative

His solicitor summoned him again to London to tell him that his former wife had died of a drugs overdose.

The office window looked over a lawn at Lincoln's Inn Fields. He stood, watching the grimy branches of a lime tree shiver in the east wind. A pigeon breasting the gusts seemed to hover, then duck beneath its force to land on the grass, jerking its head as it looked for food. He wondered why he felt nothing.

"I'll find the money somehow for her funeral. But I want to see her."

"Why?"

"To say goodbye."

It was still light a week later when he left the train and walked past river and canal to his home. He sat, sunk in a reverie, while it grew dark and he began to feel the cold. He rose, lit the fire and turned on the lights, looking around the room and at the rows of books. The logs began to crackle, a cheerful contrast to the gloomy little ceremony at church and graveyard earlier.

After a time he began to weep, a wound reopening that he had thought had healed, seeing again the body of a woman who had died without love, the closed eyes and face of despair turned away from a world that had rejected her. He had knelt by her body and asked her forgiveness, then kissed her hand and her cold forehead, then prayed, using words long forgotten, a great wave of helplessness overcoming him. He tried to remember her as she had been, to bring up memories of the vivacity and vitality that he had worshipped, but saw only her desperate search for an escape from her perceptions of her life.

In the kitchen of his cottage he wept, the numbness leaving him to be replaced with guilt, a guilt whose origins he could not identify save for a conviction that he had not done enough. She had been his wife. He had given her what he thought had been unselfish love, but how could it have been so when he had allowed her to sink into darkest addiction, to forget her? So Aengus accused himself and grieved for his dead wife, and perhaps for himself, the only mourner at her graveside.

Presently he changed his clothes into his everyday garb, washed and tried to eat, then took his journal from the shelf and began to write. He had finished when there was a light knock at his door.

The Greek

I had a slow sail home, forced by the winds to shelter in the Libyan ports, even though it was long before the Kids set in the dawn sky. Another storm reached us off Kythera, and there we offered to Poseidon as we sheltered once more. I was relieved when the Hyblaion hills rose from the clouds on the horizon. I saw the familiar low line of the walls of Syracuse draw closer and the golden figure of Athene loom above them, every high building on Ortygia in clear outline.

The ship rounded the foot of the island and tacked into the Grand Harbour. When it came up to the dock I jumped on to the wall and ran to the temple, thanked the god for a safe voyage, and hurried across the causeway to Akhradina. I had written to my father to tell him of my return, but he could not know when I would arrive.

When our house came into view I stopped suddenly, seeing a tall figure leaving it before he saw me. His hair was whiter than when he had stood on the harbour wall to say goodbye, and he looked thinner, but otherwise he was unchanged. He turned and saw me.

– *Khaire, Arkhimedes*, he said. – *You have come home.*

We settled back into our house, Stranger, and a year later I left it again, to marry. I was not lucky. My wife died in childbirth, and I returned home and did not leave it again. I completed my book on the measurement of the circle then, as I told you, and began work on the sphere and cylinder. Pheidias was growing old gently, working as quietly as ever, still observing the planet he loved, still unable to explain its movements. I did not marry again and our household settled into a routine of work and discussion. The ships brought us news of wars everywhere except in Syracuse, while the Tyrant kept his alliance with Rome even as his daughter Demarata suggested to him, it was rumoured, that her husband Andranadoros should be the guardian of his grandson if Gelo did not live long enough to succeed.

As the years passed I did some of my best works on conoids and spheroids, on the lever, on irregular solids, and on floating bodies. These works went out into the world where they were well received, and I plunged into the next. I was happiest when working on different projects at once, considering a problem in geometry while I dealt with another in mechanics or hydrostatics.

One day I opened a roll from the Librarian at Alexandria that a messenger brought from the harbour:

> *Apollonius to Arkhimedes, greetings. I bring you news of a young man, Eratosthenes of Kyrene, who follows you closely and admires your work, and who wishes to meet you. He has been here at the Library where he devised an ingenious system to discover prime numbers, and he is also poet, geographer and astronomer. He visits friends at Katana, and I have taken it upon myself to persuade him to call on you at Syracuse, where I know he will be welcome at the house of a fellow philosopher. Farewell.*

I had heard of him from Konon, and when some weeks later a young man with intelligent eyes and a pleasing face called I welcomed him warmly, bidding him stay with us as long as he would. Pheidias was particularly pleased to have a fellow astronomer at hand.

We three conversed night after night, talking about each other's work. On the evening before his departure Eratosthenes spoke of a method he had conceived to calculate the circumference of the great circle of the earth, by measuring the elevation of the sun at midday on the summer solstice at two different places at a known difference from each other.

He came to us every year from then on, saying that he was eager for anything we could teach him, but in truth he passed much to us, including a hunger for arithmetic to me. His visits ceased when Apollonios died, and Pharaoh summoned our younger friend to be the next Librarian of Alexandria. By then he had calculated the circumference of the earth, generously giving me credit for the resulting measures of its diameter and of the area of its surface.

Those and the years that followed were a wonderful part of my life because they were the most creative. I found proofs of theorems that seemed beautiful to me. A cone or a spiral or an ellipse were not objects in themselves. They were the starting points of successive mysteries that I imagined, then attempted to solve. Perhaps these discoveries in geometry pleased me because they had no value to anyone other than to another philosopher who could built propositions, in turn, from them, yet they possessed a reality that seemed eternal. I confess to you that there is also a shameful, secret pride in seeing the deductions of your mind finding their way formally into a proposition of a mathematician you have never met.

I kept up my correspondence with Eratosthenes and other friends at Alexandria after Konon died. Eratosthenes, knowing how I grieved for my friend, offered the help of young Dositheos, Konon's pupil, in distributing my work, but from then on I sent only the propositions, not the proofs, of my work to Alexandria, as I suspected that some of the younger mathematicians were not above claiming it as their own. The ships brought rolls from Alexandria and carried rolls in return. Invitations came to go there, while more came from Athens and other cities throughout the Greek world, but my work bound me to Syracuse. Friends came to our house and it rang with argument, often with music, but our work filled most of our time. My father and I continued our walks, but not as far as before, as the years were beginning to drag on Pheidias, although he continued to work, as did I with increasing momentum and success.

Finally one evening he said that he did not have long to live. When the time came he would leave the world peacefully, he said, his only sadness that he would miss my company.

I said he would live for many years, even though he was then very old. He smiled and waved my protests aside.

– *I ask you not to grieve too much for me when I leave you. Give me a simple funeral without hired dirge singers or sobbing slaves, and let me lie in the exedra on my own couch so that I face my friends when they come to say goodbye. When your time comes I would like you to lie beside me and your mother.*

I began to weep, ashamed of my weakness.

– *Do not grieve so*, he said. – *I have had a wonderful life, but you and I were not to be favoured by the gods in one thing. I am lucky. I have a son. You seem destined to be alone. Perhaps one day you will finish your work. If so, perhaps you will also finish mine. Promise me you will only do so if you have finished yours.*

I gave him that promise. He left me soon after, Stranger, but not before he had numbered and arranged his work into shelves of rolls in his room, tier upon tier. He went to sleep one early morning. When the sun reached his bed he was dead.

We washed and perfumed him and laid him out in white, a honey-cake by his side, his feet pointing towards the door of the house that had become mine. In his casket that night I placed the instruments that he made with his own hands to observe the heavens. I mourned him and gave him only the ceremonies he had requested of me, but all of Syracuse seemed to visit him, a long line of citizens forming to take lustration in the water *ardanion* we placed in front of the house. The Tyrant came, and wept beside the body, touching the great head with its crown of vine leaves, insisting that he placed Kharon's obol in the coffin himself. Soon after we buried him in the *nekropolis* where I would one day lie beside him. Some time after the funeral rites I placed a stele by his grave with the circles of the planets, the moon and sun carved upon it, to remind me of my promise to him.

I worked alone from then on, but sensed his closeness. Much later, when my hair was as white as I remembered his, I would be reminded of the other vows he had me take when I became a man.

Narrative

A chink of light caught her face when he opened the door. Behind her the river ran high and the willow's branches waved wildly. Water ran from her hair.

She saw his face as he closed the door behind her. "What's wrong?"

"I buried my wife today," he said.

She lifted her hand up as if to touch him, then let it fall.

"What happened?"

"She was an addict. She took an overdose."

It began to rain heavily, the windows streaming, the cottage gutters overflowing.

She was silent for a moment, then said quietly: "And you blame yourself." It was not a question.

"Yes."

"Don't. Blame Seth."

"Seth!" His voice sounded like an explosion in the little room. Water splashed from the gutters.

Her voice was certain. "He turns people like your wife into addicts. She did not die because of you."

After a time the rain stopped as abruptly as it had begun. She lifted her arm and put her hand on his shoulder for a moment, then sat for an hour in silence while he talked, her eyes full of compassion. He told her of his childhood, his upbringing, his married life, episodes he had omitted before. When he finished he looked drained, emptied of emotion, and she chose that moment to leave, knowing he would sleep.

The Greek

I am torn by what followed. In justice, I had no choice, as I had taken an oath to my city-state. When the Tyrant of Syracuse told me to defend it, it became a sacred obligation to do so. As a philosopher, I wished for a different path, but as a man I did what any loyal citizen would do.

At that time, you will remember, Syracuse was an ally of Rome in the war against Carthage, long our enemy in Sicily. As Hannibal swept down through Italy, so the Tyrant grew concerned that Carthage might attack Syracuse once more. Soon after the news came in that Hannibal had defeated the Romans in a great battle, Hiero summoned me.

I had seen him rarely in recent times, and then only when I inquired after Gelo. I assumed that he had almost forgotten me. My name was not among the fifteen men who had recently been proclaimed guardians to his grandson before he would become an *ephebe*, much to the pleasure of the courtiers who were jealous of the Tyrant's favours. When the summons arrived, therefore, it came as a surprise.

It was very hot, and by the time I reached the gates of the Palace the sun was at its highest. There, as if I were a slave, the mercenaries stopped me at spearpoint and questioned me, as the guards of Dionysios of old had once questioned visitors.

I waited in the blazing sun, dismayed by such suspicion, while the messengers ran back from the guardhouse and the barbarian guards eyed me grimly. Eventually they searched me for a hidden weapon and escorted me through the gate where before I had walked unhindered, and took me to a chamber unknown to me where Hiero, with an obvious effort, rose to meet me.

He seemed distant at first, deep in troubled thought, much thinner. After the preliminary greetings – briefer and more formal than usual – he lapsed into silence. His eyes wandered around the chamber, occasionally coming to rest on me for a moment before moving on once more. I, who had known him all my life, was shocked. He had aged much, and for a time I wondered if he knew who I was. Yet when I suggested gently after a long silence that I leave him, his eyes regained something of their old sparkle and fixed on me. He smiled briefly then, but there lingered a lack of trust in his voice as he said:

– *You are learned, Arkhimedes. I, an old soldier, am not, yet I have been reading Xenophon, an old soldier too, but a wiser one than I. I had forgotten how clever he was. He knew much about tyrants.*

I thought it wise to say nothing, although I still wondered at the great changes in him. He seemed very frail. I wondered if his great age or the illness of Gelo had deranged him. Rumour also spoke loudly that his son-in-law Andranadoros plotted to succeed him directly, or to rule through Gelo's young son, Hieronymos, when the time came.

– *You know the book of which I speak?*

I told him I did, the imagined dialogue between Simonides and Hiero I, the first of that name to be Tyrant of Syracuse, the brother of Gelo of old.

– *Then you will remember Hiero say that a Tyrant may trust no-one, his people, his friends, his guards, not even his family* – he paused – *especially his family*. He gave undue emphasis to the last words, and watched me closely. His smile had vanished.

Perhaps he included me in his family. I felt cold suddenly, and wondered if I were to be arrested on a false charge, but replied: – *Kyrie, I do, and I remember the advice Xenophon has Simonides give him.*

– *Repeat it to me, Arkhimedes.*

I searched my memory. – *If you make the state you rule flourish more than any others, then you will be the victor in the noblest and grandest contest in the world.*

The passage seemed to reassure him. He was silent for a time, then sighed: – *I should have known better than to question you, of all people I love.*

I saw that he still watched me intently from the side of an eye, and kept emotion from my voice: – *I took an oath, Kyrie. I took it by the side of my father, your kinsman, once at the altar by the Temple of Athene, and again by the place where Leonidas died.*

The Tyrant nodded, his familiar briskness seeming to return. – *I know. Pheidias told me.* He was silent for a time while I waited respectfully. He seemed to gather his thoughts before he spoke again, this time decisively: – *I will tell you why I summoned you.*

He rose and motioned me to a couch, then said:

– *Syracuse flourishes. No citizen goes hungry, none lacks a slave. Many are rich. Yet it can only continue to flourish if it cannot be taken. I have allowed the defences to decay. The city is in danger.*

The Tyrant paused and looked at me, perhaps expecting me to mollify or contradict him. As he spoke the truth, I did neither, but waited.

He continued:

– *I will take the advice of Xenophon and spend my own fortune on the city, on the walls, the fort of Euryalos, the latest war engines, on weapons for every man. I will spend all I have if necessary, every talent, drachma, my last obol, but if I give the money to the generals they will steal it, or someone will steal it from them. Instead, Arkhimedes, I intend to give it to you.*

This took my breath. I protested that I was an old man, a peaceful philosopher who knew nothing of war, someone whom he himself had excused from military duty when I came of age, and who wished to be left alone.

He listened, showing me at last something of the courtesy and affection of easier times, then said in a low voice: – *I confide much to you now, as Gelo cannot help me. He is very ill. I have put it about that he is better, but I fear he will not live long. My grandson is still a child, and seems headstrong, too ready to yield to his impulses. My daughters, especially Demarata, beseech me to announce him to be my heir, but they do so only because they wish to rule through him for a time, while he is still a child, before they exile or kill him. Their husbands profess loyalty to the alliance with Rome, but lean secretly towards Carthage – particularly Andranadoros, who wishes to be Tyrant himself one day. He is vain, much influenced by Demarata who believes Carthage will win. She was always the strongest and most self-willed of my children.*

He paused then, and lowered his voice. – *They believe I am ignorant of this, as if I could rule for such a long time without knowing what takes place in Syracuse and all Sicily. They do not suspect that I know that two of Hannibal's envoys were in Syracuse this very week, disguised as common merchants. They had several meetings with Andranadoros, and I have the message of friendship from him they tried to take back with them to Hannibal. Our agents robbed them of it when they stopped at Zankle to take ship to Italy. We killed them both, of course.*

He paused again, a little breathless, then went on: – *You see, therefore, why I do not trust my family, and why I fear that Sicily will be in flames after my death. Syracuse and the other Greek cities are too important for either Rome or Carthage to leave alone, but the Romans will treat Syracuse with respect, perhaps even with enough loyalty to leave us as we are, if we do not betray them. They could point to us and say they left us as we were because only a foolish ruler would breach an alliance with them, that their allies were rewarded for standing by them when the Carthaginians challenged their very existence. They will treat us with even greater respect if we are also strong, if we make our city safe from attack, but they will never forgive us if we break the alliance.*

– *Syracuse must be made unassailable while I try to ensure that my grandson prepares to rule wisely, with the support of the citizens and the generals. Walls alone, however tall, however strong, will not keep the enemy out. It will need more than that in this age of modern siege weapons, with the new rams, giant catapults, and ships so large that a small fleet can transport an army. Therefore, Arkhimedes, I command you to use your knowledge to build engines so powerful and deadly that he who attempts to take the city will wish he had not come. You cannot refuse me, and you must begin at once while we have time. Do not forget, I have seen what you can do.*

Once I had told him, rashly, that I could create deadly engines of war, after he and Gelo had seen the powers of the lever in a demonstration I had given at his command. I told him he placed too much confidence in me, but he waved aside every protest, and I saw that his decision had been forming long before he summoned me.

He extracted my promise, of course, then continued to speak freely. The victim of every sacrifice he had made had told him that Rome would triumph, as had the oracles. Hannibal, strong in tactics but weak in strategy, had surprised the Romans, but they would recover and win the last battle because they were the most resilient and ruthless people on earth. That would take time, more time than he had expected, probably more time than he had to live. In the meantime Syracuse needed to prepare for the greatest battle in its history. He embraced me then, and I left.

Narrative

The enigma of Kate and the darkness of her image continued to elude Aengus, but the terrible presence of Seth eventually came to trouble him more. Here was a reversion to the primordial, he thought as he watched the man leave and enter his house. He remembered the basilisk eyes that threatened to kill with a look, and reflected that Seth seemed to belong outside the mainstream of humanity, to be as inhuman as a Titan.

The mythologies teemed with such images, Cyclops and Titans and skygods, the brother of Osiris who killed him, dismembered his body and threw it in the Nile, the frenzied Bacchanalians who killed Orpheus, the avenging Furies. Each was an archetype of violence and destruction in the human psyche, the images that troubled man from the beginning.

The Greek

I supplied the mathematical proofs for the law of the lever in my work on statics, *On the Equilibrium of Planes*. (I used the law in geometry, too, much to the surprise of other mathematicians, and described an example of this in my *Method*, upon which a group of philosophers at the Academy in Athens wrote to me to say that I had sunk to the level of a *tekhne*.)

I tell you briefly what I saw at Korinth when we went there on our way to Thermopylai, as that is where the challenge of calculating both resistance and force suggested itself. The city stands on a narrow isthmus between two gulfs. To sail from one to the other – from the Aegean to the Ionian in the case of a ship sailing from Peiraias to the western islands – involves a long journey around the entire Peloponnese peninsula, fabulous for its dangers. So Periander, ruler of Korinth a hundred Olympiads before my time, cut a deep road across the isthmus, from one gulf to another, and he paved this road with great blocks of limestone, to fit so tightly that they made an even bed of rock. He considered cutting a canal, but his people evidently persuaded him that the height of the sea in each gulf was different.

Along this road the smaller ships travelled, avoiding the terrible dangers of storms and rocky shores. They were carried on the *olkos*, a great flat wagon that was pulled by so many oxen that we lost count. We watched a ship rocking on the great car, the beasts toiling and bellowing as they heaved it up the slope, men shouting and pushing the wagon from behind, fearful that it would run backwards and crush them. Others marvelled at the sight. I saw only wasted effort, and while I was still at Alexandria I calculated the proportions of a *trispaston*, which is merely a system of pulleys and ropes that magnifies by many times the force applied.

Those proportions were the foundation of the law of the lever that I demonstrated to Hiero and Gelo when I used a refined *trispaston* to pull a ship on a series of wooden rollers up the beach at Syracuse without the assistance of another person. I did so only to show that a simple machine could duplicate the force of files of men pulling on ropes, and that the slaves could be better used elsewhere. This simple feat, of course, was to be magnified by everyone present, including, I suspect, the Tyrant himself. For many years I was to be congratulated on impossible achievements, even of pulling the largest ship in the world, without rollers, its keel grinding on the sand, along a beach for several stadiums. When I protested at this nonsense I was told it must be accurate, as it was the word of Hiero himself, witnessed by everyone at his court who would swear to its truth.

At the time I simply told the Tyrant that the purpose of the lever was to magnify a force, a force that grows in direct proportion the further it is distant from the fulcrum, and that this had been known since early times. I showed him and his court how simple, and how pleasing, the essential proportion is. Take a plank, put a weight of two talents halfway from the fulcrum on one side and a weight of one talent at the other end. The plank will balance.

Every sailor, I said as I waved at the ship on the beach, knows that the force of the wind is greater in the upper part of the sail of a ship where the mast acts as a lever and the ship's masthole, the *lenos*, as a fulcrum. Set the sail too high and the mast will split. Set it too low and the speed will diminish. Similarly, every oarsman knows that the thrust of an oar is greater if the oar is longer, providing that the power exerted by the oarsman is in proportion and providing that the oarhole – the fulcrum – is optimally placed. All must be a balance of mechanical relationships. All parts of the machine must be strong enough to overcome the resistance of the body to be moved. Mechanics, after all, is simply the action of a force applied to a resistance.

In the simplest of terms I explained all this to the Tyrant and his court, as I say, and a year or so later I set out the law I had deduced by then in a book and followed it soon after with a second that dealt mainly with the implications of the law for the centres of gravity of parabolic segments. The importance of the law was that it enabled those involved in mechanics to calculate in the abstract, to begin with the postulates that equal weights at equal distances are in equilibrium, and equal weights at unequal distances are not, but incline towards that weight which is at the greater distance.

The law is used to calculate at what point below a lever a fulcrum can be positioned to move a given weight, if the lever is of sufficient length. In theory, any body can be lifted, provided lever and fulcrum are sufficiently strong and in the correct positions. As I said this on the beach at Syracuse that day I saw that the faces of those around me reflected a mixture of wonder and total incomprehension, and a simple statement was to be wildly distorted, its essential conditionality dismissed into the air like smoke, told and retold until I grew sick of it, of how I wished for a fulcrum big and strong enough that I, Archimedes, might move the earth. I hope I am not remembered for such a thing.

Let us return to reason. There are many machines in mechanics that obey the law. A *trispaston* is one such, and a *kharistion*, a beamed weighing machine with a counter-balance which uses the principles of the lever, is another, as is a wheel that can be rotated to lift or pull a weight far greater than the force used to turn it, as a feeble old woman may turn a winch to lift a heavy bucket of water from a well, or a soldier may magnify the force of a windlass to twist the sinews of an engine to bombard an enemy with projectiles. These are machines that simply multiply the amount of force applied, and I can tell you that to me the proportions in the law of the lever are as beautiful and as satisfying as many of the proportions in geometry. They also allowed me to make the most terrible engines of war in history.

The Book of Aengus

The fame of his engineering achievements at the time probably dwarfed that of his mathematics, at least as far as the Tyrant and his court were concerned. Later, they were to be exaggerated further, until numerous inventions were attributed to him, including giant mirrors that set enemy ships on fire. His myth acquired a deeper patina through time. Petrarch, one of the early Humanists, said he had invented artillery. Tartaglia, an Italian mathematician of the sixteenth century, credited him with gunpowder, while Leonardo believed he designed and built the first steam cannon. It seems more likely that in the main he took existing inventions like the catapult, the balance or steelyard, the crank and windlass, and the compound pulley and applied the laws of mechanics, often those of the lever, to their design.

Plutarch also appears guilty of distortion. He seems to have attempted, against the weight of evidence, to have retrospectively turned Archimedes into a Platonist concerned only with the purest of mathematics. Yet the evidence I have is that he tackled every problem, whether mechanical or mathematical in the abstract, that took his imagination.

We may be on the point of hearing not only of those terrible war engines, as he calls them, but of how he was the first person in history to develop war into a science.

I watched for hours today. I saw only Seth, but I know Kate now.

Narrative

He studied the man's face through his binoculars. Such a being might not belong to a modern civilisation, yet this one trod the ground as a free man. That he could hold his half-sister in a prison of his making in the twenty-first century had seemed incredible to Aengus at first, something that belonged to a different age, yet the newspapers regularly reported with relish and detail similar events regarding men who held their relatives captive for years, decades even, in cellars and other secret places, and only a day or so before Sid had commented on a case that was a one-minute wonder to the viewers of the nightly television news.

Darkness fell and still he stood there, watching the house, wondering at the extraordinary tensions between the three who lived in it. The night was almost as black as his images, a moonless night with a few stars showing above the cloud wrack. Perhaps because he thought more about Seth and less about Kate, other images of the woman who was not a whore began to surface, pushing through to his consciousness while his guard was down, and he saw her for what she was.

The Greek

On the day after the Tyrant summoned me I stood on the old lookout point of the ruined wall of the Fort of Euryalos, the westernmost defence of Syracuse on the plateau of Epipolai, watching a sail at sea. A fresh wind, wonderfully cool, came from the west, and in the distance I could see a heavy cargo vessel with a rounded bow steering upwind for the harbour of Syracuse, the breeze obliging it to make frequent changes of course which it seemed to accomplish easily.

I was reflecting on the properties of the ships of battle used by both the Carthaginian and Roman navies. My mind had drifted to the early Greek warships, the *pentekonter* with its single bank of oars, twenty-five to each side, then to the bireme, which introduced an additional bank of rowers, and finally to the trireme, the most graceful warship of all, which introduced three, the maximum practicable. I recalled the stories, told and retold in every *oikos* when I was a boy, of how the Athenian triremes defeated the Persians at Salamis, and, later, of how the Syracusan warships had destroyed the Athenians in the waters below me of the Grand Harbour of Syracuse.

Since then, there had been a great change in warship design to accommodate the new tactics ushered in by the wars between Rome and Carthage.

The trireme, with its three files of oarsmen, the *thranites*, *zygites* and *thalamites* seated on either side of the gangway or *parados* that ran down the middle of each ship, had once been viewed as the most deadly polyreme to be built, slim and fast and very manoeuvrable. It was the perfect machine for its time, when to ram an enemy ship was the accepted tactic at sea. Of all the variations, the Attic trireme, the racehorse of the ocean, was at one time deemed to be the finest because of its speed.

Then, as I said, Dionysios I, tyrant of Syracuse, built the first *penteres*, the five, the ship the Romans later called the quinquereme, which had files of five oarsmen to each side, still with three benches of rowers, but two of the oars were manned by two rowers rather than one to give it greater power, though not speed.

That was the beginning of a race of a different kind between every city and every kingdom that aspired to be a power, not only at sea but on land. Monstrous ships were built, sixes, sevens, tens, sixteens, and so on, so large they were hydrostatically insane, but reflected different rulers' desire to impress their rivals.

It was the five that Carthage and, later, Rome were to take as their own, the Romans copying a captured ship of the Carthaginians, plank for plank. They did not do so because of its speed – it was slower than the trireme – but because it could carry twice as many troops or *epibatai*. Remember that the Romans were soldiers, not sailors.

This, Stranger, was the essence of the new naval tactics.

Ramming, the tactics of the Greeks since naval warfare began, had become, if not completely a tactic of the past, a more distant objective. The aim of the new tactic at sea was to board the enemy by throwing a bridge called a *korax* between the ships and so overwhelm the enemy by numbers of fighting men. The secondary aim was to transport large invasion forces quickly by sea, striking the enemy by surprise. The five was suitable for both of these tactics. It was also strong enough to resist all but the largest projectiles from all known *katapeltes*.

I reflected on these changes as I stood on the wall in the breeze. It seemed to be the fate of every great design to be overtaken by another when it appeared that further refinement was impossible.

Such had been the fate long before of the legendary Attic trireme whose strength had been unduly sacrificed for speed, a weakness that the wily Korinthians had exploited by charging it head-on with shortened beak and strengthened catheads, tearing the Athenian ship to splinters.

I paused then and my head began to swim a little as I looked back into the histories to guide me, and thought of the clever Korinthians who had sought a weakness, and found it, in the Athenian three which was deemed to be undefeatable. I thought of the possibility of discovering similar, fundamental design weaknesses in the structure of the five. I could visualise little that could be effected against an enemy at sea, as the navy of Syracuse was merely a token one in this era of far greater powers. Something, however, might be done nearer at hand, particularly at close quarters if the enemy decided to throw his forces into a confined area. Remember how the Spartans held the pass.

I reflected that the strengthened timbers of a *kataphract* – a fortified ship such as a five – including the heavy oarboxes built to protect the outer bench of the *zygite* oar from missiles, the strengthened decks, and the much increased burden of the additional rowers and troops, would together not only increase the weight of the ship, but would especially increase the weight of the upper part of the vessel as a ratio of the whole. This last point, in particular, held my attention.

I had already in mind different weapons to deal with the enemy at relatively close quarters, but I began to think of another that might surprise – and, particularly, demoralise – them further if they brought their ships to the walls, and packed them so closely they could barely move. I knew that surprise in battle is close to a battle won, that it was the enveloping body armour of the Spartan *hoplites* that was such a surprise to Xerxes, who fitted his men with mere wicker shields. To make the attackers lose their courage through such a surprise is to bring victory even closer. What I sought that day at Euryalos, in addition to the weapons I had already begun to design in my head, was something entirely new, something completely unexpected that might be produced at a critical part of a battle, something expressly suited to a city whose walls towered over the sea.

I took my stylus and drew in the wax a five, alongside a three, and mentally compared them, using rough numbers to calculate. After I had drawn a series of such diagrams it seemed to me that the centre of gravity of a five would be almost a cubit higher than that of a three. I wondered if the designers had thought of the possible consequences. Surely, I thought as my pulse quickened, the wale at water level in a five, and the framing behind it, would need to be much stronger than in a three because the five's slowness made it vulnerable to ramming. That would add further to the weight of the ship above the waterline. I added up the possible increase in weight, then calculated the comparative stability. My pulse again began to race, as it did when I neared a possible solution to a problem.

The lateral buoyancy of a five seemed to be only half that of a three. Given certain conditions these battleships could be turned into traps of death.

Time slipped by me as I reflected that the fives might carry twice as many soldiers, and be invulnerable to ramming because of their heavy protective timbers. Yet they would be as feeble in certain circumstances as the Attic trireme proved to be after the Korinthians had seen its weakness.

Leaning against the wall to rest my aching back, I began to think of what those circumstances might be. The cargo ship had disappeared from view as it entered the harbour. Dusk was descending, but I remained, recalling different propositions I had proven. I had completed the proof of the law of buoyancy in my work *On Floating Bodies* some years before. This law helped to design a large ship called the *Syracusia*, which the Tyrant had commissioned as a present to Pharaoh of Egypt. I had ships and their different qualities of buoyancy in mind when I worked on Book Two, and I had used a floating paraboloid in my propositions because the shape of such a conical cut also represents the cross-section of a ship.

Every shipwright and sailor knows instinctively that a floating vessel will revert to an upright position in line with its centre of gravity in the absence of other factors such as wind pressure. I had supplied the proofs of that in Book Two, reflecting on the mathematical proportions between length and beam and on the impairment of lateral buoyancy in all polyremes, built as they were for speed. I had also, in my work on hydrostatics, calculated the relative weights of water displaced by different vessels.

It was obvious that the enemy – in this case I assumed it would be Carthage – would need to storm the defences by land or sea, or both. If it were by sea they would need to bring their ships to the walls, probably to send their soldiers ashore as a concentrated force. The place they chose would be my pass, and I would endeavour to leave them little choice as to where, unsuspecting, they would attempt to come ashore.

When I began my descent to the city the ideas that were based on my work on buoyancy and on the lever, two fundamental laws of nature, were already formed in outline.

In my mind's eye I saw a Carthaginian five lying defenceless alongside the sea walls of Syracuse with a lever suspended above it.

I was to spend several years on the defences of Syracuse, not only in designing and making different war engines, of which I made many, thanks to the open-handed nature of the Tyrant, but in strengthening the fortifications of the city in such a way that the enemy would be induced to attack where we could hit them the hardest. I studied the walls of Syracuse by land and from a boat, pondering the nature of a possible siege or an attempt to take it by assault, either from land, or sea, or both. I climbed to the highest points above the city and looked at the ground below, then at the harbour, thinking all the while and making notes and designs.

The military men were as divided and obtuse as Hiero expected, some maintaining that the defences were many times better than they had been when the Athenians tried to take the city fifty Olympiads before. The walls simply needed to be restored, they said. I did not openly disagree but told them that siege tactics in general, and siege engines in particular, had changed greatly over two hundred years and that a modern ram could breach the strongest wall before a short candle burned to its end, that in the present era it mattered most to keep the rams from reaching the walls. Others maintained that the seaward walls were sufficient to withstand a naval assault and that an attack would only come by land, probably in the form of a long siege. We must look, the generals said, to the walls that faced the rest of the island, the walls of Dionysios.

My view, which was shared by some of the younger commanders, was that any force that intended to take Syracuse by the spear would be very large, and very well-armed, greedy for the riches of the Syracusan Treasury, and that the soldiers of the enemy would be led well and would be prepared to sup with Hades on the same evening. Furthermore, none would attack Syracuse without a series of detailed plans. If one tactic did not work, another would be used at once. Therefore the defences would need to be not only thorough, but to contain deadly surprises that would rob the attackers of a desire to fight.

I decided, with the full support of the Tyrant, that the city must prepare for a full assault from both land and sea, at the same time, and for a long siege to follow.

Privately I went through the histories carefully of how the Athenians, two centuries before, had tried to take the city. For their main base they had used the area around Lysimeleia, a feverish, marshy part outside the walls on the north-western shore of the Great Harbour, and they built a wall from there north-eastwards towards Epipolai to contain the defenders, but the plateau, though it dominates the city because of its high ground, does not have a supply of water, as the attackers discovered to their cost.

They also built a secondary base at the headland of Plemmyrion, at the southern entrance to the Grand Harbour, almost opposite the island of Ortygia. Plemmyrion, although a good vantage point, similarly does not have water. In the end the Syracusans frustrated the Athenian attack by building three counter walls across their path, preventing supplies of food and water reaching them, and so halted work on the Athenians' wall across Epipolai until the Spartan general Gylippas came up.

That strategy of attack was unlikely to happen again. Some years after the defeat of the Athenians the Tyrant Dionysios I wisely constructed, at enormous cost, a fortification, roughly triangular in shape, that ran from the city to Euryalos – where he built an almost impregnable fort – in the west, then east to the sea, enclosing the strategically important plateau of Epipolae within the walls, then along the coast above the shoreline, to deny any point of weakness to an enemy. These were the walls I was to inspect and raise, repairing the towers along them and breaching apertures the breadth of a hand. Through these apertures the defenders would fire a constant series of arrows from a machine I designed that shot short missiles more quickly than an archer, and with greater accuracy and force, sufficient force to pierce the hides shielding soldiers bringing up a ram, in particular. We named this the *skorpion* because of its shape. Its concentrated fire would make it difficult for the rams to reach the walls.

If the enemy attacked from the sea, they would probably attempt to storm the sea walls to the east, as if they attacked and took Ortygia they would still need to pass along the causeway into the main city. The causeway would be simple to defend, as a wall ran between it and Akhradina, from the time of Dionysios. A small body of soldiers, in the manner of Leonidas, could hold it indefinitely unless they were flanked from the water. Their spies would tell them that. They would also tell them that Akhradina itself was a walled quarter, designed to be held if all else fell. Nor would the enemy risk entering the little harbour of Lakkios on the northern edge of Ortygia because they would be attacked on three sides, and because the Tyrant Dionysios I had fortified it so that only one vessel could pass through at a time. It was much more likely that they would bring their fives up to the walls that ran down to the sea at Akhradina, between the little harbour and the Stoa Skutike on the northern edge of the city, and send so many *epibatai* up these sea walls under a covering fire from the archers, slingers and javelin-throwers that the defences would be overwhelmed and the city taken quickly with little cost.

The aspect that interested me was that this length of sea wall covered a distance of only five stadiums. That was the pass I sought, an area of apparent weakness which we must hold at all cost, and it was where I would place the bulk of my engines. If we held those walls we might then force the enemy into a long siege during which Syracuse would be fed from the farms in the *khora* until the city was relieved, or the besiegers recalled.

Such was the strategy that I finally proposed to the Tyrant. After a discussion that surprised me for its brevity, he agreed to all.

The work fell into two parts. The first was to repair and, in many cases along the land side, to raise the walls of the city, and install in them the small openings of which I spoke. There were many objections to this work, chief among them the expense, but the tyrant opened the *thesauros* and ordered every able-bodied citizen and slave to help, telling those who dared to question him that if they wished for peace they must prepare for war.

The second labour was to build the engines themselves.

I designed four types for different eventualities. The largest were built to throw rocks of a great weight a long distance at advancing vessels approaching the walls. It was essential to surprise the enemy when they approached by sea, so I knew I must design engines that could throw larger missiles than any other, at a distance an enemy would not expect, with a force that would overcome the stoutest timbers. In addition, the *katapeltes* must be able to vary their firing range as the enemy drew nearer.

We built the most powerful *palintonons* in the world, engines to send rocks so large that the Tyrant had to extend the quarries and open another. The generals looked at the missiles as they were weighed on the special *kharistion* I had designed and said nothing could throw objects so heavy for such a distance, but I had spent much time on checking the mechanical force required. They would do as I expected.

We then built smaller *palintonons* for shorter-range work, and many *skorpions* that used the same principles but fired arrows instead of rocks. They were very mobile and could be pulled quickly to where they were needed.

We took these machines to a cliff to the east and experimented in privacy for many days before I was satisfied that they would throw the weights the desired distance and with the accuracy I thought essential.

The next series of weapons were great levers, fitted with chains and pulleys. The first type was simple, designed specifically for high, sheer battlements. One end would swing out over the walls, above the enemy, and drop heavy stones weighing ten talents apiece on the ships below. No *kataphract* could withstand such a force from above.

The other levers were the ones I had conceived that day at the Fort of Euryalos. They were designed to lower iron grapnels that would seize the ships by their projecting oarboaxes and overturn them from the side, capsizing them and drowning the *epibatai* and the crews. They would be effective only if the enemy ships were directly below us, packed so closely that they were unable to move.

They would probably do little numerical damage, but they might turn a battle because they had not been used before, and if they were brought into use at a critical moment.

The laws of the lever and the laws of buoyancy came to my aid when I designed them. I had calculated the weight of water that would be displaced by the heaviest five. I then, by a process of simple proportions that I supplied in the Law of the Lever, deduced the force required to lift each vessel.

Each great lever, which must be concealed behind the walls until the enemy reached them in his ships, was suspended on crossbeams so strong that it could take the weight of not one but two ships. Each had a counterbalance of a lead weight heavy enough to create an equilibrium with the weight of the ship if the fulcrum of the lever were in the correct position. The weight must be adjusted quickly to move outward along the lever beam as the weight of the ship came on the other end, until equilibrium was reached. Once the inward end of the lever was firmly attached to the ground behind the wall only a relatively small force would be needed to lift each ship and capsize it. We named this machine the Claw, and I was secretly proud of it. The Romans were to call it the *ferrea manus*, the Iron Hand.

I built these openly using various pretences, including one that I experimented with machines to lift cargoes from vessels, and I trained the most trusted soldiers in their use in the early mornings, before the citizens were about. Speed was all, I told them. Once the ship was hooked it must be drawn up quickly. They took me at my word, capsizing ships with a rapidity even I did not expect, shouting in triumph each time a keel lay exposed to the sky.

My last act before I finished the work was to copy Pharaoh. We built a system of beacons to relay fire signals from one end of Syracuse to the other, and trained the signallers in a simple code of our own. When we were done the signallers could relay accurate messages within moments.

Finally the work was completed. The city was in a state to defend itself against almost any force, even a very long siege against an enemy that had total command of the sea and the rest of Sicily, as long as discipline held. The Tyrant allowed me to return to my work, but not before I had promised that I would inspect weapons, walls and men regularly. He extracted a further promise. If called upon I would conduct the defence in an attack.

The Book of Aengus

Anyone who attacks Syracuse must be prepared to eat with the god of the underworld, he says, taking his theme from Leonidas who is said to have told the Three Hundred on the morning of his death at Thermopylae: *eat, drink, and be merry, for tonight we sup with Hades.*

It is strange to think that he did not know at that stage who would be his enemy, Rome or Carthage. The word he uses – *epibatai* – was used to describe naval soldiers or marines. Much the same word – *epibate* – was used by the Romans, who considered those serving in the navy to be the lowest form of life.

I searched the woods for her this morning, but she didn't appear. Yesterday she seemed very low.

The Greek

I was working in the *exedra* of my house when the porter came to tell me there was an urgent message from the Palace. The Tyrant was dead.

The gods had taken him from us at the worst possible time for the city, when Syracuse still supported Rome in its war against Carthage, a decision that the Tyrant had taken against the advice of many of his followers. The early stages of the second war between the two had increased their unhappiness with his decision, as the daring Hannibal was to win battle after battle against the Romans, crossing the great icy mountains into Italy from the North and defeating the Romans at Cannae, a place so far south that many in Syracuse panicked. Soon they were comparing Hannibal with the great Alexander, angering Hiero who said the Carthaginian general was brilliant and daring, but inconsistent.

Syracuse, in hindsight, was split in two, but as long as Hiero lived the fissure was only a matter for private opinion. Up to the time of his death I was at my work, withdrawn as far as possible from the politics of Syracuse, and had last seen him at the funeral of Gelo, whose death had clearly affected him strongly but had not altered his determination to keep the alliance with Rome.

I had heard in the *agora* on several mornings that many of the Roman soldiers had deserted at Cannae and that some had fled as far southwards as Sicily itself, fearful of retribution and intent on seeking safety in our city, but I did not know whether this was true, nor did I pay it much attention at the time. I was already old and, while my health was good, I was very conscious that I had little time left to me in which to complete my work. Yet when Hiero died I grieved deeply for him, as every loyal citizen wept and feared for a future without his wisdom and benevolence. During the mourning and the funeral games I remembered my promise to him, a sense of premonition growing.

Hiero's death might not have been calamitous had Gelo lived, or had the Tyrant's heir been a person of strong will, but his grandson Hieronymos was very young, still a boy, so vain of appearance he wore the splendid garments of a tyrant in his public appearances, unlike his father and grandfather, and he was weak where the voices of his aunts, Hiero's two daughters, and their husbands were concerned. Hiero's will, read in public before the *ekklesion* building, proclaimed Hieronymos to be his successor, but rumour quickly spoke that Andranadoros looked upon Hieronymos as his instrument to break the alliance with Rome and to unite with Carthage. Within weeks of the end of the Tyrant's funeral games I was to hear it said in the *agora* and outside the temples that Hieronymos had sent ambassadors to Hannibal offering an alliance. I dismissed this as idle talk at the time, but Syracuse frothed with such rumours, and soon two Carthaginian brothers, grandsons of a Syracusan, rode through the Hexapylon gates and appeared in public with the Tyrant. Very quickly it became known that they were Carthaginian generals, agents of Hannibal, and were already hardened in battle against the Romans. They were called Hippokrates and Epikydes.

Ambassadors from Rome came to reason with Hieronymos, to be spurned by him. These envoys wrote to the Senate in Rome that he had insulted them when he taunted them with the humiliations of Hannibal's victories. Whatever the truth of that, it was certain that Rome would seek revenge.

Some months later the pro-Roman faction of Syracuse murdered the young Tyrant while he was on a visit to Leontinoi, then set out to destroy the Carthaginian sympathisers.

I can tell you little for certain, such were the rumours, but a terrible division, the outcome Hiero had dreaded most, followed his death. Citizen argued with citizen. The streets filled with angry factions. The citizens' assemblies met for the first time since Hiero had died, the moderates sometimes winning time by their rhetoric, sometimes losing. One met and appointed Andranadoros as one of its leaders, even as he, it was said, plotted to take power. The plot, if it was a plot, was betrayed, and the assembly guards killed him and Themistos, husband of Gelo's daughter Harmonia, who was said to have plotted with him. Inflamed citizens, convinced that Hiero's two daughters were part of the plot, murdered Demarata, and Heraklia her sister who had sought refuge in a temple with her own daughters. These last two were also killed, perhaps raped as well. Harmonia, too, was murdered. If Heraklia's husband Zoippos had not stayed in Alexandria, where he was Syracuse's envoy to Pharaoh, they would have killed him as well. The violence enveloped the streets of the city, and when it was over Syracuse was openly allied to Carthage. Officially the city was to be ruled by the assembly, but in effect this power was given to Hippokrates and Epikydes and such supporters as they chose.

Word soon reached Syracuse that the Roman Senate, incensed by the change of alliance, had appointed Appius Claudius Pulcher as pro-praetor to command a force by land and reinforce the existing Roman legion in Sicily which had been in the west of the island since Rome had defeated Carthage in the first war between the two. Marcus Claudius Marcellus, who had been appointed consul for the third time, was to lead the Roman expeditionary fleet. This was rumoured to be very large, composed of sixty quinqueremes, a force so large and powerful, packed as it would be with fighting men, slingers, javelin-throwers and archers, that the bravest of Syracusans examined their courage.

Not all believed this, as so many rumours swept Syracuse at that time, but then we heard that the Romans had taken and sacked Leontinoi, and news reached us that Marcellus had beheaded as many as two thousand Carthaginian sympathisers in the city. At this point Hippokrates, barely concealing his uneasiness, sent for me.

All factions in Syracuse, I told him when we met, had blood on their hands. One set had murdered Hiero's legitimate successor, foolish though he had been, and left him unburied and unsung, a foul deed that the gods would surely avenge, if the hags did not. His murderers had gone on to commit the worst of atrocities, so much so that they had incited their opponents into power. It was he and Epikydes, his brother, who had, by their cunning, persuaded the Syracusans to break the alliance with Rome. None of this could be forgiven or condoned. Sicily was already in flames, as Hiero had predicted, with the Romans reinforcing and advancing and the Carthaginian general Himilco arriving to meet them with an army and a fleet.

When I told him this he looked angry for a moment but responded, cleverly enough, by saying that whatever events had taken place, they were then past, and that Syracuse was at least united in its desire and need to protect itself. It was I, he said, who knew every detail of the strategy to defend the city, as it was I who had drawn it up. As a loyal citizen who had sworn to conduct its defence, regardless of who the enemy was, it was my duty to obey its rulers and to honour my oath if the city was to avoid a repetition of the Roman atrocities at Leontinoi. If I did not, I would have the blood of every citizen on my hands, and the vengeance of the gods for eternity. So he spoke, and as he did I saw, through my anger with him, that what he said was true.

The Book of Aengus

Let us glimpse his new enemy, of whom he talks as casually as though he were a minor official. Marcus Claudius Marcellus was joint Head of State of the Roman Republic, and therefore the most important and powerful Roman of all. He was also one of the finest Roman generals, the saviour of the city of Nola, and the slayer of King Brithomarthus the Gaul in single combat. This was the Roman who was leading the mightiest force that Syracuse had seen throughout its violent history, bringing it into battle against a divided city whose defences were conducted by an ageing mathematical genius who had never thrown a spear in anger.

Plutarch says that Marcellus was 'skilful in the art of war, of a strong body, valiant of hand, and by natural inclinations addicted to war', and adds that he revered Greek learning and discipline, as Alexander had. Many saw him as a new Alexander. That is not a title one would easily give to his opponent, a frail old man who often forgot to eat and spent much of his time dreaming about the frustum of a cone or the properties of a sphere.

History sometimes chooses its heroes by a circuitous route, and one could forgive the Roman Consul if he felt a surge of confidence when his spies brought the news that Syracuse was divided and that its defence would be led by an old man, a philosopher – the greatest mathematician in the world at the time, but one who had never charged an army of Celts, as Marcellus the Consul had done, an army of Celts, the only nation that the Romans feared since Brennus had casually taken Rome in the previous century. Marcellus had defeated this army of Celts, against superior odds, taken their city of Mediolanum – modern Milan – and been given a triumph by the Roman Senate as reward, at which Plutarch says he carried the sword and shield of the Celtic king nailed to a block of oak, which he dedicated to Jupiter Feretrius, Zeus the Thunderer. Marcellus, says Plutarch, 'carrying this trophy, ascended the chariot; and thus, himself the fairest and most glorious triumphant image, was conveyed into the city. Rome went wild with joy that day in celebration of the end of the war with the most feared enemy of all, showering garlands of laurel on the general and his legions, and sent a golden cup weighing a hundred pounds to the Oracle of Apollo at Delphi' – and also, Plutarch says, many presents to King Hiero of Syracuse, their friend and ally.

It was at the city of Nola, after Hannibal and his army of Carthage had invaded Italy and defeated all before them, that Marcellus achieved his most notable victory. There he outwitted Hannibal, who believed the city to be empty of Roman forces of any consequence. Marcellus had commanded his soldiers to be silent and the citizens to stand down from the walls, and from there he surprised the Carthaginian invader by throwing open the gates and charging Hannibal and his men. The Carthaginians resisted at first, then retreated to their camp, their first reverse since they had crossed the Alps. Rome breathed its relief and began to believe, for the first time, that Carthage and Hannibal were not invincible, in spite of their years of military success.

Marcellus was once more recalled to be consul, but Jupiter thundered.

Every chronicler and student of Roman history has had to understand a singular quality about its citizens and its leaders. Romans were obsessed with omens and auguries. All nations were religious, all had their superstitions, all sought oracular or divine guidance in some form or another, but none carried it to the superior level of the Romans.

Perhaps it was because they fought so many wars. From 510 BC, when the Romans founded their republic after they had revolted against the Etruscan King Tarquinus, the Romans seemed to fight everyone within reach – the Etruscans, the Volscians, the Aequians, the Latin League, the Samnites, the Gauls or Celts who took the city in 390 BC, and, over a period of 58 years in what are known as the Punic Wars, the Carthaginians. It is not surprising that Rome's heroes were its successful generals, steeled in battles. Marcellus was the most successful of them of his time, yet he was as subject as the humblest legionary to the interpretation of the omens.

Divine intervention in war was unquestioned then, as it was to the Greeks at Troy, but in effect the Republic had a State religion, unlike the Greeks, and every appointment to a Roman magistracy – the two Consuls, as nominal Heads of State and after whom the Roman years were named, the occasional Dictator (not a dictator in today's sense, but someone given temporary power in a crisis, as Cincinnatus was recalled from his farm to fight the Aequians), the Pontifex Maximus (responsible for all religious matters), the Censor (public morality), the Praetor (laws), the Aedile (public works), and the Quaestor (finance), the magistrates together holding the power collectively called *Imperium* – could not be made by the Assemblies (of which there were five, with the Senate easily the most powerful, and therefore the most corrupt) without the most elaborate and strict rules and vigilance on the part of the Augurs, the priesthood who barred a candidate from office, no matter how powerful or popular, if the *Dirae*, Rome's informal encyclopaedia of signs of ill omen, said *No*.

Silence was essential when the auspices were taken. If it was broken by a sudden sound the gods clearly did not favour the business at hand. The Roman day began at midnight, and Livy writes that if a consul was making an appointment he would wait, then rise in the silence of the night to minimise the risk of a sudden noise. No rules could be more definite. When Minucius the Dictator named Caius Flaminius as master of horse, a mouse squeaked. Both men were immediately and automatically deposed.

Among the most significant of the omens were the heavenly signs, the unmistakable expressions of the will of Jupiter, the chief of them a lightning bolt. Thunder was an evil omen, but the course of a lightning bolt determined all. If it struck to the watcher's left, it was lucky, on the right, unlucky.

In the case of Marcellus, the lightning fell to the right. He immediately resigned the consulship to avoid embarrassment to the other magistrates, but kept his command and, as pro-Consul, returned to Nola to continue the fight against Hannibal.

One can forgive the stunted religion of Rome in this case, as the omens, by a bolt of fate or a flash of luck, brought about a desired result for the Republic. Marcellus followed the Roman policy of declining a set battle with Hannibal, but surprised a large Carthaginian force sent out to plunder the country, and killed five thousand men, the worst disaster thus far in Hannibal's career.

Marcellus was made Consul for the third time. The auspices were taken and the *haruspex* who stood by announced, as a matter of form, that lightning had been seen on the left. The mice were silent.

The man they called the Sword of Rome soon sailed with a mighty force to take Syracuse, the city state that had gone over to Rome's enemy.

The Roman quinquereme, known as a *penteres* to the Greeks because it carried five-man files of rowers on each side of the midship gangway, with three hundred men manning the oars in each, was copied exactly from those of the Carthaginians, who were better sailors. It was more than one hundred feet long, held four hundred and twenty men including one hundred and twenty marines and when fully loaded, as these were, displaced one hundred tons.

In total, the sixty battleships sailing to Sicily carried upwards of twenty-five thousand men. Rome was throwing a quarter of its entire naval power, under its best general, at its former ally, and the auspices were favourable.

Narrative

Livy and Plutarch lay on the kitchen table when there was a soft knock at his door. He opened it and she stepped inside. Outside a gale rocked the tops of the trees.

She had told Kate she needed air. Seth had left, probably until the next day. Aengus kept his resolve not to question her, sensing that she wished to listen rather than speak, and as the wind rose outside and the little fire blazed he found himself telling her of the weather on his travels, of a storm outside the holy city of Q'om that filled the sky with sand and almost drowned him, how the Ramganga river had overflowed its banks and flooded the jungle, sending chital, sambar and leopard into the open to search for high ground as he watched from a height, and of the new life on the Nile when the flood arrived.

He told her of storms he had seen when the very ground had rocked with thunder and the sky had been black, riven with flashing blue bolts. He talked of the gales in Scotland that he had feared would blow his roof away. He spoke of the fauna of these places, then of an old dog otter in Scotland that came downriver with the ebb under darkness to whistle at his back door for food. She listened gravely throughout, not interrupting or questioning.

Presently, as he rose to put another log on the fire, she spoke, to tell him of how she had seen herself as strong, courageous even, with a zest for life, yet recently she was losing her sense of identity, overwhelmed by a feeling of claustrophobia and helplessness. On the previous night she had dreamt she was in a tunnel, running towards a light at the end. Then the light had gone out.

He was silent in turn.

After a pause she went on: "Yet the feelings that trouble me more are when I wake, thinking that I'm back in my home, and realise I'm not. I still have that dream, although I know I won't see my home again."

The wind was dying and the cottage was very quiet, the sound of the old alarm clock suddenly magnified. The log flamed into life.

"Did you have a happy childhood?" she asked suddenly.

"I did, though a solitary one," he answered slowly. "I cared more for animals than humans at one point. Perhaps I still do, in a way." He watched her gazing at the flame, a strange certainty growing in his mind.

He sat for long after she had gone, his mind in a tumult. Who was or were the other person or persons at her old home? Parents, a lover, a husband even? He stirred uneasily in his chair. Perhaps it was a child. No, he thought, she did not seem like a mother. What hold did Seth have over this other person, enough to give him power over Bridget? A darker question surfaced. Did the girl herself have something to hide, something so serious that she did not dare to have it exposed? No, because she would have escaped rather than live as she did. A bond of some kind held her captive, but which? Of the possibilities the most likely was that someone close to her was threatened by Seth. That was the chain that kept Bridget a slave in a hovel, her beauty hidden, her youth wasting. As he watched the fire die he was certain of it.

He went to bed as his brain still whirled with questions, fell asleep eventually and woke soon after midnight, sweating. He had heard the terrible cry of a woman in pain, so real he thought it must have come from nearby. He rose and scouted around the cottage in a blustery wind, but saw nothing unusual. He returned to bed and woke an hour later, sweating again though it was very cold in the room, hearing not the voice of the Greek but the memory of it as Archimedes spoke of the goddesses of Eleusis. When dawn woke him the memory surfaced.

Soon after he went to the public telephone box on the main road and called his lawyer.

"I wrote to you this morning," said Simon. "You're rich."

He tried to concentrate as the lawyer told him that one of his private equity investments, all that was left after his divorce, had been lucky or inspired. He need not work again.

"I live as I want to live. I don't need money. I'm happier without it."

"Why did you call me?"

"I want you to find someone for me. I have the surname, providing it's the same. It's probably a woman."

"Is this the person you spoke of?"
"No, but I think it may be her mother."

The Book of Aengus

The gale has blown itself out at last. The owls and bats are busy hunting. It's a clear night and the sounds of the river comfort me, although I begin to miss the sea and the great changes in its moods. I miss the estuary and the waders, the cormorants and gulls riding the high winds, the shrill cries of the oyster-catchers and the sharp smell of seaweed and saline mud at ebb tide. I don't miss the damp, the weeping walls of the grey town on a wet day with the wind in the north-west, any more than I miss the dry plains of India, but part of me wishes for a change from this sheltered country where the chimney doesn't rock in a gale.

We've set a hound running without knowing what it might flush. Sometimes that can be dangerous, a move that produces an unwelcome surprise, but I must do something. Perhaps I see my myths as real, but that cry is with me still.

I'll wait with an easier mind and while I wait I'll keep my mind occupied with the possibility that I may hear soon an account of the defence of Syracuse against Rome. We know the outcome, of course, but all evening I have been reading about Carthage, the strangest of empires, and the flows of history that placed Syracuse between the Sword of Rome and the spear of Carthage.

Think of Carthage and think of the Phoenicians, from which the word *Punic* comes. The Carthaginians were Phoenician colonists, merchants and traders to a man, descendants of a Semitic people who worshipped the Great Goddess as Astarte and gave their alphabet to the Greeks. They were not naturally a belligerent people, as the Greeks and – later – the Romans were. They were learned and creative. Thales of Miletus, the first scientist, was at least half-Phoenician through his mother, and the father of Pythagoras came from there, the land of Tyre and Sidon.

Tradition has it that Carthage was founded by Dido, whom Virgil portrays as the tragic lover of Aeneas. Dido was the daughter of a king of Tyre, and a legend says that in 814 BC she was borne to a headland on the Mediterranean coast of Africa where the Phoenicians laid the foundations of a trading outpost they called New Town, or *Kart Hadasht* – Carthage – renting the site from the Libyans, as Africans were known then. It was one of many such Phoenician trading towns, and it was close to another called Utica, one of a chain that stretched from Asia Minor to the kingdom of Tartessus in Spain, which was rich in silver.

They prospered, then a century or so later the hungry Greeks arrived in Sicily, seeking colonies and prepared to take them by the spear. They were successful, as the histories of Syracuse, Gela, Akragas, Leontinoi, Megara Hyblaea and so on testify, and they began a trade of their own. The Phoenicians armed, and united under the strongest town, Carthage, some of the town-states joining as sovereign allies, others paying tribute to Carthage, and the empire began, an armed common market which made friendly treaties with Rome and the Etruscan cities and tried unsuccessfully to expel the Greeks from Sicily. At home the Carthaginian merchants became landowning aristocrats and the empire expanded at an astonishing rate, building a formidable navy, its armies driving south into the African hinterland, into Sicily when they would hold cities in the north and west of the island, into Spain and Brittany and Cyrenaica. Its population was too small to support such an expansion, but its wealth was not, so its fighting was mainly conducted by mercenaries, and its purposes were to protect its existing trade and to acquire more colonies and so conduct more trade.

It seems that the only thing that united two or more Sicilian Greek cities was a Carthaginian. The Greek states in Sicily squabbled like fishwives, but when they decided in the fourth century BC that Carthage was their common enemy, Agathocles, the Tyrant of Syracuse, the strongest of the Greek states on the island, took the war to North Africa and was so successful for a time that the Carthaginians feared for their principal city, and when he died two years before the birth of our Greek, Carthage in turn laid siege to Syracuse – threatened it with such menace that the Syracusans appealed to King Pyrrhus of Epirus, he of the expensive victory and son-in-law of Agathocles, for help, which he gave, crossing over with his war elephants, but then he left to create another cliché, and Carthage pushed its territorial hold to the walls of Syracuse, occupying Neapolis itself and destroying the temple of Demeter immediately above the theatre, before being driven off.

I omit great tracts of history here because the history of Syracuse and its involvement with Carthage is convoluted, full of ebbs and flows and complications such as the constant conflicts with the Mamertines, a collection of brigands who worshipped Mars and held for a time the city of Zankle (Roman Messana, modern Messina) on the Sicilian shore of the straits between Sicily and the mainland of Italy.

Yet two broad strands stand out. One is the constant desire of Carthage to pursue trade without war. The other is the extraordinary disunity of Syracuse, whose history resonates with a series of episodic internal struggles as tyrant followed tyrant, many of whom were murdered, including Agathocles whose nephew killed him. In all, there were more than twenty-five civil wars in Syracuse before Archimedes was born.

We are moving fast towards the cause of the first of the Punic Wars, the third of which would see the end of Carthage and the beginning of the hegemony of Rome over the Mediterranean basin, to be followed by its dominance of the Western world and much of the East. The key character in these events that are to shape the political character of the Mediterranean and the West is Hiero, tyrant of Syracuse and relative of Archimedes.

Hiero, whom I picture as a benevolent absolute monarch at the end of his very long life, distinguished himself as a young soldier against Carthage, rose rapidly and as head of the army led yet another Syracusan coup, eventually to become tyrant. He went to war against the Mamertines and was so successful that Carthage, fearing he would reach for all Sicily like Agathocles, duped Hiero into staying his hand while they shipped a small force into Zankle, making it a Carthaginian protectorate.

Hiero retired to Syracuse to consider whether he wanted war with Carthage and in the meantime the Mamertines decided that Rome would be a better protector. The Romans consented, anxious to take control from Carthage of the strategically important straits that divided Sicily from the underbelly of mainland Italy. The Mamertines persuaded the Punic leader to withdraw his force, for which he was crucified when he returned home. Hiero entered an alliance with Carthage and both went to war against the Mamertines. Rome sent a consul with an army of twenty thousand men to relieve Zankle and the Mamertines. The First Punic War had begun. It would last for twenty-three years, and end with an uneven truce in 241 BC that rankled because, under its terms, the Carthaginians left Sicily.

What of Hiero and Syracuse? He believed that Carthage had betrayed him and had deliberately allowed Rome to land its forces in Sicily. He returned to his city and when Rome later sent its envoys to him he accepted their offer of friendship, agreed to pay a tribute of a hundred talents and entered into a treaty under which he would help Rome when called upon. In return, Syracuse would enjoy the protection of the republic. Hiero settled down to spend the remainder of his life at court as the ruler of an independent city state. He would do so for around fifty years, and retain his alliance with Rome even as the Second Punic War began in 218 BC and Hannibal crossed the Alps into Italy.

The Greek

I resume, Stranger, with the story of a beautiful dawn revealing a light mist drifting over the sea to the east, a cool morning in early summer, ideal for a peaceful walk to the *agora*. It was a time that showed Syracuse at its best, yet every citizen knew that by nightfall the city might be in flames. I stood by the battlements on top of the sea wall in that part of the city called Akhradina, near the Stoa Skutike where the shoemakers had displayed their goods, seeking the first glimpse of the Roman fleet of Marcellus that we knew was approaching.

We had sacrificed a goat to Artemis Agrotera and prayed to Poseidon for a tempest on the day that our spies told us that the Roman fleet had sailed to round the cape to the north, a tempest or even a moderate gale, as the Ionian Sea, with its great rolling waves, is a dangerous place to be in a warship during anything other than a calm. The wind, however, did not come, and I saw with disappointment that the seas met the reef off the little harbour and the crags below us with scarcely a break. If we were to repulse the Romans, we must do so in fine weather.

We knew that a great force of Romans had marched overland to the north of Syracuse, near the Hexapylon gates in our northern walls. I had told the *strategoi* not to meet the Romans on open ground, but to harass them with the archers, while the main Syracusan forces stationed in the north were to remain within the walls.

They had followed their orders. The Roman land force, under the command of Pulcher, arrived at the walls to the north at dawn on the following morning, while the fleet, with Marcellus in command, sailed around the walled cliffs towards Syracuse itself.

The city had slept little on the previous night and was in a great state of excitement. We had been busy since dawn, testing the machines which were ranged along the walls beside me. Every man who could walk had been ordered to the defences, every beast of burden seized to bring up the great stones for the *palintonons*.

I had spent the weeks following the Roman sack of Leontinoi in the organisation of the machines and the disposition of the army and the citizen militia, as Hippokrates and Epikydes had left the city to join forces with the Carthaginians, hoping to meet Pulcher's forces and cut them off. Evidently the Romans had not taken the route they expected.

Presently the runners reported that Pulcher had begun his attack. As the news came in the Syracusan soldiers nearby seemed cheerful, if grave, having sacrificed to the gods that morning, as I had, asking Artemis to protect her city from the barbarians.

A sentinel placed on the high ground above Tykhe saw them first, sailing through the morning mist. The next runner reported that the Roman sailors had brailed up their sails, struck their after-masts and, under oars, were steering to round the point.

A great murmur went up, with anxious cries from the women at the rear. I told them to be quiet, calling out to the soldiers that we would rain death on these Romans and repel any of them left alive if they would obey my orders, and that Artemis would protect her city as she had done before. Remember how Syracuse shattered the Athenians, I told them, surprised at how calm my voice sounded, even to myself. We waited quietly for the first ship to round the headland.

The sun had burned some of the mist from the sea by then, but from that which remained I saw the beak of the first Roman battleship emerge, like the head of a monstrous seabird or a dragon in a fable, pushing through the mist straight for us. We saw the oars breaking the sea with tiny white splashes and the rest of the ship came through. Others loomed on either side, cutting the surface with their rams. The mist burned off and suddenly eight battleships were in full view, oars working steadily, to be followed by a further eight until the full fleet of Marcellus, a sight to remember, lay before us, the vanguard of a great force intent solely on our destruction.

The Roman ships steered for the walls of Akhradina eight abreast, three banks of oars in each lifting and plunging in the morning air, eighteen thousand men pulling at a disciplined pace, the ships resembling beetles, creeping towards us across the shining waters, the sun then lighting the sea like polished bronze.

The standard of Rome hung from each ship, and we heard the trumpets sounding as the soldiers assembled on their decks. Again a murmur went up, which I halted at once, growing more certain that the barbarians expected a quick victory, as at Leontinoi. As they drew closer, the approaches seemed to fill with ships, and we could see the faces of the nearest Romans looking up at the high walls of Syracuse, and at the rocks below them. Even to soldiers such as these, the defences of Syracuse must have appeared formidable.

Behind the second line of ships I saw a larger vessel, evidently a six, and this I deduced to be the ship of the Consul. If we could sink that vessel, it would be half the battle, but we must take each target as it came within range.

The *palintonon* crews stood by their engines, with the soldiers taking up their posts at the walls. All the pipes of the heavier machines had been loaded with stones. I ordered the arms to be drawn back. Along the sea wall of Akhradina the sound of windlasses turning was heard, a great creaking of timbers accompanying it, silencing the excited murmurs of the crowd.

The ships drew nearer, and we waited, nearer still and the moment for which I had prepared for years was at hand. I heard a trumpet call from a Roman ship in that silence, probably from the ship of Marcellus. Still we waited, hearts pounding, until I judged the ships were within range. I gave the order to release the first missile.

It was a rock of five talents and it bounced against the side of one of the ships in the middle, smashing the wood but not sinking the vessel. Three of the succeeding rocks missed, but the fourth stone hit the bow of the ship on the right of the fleet, sinking it instantly amidst great cries from the Romans who believed they were not yet within range.

Our people, astonished at the damage, halted to cheer, but I called to them to sink the nearest ships before they came close to the walls. They did so, directing the great rocks across the water at the Roman vessels, sinking some of them and causing others to collide as their oars were smashed. We heard shouts of command from the ships behind and, presuming that some of these came from Marcellus himself, we stepped up the attack on the six, hoping to sink their commander and so leave them leaderless, but the Consul, when he saw the sea foam as the rocks fell around his vessel, retreated to direct the battle from a greater distance.

The command must have been to change tactics, as the Roman ships quickly reformed, some of the oarsmen backing water while the other fives came up to join them until they were twelve abreast, remorselessly resuming their course for the walls on which we stood. It was clear that the tactic of Marcellus was still to try for an immediate assault, and to assume that sufficient ships would evade our bombardment to put his soldiers ashore.

Behind the leading vessels I saw a different force coming up, making the Consul's intentions plain. The approaching force was composed of ten quinqueremes, lashed in pairs, moving more slowly as only the outer oar banks were in use, each pair with a large wooden structure that projected beyond the bows of the vessels. The battle quinqueremes attempted to shelter these ships from view, but we identified the wooden structures on their decks immediately as sambucae.

These sambucae, so called because they resemble a harp in shape, are siege machines of stout ladders with wooden platforms at the top, the platforms shielded from the defenders by high wicker screens and a roof of the same material. Each platform holds four soldiers. When the ship approaches the wall the crew in the stern of the ship haul the ropes that attach the tops of the foremasts to the sambucae, and so pull it upright, while those in the bows prop it with long poles. The sambucae are then pushed against the wall and the soldiers ascend by the ladder. When the platform is level with the walls the soldiers open the wicker doors and jump onto the battlements. This was the method that had worked so well against other sea cities. The Consul evidently intended to use it once more, seeking a shock assault that would take the defences with the concentrated force of a phalanx.

I called on our people to direct the bombardment on the lashed fives with the sambucae on board and, while the battle quinqueremes attempted to screen them from us, we quickly succeeded in sinking two of the pairs, but the others came on. Throughout this the noise of the battle grew deafening, the Syracusans shouting exultantly as the ships were sunk or hit, the Roman archers and slingers shouting defiance and threats from the ships nearest us. Showers of arrows, fired into the skies above us from the ships, began to come in over the walls, but the long shields we had built protected the defenders like a roof.

In the meantime, messengers brought news from the north that Pulcher had attempted to storm the walls, bringing up his penthouses and rams under a heavy bombardment from the machines we had concealed. The first waves had been repulsed by the Syracusans.

This news greatly encouraged the defenders and the rate of fire from the *palintonons* quickened. I ran along the line of weapons, urging the firing teams to slacken the tension on the arms of the machines to allow for the shorter range. I slipped in a pool of blood and almost fell, drank quickly from one of the *krater*s of water placed beside each weapon, then turned, very hot, to judge the state of the battle.

The Romans were taking terrible punishment. The Syracusans had found their range. I heard the crashes of splintering wood and the screams of wounded men as I watched. A pair of lashed quinqueremes drifted in on the tide to the rocks below us, most of the oars shattered, the sambuca a splintered mess. The Syracusans were sinking them by dropping lead weights and rocks, in spite of the cries for mercy and pleas from the remaining marines and crew. Smashed bodies lay on the decks, and blood ran down the sides, staining the water red. I told the men to stop, that the wrecks no longer threatened us, but a great rage and thirst for blood consumed them and they took no notice, continuing to rain rocks on the ship until both sank, one bronze ram protruding from the water until it, too, vanished from sight. At that point I saw Marcellus wave to his ships to withdraw.

He stood in the prow of the six, watching the battle and calling directions, apparently calm even though his men were dying in their hundreds and a shower of darts was aimed at him.

I looked down across the water at the Consul who was called the Sword of Rome and saw a fine man past his middle years, dressed in a simple tunic, his pate bald at the crown. I saw him glance at me and wave even though the waters beneath the walls ran red with Roman blood, and though our people were then cheering and dancing as the Roman ships began to turn, banks of oars throwing spray everywhere in their haste, I sensed that he would return soon, perhaps when darkness fell.

I shook my head to clear it and put the long-range machines into action again to bombard the Romans as they left the harbour. We sank a further two quinqueremes.

The citizens danced in jubilation then, even as I told them that we must not assume that the battle had been won, that what had taken place was merely the first act in the tragedy. They took little notice, offering more wine to the defenders, many of whom were already drunk, so I ignored them all, growing more impatient as the noise and cheering grew louder.

Some of the generals were confident that the Romans would not return by sea. To listen to such talk from the citizens was one matter, but to hear the military men, with all their training and wisdom, proclaim such nonsense was more than I could allow. I said to them that a consul of the standing of Marcellus would not bring sixty battleships full of soldiers and siege engines to Syracuse without satisfying himself that to take the city by a quick assault was impossible. We had simply surprised the Romans with the effective use of war engines which had not been used before, and they would become wiser quickly as a result. I was an old man unused to war, I said, but even I was able to tell them that a general with the reputation of Marcellus would not leave Sicily until he had taken Syracuse, died in battle, or was recalled by the Senate. Was Rome not the state to which the late Tyrant had allied Syracuse, I asked, and to which he had concluded we should pay tribute? Were the Romans, in spite of their reverses against

Carthage, to be taken lightly, like an army of Sybarites on dancing horses? Only a few hours before, I asked them, as we first saw the Roman fleet, how many hearts had quailed at the sight and accepted that they must die this day? Marcellus, I said to the doubters, would return.

The messengers came in from the north to say that Pulcher had withdrawn, leaving many dead below the walls. I ordered fresh sentinels to be stationed at the critical points, then told the generals I expected the Romans to return when it was dark.

The Book of Aengus

That matches most accounts of the daylight battle, which say the Syracusans repelled the first attack before it reached the walls.

I have a description of the catapult that the Greeks called a *palintonon*, the Romans a *ballista*. Two heavy wooden beams cross to form the base from which run two uprights, each the thickness of the base timbers. Two horizontal beams join the uprights, one halfway, the other at the top. The middle timber supports a frame on each side. These hold a series of twisted ropes or animal sinews under great tension, and into these twisted ropes two strong wooden arms have been inserted. At the ends of these arms are ropes attached to a ring behind the firing end of the machine.

A long wooden trough or channel, open at the top, runs up from the base at an angle of thirty degrees to rest on the middle horizontal, its front end protruding. This is the Pipe, and at its base is a windlass attached to the ring which draws back the arms, under increasing and enormous tension from the twisted ropes, to release the missile along the channel of the Pipe.

That was the machine that sank the Roman quinqueremes, ambushed the greatest Roman general of the day, and forced the Roman navy to retreat from Syracuse. Its smaller brother, the Scorpion, which worked on the same principle, killed many of its marines with an efficiency hitherto unknown in war, releasing arrows with an accuracy and speed never seen before.

It's too soon to expect any news from Simon.

I went to my house, forced myself to eat and drink, and sat in the *exedra* with my maps that I had drawn of Syracuse, studying them for the thousandth time until the sun began to sink, regathering my thoughts about the possible next phase of the battle, seeking flaws in my plans, pondering yet again what I would do if I were Marcellus.

He would almost certainly return that night and bring his ships quickly to the walls before we could begin to pound them. Darkness would be his cloak. He had chosen his timing carefully. There would be not be a moon. Artemis could not help us, as she had helped Syracuse against the Athenians. Pulcher would attack the walls to the north at the same time, choosing a single point where he would bring his rams to beat an opening. That seemed obvious. Yet each had many men available, enough to create a diversion, perhaps even for a third attack by a separate force. I expected the last, knowing how cunning was the Roman Consul. He would certainly have Greek traitors in his pay to guide him who knew the waters and the shoreline around Syracuse as well as we did.

If I were Marcellus I would plan to land a third force from the sea to the north of the city, on the eastern shore, and leave it to scale the walls there while the main naval force carried on to the city itself. Such a third force would still have the inner walls of the city to storm, but if it succeeded it might flank the defenders, causing the confusion of which Marcellus was master. If it did not it might still draw enough Syracusans for his purposes away from his main point of attack, which I thought would be the same walls of Akhradina that he had attacked that day. He had seen that we could defend those walls in the light. My instinct was that he did not believe we could do so in darkness, particularly if a third attack flanked us.

Some time before Marcellus attacked I had decided that the best means of defending the city against such a third force was to attack it as it disembarked. Here I gambled, as I could not be certain which point Marcellus would choose, but I thought I could reduce much of the risk. I had walked to Hexapylon and back many times, looking at each possible landing point with great care, and finally I had selected the point where I expected this third attack, on the coast towards Trogilos six or seven stadiums to the north, an indentation in the shoreline where the waves were sheltered from all but an easterly wind. There the shore would allow a number of small boats to be quietly positioned, if the seas were calm, and the Romans to disembark without causing an alarm. I had put the youngest general, Hermokrates, in charge of the defence of that place, told him to pick his men carefully, to place the fastest runners along the walls from Akhradina to Hexa-pylon to watch other possible landing places, and instructed him on what to expect. If they saw or heard the Romans ground their boats his archers were to throw lighted torches over the walls and pick off the attackers as they waded ashore. At the same time, he must light a beacon to warn us, and follow it with a second if the attack was beaten off. Whatever happened, I said, the Romans must not scale the walls. He, my favourite among the generals of Syracuse, said he would die first.

Those were the plans I had put in place, and as dusk fell that evening after the daytime battle and a new day began I went through them again, searching for contradictions. I dozed for a short while, then rose to return to my place in battle.

When I reached the walls it was very dark. I occupied my time inspecting the *palintonons* and *skorpions*, speaking quietly to the men, satisfied they were ready. Our people seemed cheerful when we called them to their stations. The torches lit their faces to show a determination that reassured me. The supplies came up without interruption from the underground galleries and the heavy machines were loaded. I went on a round of the sentinels at each observation place, checking they were awake and watchful, telling each that the fate of the city might depend on him.

Then there was nothing to do but wait. I occupied myself as best I could, but inwardly I seethed with excitement and self-doubt. After what seemed an age I heard a shout and saw a runner come in. I waited for him, apparently calm while they directed him to me. I listened carefully, questioning him until I was satis-fied he had told me everything he knew, the generals interrupting frequently. The runner had come from Hermokrates. One of his men – a soldier known for his sharp eyes – believed he had seen the whiteness of the splashes of oars and the loom of several Roman quinqueremes in the starlight as they passed him.

Hermokrates could not be sure that this was the main Roman force. It seemed to me probable that it was, that Marcellus had steered inshore for a purpose – to detach a third force, then to carry on to the city itself where we waited.

Soon after that we saw fire signals from Epipolai, relayed from near the frontier with Megara. They told us that Pulcher had already begun his attack in the very north, near Hexapylon, and shortly after a runner came in to say that one of Pulcher's rams had already been abandoned after the *skorpions* of Syracuse had killed many of his men, but the lights continued to signal fresh attacks. Clearly the Syracusans were fighting a great battle in the north. Perhaps, I thought, I was wrong, and the main attack would be on the northern walls – or perhaps, I reflected, the Consul wished me to believe this.

Still there was not a sign of the main fleet of Marcellus, not the splash of an oar, or a muffled order from the open sea, though I and all the others looked out until our eyes hurt. In the hateful silence I began to wonder whether the Roman Consul, if he truly planned to attack the city itself, had chosen another point in the darkness, perhaps evading a line of sleeping sentries. Possibly at any moment we would hear the alarm raised as the Romans began to come ashore where they were least expected. The waiting seemed to be without end.

At length a runner came in, sent by a sentinel stationed at the wall to the north of the Stoa Skutike. He had seen at least three quinqueremes together, perhaps the vanguard of the fleet, approach closely, then row away at once. I grew very tense at this news. For a moment I wavered and considered sending the bulk of our archers and machines to defend that part. Then I reconsidered, forcing myself to reason clearly. The cliffs at that point were high, and so steep they were almost sheer, which would slow the Romans seeking to scale them. The quinqueremes might have been sent there as a ruse. The logical point for Marcellus to attack with his main force remained Akhradina where, if he quickly landed sufficient soldiers in the darkness, the walls could be scaled because of their comparative lack of height. I stayed with my instinct and instructed the messenger to report immediately if the Roman ships were sighted again. After I announced the decision and sent the soldiers to their posts I waited, stubbornly resolute to those who might look at me in the flickering torchlight, but inwardly I wondered if I had made a terrible mistake, or a number of them.

I would have given anything then for a moonlit night. I sensed that the generals were doubtful, talking among themselves in low voices and occasionally glancing in my direction. Still we waited. Then, as I resolved to send another messenger to the sea wall to the north, a runner arrived to say that Hermokrates had lit his beacon. One of my guesses, at least, seemed to have been correct. The Romans had detached a third force, and it had landed.

Still we waited without a sign of the main fleet of Marcellus. The night was as black as before, almost windless, the sea stirring gently below the walls as the tide rose. Only the bells of the sentries and the low murmurs of the men disturbed the quiet.

Suddenly the water below us was full of ships. The Syracusans shouted in alarm. The Roman quinqueremes had emerged from the darkness without a sound and were shockingly close, entering the faint circle of light from the torches, ten abreast this time, almost directly below us. This time the ships that bore the sambucae were in front of the others, touching the walls.

The Romans attacked at once, their tactics well prepared. Stones flew in from the slingers in the outer ships, while a hail of arrows and javelins was launched at us, high above the sea though we were. Marcellus, silent as a fox in the night, had surprised us.

I called to the archers at the *skorpions* to hit the Romans at once. The men at the *palintonons* kept their discipline, shortening the range of the engines quickly as I shouted instructions, and while they did so the defenders at the walls rushed to the piled rocks and began to rain them by hand on the ships below.

We began the bombardment from the *palintonons* soon after, but the quinqueremes were already at the walls. We had damaged only one of them by then, and urgently turned to the levers, but nothing could prevent the bulk of the Roman vanguard from reaching the walls. The Romans saw that, too, and raised a loud exultant noise as they sensed that Syracuse would soon be theirs.

We swung the levers out and dropped lead weights into the ships. By then the Roman slingers and archers who stood on the decks of the outer quinqueremes were keeping a constant, accurate fire on any defenders who showed themselves. If that continued the marines would scale the walls almost unscathed.

We moved the *skorpions* quickly, concentrating on these slingers and archers to the exclusion of all else. The days and hours of practice rewarded us then, as we swept the decks clear, killing them in great numbers with a terrible efficiency. The levers dropped more weights, the men calmer as they handled them, their accuracy improving as the enemy marksmen took cover. The yells of drowning Romans added to the clamour, and I saw the marines hesitate for a moment, but more ships came to the walls out of the darkness, and the hail of javelins, arrows and stones from the slingers in the arriving ships increased as the sailors attempted to bring the sambucae into use. Syracusans begin to die in numbers but the courage of the men who were defending their city against the barbarians held. I ran along the line, telling the men to kill the slingers in the outer ships because they did the most damage. Our archers responded, disciplined and concentrating their fire. A great crashing of wood and screams from below told me the hail of rocks and blocks of lead dropped from the walls had found a target. I looked and saw a sinking quinquereme, the marines leaping into the water, and as I did so a messenger came in, breathless, to say that Hermokrates had lit his second beacon. One danger, at least, had been successfully anticipated, but a greater one confronted us.

It was the Claw that was to cast the greatest fear into the hearts of the attackers. It may have swung the battle. I do not know. Perhaps it did. It sank only a few ships that night, but it spread the fear of the unknown among the Romans who had packed their ships too closely to the walls by then. I swung the great lever with its long chain and iron grapnel over the side of a quinquereme immediately below, choosing it because it was hemmed in by others, unable to manoeuvre. There was a pause in the fighting for an instant, then a javelin from one of the ships passed close by my head. The Roman crew in the torchlight looked up at the Claw, surprised and suddenly fearful. The grapnel swung, hooked on the rowing box, and we immediately drew up the lever and secured the inner end.

A Roman captain, a brave heart, ran to free the ship, but he was too late. The quinquereme seemed to shudder as the strain came on the lever, then abruptly the deck began to cant as the side came out of the water. The oarbox held. The ship turned on its side, the oarsmen abandoning their sweeps and leaping into the sea. It capsized in a crash of yellow foam, its false keel a swaying dark line in the torchlight.

There was silence for a moment as attackers and defenders paused to look at the terrible sight of a Roman battleship which only a short time before had been poised to send its troops to the walls, then lay like an upturned turtle on the tide. When the battle resumed, the Syracusans seemed to fight with renewed zeal while the Romans appeared increasingly uncertain and desperate, as though they wondered whether we had more weapons they had not seen before. We capsized two more quinqueremes and smashed the side of another whose oarbox tore away, the released claw hitting the Romans on its deck as it swung across the ship like a maddened axeman.

So great were the numbers of ships and the numbers of Romans in them, however, that already two of the pairs of quinqueremes had propped their sambucae against the walls. While our people dropped great stones and blocks of lead on these ships, I ordered the men at the *skorpions* to turn their arrows on the soldiers entering the first sambuca. All of the first wave of soldiers hastening to climb the ladder were killed or wounded, and we could hear the captains shouting to the men in the ships to follow them, waving their short swords and beating them while we fired arrows and threw spears into them.

I hurried to the part of the wall where a sambuca was propped, calling to our people to bring up the long poles that lay by the walls. They did so and we pushed the sambuca over, hurling the soldiers into the sea and smashing the Romans on the deck of the lashed pair of quinqueremes. The Syracusans hurled lighted torches into them. In retaliation a wave of arrows came in over the walls, killing two men to my left and wounding one on my right, yet I was untouched. The Syracusans near me cheered at this, their spirits lifting as they sensed victory. The Romans had been quick to throw most of the Syracusan torches into the sea, but one of the ships was on fire.

For a short time the Roman navy retreated into the half-darkness, throwing the wreckage of the burning sambuca over the side, safe for the moment from the Claws and from the firebrands the Syracusans threw at them. There was a shouted command, and they came back to the walls, throwing everything into the fight in a single effort.

We did terrible damage to them then. Flames rose from another ship, to light part of the waters like day, and every Syracusan gave his all, knowing what would happen to his family if he did not. The waters below us rapidly filled with dead and drowning Roman soldiers and sailors. There was wreckage everywhere below us, smashed masts and rigging, floating planks, some with bleeding *epibatai* clinging to them, broken oars, Roman shields, the winged thunderbolts on some of them visible in the bright light of the fires, but still the Romans came on, propping sambucae against the walls. Successive waves of arrows flew at us from the archers in the rear ships, heavy lances and the lighter *pila* were hurled ashore in great numbers in spite of the height of the walls, and a deadly stream of stones came in from the slingers. More of our people were killed and many badly wounded, the battlements grew slippery with blood, but the Syracusans held, seeing their enemy clearly in the light of the burning ships, watching them die in numbers, sensing that the decisive moment of the battle was approaching.

A party of Roman soldiers emerged, short swords thrusting madly, from a sambuca at the top of the walls and began hand to hand combat with our people, successfully at first, but then our archers turned the *skorpions* upon them, killing whole files of marines, doing such damage that the Romans wavered, then jumped back onto the walls and into the sea, shouting to their comrades to rescue them from drowning.

Still Marcellus did not yield, attempting once more to get his sambucae to the walls, his ships darting to different parts, but each time we pursued them, bringing the attack to them. The waters in the light below me were a terrible sight. The Claws kept the Roman ships from packing against the walls, but our people were doing devastation with rocks and weights and fire. The *skorpions* swept the Roman decks clear, killing archers and slingers in increasing numbers. The Syracusans, maddened with blood lust, threw more burning torches, bound with wool and soaked with pitch, into the ships below, and soon the view was as bright as day, lighting a terrible sight I would not forget, and will spare you from, but the noise was terrible, triumphant cries from the Syracusans, shouting and screaming from the ships below, and through it all came the crackling of the fires on the Roman ships, sending clouds of smoke across the water.

I attempted to follow the number of ships I had seen sunk or burned since the Roman ships first appeared. When Marcellus finally recalled his ships and the oars thrashed the waters once more as the Romans retreated, I had lost count, but I believe the Romans lost a fifth of their fleet in the two attacks.

The sentinels sent word that the ships had hoisted sail, cleared the point and could no longer be seen in the starlight. I sent files of soldiers with torches to round up such Romans as had made it ashore, many of them badly burned, then posted fresh watchers. News came in from the north that Pulcher had withdrawn, and the cheering and dancing began anew. A runner from Hermokrates told us that the remnants of the Roman third force had taken to its boats and vanished in the darkness, leaving many bodies in the tide. The immediate dangers, at least, seemed to have passed. We had many dead to sing for, most of them Roman, though I shrank from the wails of the Syracusan women as they searched for their men and found them among the slain. I was very weary, but I stayed at the walls until dawn, awaiting each runner as he came in with news. I remained there, surrounded by sleeping defenders, in case Marcellus, against my expectation, returned. He did not. Perhaps his men would have mutinied if he had. Syracuse had defeated the Roman navy, creating a terrible setback for the Sword of Rome, yet all I felt, as the sun came up and the singing citizens prepared for a great sacrifice at the Altar of Hiero, was a sense of shame.

The Book of Aengus

He was probably exhausted. The value of the Claw was probably its novelty. It would work, as he said, only when the Roman ships were so closely packed together they could not move. The genius lay not only in the concept but in the calculations embedded in their design, allowances for his estimations of the weight of water that each quinquereme displaced, its dimensions, and the mechanical force needed to lift and overturn it. He saw, early on, the inherent weaknesses in a warship that was designed to transport and board, and developed a weapon to capsize it when the soldiers it carried felt sure of victory.

I note his remark about securing the landward end of the lever before the lift was applied. Polybius, who was early enough to have spoken to the survivors, is the only historian to refer to it.

The ruins of the Altar of Hiero lie close to the ruins of the Theatre, near the quarry where the Athenian prisoners were held in an earlier era and whose entrance so caught the imagination of Caravaggio that he named it the Ear of Dionysius. This altar was a vast sacrificial site of cut stone, the length of a stadium, and upon it as many as four hundred bulls could be sacrificed, the burned intestines offered to the gods above, the bladders to the gods on earth and below.

I see her on the path.

Narrative

Little by little she told him some of her history, of her early life in the valley of the Wye, close by Tintern. She was the second child of a gentle doctor, and the first of a young woman who had fallen in love with the widower. His first marriage had been to a wild creature, an addict from a violent, criminal family, and had been a failure from its beginning to her death. The woman had died while still young, when Seth was in his early teens. Seth had hated her, probably because he saw so little of her.

They were sitting outside his cottage, the weather mild for once, sheltered from view by the big crack willow.

Her father, who had never questioned aloud whether Seth was his child, had married again three or four years later. They were happy together, happier still when they had a daughter.

"And Seth?"

"He was a terrible boy who grew into a worse youth. Sometimes, when my father thought no-one was looking, I saw his face when Seth's name was mentioned. All I saw was pain."

The Greek

I slept little on the morning following the battle for Syracuse, hearing the echoes of the screams of the burning and drowning.

When the sun was high I walked out into the *khora* towards Epipolai, my heart heavy.

I re-entered the city later in the day, and went to the temple where I made an offering. Two days later a messenger came in from Hippokrates to say that Himilco, the Carthaginian general who had been at sea with a fleet hoping to intercept Marcellus, had sailed for Carthage to ask for reinforcements. Hippokrates had no doubt they would be forthcoming. The setback the Romans had suffered at Syracuse made that certain. If Carthage took all Sicily, the soft underbelly of Italy would be at their mercy, and Hannibal might quickly win the war.

Spies from the north brought news that Pulcher had withdrawn to his camp and summoned his tribunes, who told him that an assault on the walls was not practicable, and that the city must be besieged until it starved or surrendered.

It was not a surprise to hear that Marcellus had agreed to this. He had decided with Pulcher to divide the Roman forces so that they could attack other cities in Sicily that were allied to Hannibal. Marcellus would take a third with him in pursuit of that aim, while Pulcher remained with the rest to lay siege to Syracuse. Two days later the Roman picket ships lay off the Grand Harbour. The city was surrounded, sealed from the rest of the world, while we awaited the arrival of Himilco, and Hippokrates who had ridden to meet him. Himilco had brought a force of twenty thousand soldiers and three thousand cavalry. Carthage was taking the fight to the Romans in Sicily in earnest, fulfilling Hiero's prophecy that the island would be in flames after his death.

In the meantime Marcellus captured Helorus, a city to the south, then, in the worst atrocity of the war thus far he took Megara Hyblaia and murdered every citizen, as a clear warning to Syracuse. Before that Hippokrates and Epikydes decided that I was too powerful, too dangerous to their cause, and removed me from my post.

The Book of Aengus

Those were the final years of Syracuse, the prize of the Mediterranean, the city that began when the Greeks were migrating from their arid valleys on the mainland.

It reached a pinnacle of riches and power under the Tyrant Gelo who led the Syracusans and others to victory at the battle of Himera over Carthage in 480 BC. Gelo's praises were sung by Pindar and Simonides – not because of his military skills which led to his rule of all Sicily, but because of his horsemanship at the Olympian and Pythian games. Herodotus writes of him as a ruthless, greedy man who did not send reinforcements to Greece when the Persians invaded. Yet he loved his drama. Aeschylus was honoured at his court and travelled on to Gela on the south coast of Sicily, where legend says he became the first man to die from baldness. An eagle carrying a tortoise, seeking a stone far below to drop it on to crack its shell, mistook his hairless head. Whatever the truth of that, it entered the legends.

I have the reference in Thucydides to Artemis saving Syracuse two centuries before our Greek's death. In 415 BC, during a temporary peace or truce during the war between Sparta and Athens, the Athenians launched an expedition which ultimately led to their defeat in the Peloponnesian war. Ostensibly it was to relieve a city allied to Athens in Sicily, but in reality it was meant to conquer and sack Syracuse, which was allied to Sparta. It consisted of 134 triremes and more than five thousand *hoplites*, and was too costly for the Athenian treasury alone, so enthusiastic Athenian citizens, in a frenzy of patriotism and greed, poured their wealth into it.

Alcibiades, rich, gifted, vain and aristocratic, was appointed to be one of its three generals, but he was accused of impiously mutilating the *Hermae*, the busts of the god Hermes that guarded the streets of Athens, and was forced to leave on the expedition before he could be tried, a picture of frustration and injured vanity as libations were poured and hymns were sung and the fleet put to sea. Its leadership was divided, yet it was successful in parts until the generals quarrelled. As winter arrived, they sailed into the Grand Harbour of Syracuse, pitched camp opposite the walls of the city, then quarrelled again and left for Catana, below Mount Etna. There a vessel awaited Alcibiades to return him to Athens for trial.

He jumped from this ship in southern Italy and reached Sparta, disclosing the secrets of the expedition to Athens' greatest enemy, and urged it to help Syracuse. While this went on the Athenian army landed near Syracuse and took the heights of Epipolae. The

Syracusans sent for help from their allies, built walls to prevent the Athenians from finishing theirs, and through a gap in the unfinished wall of the Athenians came the Spartan general Gylippas and his soldiers who had arrived to relieve the city. Gylippas trained the Syracusans to be good soldiers, the Athenians sent for reinforcements of an additional fleet of triremes and soldiers, yet in the end they, outmanoeuvred by Gylippas, decided to withdraw under darkness. When the hour arrived to leave, Artemis intervened.

She appeared in full that night, then abruptly vanished. All grew suddenly dark as the earth passed between sun and moon. A lunar eclipse was a terrible portent to the Athenians. They summoned their soothsayers, who advised them to delay their departure. While they did so, the Syracusans blocked their escape routes, then attacked the Athenians with their heavier triremes. In the cramped space of the Grand Harbour the Athenian ships suffered terrible losses and made for the shore. The warships were abandoned, the Athenians fled inland, then were separated into two forces, to be cut down or captured, the survivors imprisoned in the quarry beside the Theatre of Syracuse in terrible heat and finally sold as slaves. Athens was fatally weakened.

Alcibiades rediscovered his loyalty to Athens in spite of his vanity, and was an eyewitness at the battle of Aegospotami, the final triumph of Sparta over Athens in the Peloponnesian war. In 405 BC, from his exile on a promontory above the Hellespont, he overlooked the sea on both sides and saw the Spartan fleet under Lysander about to surprise the Athenians who, unaware of the Spartans' presence off Aegospotami, had drawn up their ships on a beach. He rushed to warn his fellow-citizens, who told him to go away. The Athenian exile watched helplessly as Athens lost 160 of its 180 ships. Soon after, on the anniversary of Salamis, the Spartans entered Athens and the war was over.

In many ways Dionysius I was the most remarkable Syracusan Tyrant of all. He rose from a clerkship to save Greek Sicily from the Carthaginians, scheming and manoeuvring his way to a generalship until he became Tyrant. He reigned for 38 years and became so fearful of assassination that he turned all of Ortygia into his own fortress where he slept by a raised drawbridge, refusing to allow a barber to shave him. Cicero says he ordered his daughters to singe his beard instead with hot walnut shells. It was Dionysius who built the great walls that Archimedes repaired, seventeen miles of them in a rough triangle, enclosing the commanding heights of Epipolae within them, and it was he who tired of the oiled flattery of his courtier Damocles and invited him to dinner. Damocles, in the middle of a panegyric on the qualities of his patron, looked up and saw a great sword, suspended by a single hair, immediately above his head, an episode that has provided indifferent writers and speakers with a favoured cliché for more than two millennia. Dionysius wrote very bad verse plays and raged when he failed to win a prize at a drama competition in Athens for *The Ransom of Hector*. He was succeeded by his son who was tutored by Plato – unsuccessfully, as Dionysius II tired very quickly of Euclidean geometry and Pythagorean numbers. Plato returned to Athens, narrowly avoiding his death. The Syracusans in turn tired of Dionysius II and deposed him after twelve years. He wasn't half the chap his father had been.

Narrative

It was raining heavily when he went to the telephone box the next day to call his solicitor, who had nothing to report.

"All you've given me is a possible surname. That's not much to go on." Simon suggested a solution, to hire a private investigator. "You can afford it."

"Do you know one?"

He did, a former policewoman who had retired early. "She mostly does divorce work. She's good at finding people."

Aengus thought for a moment, then saw that the impending arrival of summer made the decision simple. He agreed.

The weather kept the men indoors that day, doing maintenance jobs on machinery, sorting tools. He found it hard to focus on his work, his mind elsewhere, and as the working day neared its end he decided to begin his nocturnal watch earlier than usual.

He left his cottage soon after darkness, hearing the calls of the owls and a fight in a heronry, paused to look at the dull shine of the river in the almost total darkness, fastened his old waxed coat to keep out the misting rain, and set off.

He followed the riverbank for a few hundred yards, then cut into a wood, the wind keening through the tops of the trees overhead, as if lamenting the wet spring. He walked steadily like a man who knew his way, using an inner sense of direction to bring him out at the point he sought.

That point was close to the main road, beyond Seth's house. He crossed that road in the darkness, waiting until the headlights of a car swept past, then vaulted a three-barred gate and circled across the field behind the building. This would bring him to Seth's back yard. As he crept closer he saw torch lights in the yard and as he grew closer still he heard low-pitched voices drift to him on the wind. He crouched, satisfied that Seth was at his work, and waited.

At first he heard only a few snatched phrases. Then he saw the shapes of two men when a torch was briefly switched on, one a thick-set figure who seemed displeased. Aengus settled to watch and listen.

He heard the sound of a car's engine a few minutes later and saw headlights swing towards the yard, and ducked, concealing himself behind a broken water-barrel. The car drove into the yard, catching Seth and a small thin man in its headlights. Seth gesticulated and the yard went dark. Aengus saw little then, catching only a few words as the three huddled together in the light rain, talking urgently, but thought he heard Seth say: "Do the job and leave. Take this. Throw it in the canal when you finish."

Aengus strained his eyes in the darkness but could not see what passed between them. Drugs? No, they would not throw those away. A weapon of some kind, a gun perhaps? His spine felt cold. The man answered in a low voice, then went to his car. The courtesy light showed a glimpse of a neat man of medium-size, wearing a tie. He might have been an accountant, or a local authority clerk, Aengus thought, were it not for the presence of Seth. The car drove away.

A torch flicked on again as the two figures crossed the yard. The back door of the house opened. A tall woman showed in the gap of light, standing there while Seth and the smaller man passed her. Aengus tensed, then relaxed. The figure was that of Kate. The door closed.

It opened soon after, disclosing Seth and the small man, their arms loaded with bags. The yard was dark once more until the little man turned on a torch and pointed it at the open rear doors. Seth grunted as he laid down the load, and while the other's sack was also laid on the floor of the van he said: "Clear?"

"I got it all right," said the van driver nervously. "I got my head screwed on."

"Keep it there," said Seth, and slammed the van door.

Aengus crouched while the van drove away, then saw Seth enter the house. The rain pattered unnoticed on his coat. He felt cold, then hot, wondering whether he had witnessed the prelude to an execution.

His immediate instinct was to leave, to put distance between himself and the menace of Seth. The rain grew heavier, and he stayed at that spot as if his feet had taken root there, slowly recovering. Perhaps he had been mistaken, he reasoned. Perhaps all he had overheard was merely a sordid drug deal, and his imagination had supplied the rest. Then he remembered the purposeful look of the man in a suit and the calm way he had dealt with the menace of Seth. Still standing in the rain, he replayed Seth's instructions in his mind, knowing in his heart that the man was someone far more dangerous and terrible than a drug dealer.

At the same time his instinct told him that he must follow events where they led him. The feeling of horror began to subside. He would wait a little longer. He saw lights go on in two of the upstairs rooms. The curtains were open in the bedroom at the left of the house and as he watched he saw a slight figure come to the window and stand there, silhouetted against the light in the room. It stood there for so long that Aengus thought he had been seen, then realised that that was impossible in this light. The figure closed the curtains, but not before Aengus had recognised the figure of the girl. For a wild moment he thought of attracting her attention by throwing something to rap against her windows, but the moment of madness passed.

Was Seth going to bed, too? As he waited he saw the light in another upstairs room go out, but a downstairs light remained. Had Seth forgotten to switch it off, or did he mean to go downstairs again? Perhaps he already approached the door and was about to appear at any moment.

It grew colder, but he did not notice, gripped by a conviction that the events of the night had not finished. The tawny owls were out, calling in the woods behind him, keeping him company. The downstairs light still shone.

When his limbs began to cramp he moved a few feet, taking a fresh position by a broken fence post, his eyes rarely leaving the back door, yet he was taken unawares when Seth left the house.

It was the sound of a light footfall at the side of the building that alerted Aengus. He peered into the darkness to his right and saw a strange silhouette, like a hunchback, against the starlight. The silhouette straightened, and Aengus heard the slight sound of metal closing against metal. Seth the cunning, unaware that he was watched but careful by instinct, had left the house through a window. Aengus shook his head. For all his own nightcraft, he knew that Seth would have eluded him had he not closed the window so firmly. How he had manoeuvred his bulk through the window with scarcely a sound was a mystery, but a clear signal that Seth was a formidable enemy.

He listened to the man making his way across the yard, wondering whether Seth would drive or walk. He stared into the darkness, listening for a footfall or the click of a car door. As he did so the headlights of a car on the road betrayed a shadow on the wall near the cottage's front gate. Seth had ignored his car and was setting out on foot. Aengus moved silently to his left along the fence and waited. In the waning rear lights of the car he saw Seth's outline as he crossed the road at an unhurried pace, waiting until he would not be visible in the driver's mirror.

Silent and furtive though Seth was, he could not conceal himself completely as he turned into the lane that ran down to the river. Lights from the nearby cottages caught him as he passed them in a crouch. The headlights of another car outlined him for an instant before he ducked behind a wall. Then he was down the lane and into the darkness.

Yet Aengus could follow him here, as he knew the ground as well by night as he did by day. Once he had satisfied himself that Seth had not crossed the wooden bridge at the end of the lane, Aengus turned into the wood, ran through it until he reached a clearing, and waited, knowing that Seth could not pass without outlining himself against the lighter surface of the chalkstream. If

Seth were making for the estate buildings, pass he must unless he had also taken to the woods. Aengus guessed he would feel more secure if he kept to the riverbank.

He had waited only a few moments before the commotion began. A moorhen, deep in the reedbeds, sensed the vibration of the heavy man's soft footfalls, shrieked, and scuttled across the dark river, alarming a flight of mallard that had been asleep under the willows on the opposite bank. The mallard began to run across the water, wings flapping, quacking, alarming the roosting wood-pigeons in the woods. The riverbank rang with noise.

Aengus smiled grimly. Seth might be expert at leaving buildings like a wraith, and could probably disappear in a town or city without a sign, but he plainly did not know a riverbank at night.

The quacking and squawking diminished. Apart from the occasional mutterings from the moorhens and the chuckle of the chalkstream, the area was quiet. Seth would probably wait to see if anyone responded to the noise. A fox or a deer might have caused the same commotion, although a fox might bring a keeper with a rifle and a lamp.

The wind was rising, bringing a spattering of rain. It passed through the wood with a swishing sound, the trees swaying around Aengus as he waited, crouched in a thicket, head cocked.

He saw Seth's outline against a rare patch of moonlight a few moments later. The burly figure had moved nearer the wood, presumably to avoid the wildlife. It moved on a few yards, then stopped abruptly when a figure like a white crucifix rose to attack it.

Aengus could hear the furious hissing above the rain as the cob swan, its wings spread wide to magnify its size, rose angrily from the nest on the bank. He saw Seth draw back, flash his torch at the creature, and give the enraged bird plenty of room as he circled it.

Aengus re-entered the wood, moving swiftly once he was beyond earshot, planning to arrive at one of the upstream bridges before Seth reached it. When the figure approached the bridge and remained on the same bank, he saw that Seth was not crossing the estate, but heading for its centre.

The rain's intensity increased, a building up of the weather that had made this spring one of the wettest on record. He drew his hood over his cap, and pondered. Seth was trespassing on the estate, and had been since he reached the lowest bridge, but that was of little account in law. Aengus could face him and probably force him to return to his house, but Seth could simply return on another night, and by then he would know that Aengus watched him from the darkness, that Aengus might even have observed the events in the yard. The element of surprise would be lost, and the initiative would pass. Aengus would be in danger himself, judging by Seth's record and the words that he had overheard this night.

He pursued the figure with determination, again used his tactics of circling through the woods and heavy thickets before dropping down to the riverbank to wait for his man. At one stage Seth came close to surprising him, arriving before Aengus expected him. Only the sound of heavy breathing as the figure moved at a pace unusual for so large a man saved Aengus from crashing into him. Had Seth flashed his torch a yard to his right he might have seen his follower, but the man seemed oblivious, intent on reaching his destination as quickly as possible.

By then they had reached the point on the estate where a carrier joined the river, near the path to Aengus' cottage. The farm buildings and estate offices lay to the north-east. Open fields lay between river and buildings. If Aengus were not to be seen in the lights from the buildings, he would have to take a chance on Seth's intentions and reach the outskirts of the buildings first, to lie in wait. He moved very quickly, using the cover of the hedges and the outskirts of the buildings, and reached a low wall that enclosed a cattle yard.

It was then that he lost Seth, and knew his guess had been wrong. He waited for ten minutes, crouched behind the wall, until it was clear that the man had not chosen the route that Aengus had expected him to take. He moved to the other side of the yard, expecting to glimpse him against the lights of the farm buildings, hoping that the agent's dog would sense the enemy within the walls. There was nothing to catch his eye, and the dog did not bark. Aengus grew more concerned. What was Seth's purpose tonight?

He waited for a few more minutes, a deep sense of urgency gripping him. It was raining hard, the steady downpour deadening the usual nocturnal noises of a farm and the little hamlet of the estate, sharply reducing his chances of hearing a chance noise of an intruder. He felt a moment of despair, then forced himself to think clearly.

He had lost his man. To blunder around in the hope of finding him invited discovery, or worse. He would return to the main road and telephone the agent from there, he decided, cursing himself for not having a mobile phone, a luxury he had not realised he needed.

He set off, very quietly, choosing the quickest route that would pass his own cottage. The rain was dying, the wind rising, driving the clouds before them. A raven croaked, once, twice. Aengus halted.

The half-moon appeared intermittently in the gaps. In its light he caught the smallest glimpse of a sinister face under the crack willow and recognised it. Seth crouched there, watching the cottage of Aengus.

The Book of Aengus

He is well named. An earlier Seth murdered his brother Osiris, dismembered his body and threw the parts in the Nile. Isis, sister to both and wife to Osiris, searched the river, put the body together again and Osiris was reborn, as he would be every year in the annual rebirth of the Nile, as the living god, the first Pharaoh.

Seth, a primitive, angry god who ruled Upper Egypt before the dynastic kings or Pharaohs arrived, was introduced into the Osiris/Isis cycle as the embodiment of evil, the ritual slayer of Osiris. Horus the Child, son of Osiris and Isis, avenges him and the stories of their battles are told in the temples and in mystery plays during successive ages.

I saw the other, living Seth as an aboriginal, angry god last night as the moon caught his face. It's hard to control your imagination when you see murderous evil lurking beneath a tree, watching your home. It's even harder when your imagination shrieks that he's not mortal.

I waited for him as he waited for me. Each minute seemed an age as my pulse raced and I tried to breathe slowly. I glimpsed him only occasionally when the clouds parted. After a time – perhaps half an hour – I looked again and he wasn't there. I closed my eyes for an instant, convinced I was wrong, but he had vanished without a sound. I was careful not to enter the cottage, but slipped away and did not return until dawn, when I found his footmarks beneath the willow.

Narrative

The agent brought them news the next day as they worked.

"Did you see the police car at Seth's house this morning?"

Aengus waited, dreading what might come next.

"Can't say I did," said Sid, glancing at Aengus. Bill looked expressionless.

"He's being questioned again," said the agent, resting his boot on the side of the Mule. "They've been to see me, asking if any of us saw or heard anything last night." All three were quiet, waiting.

"None of you? We were probably all in our beds by then."

"What's up?" asked Sid quietly, speaking for all three.

"Some criminal was killed in Swindon last night as he opened his door. The police say it was more like a cold-blooded execution than a murder. They think Seth is connected."

"Sounds like it," said Sid phlegmatically. "Wouldn't put it past that bugger."

"Of course he had the women as his alibi," said the agent with contempt.

Aengus cleared his throat, his mouth suddenly dry. "Did they back him up?" He was conscious of the sudden gaze of the others.

"Must have," said the agent. "What do you expect from people like that?"

He made his excuses to Sid and left, hastening towards Seth's house. When he paused to think he heard Seth talking to the quiet man wearing a tie, then saw the sinister face waiting under the willow. He could not wait. Bridget must be told that his cottage was watched.

His luck held. He saw her leave the house to walk in the woods and waited for her on the path.

She gave a low cry of alarm when she saw him, then listened as he told her of how he had followed Seth and lost him. "When I came past my cottage I saw him hiding there, watching. At dawn I found his footmarks under the tree."

Surprise turned to concern. "You might have died." She looked directly at him and said: "He has killed many times. It's his nature, and now he suspects you."

"Of what?"

"Of knowing me."

His eyes searched the clearing, ears cocked for unusual sounds, but heard only birdsong.

"He has killed someone close to him before." Her voice was barely audible.

He stiffened. "How do you know?"

She lifted her head. "He told me."

"Who did he kill?" He kept his voice gentle.

She looked down, her voice scarcely a whisper.

"He killed his mother."

The Book of Aengus

He killed his mother, almost certainly by poisoning her, then set off on the life he has led since. Bridget has known this for a short time, since Seth somehow forced her to live in his house. Her father never knew. The woman would have died in time, but Seth could not wait. He had to kill.

He killed her because she forsook him as a child, he told Bridget one night when he was very angry. She left her husband and her son to drink and sleep with any man who wanted her. Her husband forgave her. Her son did not, and before he reached adolescence he began to plan her death. He told Bridget that he had killed her in such a way that only a postmortem would have detected it.

Why did he tell her? I can think of only one reason. To convince Bridget he was prepared to kill someone else.

The ancients thought matricide – even what some might call justifiable matricide – to be the worst of crimes. Aeschylus sets his trilogy of the *Oresteia* – his greatest work – around the death of Clytemnestra at the hands of her son Orestes, who kills her in revenge for the murder of her husband Agamemnon.

I have the lines of the chorus of the captured Trojan women:

And though all streams united gave
The treasures of their limpid wave,
To purify from gore;
The hand, polluted once with blood,
Though washed in every silver flood
Is foul for ever more.

Orestes slays his mother and her worthless lover Aegisthus, and is pursued by the *Erinyes*, the Furies, the hell-hags with brass wings and claws who carried out the vengeance of the gods. He is favoured by Apollo who condones his crime and takes him to Athene. She casts her white pebble in favour of his pardon and placates the Furies, renaming them the *Eumenides*, the kindly ones. The *Oresteia* is a quarrel among the gods themselves, half of them siding with the Furies, just as they divided their allegiances between Greeks and Trojans. If they were with us today none would side with Seth of the foul hand.

The Greek

Hippokrates being with Himilco and the Carthaginian army in Sicily at the time, retaking cities from the Romans, it was Epikydes who sent his men to seize me and bring me before an assembly he had secretly convened, an assembly made up of the men who represented the most corrupt and unscrupulous factions in the city.

The spokesman said I had been implicated in a plot, that I was known to have been sympathetic to the former alliance with Rome, that I was related by blood to a tyrant who had denied the citizens of Syracuse the liberty that had now been restored to them, that it was known that I had admired and loved this tyrant, but that they would be inclined to spare my life if I retired from politics and remained in my house. Epikydes would take charge of the defences.

I saw that they feared me because I was popular with the citizens and the soldiers, and told them such charges were baseless. I challenged them: when had I engaged in the politics of Syracuse? How could it be, when I had responded to Hippokrates' order to take on the defence of the city, and conducted that defence so loyally, that I could plot to turn Syracuse over to the Romans, who would slaughter the citizens with greater eagerness than they had at Leontinoi? Let my accusers come forward, I said. There was a silence while they looked at each other, then I turned to leave. As I did so, Epikydes took me aside and told me in a low tone that I should let it be known that I was sick, fit only for rest, unless I was tired of life. I saw then that they did not dare kill me.

I was abruptly dismissed, without the meanest courtesy. A file of soldiers, deeply shamed by my treatment, escorted me to my house. I was free to walk in the *polis*, but not to attend any meetings of the citizens, secret or otherwise. My movements would be watched. If any Syracusan questioned this, he would be told that my mind was deranged by strain and age.

This was shocking treatment, but worse was to follow for the *polis*. The generals I had temporarily appointed or promoted were demoted or removed. Hermokrates was assassinated, as were his wife and family. They said he plotted to turn Syracuse over to the Romans, although he had done so much to save it. The rulers promoted their friends or relatives, mainly the generals whom Hiero did not trust, and one by one they murdered their enemies. Some of the oldest Syracusan families, the backbone of the *polis*, suddenly disappeared. A few who had been sympathetic to the Romans escaped. Others were executed as traitors. Their wealth was confiscated on one ground or another. The period seemed even worse than the Rule of Thirty in Athens when the Athenians lost the war with the Spartans. Religious festivals were neglected. The Syracusans became fearful and distrustful, the unity forged in the battle dissipating. Our successive victories seemed forgotten. Few dared to speak to me. Trade ceased, the ships rotting on the beaches. As the siege tightened, I became isolated, viewed as a mad old man. If there were those who knew otherwise, they held their tongues, perhaps as fearful for my life as for their own. My work for Syracuse was finished, however I might wish otherwise.

For a time I did little, unable to absorb this terrible change. I found it impossible to work, even to think clearly. My sense of purpose seemed to have vanished. The nights were particularly disturbing, long hours of unsleeping anguish, filled with memories of those I had lost, those who had gone before. Images of friends and family haunted me. The shades of the dead, Greek and Roman, surrounded my couch until the hopeless dawn.

One night, unable to bear their presence, I sat at my table in the *exedra*, despairing of sleep. The air seemed heavy, the night clouded, the trickle of the clock the only sound. My spirits were as low as I could remember. My mind wandered aimlessly, hardly conscious that the moon had appeared from behind a cloud, seeming to hover in the sky. The *exedra* filled with light, I looked up, and my senses began to clear. After a time I rose from my bench and offered to the Goddess, then watched the moon go down, as I had watched it as a boy, before I went to bed. I slept the sun around and awoke fresh and determined, my mind as sharp as it had ever been. I began to consider the future once more, and my own situation.

I despised these rulers and the men who fawned on them, but unless I engaged in some ugly plot, my work for the defence of Syracuse was finished. That was not a choice. Such plotting repelled me. Every part of my being shrieked against it. For good or bad I had taken an oath not to engage in one.

I was left, then, with nothing but a strange freedom that had been denied to me for several years while I did all I could for Syracuse. My sense of having a purpose returned, slowly and almost imperceptibly, but definitely. Over the next few days I began to sense what that purpose was, that such time as remained to me would be devoted to my final work, the fulfilment of a promise to Pheidias the astronomer, accepting his last request as a sacred command. It had rung in my mind every day since his death, a persistent call, yet one that had a curious form of fatalism underlying it, as I began to sense that one last great labour might remain, and that my only course was to pursue it. The moments when my pulse began to quicken, absent for some time, came back to me.

An idea took and broke ground over the following weeks, without the certainty of a mathematical hypothesis where the proof frequently came with the proposition. It originated from someone whose work I knew well, and whose hypothesis had constantly returned to me even when I was occupied by the urgency of the labour Hiero had given me. Philosophers from

Pythagoras to Plato to Aristotle and the Stoics had told us the earth lay at the centre of the cosmos, but some years before I had studied the work of Aristarkhos of Samos, who wrote that the order of the heavens was much different to that we supposed.

I had seen him at Alexandria, but he was considerably older than I, and rarely visited the Library when I was there. I knew only that some of the astronomers thought he was too obsessed with his own theories. He said that, contrary to all accepted philosophical thought, the fixed stars and the sun did not move, the sun was more distant than the moon, the cosmos was much larger than we believed, and earth and planets revolved around the sun in a circular motion. As my energy returned and Epikydes' men followed me everywhere, I began to consider whether his hypothesis might be the basis of an explanation of the movement of the planets, the explanation that Pheidias sought.

I pause here to say that I came to know the work of Aristarkhos well after he died, and you may know that I had used his hypothesis about the size of the universe in my work *Psammites*, or *The Sand Reckoner*, but I had done so only as an excuse – a means of rising to a challenge – to create a numbering system that possessed a power hitherto unknown to mathematics.

Let me be very clear about that. Aristarkhos had proposed a cosmos of an almost unthinkable size. That had set me thinking at the time only about one of the challenges such a size presented. I had wondered whether it might be possible to calculate how many of the smallest objects that existed would be needed to fill it, taking a grain of sand as an example of the infinitesimal and assigning a given volume to it. So I had constructed a number system to show how a mathematician could calculate the size of the cosmos itself, even a cosmos of the size that Aristarkhos suggested. I had used these numbers to demonstrate how many grains of sand it would take to fill it. I wrote a work on it called *Archai*, or *Principles*, which I sent to Zeuxippos, but I repeat to you that at that time I had not seriously considered the validity of the hypothesis itself, only of the challenge to deduce a system of arithmetic that could simply and easily produce number to infinity.

As a further aside, I tell you that the choice of a grain of sand was inspired by a philosopher whose work, you may remember, I studied closely at Alexandria. Demokritos of Abdera, whose nature was said to be so good that he laughed at everything except his work, had long before hypothesised that everything in the cosmos was made up of individual pieces of matter so small they could not be reduced in size. Each was an *atomos*, uncuttable, so tiny it could not be seen. The hypothesis could not be proven, of course, and Aristotle was to dismiss it, but I had the *atomos* of Demokritos in mind as I chose the grain of sand as the smallest unit we could see. Let us move on from there.

I began my task by reading again the works of Aristarkhos, and of how he had attempted to measure the relative distances of the moon and sun. He concluded that the sun was far more distant from the earth than we believed, and therefore much larger. Just as the moon orbited the larger body of the earth, so earth and planets revolved around the larger body of the sun. He said that the sun is further away from the earth than the moon because he had read carefully the records of how the moon eclipsed the sun.

Aristarkhos chose a special time for his observations to judge the relative distances from the earth of moon and sun, a part of the day when the moon was still visible. For such an observation, the moon must be half-full, so the line of light bisects its surface. This line is therefore at a right-angle to the sun when viewed from the earth. He measured the angle of the sun from the earth, using a staff which pierced a small leather disc. He pointed the staff directly at the sun, protecting his eye by adjusting the disc forwards or backwards along the shaft to blot out the sun's surface, then took the angle of the staff's direction. From the result he created a right-angled triangle, with sun, moon and earth at each vertex, the point where the sides meet, and, using the law of the right-angled triangle that legend said came from Pythagoras, he was able to say, from the length of the hypotenuse, that the sun was as much as twenty times further from the earth than the moon. This was incredible to other astronomers.

As the watchers outside my house grew bored and the fighting went on elsewhere in Sicily I, an outcast in my own city, settled to concentrate on what I knew would be my last work, this time not as a mathematician such as I was, but as an astronomer, a task for which my father had told me long before that I did not have the necessary patience. I was about to test the truth of that as I prepared to acquire as much knowledge about the movement of the planets as I could. To do so, I must enter a shrine.

I knew I must read through every roll of observations that Pheidias had left, including the copied work of the Babylonians, and examine them as closely as I could. To do so meant I must enter his room which I had left untouched since his death, and remove every roll he had stored there. That may seem a simple task to you. To me it felt as if I disturbed his grave.

It was several days before I summoned up the courage, but one dawn I entered his room for the first time since his funeral. The silence when I did so seemed very solemn, yet welcoming, reminding me of how close we were. His presence in it seemed real, as if he would appear at any moment. I caught my breath. There were the rolls and his wax tablets, his styluses and the long sighting tubes that I had not buried with him, all neatly arrayed in rows and tiers as he had left them. Then I saw, with a great sadness, that they were covered in a fine layer of dust, and I remembered that I had banned the slaves from his room.

I took the first roll, gently brushed the dust from it, and opened it slowly, with great care. It contained a series of observations, each neatly titled by time, a certain day, in a certain month, in a certain year of an Olympiad, with brief descriptions summarising his thoughts.

With a heavy heart I removed them all to my own room, began to read, and Pheidias' relationship with the heavens gradually began to open to me. He had clearly intended these rolls to be read by a successor astronomer, and had left behind him every possible aid to help that successor.

Even so, they took months of intensive reading, starting with the first, and I have to tell you it was the hardest task I had ever undertaken. Every observation reminded me of him, and the number of angles he took was almost bewildering. Each *parapegma*, the calendar of each constellation's rising and setting, was filled with detail written in the hand that I remembered so well. His notes on the Babylonians' observations filled some of the longest rolls, long enough to stretch around the *exedra*. I waded through them all as through a strong tide that flowed against me, patiently, frequently comparing an earlier observation with a later one, filling rolls of my own. There were many diagrams in addition, carefully drawn, all attempting to show the movements of the red planet, together with possible explanations. Without his explanatory notes the task would have been impossible. I knew him to be thorough, sometimes almost ponderously so, but even I was surprised at such thoughtful detail, such acts of kindness to a possible successor who might never appear. I thought how strange it was that it should be me. Even then I did not guess the truth.

When I reached the last roll I saw for whom they were intended. Inside, attached to a diagram that projected the movement of the red planet on to the papyrus as a series of loops or spirals, I found a letter written only days before his death.

My son, this is the culmination of my work.

Long before you were born I read Plato and his belief that the cosmos did not come about by chance, that its order was too good for it to be in a state of chaos. I put aside his geometrical god, his demiourgos, *but saw both logic and beauty in his arguments that the best principles in geometry were present in the proportions and harmony of nature. That came as easily to me as it will to you.*

Plato used the argument of teleology, as Aristotle did after him. Each said that this order had a purpose, that it was directed to an end, which Plato said was to produce the best possible order of the cosmos, that it was so because it was best for it to be so.

I could not explain why teleology was not central to the cosmos, but I instinctively shunned it. There is a logical, physical explanation for the movement of the planets, and it can be proven by observation if the astronomer does not rely only on appearances. That was my guiding principle throughout.

The Pythagoreans proposed that the earth is a sphere, and observation of the earth's shadow on the moon proved this to be true, a proposition that created a sensation at the time among philosophers and those who understood the implications of such a statement.

Ekphantos the Pythagorean proposed hypothetically that the earth revolved on an axis, on the basis that, as the stars are fixed, the revolution of the stars above our heads is apparent although unreal, that it is the nightly revolution of the earth that causes them to revolve. That seems probable to me. It is easy to see that the stars that appear to revolve at the quickest rate are those above the northern axis of the earth, such as the constellations of Kassiopeia and the Great Bear. Heraklides of Pontus supported this, as did I, who met Heraklides. Yet none of this explained the wandering movements of the planets.

I will stop here, lest I influence you too much. I will only add that one day we should be able to predict the movements of the planets as easily as the Baby-

lonians could predict an eclipse of the moon. When we do we will begin to know the cosmos.

These works are my gift to you in your labour. Farewell.

Psammites or *The Sand Reckoner*, the work that most appeals to me – perhaps because even I can understand it – was a wonderful achievement, particularly if you are reminded of how clumsy Greek mathematical notation was, based on their alphabet of twenty-two letters, each with a tick to indicate its value. It was a cumbersome system, one of the reasons most Greeks preferred geometry to arithmetic. The work he sent to Zeuxippus vanished.

A myriad was 10,000, and the revolutionary step that Archimedes made in *The Sand Reckoner* was to invent an entirely new number system, using his own symbols, that took the powers of a myriad times a myriad, a myriad times a myriad times a myriad, and so on, up to an astonishing eighty billion ciphers, similar to our own system of inserting as many zeros as we need.

It was beautifully simple, yet totally new, the product of an original genius, and the book that contains it has a dramatic flourish to it. Netz, the scholar who probably knows the works of Archimedes best, says he solved a problem, not like a schoolmaster, but like a conjuror, producing an effect of awed surprise from an audience. It was as if he suspected that the mysteries of the cosmos, ranging from evolution and natural selection to the size of the universe, would require dimensions so great to be calculated that they were beyond the ability of known systems of arithmetic. Very well then, he might have said, he would invent his own. As it turns out, his system would be powerful enough to calculate the number of atoms that we now know are in the entire universe, incredible though that may seem, but I think even he would have been astonished to learn that his grain of sand, the closest he could visualise to the atom of Democritus, contains trillions of the atoms that Rutherford found in the twentieth century.

Orthodox Greek astronomers rejected the ideas of Aristarchus and continued to believe that the earth lay at the centre of all. They had good reasons for doing so. The best of them recorded what they observed, and built their hypotheses from those observations. These hypotheses were to lead to the works of the astronomer Ptolemy of Alexandria and his predecessors, who created the theory of epicycles to explain why some of the planets appeared to travel backwards in loops, and whose teachings were taken as truth for a millennium and a half. Ptolemy's *Almagest*, written around AD 150, explained and accurately predicted the celestial motions, the eclipses and the movements of the planets as they appeared to an observer on earth. Without telescopes, Greek astronomers could record only the movements they saw along their sighting tubes, and they modelled the universe according to what they saw without attempting a physical explanation for its movements, a method known to philosophers as *saving the appearances*.

Even when Copernicus suggested, in the earlier part of the sixteenth century, that the earth travelled around the sun, he clung to the Greeks' epicyles, probably because he was too timid to demolish them. It would take the work of Tycho Brahe and Johannes Kepler to remove them for all time.

I witness the creative energy of Archimedes who invented his version of the calculus to bypass the weakness of the clumsy Greek numerical system which used the letters of the alphabet with dashes and accents and horizontal strokes to distinguish different values, lacked a zero, and wrote fractions as ratios.

Teleology means literally *end-directed* and would afflict philosophy and religion long after Plato. Aristotle believed in it, though not in the Demiurge, a neuter god invented by Plato, a craftsman deity who brought necessary order from chaos to the cosmos. To Aristotle the universe required some form of teleology to come about as it did, and the views of Aristotle dominated philosophy in the West until the seventeenth century, by which stage many religions were infused with the belief that the order of the universe had a divine purpose. Then in the nineteenth century Darwin published his *Origin*, whereupon Marx proclaimed the end of teleology, and Nietzsche hailed the new freedom of man without God.

Narrative

An uneasy truce descended on the area. The weather had turned for the better at last. Seth was quiet, perhaps brooding over his questioning. He did not have visitors, and kept to his house when in the area, sometimes driving away and reappearing at unpredictable times, sometimes not returning for days.

They would have been days of relative peace for Aengus had he not decided to follow Seth in Sid's van. Twice he did so, and twice he failed because he could not risk being seen. The first time he lost Seth on the Cirencester road, the next he trailed him to Lechlade where Seth crossed the Thames and disappeared. He stopped then because the risk of discovery was too great. The solicitor also had little to report, other than that the search continued.

He sought the open skies for relief and climbed the chalk hills to the west of Newbury on a warm Saturday afternoon and rested by Combe Gibbet and the remains of the Iron Age fort. Combe Down gave him a view through his binoculars that was long and clear. He saw the rooftops of the village of Inkpen and the gleam of river and canal, the fresh air filling his lungs. In the distance he saw a large bird circling. He scanned the ground below, idly, and focused suddenly on the tiny figures of a woman and a dog ascending the hill from the north. He watched them for a while, recognition growing. "They're a long way from home," he thought, conviction hardening that they were following him. The figures disappeared behind a fold in the ground, then came into view again.

He waited for them, seeing the figure of the woman grow taller in the clear air, a light breeze ruffling the grasses on the sides of the track in the sunlight. Her dog stopped suddenly as he saw the man and Aengus heard a deep growl that silenced the lark above his head.

As she approached he saw once more, this time closer at hand, a mass of black hair above a face that was almost handsome, a long, bony face with heavy eyebrows, a thin, straight nose and a strong chin. She walked with an easy yet purposeful gait, and as she came up to draw level with him he saw that her eyes were green and that she was almost as tall as he. The dog growled again, the sound coming from deep inside its great frame. When it showed its teeth he was glad to see that its leash looked new. She silenced it immediately with a sharp word, but it continued to glower at him, a deep sound coming continually from the back of its throat.

"You waited for me," she said, her voice surprisingly agreeable.

"You don't mind?"

"Why should I? Our paths have crossed before."

"You know me then, Kate?"

"I've seen you many times, perhaps more times than you know. Now let me sit here, as my legs are tired, and I'm no longer young." The dog settled beside her at her gesture, eyeing the man.

"Yet you look strong."

"I'm strong enough," she said as she settled on the grass. He felt her look as she scanned him. He returned her gaze, but saw nothing but darkness beyond the green depths.

"Do we meet by chance?" he asked after a pause. A pair of walkers gave them space, wary of her dog. She did not reply until they were beyond earshot.

"You mean, have I followed you? Perhaps I have, but it's time we spoke." Her jet-black hair rose as the breeze strengthened, exposing the gaunt face and the long ear-rings that seemed her sole concession to femininity. She savoured the cool air, head held high as she turned to him, her presence remarkably forceful, projecting a power he could not explain.

"You're curious about me, aren't you?" she asked, "curious enough to follow me."

He saw little to gain by evasion. "Yes. I've followed you, as you've followed me."

"What do you want from me?" A party of walkers circled the double gibbet, one of them gesticulating and talking loudly in a voice that carried on the breeze. A woodpigeon flapped away to the higher ground.

"I think you know," he said evenly. "She needs help." The voice of the guide grew louder. The walkers passed near them, adjusting their rucksacks. The dog watched them, a rippling shiver running along its pelt.

Kate waited until the walkers were out of earshot. "Perhaps she is beyond help."

He waited. She turned her gaze back to him.

"Perhaps you are also beyond help," she said matter-of-factly. "Tell me, what do you see when you think of me?"

"I see a blackness," he said, almost brutally.

"You see very well," she said easily. "You also have a gift. What do I see when I look at you?"

"Well?

"I see three things. A full moon that lights emptied fields. A hill. Death."

She left him, rising gracefully from the ground, her dog pulling at its leash, and walked on up the hill. The shadows were lengthening, the sun sinking into the darkening green as he left the down.

The Book of Aengus

The full moon that she spoke of may be the harvest moon, when the fields have been cut, but I think she meant *Lughnasadh*, an early harvest festival in August. The Neolithic people were agrarian. Unlike the earlier nomadic peoples, they sowed and harvested. We know the Celts divided their year according to the harvest cycle, and it seems likely that they inherited this from the Stone Age peoples, so I'll rely on that as my guide if I'm to take her warning seriously. For some reason I do.

The Celts or Gaels in pre-Christian Ireland had eight big festivals each year, adhering to a solar calendar as the Egyptians did, beginning with *Imbolc*, or St Brigid's Day, the first day of spring, which is probably of Stone Age origin. Four of these seem to have been agricultural, fire festivals, symbolic of fire deities. These are known as the True Quarters, and they come down to us from Celtic Ireland – perhaps the best guide we have – as *Imbolc*; *Bealtaine* or May Day – the first day of summer; *Lughnasadh*, autumn; and *Samhain*, winter. The next festival will be *Bealtaine*, the first day of May. Is that the festival the Greek told me to attend?

A way of cross-checking the answer may be to look at the festivals of Artemis and compare them. The Greeks held a very large festival to her at the full moon in late March or early April, but the succeeding one does not seem to occur before the last day of May and, while it specifically honours her as the goddess of the full moon, the dates seem too far apart. That may rule out *Bealtaine*. There is a festival to her at the full moon in August, and that would coincide with *Lughnasadh*. I think *Lughnasadh*, or Lammas, is our festival, as it honours the Great Goddess whose symbol is the moon.

One of the difficulties with knowing Greek mythology is that it was constantly changing. Deities were promoted, demoted, or welcomed for the first time, probably from another civilisation. By the Hellenistic era Artemis seems to have become a secondary goddess in different parts of the Greek world, except perhaps in Asia Minor. The fact that in the Olympian pantheon she is the daughter of Zeus and Leto and twin of Apollo is a clear example of the arbitrary way in which they changed the chronology, as Artemis is much older than Zeus, who was a late god in his Olympian role. The Greeks also seem to have performed similar anachronisms with Leto, who was originally much earlier than Olympian Zeus, but was later presented as his contemporary.

All the evidence I have is that Artemis is an original moon goddess. Perhaps it was later that she became part of the lunar trinity as the goddess of the full moon, Selene being the waxing moon, and Hecate the waning, the dark deity who turned the moon into darkness for three days and who later came to be seen as a witch. Cerberus, who guarded the gate into Hades, was her dog, and dogs were strongly associated with Hecate, as Virgil knew:

The Earth began to bellow, trees to dance
And howling dogs in glimmering light advance
Ere Hecate came.

Brigid is said in some legends to have borne children, which is more suggestive of the Mother Goddess. Both were virgin goddesses, but the image we have of Artemis, as a chaste, beautiful virgin who had Actaeon hunted to death when he saw her bathing naked, is probably a late one, and the evidence points to her originating during an earlier era, one at least as old as the Bronze Age. There seems to have been a connection with Minoan Crete, which would make her very early and more clearly identifiable as the Moon Goddess. The early Minoan Period seems to have had a wholly matrilineal society. It was probably during a later period that the myths evolved of the cow goddess and the bull god, clearly symbols of moon and sun.

Celtic mythology was as liquid as Greek, with deities promoted, demoted, merged, or allowed to languish, but it is very clear that most of these deities pre-dated the Celts in Ireland, and probably the Tuatha de Danaan, the people of that other moon goddess, Dana. It pre-dated, too, the Fomorians, and the Firbolgs, if those people indeed existed, and may well take us back into the Stone

Age. That's conjecture, and very unscholarly, but we have enough to my mind to enable us to identify Artemis, among many others, as a Great Goddess.

What do I do with all this? Obey. He tells me to go to the next festival to Artemis. I estimate that to be early in August. I will go. Where? Probably Silbury Hill. The evidence, at a minimum, points to it being a votive hill where the Great Goddess was worshipped, particularly at harvest time, and it was where I believe I felt a communion with her.

We know now at least part of what Archimedes seeks, and it should not surprise us. His father was an astronomer who left him a mystery before he died, and many people return to the questions of their youth as they grow older. His search seems a natural evolution in his life, particularly in view of his later work when he had moved on to arithmetic, to invent his own language of mathematics.

He probes the mysteries and proportions of the universe like a good philosopher, in the belief or hope that these will one day yield the secret of the planets, possibly even the secrets of Creation itself. Perhaps he expects the Goddess to reveal some of these truths to me at Silbury Hill, and perhaps that is why Kate tells me that the full moon at *Lughnasadh* will be a time of great danger for me. Yet I have no choice and, if I am truthful to myself, I wish to go.

Narrative

The riverbank was alive with bird song and the sun was lifting above the alders when Aengus heard the raven call and opened his cottage door. Seth stood on the path, a stone's toss from the cottage, unmoving.

He looked as menacing as before, his shock of reddish hair gleaming in the sunlight, the reptilian eyes fixed on Aengus.

"What do you want?" Aengus called, recovering from his surprise.

The man considered him.

Aengus spoke again: "Why are you here?"

The figure turned without a word and walked away.

The air, full of tension a few moments before, seemed to clear again as the thick figure receded down the riverbank.

Aengus looked up at the raven whose tail swayed in the fresh breeze. "He's mortal, after all," he said to the bird, who cocked an intelligent eye at him. "We flushed him out."

The raven croaked, rubbed its beak on the eaves, then looked greedily at Aengus, who fetched a piece of gristle for it. It hit the roof, ricocheted, and landed on the ground. The raven dropped from the roof and approached the morsel with a slight swagger.

Aengus tried to analyse his reaction to the appearance of Seth. To his surprise, it did not affect him as it had when he had seen Seth watching his cottage at night, and he found himself looking about him with approval and pleasure instead of the sense of horror he had felt before. The young catkins on the willows and the colourful bursts of primroses cheered him. He saw a kingfisher dart by an alder on the far bank as he walked upstream. The sun caught a flash of iridescent colour as the bird hovered, wings whirring, entered the water with a little splash, re-emerged with a tiny chub and disappeared in a hole in the side of the bank.

The walkway led through banks of daffodils, swaying stooks of yellow and green in the warm spring breeze. Willows and alders were alive with nesting birds. The sounds of mallard and moorhen came from the reeds. A trout rose to take a sedge, leaving a ring of circles on the water.

The Book of Aengus

Strangely, I wasn't afraid. I sensed the menace of the man, and knew his threat was real, yet I felt relief because at last I know him for the enemy he is. The horror I felt of him on the night I found him watching my home receded, to become something real, human, tangible, instead of a fearsome, amorphous shape in my imagination. I feel I am coming closer to understanding him and that great inner power he radiates, closer to comprehending the nature of the evil which programmes him to possess and kill and hate. Bridget has yet to grasp this, naturally enough. She feels off balance, appallingly vulnerable, unable to measure the threat and therefore to deal with it, probably because he's almost always present. I'll try to deal with her fear, to pin it down and place it in some form of perspective, to show her that at least part of it springs from her own imagination. That would be a great step forward. I'd like to take her to the outdoors, on to the Downs where the wind will breathe fresh vitality at her, to Avebury and Silbury perhaps, and persuade her that there's hope. If I can't, I must act alone.

His curiosity has the better of him. He watches my cottage because he wishes to know who or what stalks the woods at night and sets the cocks crowing, whether it's human or spirit, whether it's something he can deal with as he deals with every mortal enemy. I'll keep him guessing. He'll kill me without a flicker of remorse if he finds me with Bridget, yet I know I do not have the supernatural to fear, but a throwback to a level of evil that the fools of the modern world think has vanished into myth.

The other Seth, the aboriginal god of Lower Egypt, possessed the same terrible anger, and was a paradigm for Satan.

Narrative

A light breeze ruffled the beeches on the tops of the downs as Aengus and Bridget walked past Old Eagle, along Temple Bottom to Glory Ann, then across Monkton Down towards Avebury.

It was a Saturday, a week after his meeting with Kate. Seth had gone, telling Kate he would return on the following day.

"Come with me," said Aengus.

"Where?"

"Into Wiltshire. To the Downs."

She looked at her shoes. He followed her look. "They'll do." He smiled and saw she was torn, unsure of this fleeting freedom.

A longing for an open sky overcame her doubt or fear. She gave in and sat on the bench, waiting for him while he made sandwiches, her gaze resting on the lines of daffodils along the riverside paths, below the greening alders and willows. Blue tits, robins, blackbirds and wrens, all seemingly tame, hopped back and forth to the porch rail to take the seeds Aengus had placed for them, while a goldfinch turned its bright red face to her as it wrestled with an insect on the grass a few feet away.

They set off, waited for the bus and when it arrived he sat as close to her as possible. Then they walked, following the rights of way and the bridle paths, Aengus accommodating his long stride to hers.

The sun came out and the young wheat and rape created a fresh, green landscape that rolled away from them to the tall beech stands in the distance. The hedgerows were filled with primroses, celandines and nesting birds. A lark sounded above to their right, and the rarer corn buntings called to them with strange cries. She watched a raven circling a rookery, her eyes regaining a sparkle.

He spoke as they walked of the chalk country of Wiltshire, more than half of the county, that stretched from Burbage to Devizes. On the other side of the Vale of Pewsey was the Plain. "We're on the Marlborough Downs here. It's full of history – Stone Age history in particular. Yet the landscape is recent in many ways."

"How would it have changed?"

Once, of course, it had been covered by small-leaved lime trees, before man had begun to clear it. When it was too bare, man had relented. The beech clumps on the down tops, for one thing, he said, were not native, but planted to enhance the landscape two centuries before. "The chalk is thin and won't support trees with deep roots, but beech has shallow roots and likes lime." He pointed to the fresh green foliage on the trees whose leaves a few weeks before had been a reddish colour. "There's a lot to be said for a wet spring."

He told her how the downland seemed at its best in darker weather, when the light changed constantly, creating shadowy profiles along the ground, with wide skies that looked as if they had been pulled and stretched.

Alarm calls came from the beeches. They stopped and saw a raven swoop. Rooks flew in all directions, cawing madly.

"What's that bird doing?"

"He's flushing the rooks from their nests."

The breeze shifted to the west and Aengus looked across the down. "Do you see that pair of birds over there? Deceitful lapwing."

"Deceitful?"

"Chaucer called them that. The female draws the attention of anyone who approaches her nest by pretending she's broken a wing or a leg. They're natural actors. She'll flap along the ground as if she's crippled, and sometimes even lie as if dead."

She took his binoculars, unaware that they were used frequently to spy on the house where she lived, and admired the crests and the glossy green backs. "What handsome birds!"

"You talked about weather. There's rain coming."

Her face changed. "Once I liked rain, but now I hate it," she said.

They crossed the escarpment and Monkton Down and came to Avebury, the freshening breeze in their faces, the edges of the henge a blaze of daffodils. The road through the village was busy with traffic, so they moved quickly to the outer ring. He showed her the stone circles and the standing sarsens, male and female.

She stood beside one of the larger stones, dwarfed by its size, her paleness accentuated by the greyness of the sarsen. He studied her covertly, thinking how natural she looked in this setting. The first raindrops fell, but she did not move.

After a time she stirred, a distant look leaving her face, and looked around her at the circles. "A great people must have built this," she said slowly.

The rain passed over quickly. He looked at the sky and saw that another shower would follow.

"They were a clever people, though we know little about them, except that they knew their mathematics," he said, gesturing at the stones, "just as the Egyptians knew theirs. The Stone Age people here studied the heavens and used their astronomy to bring them into a perpetual communion with time, and therefore with nature itself, building their circles that were aligned to the solar calendar, asking the Goddess to bring in the new year, not to let the sun die, or the moon, her manifestation, to lose its power to heal and give fertility."

"I've read of how important the moon was," she said, "and how close they were to it."

"It was everything, in a way. The moon was the source of rain, and therefore of fertility. These people sowed crops, so rain was life to them, and the timing of the equinoxes and the solstices was very important for the same reason. They saw the moon as the source of that rain, and of their own fertility as a people. "

"And the sun?"

"It was important, of course, because it told them when a new year began, how the seasons progressed. They possibly worshipped it as a god, as a distant father, but the Great Goddess was far more important to these people. We make an artificial distinction between ourselves and Nature, whereas these people were at one with it. It was much the same the world over – in Europe, India, the Americas. Many societies were matrilineal then. Even the beautiful goddesses of Greek and Roman mythology were manifestations of her. So was the Virgin Mary, and so was your namesake."

Aengus was looking south, past Waden Hill, at the conical shape of Silbury. She followed his gaze, but sensing that he did not wish to talk for a moment, she looked across the escarpment at the beech clumps on Avebury Down, watching a squall of rain chased across the fields by the returning sun.

"Yet she faded into little more than a myth," she said at last, following his gaze.

"Societies probably suppressed her in favour of a male god," he said. "In some mythologies the sun god fights the moon goddess and wins. In Greek mythology Apollo gradually became more important than Artemis, who was his twin, but in a very civilised fashion, as you would expect from such a civilised and thoughtful people. A dominant male god is relatively recent in historical terms."

She looked again at the standing stones, trying to imagine the site crowded with Stone Age people arriving off the Ridgeway, dancing in the circles or waiting for the solstice, then at Aengus who suddenly seemed far away, his gaze resting on the path that led south-east to the Sanctuary.

"You speak as though she were real," she said, looking directly at him.

He met her gaze. "She seemed very real to the people who worshipped here. There are pottery figures of her everywhere in the world, most of them seemingly very basic and crude, yet they all have fertility as their essence. The Egyptians saw her as Isis, who married her brother Osiris and when he was hacked to pieces by his brother" – he hesitated for a moment – "by his brother, she searched the Nile until she found the pieces and put his body together again. Hence the reborn Nile each year, and hence the act of mummification. His body was wrapped to keep the parts together, so they mummified Pharaohs from then on. The Greeks gradually refined the same Great Goddess from a figure like Gaia into a thing of beauty and grace, generally a virgin goddess, yet they kept the Terrible Mother aspect, even in the most beautiful images of Artemis. Hecate, who was one of the Triple Goddesses of the Moon along with Artemis, was usually the Terrible Mother – the crone, sometimes portrayed as a snake-goddess, a hag who later became a witch – because she took the moon away every month. The Stone Age people feared that it, the source of all goodness, wouldn't return. Yet Artemis, the good goddess of the Greeks who brought the moon to its full each month, could also be capable of terrible acts of vengeance."

They began to walk towards Silbury Hill. The sky was clearing, the wind rising.

"I see you as a romantic, but I don't see you at Stonehenge during the winter solstice, dressed as a druid and chanting something." She smiled then. "Or dowsing among the crop circles."

He smiled in return, glad of her teasing, and turned to look back at the grey stones. "There are dowsers who think we're on a ley line here, a line that runs through the churches of St Michael all the way to St Michael's Mount near Land's End, a channel of psychic magnetism of some kind, but ley lines and dowsing have never appealed. I can't take them seriously."

They walked on, both silent for a time. Silbury Hill loomed as she said: "Yet you take the goddess myth seriously. You keep returning to her."

He stopped and said: "She exists."

She looked at him searchingly, and he quickly said: "Not as you and I do, but as an archetype, one of many such images in the human psyche, images at work all the time in the unconscious mind. Jung saw that clearly. He saw it in his patients when he treated them for psychic disorders. I think he saw it in himself."

They were nearing the hill, close enough to see the awakening grasses on its flanks.

She studied his face for a few moments, began to ask a question, then stopped herself, realisation dawning. "You see it in yourself, too," she said, "and you see it in others. You see it in me, don't you?"

He nodded.

She went on: "Not necessarily the Mother archetype, but others, some of them terrible." Her face set with a sudden conviction: "That's why you brought me here, to tell me this, isn't it?"

He looked directly at her, and saw courage where he had feared he might see trauma. "I hoped it would help. You're brave enough to face your own fears, even if you can't share them."

"You mean I have to face fear head on. Are you convinced that it helps?" He saw the stress in her face as an acute sense of her plight returned to her. He waited, felt the keenness of the wind, then led her under the lee of the hill.

"I'm very careful about what I allow myself to believe, but instinctively I am, yes," he said when they were more sheltered. "The fear you have is based on the images you have. You forget that the real threat to you does not come from an image, but from something very human – cunning, brutish, but human. He can be overcome."

She turned her head from him, her shoulders trembling. She looked cold and vulnerable. He wanted to hold her, but sensed it was not the time.

"I'll help you, if you want," he said instead. "I made up my mind early that I wouldn't question you, to force whatever secret you have from you." His voice shook a little. "I still hold to that, but if you'll let me help, I will."

She turned to face him, her cheeks slightly damp, the beauty of her face a naked thing, and slowly shook her head. "We should get back," she said, and he knew he had failed.

The Greek

I went down to the harbour of Syracuse when the moon was up, thinking of the triangle of Aristarkhos, and there I had a revelation. I watched the silver light on the sea and felt the wind clear my head. There was a very high tide that night as the moon grew full, and suddenly I saw what I, blind as I was, had not considered before. The moon was pulling the tide, yet it could not do so unless it was pulling the rest of the earth.

The moon is smaller than the earth, as we know from the size of the earth's shadow, and orbits it every month. Therefore it must be connected by an invisible force, evidently an attraction of a smaller to a larger body. Below me was the evidence that the larger body was also attracted to the smaller. If the moon pulled on the sea, it pulled on the entire surface of the earth with the same force.

I stood there in the wind, ignoring the sentinels who patrolled the walls, and the spies who watched me. I was oblivious to all except my thoughts. Memories flooded in.

I remembered that the ancients knew that the moon exerted a force upon the tides and the female cycle.

I remembered how the speed of the rocks thrown from the *palintonons* had appeared to accelerate as they fell, as if the rocks were pulled by a force. There was nothing original in such an observation. Strato of Lampsakos, when he was at the Lyceum at Athens, had already written of it in a book called *On Motion*, around the time of my birth.

The rain soaked me as a different memory resurfaced. I recalled with a jolt how Eratosthenes, who sent me letters and blank papyrus from Alexandria that I might correspond with him, had described how the adventurer Pytheas of Massalia claimed that during the time of Alexander he had sailed so far to the north that there was almost constant daylight during summer.

The part of particular interest was where Pytheas observed that different levels of tide coincided with different phases of the moon, and kept records of this. Many called Pytheas a liar. They said he had invented the voyage, but the rolls recording his observations had been discovered recently at the Library of Alexandria and shown to Eratosthenes, who studied them closely, had them copied and sent them to me. I had read them briefly, then put them aside, fool that I was.

The wind strengthened and the clouds again covered the moon over the Grand Harbour of Syracuse that night as these memories tumbled into one concept. It continued to rain but still I stood there, deaf to the noises of the city as I thought of how Aristarkhos, a lone mind, had concluded that the earth is twice the size of the moon, and only a sixth the size of the sun. Pheidias used the same method and estimated the last to be one-twelfth. From curiosity I had taken observations of my own. These showed the angle to the sun to be even more acute than either said. That placed the sun at an even greater distance and implied that it was much larger. There I had left it, to move on to other works, just when part of the solution to a great question was at hand. That night in the rain I realised that if the sun was large enough it might pull the other heavenly bodies around it through an invisible force, as the earth pulled the moon and the moon pulled the tides.

I emerged from my reverie, cold and very wet, and ran to my house. The streets were deserted. Piles of stinking refuse flowed down them as rain swept them clean.

I reached my home at a high pitch of excitement and, late as the hour was, I called to the slave to prepare a bath as hot as I could bear and to anoint me with oil. The cold fled my bones. I drew diagrams on a wax tablet, in a fever to return to work when I would plot the possible movement of the cosmos with the sun at its centre, to test each against my father's observations.

It did not matter at this stage whether the sun was twenty or one hundred times the earth's distance to the moon. That would be established by observation. What did matter was that the sun lay at the centre of the cosmos, and the force it exerted on the earth and planets was the same force that pulled the tides. I could not yet prove it, but I knew it, just as I knew the law of floating bodies before I had the proof. The sun's apparent transit across the sky, so deeply embedded in our astronomy and in our daily life, was not real.

Yet there remained the mystery of why the planets at times appeared to fly backwards.

The slave brought a towel and dried me, urging me to eat, coaxing me to drink something, reminding me that I had had nothing since morning and very little then. I could hear his voice but what I saw in my mind was the diagram of Pheidias with its image like a volute on an Ionic capital, the shape of a ram's horn, and I knew that I had found it.

The Book of Aengus

He and Aristarchus have discovered some of the great secrets of the universe, eighteen hundred years before Copernicus and Brahe and Kepler. Perhaps that should not surprise us too much, as plenty of circumstantial evidence has come down to us of his astronomy as well as his mathematics. Macrobius, in about AD 430, wrote in passing that Archimedes had already discovered the distance of the planets, and Hipparchus refers to Archimedes' work on discovering the length of a year, which he has told me he learned in Egypt, so his astronomical work was known to the scientists that followed, even if it was not to us. Livy calls him *unicus spectator caeli siderumque*, while Dijksterhuis states that posterity appreciated his astronomical work before his mathematics.

Today we would also call him a physicist, as he has taken a great step towards discovering the laws of gravity.

I've failed to convince Bridget. I must act alone, if or when the time comes.

Narrative

Seth had returned and the watching Aengus spied once more from the edge of the woods to the north of the house. He listened to the calls of the tawny owls in the woods and the barks of the vixen in the field to the side, calling to her cubs while the dog fox set forth on his hunt.

Sometimes, to relieve the boredom of his nightly spying, he hooted to the owls, and sometimes he barked to the foxes, listening to the confusion he caused. One night under a waning moon a barn owl perched on a branch close to him, turning its head full circle while its body still pointed in the opposite direction, its facial disc feathers yellow in the flickering moonlight, to stare at him, unblinking. Then it began to grumble, to scold him for diverting it from its hunt. He talked to it in a soothing voice while it turned its head to the front, listening for tiny vibrations on the floor of the wood. Then it gave him a last look before floating off silently across the face of the moon.

The Greek

I saw a spiral and I saw the diagrammatic projection of the looping path of the red planet Ares that it resembled, which my father had drawn from many years of observation, and I thought how that looping path could be explained if I took one simple hypothesis.

The hypothesis was so simple that I stood silently for some moments, hearing the slave's voice from far away, again telling me I must eat.

In my mind I saw the planets circling the sun at different distances and therefore at different speeds in relation to it. The planets closer to the sun than the earth might take a shorter time to complete their circles.

If the planet Ares were further from the sun than the earth, then it might take longer to travel around it. As the earth overtook it, Ares would appear to travel backwards in a motion that looked like a loop.

Narrative

His sleep after the visit to Avebury was deeply troubled by different images, so much so that he tried to remain awake even after he had gone to bed. He saw Kate in these vivid nightmares, her mouth open in a soundless shriek as she cursed him. He saw Seth, as in a Blake painting, with a molten sun behind his reddish head, brandishing in triumph a knife that dripped with blood, standing in an ochre desert while a lone female figure in the background hastened past the date palms along the bank of a wide river, searching. He saw these images and quailed, his body breaking into a sweat, then the protective carapace he had inherited or acquired to retain his sanity returned and a succession of visions followed of a young woman, her face concealed by a cloak or shawl, undergoing some rite of lustration before approaching a holy well set at the foot of a small mountain that looked a familiar shade of green. He clung in sleep to the images of this lissom woman, begging her to stay with him, his survival instincts guiding him back to her each time the images of the terrible mother and the aboriginal god of the desert tried to return. He felt the different forces at war in his psyche and recognised them, seizing the image of the lissom woman for his own as he saw the figure of Bridget standing before the stones of Avebury.

This stirred a great impatience in him next morning as he felt an urgent need to make the most of the time left. He rang the lawyer repeatedly, to hear that the search continued without result.

The three men worked on the spring chalkstream, cutting with long chains the crowfoot that waved from the dappled bed, and the grass on the banks with a gang mower. The fishing season would open in a few weeks when bluebells carpeted the floor of the woods.

The river wildlife had re-emerged fully after a long winter and a wet spring, and the early migrants had made their homes in trees and bank and hedgerows. On the edges of the trees, Aengus saw the wood-sorrel nestling in hollows, its fragile white petals singing of spring.

The fertile swans would have ripped much of the weed from the riverbed were it not for Sid's birth control. He paid secret visits to their nests, armed with a twin-pronged pole, on the darkest nights, when he held off the charges of the cob, ignored the furious hissing of the pen and removed all but one of half-a-dozen eggs, took the others to his deep freezer for four or five hours, and, mindful of interfering eyes, returned them to the nest before dawn.

On one blustery, sunny day Aengus counted five kingfishers, one of them fluttering its wings while it hovered over a shoal of little grayling, and gloried in the sight. By then he knew where each nested in the holes on the bank, and sometimes watched for a blue-green head to appear and look about it for danger signals.

Early one morning he saw a rudder swirl in the water as an otter took a perch, but turned his head away and said nothing. Later that day he saw a long, menacing shape glide close to the bank and open a fearsome jaw to take a water vole swimming for its life, and this time he called to his friends and they netted the pike successfully, knocking it on the head as it thrashed furiously. They threw it in the undergrowth for the birds.

Most sightings on the river pleased him. One was of the brave moorhen that guarded its eggs and young so fiercely. He saw a cock bird one day attack a crow that had landed on the wall of the nest to steal its eggs, and watched as the moorhen rushed at the crow, knocked it in the water and drove it away. The keepers accepted that the moorhens ate a little trout ova from time to time, but praised them for their destruction of the larvae of the dragonfly which fed greedily on ova and fry after they hatched.

The moorhens' cousins, the coots, were the sentries of the chalkstream, their sooty feathers and white foreheads instantly identifying them as they turned to give the alarm if a stranger appeared, flapping their wings and running simultaneously along the stream's surface as they fled. They generally remained unflustered when the keepers appeared, aware that the men were friendly. The lazier old coots continued their favourite game, robbing the energetic younger birds of their prey when they returned to the surface after diving for food.

Moorhen and coot were tolerated and left alone, but the dabchick was not because it devoured trout eggs with a manic greed. Pretty as it was – the adult male with its chestnut-coloured neck and dark brown upper body was a handsome sight that appealed to innocent river strollers – the keepers hated it. "Bloody sight more destructive than a pair of otters," said Sid with a sharp edge to his voice, displaying the scars on the back of his hands, "and they're buggers when you catch 'em." The keepers, with a wary eye for trespassers, thinned the dabchick population by netting them as they left their big nests of reeds and flag irises, then knocked them on the head while the birds tried to stab them with their beaks.

Aengus loved the birds of the chalkstream country, resident or visitor, the spotted fly-catcher that would not arrive until a week or two before the mayfly began to hatch in mid-May, redstart and willow-warbler and wheat-ear, which had already arrived, and black-cap, increasingly a resident during the soft southern winters and whose song was nearly as sweet as that of the nightingale who, when the dark descended, would sing of joy and early summer at the end of a day when the mayfly spinners swarmed among the alders and willows.

His favourite was the grey wagtail which piped its call as it darted, yellow breast flashing through the air, from reed-top to the bright flower of the water-lily to chase its food, its long tail quivering as it prepared to intercept a mayfly in mid-air. This bird to him was nature at her best, the symbol of early summer on the river.

He watched the river one moonlit evening from the front of his cottage, and heard a light footfall on the river path. He turned and saw her, and for an instant the image of the goddess at the holy well returned.

"Seth is away until tomorrow," she said, her eyes downcast as he led her into the cottage and up the stairs to his room.

The Carthaginians marched on Syracuse. The Carthaginians were in retreat. Marcellus had been recalled by the Senate and was already in Rome. No, Marcellus had been seen, disguised as a common soldier, spying near the walls at Hexapylon. Himilco had won a great victory. Himilco was dead. Two of the rulers of Syracuse had quarrelled over a handsome Kretan boy. No, he was from Rhodes.

There was rumour everywhere in Syracuse at that time. I ignored it. Then a few survivors came in who had been with Hippokrates when Marcellus had surprised his army as it set up camp. They soon told their story. Himilco and his Carthaginian force had retaken several cities from the Romans after landing near Herakleia Minoa on the south coast of the island. Marcellus had marched to the aid of Akragas, but Himilco had taken it by the time he came within sight of its walls. Marcellus returned to Syracuse and by chance encountered Hippokrates' army on its way to join Himilco, and killed or captured the Syracusan infantry. Hippokrates and the cavalry had escaped, and reached Himilco who was advancing towards Syracuse to relieve it. Hopes rose when runners brought in news that Himilco had advanced to within a few hours' march of our city, and rose further when a Carthaginian fleet under Bomilcar slipped past the Roman navy and entered the harbour of Syracuse.

While this was happening I was at my work, aware of events yet curiously detached. I gave the earth and each planet a circular orbit, confidently testing the projections against my father's observations, using different assumptions and my large numbers to calculate the relative distances covered as the bodies moved around the sun. My spirits failed as I saw that my hypothesis did not work. The observations did not match.

The tide of war turned once more as the Romans brought in a further legion so that its forces matched that of Himilco, whose position outside Syracuse was suddenly exposed to attack. He removed his forces to attack other cities, leaving Syracuse to its fate once more. I shut myself away from the despair in the city, abandoning my daily walks. The tablets were covered with diagrams and figures that I constantly erased and replaced with another set. At night I worked under torchlight, my only variation a visit to the roof to take further observations of the red planet. Finally I arrived at a conclusion, agonising though it was. The planets might orbit the sun, but they did not do so in circles.

The Book of Aengus

We have no likeness of the Greek that could be called genuine, so can only imagine him. Torelli's celebrated edition of his works published a medallion and a statement that it is of Archimedes, yet Peyrard and Grenovius published a further two, each of them clearly of different men, and the writers on iconography, for what their work is worth, do not recognise the Greek in any portraits.

Nor do we have his original manuscripts. All are lost, many of them probably due to the fire at the Serapeum in Alexandria in AD 391. Some of the best copies that we have originate from a single manuscript copied in the ninth or tenth century. Copies were made from it in around AD 1500. Then it, in turn, was lost. The highest quality versions turned up in Venice. We hear of these and other copies, some of them translated into Latin from Arabic, coming down to us through the Library of the Vatican and other sources. Pope Nicholas V certainly had a copy translated into Latin by Jacopo Cassiani. Other copies turned up in Germany – notably the one known as *Codex Norimbergensis* – many of them with corrections added in Latin. The Heiberg Codex C, a palimpsest found a century or so ago, was the most valuable of all, as it contained the translated text of *Method*.

The Byzantines rather than the Arabs in this case are probably the scholars to whom we owe most, as they seem to have actively sought to preserve his works. Some of these may have made their way to the West when the Ottoman Turks took Constantinople in 1453 and the Vatican Library became the central repository for Greek texts. We know that a number of original works have been totally lost – not even copies exist – including that on large numbers the Greek sent to Zeuxippus, and another on sphere-making.

There is little in Syracuse today to suggest he was ever there, other than the Piazza Archimede, which was probably placed at random to attract tourists. Ask the Syracusans where he lived or where he is buried and they will shake their heads, although they can tell you that the Grand Harbour has been shrunk to half the size that it was in his day. The guides will also tell you that he redesigned the Fort of Euryalus to be a deadly series of traps for enemy soldiers who entered its basement chambers, and they will show you where, in the Ciane river, close to the other side of the neglected Grand Harbour whose shores are littered with rubbish, the papyrus plants flourish in the chalk beds. They are said to have originated as a gift from Pharaoh to Hiero to acknowledge the present of the *Syracusia*, and there is a legend that they were planted by Archimedes himself.

I find I can write nothing of Bridget's last visit, but she will not break her vow to keep her secret.

The Greek

The city buildings seemed to glare in the midday sun as I walked past the columns of the temple of Athene, tired of the confines of my house. I stood, meditating, seeking inspiration of some kind but without result. I walked across the causeway and down to the walls again and stood at the point where we had repulsed the Romans. The sea was still and listless, rolling gently over the reefs, and offered nothing. I walked on and up to the Theatre of Syracuse, passing the Altar of Hiero where the citizens had sacrificed after the victory over the Romans. My spirits were as low as they had been, and I accepted that the perfection I expected did not exist. The motion of the planets was not a circle.

It is difficult to convey how much this mattered to me. Remember, Stranger, that every theory, from Eukleid to the daring hypothesis of Aristarkhos, said that the cosmos was circular. Everyone, from Pythagoras to Plato to Aristotle, said that the circle, as perfection, was its natural motion. I could prove them wrong, but it did not please me to destroy a profound belief when I had nothing to put in its place.

I sat on a high point in the hot sun, reflecting. It was quiet. The citizens were indoors because of the heat, the loudest sound that of running water from the Nymphaion, carrying the clear liquid down from the distant hills. The great semicircular sweep of the theatre swam in front of me in the warm air, its shape distorted by the angle from where I sat. I heard the distant sounds of the guards changing, and looked across the roofs and groves of Syracuse at the harbour in the distance. The Greeks had treated the sea as their own not long before, and perhaps would do so again, but now, not for the first time, the barbarians who controlled it were at the walls of Syracuse.

I remembered Pythagoras and his theory that the spheres were in harmony, their music the sound of a mathematical perfection. The mystic was said to have died a lonely man, deserted by his followers who turned on him.

Perhaps I dozed for a time, dreaming of the mystic, and when I awoke the empty theatre lay there still while the shadows formed and the sun sank, but this time its proportions were full of meaning.

The Book of Aengus

I have a Christie's catalogue of the Heiberg palimpsest, which lay hidden from the scientific world for a thousand years. The original copy of Archimedes' work was probably written at Constantinople, then the capital of the Byzantine Empire, probably in the mid-tenth century. Two or three hundred years later a writer – probably a priest – took the manuscript and washed or scraped the surface text and diagrams from the leaves and used them to write a Greek liturgical book, a *euchologion*, turning it into a palimpsest. Such was the hunger at the time for something to write on. Underneath the liturgy lie the works of Archimedes, including *On the Equilibrium of Planes*, *On Floating Bodies*, *On the Sphere and the Cylinder*, and others, including the only copy of *On the Method*, which demonstrates clearly how he arrived at a proof – sometimes taking a mechanical approach – which mathematical historians had until then criticised him for omitting. The catalogue describes it as the earliest extant manuscript of the works of Archimedes, 'arguably the most important scientific codex ever offered at auction'. The palimpsest is in a disgraceful condition. Pages are missing, the leaves are worn and crumpled, some badly damaged, yet the estimate was more than one million dollars. A wealthy American, a friend to scholarship, paid more than two million.

Who cares what he paid? What matters is that the work showed that an ancient Greek understood the concept of infinity.

The Greek

I sat upright, looking at the outer curve of the theatre, noting with a freshening eye how its shape was distorted by the angle from where I sat, no longer circular but elliptical. I felt cold for a moment, remembering how I had calculated the area of the circle, its proportion producing an incommensurable that was still a mysterious symbol to me, and a voice inside my brain said that if a perfect shape could produce an imperfect number, then a perfect proportion might be an imperfect circle. Think of *entasis*, the voice said, where imperfection produces perfection and symmetry.

I remembered Menaikhmos who discovered the properties of cones, and the works I had completed on ellipses and the conic sections that young Apollonios of Perga persisted in calling parabolas.

I looked up at the sky, seeing beyond it into the darkness of the heavens, picturing the planets and the earth in their immense, curving paths around the sun, knowing that the symbol of imperfection that had troubled me for more than half a century had remained with me for a purpose, and that at last I knew its meaning.

The Book of Aengus

Menaechmus was born in Asia Minor more than thirty years before the Greek. He was a pupil of Eudoxus, the mathematician who gave us the basis of proportions. He was the first to show that ellipses, parabolas and hyperbolas are produced by cutting a cone at angles that are not parallel to the base, while a parallel cut, of course, produces a circle. Archimedes produced many works, supplying many of his most elegant proofs, using the shapes of conic sections, just as he proved many propositions on spirals.

Apollonius of Perga was a contemporary of Eratosthenes at Alexandra. All three were intensely familiar with the others' work. Today the work of Eratosthenes and Apollonius is ranked second and third only to that of Archimedes.

I sense a touch of mischievous humour here, as Apollonius was not much younger, and is said to have been unkind to his friend Conon. It was young Apollonius who cheekily renamed the parabola, which Archimedes knew as a section of a right-angled cone.

I must try to see Kate.

Narrative

He was working above Bull Bridge two days later when he saw her, the mastiff at her side, on a right of way past the water meadows that were beginning to blaze with buttercups and dandelions. He set off to intercept her, surprising a heron that rose hastily from the shallows and hurried, its wings beating urgently, for the woods. He crossed through the gates in the barbed wire fences, past grazing cattle, and emerged on the track.

The dog growled, a low rumble, full of menace. "Quiet!" said Kate. The animal obeyed, eyes fixed on Aengus.

"You want to talk to me, Aengus. It's dangerous. He may be watching."

"Does he always watch you?"

"He watches everything. It's his nature."

The tall woman gazed across the meadows and saw a raven circling. "Your companion is here today." She gestured towards the bird, her dark features squinting into the sun. "He watches for you. A very old bird, that one."

"I think he's my conscience," he said as the raven swung over them, croaking.

"A symbol to fear once, that bird of Apollo, who was white until the god cursed him," she said lightly. "A sacred bird down the ages, the sign of the Viking, on every sail on every longship."

"Yes," he said, "but he can't tell me what I need to know."

"No, and perhaps I can't, either." There was a pause. He waited. "She loves two people, Aengus, but not in the same way. It's weakening her. She could become very sick."

A cloud covered the sun, and the wind shifted towards the east. The cattle had gathered at the barbed wire fence, watching them. The dog saw them and uttered a low rumble. "Quiet!" said Kate, but kept her gaze on the man.

"Kate, do you know who the other is?"

"Yes."

"Is that person in danger?"

"Yes."

"What should I do?"

"The worst thing you could do is to let Seth know you know that person exists. He has killed before. He would kill again."

"I know that too well. I have another question."

"Ask if you must, but I cannot help you."

"Do you know where that person is?"

"No. Only Seth knows that." She paused while her green eyes scanned the woods beyond the water meadows. "I cannot help you," she said again at last, "but I will say this. Be careful, or you will be responsible for her death. She will not tell you her secret, because she dare not. If she does, and he discovers it, the other person will die, and your shade will join the one who visits you. You will never rest."

The Greek

I found the true cosmos, Stranger. I took a set of recorded observations of Ares, compared them with an ellipse I drew, while in my memory I saw a Roman slinger whirling his arm before releasing a stone. A pattern began to appear on the big wax tablets I used for such rough work, to loom out at me, to tell me that I must think on a higher plane, that the cosmos was so large that my mind for a time could not grasp its size. I saw that I had lacked the imagination to conceive the geometry of the heavens, that the ellipse I had was too close to being a circle. I tried again, stretching it until it was longer, narrower, as though I increased the vertical cut of the cone. Still it would not fit. I stretched it remorselessly again, my senses beginning to shriek at the impossibility of it all, until each observation began to make sense, to tell a story of its own, to connect with the others and tell me of the immensity of the planet's curving movement through the heavens, but even then the cosmos I built in the wax was not big enough. I stretched the section again, and applied set after set of observations to it. Eventually, when I had a cosmos of previously unimaginable proportions, every set began to fit, apart from some of the early

Babylonian observations that Pheidias had always regarded as flawed.

Gradually the geometry of the cosmos lay before me, and I sat and marvelled at it, the enormous space that I had found through which the planets moved, a discovery I had made on the back of brave Aristarkhos. It was as if I had walked into a cave and looked up to see an infinite sky instead of a roof.

The image came to me again of the slinger releasing a stone, the missile's speed diminishing the moment it left the sling as the invisible force took it towards its centre of gravity. The natural movement of any body therefore must be along a straight line if such a force did not exist. By contradiction, it existed.

Solutions to the problems of finding the centre of gravity of a body came back to me, as I knew them well. The centre of gravity of a sphere is obviously its centre. Therefore all bodies on earth naturally gravitate towards the earth's centre, as the planets gravitated towards the sun. The momentum of a planet, a product of its weight and speed, would, once it had rounded the sun, swing it around like a slingshot on an elliptical path until the attraction of the sun's force was once again greater than the planet's falling momentum. Then the planet would be pulled towards the centre of the sun once more. The ellipse was the natural shape for such a motion, but the ellipse that I saw made me drop the tablets and think deeply of the implications.

What was true of the planet Ares would be true of the moon and other bodies. I was sure of it, as I remembered how Eratosthenes had sent me some years before the latest estimate he had completed for the circumference of the earth. He and I had corresponded subsequently on the probable circumference of the moon, using the size of the shadow of the earth on its surface during a recorded eclipse.

Each of us had taken the arcs of degree of the moon when full, and arrived at estimates of its diameter, and so of its circumference. Each of us agreed that the moon appeared to be around one third the size of the earth. Each of us agreed that the moon moved eastward nightly on average by an arc of thirteen degrees, yet what had perplexed us was that on one night the moon would look relatively small, while two weeks later it would look significantly larger.

The implication of this suddenly seemed obvious. The moon's distance from the earth during each lunation period must fluctuate. At its perigee it was closest, at its apogee furthest. That contradicted the belief that the moon orbited the earth at a constant distance in a circle with the earth as its centre. Furthermore, our observations and those of others had shown that the speed of the moon's passage across the sky was slower at its apogee than its perigee. The moon therefore travelled more quickly as it neared the earth, attracted by its mass. The ellipse must be the answer here also, one where the earth was not at its centre, but at one of its foci. The change of speed across the sky was the cause of the difficulty in predicting when the moon would rise or set.

A further shock came when I calculated as closely as I could the relative distances between the planets and I saw how lonely a place the cosmos must be. The implications of the results again overpowered my reason for a time. So did the implied speed of our earth as it revolved. If the earth took one year to travel around the sun it must cover a distance in that time so great that its speed was unimaginable – calculable, using my large numbers, but unimaginable in terms of orthodox Greek knowledge, yet by contradiction it must be so. A year on the outermost planets was a multiple of ours.

Shaken by this as I was, I thought of the stars, the distant ones that we had viewed as fixed because we could not see them move. Their distance must therefore be many times that of the sun. Perhaps they lay in a cosmos of their own, or one of many.

I thought of the tides, reasoning that if the moon pulled them, so must the sun and even the other planets, the forces of their attraction being a product of their size or weight, or of both. Perhaps different stages of the alignments of all of these explained why some high tides were higher than others. Observation would tell us.

I had the answer, though not yet the proof, but I knew that the cosmos was one great ellipse after another, governed by the same universal law that governed the earth.

My immediate duty was to share this information, knowing I was unlikely to live long enough to supply the proofs. The discoveries must be described and the rolls sent to Alexandria, where Eratosthenes would share them with the other scientists at the

Library and the tasks of further observations and calculations could commence.

Yet as I wrote a description of the work and a rough hypothesis, knowing I would never write the proof, I was filled again with doubt, so much so that I checked the observation sets against the ellipse, again and again. They could not lie, I knew. They were too numerous, too unanimous, too accurate, as I was present while Pheidias noted some of his own and I saw the pains he took. Yet the dimensions they implied were so great, beyond anything we might have imagined, destroying a vision of the compact order of the Greeks and replacing it with one that told me that our earth was very small, proportionately not much larger than a grain of sand.

Still in a daze, I drew the relative positions and distances of the bodies of the solar cosmos. Some days later I took two diagrams to the skilled artisans with whom I had worked for many years. Time was against us, but we built two working models in bronze of the cosmos that I saw. I would send these to Alexandria with the rolls.

I named my work *On the Invisible Lever and the Motion of the Planets*, and dedicated it to Eratosthenes.

Narrative

He stood on the track after Kate left, watching her until she rounded a bend, the breeze suddenly cold, as if winter had returned.

The cattle looked at him curiously while her words rang in his head, the sentences revolving, the words resonating, disjointed nouns and verbs and adjectives tumbling and dancing, the image of the dark face and wild hair as stark as if she stood there still.

Doubt flooded him for a moment. He shook his head after a pause and returned to his work.

The Book of Aengus

He has discovered what Newton saw eighteen hundred years later, the universal laws of gravitation and, on the back of Aristarchus, the motion of the solar system. That was the mystery of the cosmos he unlocked, that and its size, the mystery he spoke of during his first visit to me.

Had he lived, he would have supplied the most elegant of proofs. As it is, we have a tragedy of history related at first hand. The documents and the models seem to have been looted or lost. Cicero claims to have seen one of them. He maintains that it was so accurate that it could predict solar and lunar eclipses. Marcellus is reported to have taken it to Rome.

We know nothing of the documents. Many of his works are known to be lost, although Pappus says that Archimedes wrote a book on the construction of the model. Perhaps the Romans threw away the rolls. What did the truth of the cosmos matter when you could not build a road on it?

There are many Archimedean propositions dealing with parabolas, particularly in *On Conoids and Spheres*, and there are many dealing with ellipses – the true paths of the earth and planets – in propositions that state: *The area of any ellipse is to that of the auxiliary circle as the minor axis to the major*, or another: *The areas of ellipses are as the rectangles under their axes*, the stuff to make schoolboys squirm.

Eighteen hundred years later Johannes Kepler officially discovered the elliptical nature of the solar system, to deliver to a startled scientific world the beautiful proportions that would have so pleased the Greek, that the cube of the distance travelled by a planet around the sun is equal to the square of the time it takes to complete an orbit. That is Kepler's Third Law of Planetary Motion, the first being the ellipse, yet it took Kepler many months to realise that the formula he had deduced for the motion of the planets was the same as the formula for an ellipse. Surely, he thought, this is too simple?

An irony is that Kepler, son of a Black Forest witch, had when younger seized on the five Platonic solids as the explanation of the different distances between the planets, convinced he had received a mystical revelation from Pythagoras. He first drew a circle, then an equilateral triangle around it, then another circle around the triangle. As it happens, the relationship between the two circles is constant, regardless of their sizes. This, by coincidence, is the same as the relationship between the orbits of Jupiter and Saturn, Jupiter represented by the larger circle. Pythagoras was correct, thought the excited young Kepler, and inserted the five perfect solids into circles. Each fitted neatly between the orbits of the respective planets, of which by then six were known. Pythagorean mysticism had returned more than two millennia after the death of its founder – perhaps Kepler, who had almost become a Protestant minister, believed he was the reborn mystic – but in time it became plain to the young German that it was not the correct explanation because the planetary orbits are not circles, but ellipses. It would take the death of Tycho Brahe, Imperial Mathematicus or chief horoscope-caster to the Emperor, to make his observations available to Kepler, and it was the great Dane's observations that led him towards the ellipse.

The Greek

News came in of a further Roman atrocity, at Henna in the centre of the island, where the Roman garrison had slaughtered the citizens, upon which Marcellus was said to have congratulated its commander. This shook me. I felt very angry, as others did, and a great wave of feeling against the Romans swept through the cities of Sicily, for Henna had been a centre of worship to the goddess Kore, and the Romans had desecrated her shrine. Soon after this news Epikydes said he had uncovered a Roman plot and summoned the citizens to hear how clever he had been to detect it. Some Syracusans from noble families who had escaped death from him during the aftermath of the siege had been helping the Romans foment a rebellion in the city and had smuggled in a slave to approach others who might be sympathetic to them. A band of discontented citizens had hidden in a fishing boat and gone to the Roman camp where Marcellus and the Syracusan exiles eagerly awaited them. More followed until a sizeable body was ready to aid the Romans from inside the walls. They were betrayed, and Epikydes put all of them to death.

If he expected the gratitude of the citizens, he was to be disappointed. I had failed to find someone to smuggle my works from the city and was returning from the harbour when I saw him retreat into the *prytaneion* as the citizens began to stone him. Epikydes sent out a file of soldiers to quell the riot. Guards from the *thesauros* joined them. The citizens stoned them in turn while

I remonstrated with them not to fight their fellow Syracusans. The soldiers beat them and in the rush I was thrown to the ground. My head hit the street as I fell. The citizens lifted me and helped me to a fountain, one calling to the soldiers that I was the man who had saved the city. I was carried home by this man, who told me proudly he had stood close by me when the Romans attacked, and who grieved for me, telling the soldiers that I was a hero. My head throbbed from my wounds and by night I was delirious.

The Book of Aengus

The city must be very demoralised when the rulers hide from the citizens.

Clearly the package never reached Alexandria, or the science of gravity and planetary motion would have flourished for two centuries before Christ. A priceless piece of knowledge disappeared, and the world continued in a state of profound ignorance of the cosmos of which it was part.

He arrived at the basic laws of Newtonian gravity in a spectacularly Archimedean fashion, giving a typical display of intuition and *nous*. The functioning of the tides is more complicated than he realises, and it was to enrage Galileo as much as it pleased Newton, who elegantly explained that spring tides occur when sun, earth and moon are aligned, and the weaker neaps when sun and moon pull from different directions. Yet the tides gave him the insight, helped by the nudge of Eratosthenes' letter about Pytheas, who is said to have circumnavigated Britain. So we arrive at the *invisible lever*, which would have been his greatest work. What a proof that would have been, a proof drummed into every schoolboy for more than two thousand years!

Neither he nor Aristarchus was able to measure the angle of the sun with any degree of accuracy because of the lack of instruments fine enough to take an angle at that distance. He did not have a telescope, so could not prove the changing parallax of the stars. Bessel would not accomplish that until 1838.

His discovery is in keeping with the spirit of Greek mathematics, which was to set itself the most rigorous intellectual challenges, to which he referred briefly when he began to visit me. One of these challenges had to do with the altar of Apollo on

Delos, an island in the Cyclades that was sacred to the god because he was born there. At some time before Euclid, Greek mathematicians imposed the rule restricting themselves to the use of rulers and compasses only in their search for the solutions to the three classical problems in geometry, to double the size of the altar at Delos, to square the circle, and to trisect any angle.

The Delian problem, as it came to be known, came about because of a plague that killed a quarter of the population of Athens, including, according to legend, the great Pericles, father of Athenian democracy. A delegation, desperate for divine guidance, went to the oracle of Apollo at Delos, who advised them to appease the god by doubling the size of the altar. The Athenians dutifully doubled each dimension. The result was to astonish them because, as any mathematician knows, the volume of the altar increased not by a factor of two, but of eight.

Archimedes was to solve the second and third classical problems by the use of a spiral (for which he gave much credit to Conon), but even he could not solve the three problems by the use of compass and ruler only. No mathematician could. Modern geometers have proved that it's impossible.

It didn't stop the Greeks from trying, and in the same spirit of adventure Archimedes took his knowledge of mechanics into mathematics, using his law of the lever to balance line segments in his imagination, as his mechanical law balanced weights. Boyer says he could be called the father of mathematical physics. That would have pleased him.

He seemed to know that the force that made the planets revolve would be natural rather than divine. Newton reached his own answer by taking Kepler's third law – that the cube of the planet's distance from the sun is equal to the square of the time it takes to complete an orbit – and calculated the force that would maintain the moon in its orbit around the earth. He reasoned that the further the distance of the moon from the earth, the weaker the earth's gravitational pull would be, and he calculated that the force would weaken inversely as the square of the distance, another proportion that the Greek would have relished for its simplicity.

Newton was sent home from his studies at Cambridge because

of the Plague, and while at home he deduced his laws. Later he wrote them up, locked the papers in his desk and left them there for years, to become an alchemist, searching for the Philosopher's Stone that would yield total knowledge, and developed an obsession with Rosicrucianism.

It was Halley of the comet who persuaded him to write the proofs, which Newton, by then a mystic, did reluctantly, devising the calculus to produce one of the most magnificent books on science, which made him the greatest celebrity of the time in Europe, and one of the most unpleasant. In the twentieth century, of course, Einstein's General Relativity was to supersede Newtonian physics, to show that gravity was a consequence of the distortion of space and time and was not strong enough to move the planets. Instead, they follow the curved deformation of space-time caused by the sun, the momentum of their orbits preventing them from falling into the star.

Mysticism seems never to have been far from mathematics, or from poetry and music, from Pythagoras down to Kepler and Newton and Mozart and Yeats. The chief reason for royal patronage of the great astronomers such as Kepler and Brahe seems to have been the casting of countless horoscopes for their masters. Even our Greek has a touch of mysticism, but Newton took it to extremes, devoting much of his life to calculating the age of the universe from the chronology of the Bible. He left behind enough material on this to fill a modest library. I think of Heer: 'The most orthodox thinkers, the church fathers of philosophy and theology, all contain their opposites in themselves.'

Narrative

It was a sunny morning broken by heavy showers when he received the news that he had awaited, and some that he had not. His solicitor told him they had found the woman, and lost her.

The person who matched the description of Bridget's mother – a strikingly beautiful woman still in her middle years – had been traced to a village in Gloucestershire, the solicitor said. The police had provided the lead. Seth's registration number was on a watch list and the police had cross-checked it when they had seen it parked outside the woman's house. The detective, recently retired, still had her friends in the force, some of them obliging.

"Is she the mother?"

"We're almost certain." The detective had gone to the village and questioned the postmistress on a pretext. She had been only too happy to point out the house of the lady who had impressed them with her quiet dignity. A neighbour spoke of frequent visits of a big man with reddish hair. The woman had moved three days before, leaving nothing but an empty house.

"We were too late," the solicitor said.

The Book of Aengus

We were, but must begin the search again. We know she exists and that Seth visits her. Given enough time, we'd find her. Time is our biggest problem, and Seth begins to exude an air of urgency.

My guess seems to have been correct. The mystery woman was tallish, bearing a strong resemblance to Bridget, and also to the description given by those who knew Bridget's mother. We now know practically everything about her, except where she is.

She may have moved so suddenly of her free will, but I doubt it. I think she left because Seth moved her on. Perhaps we've alarmed him in some way, or perhaps he is naturally vigilant.

I told Simon that the search must go on, to step it up, to double, treble the numbers if need be, but so far Seth has shaken them off. He's amazingly cunning or elusive.

The Greek

When I left my home again to seek someone to smuggle my rolls from the city I walked through the *agora* to find the citizens again arguing. I told them there could be no honour if Syracuse changed sides once more, and that the Romans would sack the city even if we surrendered it. As I left them I heard one say that the gods had destroyed my mind. I went back to this man and said that if they had, they had at least left me with my hearing.

I walked away and at the *stoa* I encountered Arkhytas, son of Diagoras, an old friend to whom I had done a kindness that he had yet to repay. He looked at me strangely when I hinted at my quest but directed me to the Lakedaimonian Damippos, an adventurer who regularly evaded the blockade of the Roman fleet by night. He I eventually found in a gambling house near the harbour, lavishing silver, in the company of a handsome boy. I took Damippos aside, and told him my mission. He came to my home on the same evening and took the rolls and the spheres I had made for Eratosthenes, saying that he planned to sail that night as there would not be a moon.

The Book of Aengus

Plutarch says Damippus was taken at night by the Romans as he put to sea, so the Romans captured the rolls containing *The Invisible Lever*. They probably threw them in the sea in disgust, disappointed not to find the beautiful coins of Syracuse instead, but kept the spheres as souvenirs, which would account for their subsequent appearance in Rome.

Perhaps, however, they kept the work on papyrus. Might the rolls have been copied, and their contents have survived? Do they lie in a library or a museum, perhaps as a palimpsest also? Might the book have been copied into Arabic and been known to the mathematicians during the Caliphate of Baghdad, when algebra was discovered and mathematics flourished under the Abbasid dynasty roughly one thousand years after the death of Archimedes? Might it, or fragments of it, have made their way back to the West, to be translated from Arabic into Latin? Might it have been burned as pagan magic? The Heiberg codex lay hidden for more than a thousand years. The specialists say that had it been available it would have advanced mathematics by centuries.

It is as dark and stormy as much of history tonight as I think of how orthodox opinion over the ages has so often been the enemy of the truth. It sank the theory of Aristarchus, but the example I think of is Heinrich Schliemann, a nineteenth-century piratical and vain adventurer who believed every description in Homer, with much the same reverence that many of his fellow Germans had for the literal interpretation of the Bible. The rich merchant, a self-made man who taught himself seventeen languages, left his business behind and, the *Iliad* in his hand, sought the ruins of

Troy. You will not find it, said the scholars, it is long gone. Nonsense, said the ignorant amateur who knew Homer by heart, it's there.

He dismissed the accepted site of the sacked city and found one nearer the sea that matched the description in the *Iliad*, and in 1870 excavated a trench that was so deep that he, enthusiastic but clumsy, went through three and a half thousand years of history in a single dig. He found not only Troy, but the remains of a further eight Troys in all, each built on top of the last. The bottom of his trench revealed the second city of Troy, built one thousand years before Priam, and here Schliemann, son of the poor pastor of Mecklenburg in northern Germany, an inspired chancer who at the height of his fame was known to tell stretchers of his own, found the treasure that made him famous and lit the flame of archaeology.

On fire with enthusiasm, he went to Mycenae to find the tomb of Agamemnon. He dug and discovered the golden death mask of a king he said had been the Greek leader at Troy, and the treasures that showed how a golden civilisation had flourished in Greece during the Bronze Age, in the second millennium before Christ. The mask was probably of one of Agamemnon's forebears who had died several hundred years before the siege of Troy, but the evidence of a rich and sophisticated civilisation was there for all to see. Nonsense, the scholars chorused in turn, a civilisation so advanced didn't exist in Greece until a further thousand years had passed. He'd found a Phoenician trading outpost, they said, in spite of the great walls and the Lion Gate, the sheer size of the city, and the evidence of the treasures, the greatest hoard until Tutankhamun's tomb was opened. Crushed by the weight of opinion, he accepted the opinions of the fools.

When he died unexpectedly in Italy his body was brought to Athens, where the King of Greece came to honour the man who had made the greatest discoveries in modern Greece's history, even though some of the treasures he had discovered had probably been sold secretly by him. Schliemann's wife and two children – Andromache and Agamemnon – stood by the bier, on which had been placed a bust of Homer, whose descriptive powers had been not only poetic, but accurate.

The meadow-pipits, small and sober in their streaked brown feathers, had wintered nearby and had built their nest in the long grass of the water meadows. They rose when they saw him, calling in a shrill pipe: *wisk, wisk!* The female was a gullible old wet-nurse, he thought, watching her jerking flight. Soon she might feed a monstrous baby.

As if on cue, he heard a call, *uh-uh! uh-uh!*, as he neared the lower bridge. He stopped to listen. It came again: *Uh-uh! Uh-uh!* The male cuckoo had arrived before his mate, whose call was closer to that of the hated dabchick. Spring had truly come, thought Aengus, watching a big trout below the bridge swing suddenly across the current to take an olive nymph.

The cuckoos had stopped calling when she came to his cottage as the sun set through the willows.

The temperature had dropped sharply with the sun. He lit the fire and they watched, without speaking, the kindling blaze until the logs began to crackle and spit. She clearly needed the silence as she had barely spoken since her arrival, and he sensed that even to touch her would be to violate her, so he sat on the opposite side of the little fireplace, content to feel her presence without intruding on her thoughts. Once or twice she looked at the clock but remained in her seat, her head sunk in reverie.

Presently she stirred and he thought she would go with little more than a usual hasty goodbye, but instead she gazed into the fire and spoke of a terrible dream she had had, so real it was almost palpable. She had heard a great cry in the night.

He waited, keeping his gaze on the fire.

"I recognised the voice," she said, and he turned to her then, catching a fleeting glimpse of pain in her face before she composed herself.

He asked: "Do you remember which night it was?"

She told him, and he heard again the cry that had woken him on the same night, of a woman keening for a lost one. That probably impelled him to break his self-imposed rule. "Do you know what will happen to you?"

He regretted the question the moment he had finished, but she did not shrink from it.

She paused instead, and said: "I don't, but I have a sense of horror that grows every day. It's like the threat of some form of defilement I cannot name, a sickening dread that paralyses me when I think of it. I feel like a victim waiting for a disgusting, bloody sacrifice."

He sat upright, but held his tongue.

"I don't know what he intends, but I feel it will happen soon, before the summer is over. I've heard him make remarks to Kate about moving, that he has matters to settle before we leave. The strange thing is that I feel unclean, guilty of something, yet I have nothing to be guilty about. It's the twenty-first century, yet I'm cooped up in a dungeon of a house without anyone to talk to except Kate and her dog, and she's silent most of the time, like a great brooding presence."

He cleared his throat. "Does he interfere with you?"

She looked down. "He seized hold of me one night and swore he would own me forever. He was in a frenzy. I was very afraid, but I wouldn't let him see that. Kate threatened him with a knife. She told him she would cut his throat while he slept if he ever touched me again. She's the only person he fears."

He watched Seth's house the following night from the wood, too preoccupied to hoot to the owls or bark at the vixen who played with her young in the pasture at the edge. A barn owl scolded him from a young oak, and he ignored it. His head was full of images of Seth who had murdered his mother and taken his sister away for some dark purpose, and as he pondered these images rage rose in him. "Evil!" he muttered, his eyes on the cottage below. "*Sker-reek!*" answered the barn owl, but gently. "Evil!" said Aengus, his voice louder. Then he thought of Bridget and regained control of himself. He had almost told her that he knew her secret, but had held back, afraid this would place her in greater danger. Instead he had told her that her courage would see her through the ordeal, and as he spoke he felt despair at his baseless promise and cursed the loss of contact with the woman whose cry had pierced the night.

He returned to his watch on the following evening. Before it grew dark he watched the dog fox charm a pheasant in the field to the side of the wood, beside patches of St John's wort and bird's-foot. It was the fourth evening in succession that the fox had done so, sauntering casually past the pheasant in the pleasant evening sunlight while the young cock gradually relaxed, eyes fastened stupidly on the moulting fox who radiated friendliness and innocence. Aengus judged that the fox would not pounce for a day or two yet, that he would wait his time until the pheasant accepted him as a friend.

When it grew dark the vixen sat by him like a tame gundog, looking up at him while he gently stroked her fur, his eyes on the cottage below. She stirred when the young barked, and left him. A moment later he saw a hare's ears spring erect in the waving grass and watched the animal make its run from its form to the safety of the hedgerow.

The Greek

Within days I heard that Damippos had been taken at sea by the Roman picket ships, and that the Syracusans had approached the Roman tribunes under a flag of truce near Hexapylon and offered to ransom him. I wondered if his lover had betrayed him to the Romans' spies. The news of his capture was a great shock to me. I had supposed the works I had entrusted to him to be safely on their way to Alexandria. I had copies, of course, though not of the spheres.

Damippos was rumoured to carry an oral message to Hannibal from Hippokrates, who had returned to the city unscathed. It was plain that they feared the results if Damippos told all he knew.

Narrative

He took her to the West Woods in a roundabout way, climbing Martinsell Hill on a blustery day of sunshine and showers, from where they saw the landscape, swathes of green and yellow, from Savernake Forest to the escarpment. They walked past the Giant's Grave and over Wansdyke. Seth had left that morning, refusing to say when he would return, but she thought he would not be back before night.

They reached the wood, its floor a hazy mist of bluebells after the wet spring and at their edge, by a patch of rosebay willowherb, they sat on the trunk of a fallen beech from which the ferns grew. A rare whitethroat, its head-feathers in a crest, clung to the flower of a meadowsweet and sang, its voice quivering with eagerness.

He glanced at her eyes and saw that her life force continued its struggle. She was thinner, her cheekbones more prominent. Her eyes, beacons of dark blue, gazed steadily at him with an honesty and a bravery that gripped his heart and for a moment he thought he saw hope in their depths before she turned away. That moment, fleeting as it was, reassured him that her courage held, that she confronted her living nightmare with all the strength that remained to her, failing though it clearly was. More than ever he mourned the lost opportunity of finding the one she loved, plunging himself into a despair so deep he needed all his own strength to surface from it. He turned away as he did so, and when his composure returned he found she was looking at him with a compassion that shamed him.

He found himself talking of Darwin and of the unceasing algorithms of the natural selection of life, then of Mendel, the Augustinian monk whose discovery of the gene went unnoticed for decades. Her gaze continued to rest on him as he went on to the creation myths and their wonderful imagery as man everywhere, from the villages of aboriginal Australia to the Valley of the Nile, constructed his visions of his origin, some of them showing an extraordinary instinct for or memory of the truths that science would reveal in time, many of them full of the vitality that Darwin saw in natural selection and Mendel saw in the rows of pea plants in the garden of his monastery in Brno, a determination to survive and replicate that was worth a million miracles from the Bible.

They passed Lockeridge and Fyfield and he showed her the Devil's Den dolmen, the landscape behind it of bare downland and sky. A warm breeze blew in their faces as they rested by the remains of the burial place of a leader of some kind from the Neolithic age and he saw that some of the hopelessness had gone from her face. Perhaps he had bought her a little time. He hoped it would be enough.

The Greek

For days, as the festival to Artemis drew near, the negotiations for the return of the Lakedaimonian continued, with Marcellus himself conducting them. When this news reached me I did not at first believe it, regarding it as another rumour spread among the citizens, but when my neighbour, whom I knew to be truthful, told me he had seen Marcellus in person approach the negotiators from Syracuse, I was suspicious, reasoning that the Roman Consul would not devote his time to the ransoming of a spy unless he sensed an opportunity to see the defences at close hand and to discover any weakness in them. Rumours reached me that some of the towers were not constantly manned as I had ordered, but the *skorpions* had kept the Romans at a safe distance from the walls until then.

I feared for Syracuse and its people, just as I mourned the loss of my spheres. I prayed to Artemis to spare her city.

Narrative

The May was in blossom. The crack willow by his cottage had flowered, the male catkins dangling from its branches. A little hatch of olives danced above the surface of the chalkstream below Bull Bridge, but the water was as yet too chilly for the trout to take the surface fly. By midday they might, Aengus thought as he passed, especially if a breeze brought the hawthorn flies onto the water.

The fishing season had begun, but the trout did not know that, and were failing to co-operate with the anglers who parked their cars by the hut and stalked the river for rising fish with an eagerness that suggested they had emerged from an urban hibernation of their own. The song of the newly arrived migrant birds, the spotted flycatchers and the rare whitethroat added to the urgent calls of the residents, the wood-pigeons and collared doves a constant background noise. The cuckoos called from the far woods. The female meadow pipit had lost her eggs, oblivious to the great bird that had rudely tumbled them from the nest and left her own to be incubated, and the little male was frantically flying to and fro with grubs and insects to fill a maw that was never full.

The estate restricted the fishing to a maximum of twelve rods and their occasional guests. The rods were friendly, most of them sportsmen whom the keepers knew well, generally older men disdainful of underhand tricks such as fishing an upstream nymph before July, or casting a wet fly downstream when the keepers were not in sight. Some of them surreptitiously returned a trout unharmed in spite of the rules that said all fish caught must be killed to keep the stock as wild as possible, but that was a venial sin that might be overlooked if discovered. Some were expert fishermen, in the tradition of Skues and Halford. All but one or two were very courteous to the keepers, who gave advice when asked but otherwise remained unobtrusive.

The keepers had plenty of work to do, in any case. That season's weed growth was the fastest that Sid had seen in his years on the river. Thursdays were set aside for all three men to cut it, a hard task that left them with aching arms and backs when darkness fell. Their good humour was unhindered by this, and by the luxuriance of the grass and the yellow flag irises on the banks and the reed growth after the rainy spring that kept the mowers and toppers busy each day. The May showers delayed the cutting until the grass dried, but the keepers were enjoying the early season almost as much as the fishermen, although they secretly delighted in watching the more pompous anglers catch a willow.

"Look at that bugger," Sid chortled as they crossed the lower bridge to see a fisherman trying to jerk his fly from a branch with his rod. "He'll break 'is bloody rod, just you see." The rod snapped as he spoke and the fisherman, unaware he was being observed, threw the broken bits on the bank in a fury. "Ow you gettin' on then?" Sid asked him as they passed.

"Can't you keep these banks trimmed?" the fisherman asked, red in the face.

"Certainly, sir," said Sid. "We'll cut that bloody tree down tomorrow. Why should the trout have all the shade?"

The nightingales had sung in the woods by Aengus' cottage for the past week, and he listened to them from his bed, feeling very alone. He had not seen Bridget since he had parted from her a mile from her house, leaving her to return the last part on her own in case Seth watched. When the birds ceased their calls he lay there, still awake, worrying. He went to his hiding place in the wood above Seth's house each night before darkness fell, to see nothing of note. He must wait and be patient, he knew, and found that to be the most difficult part to endure, as Bridget's warning of Seth's intention to depart echoed in his mind.

On the evening of the day that he saw his first mayfly of the season there was a light knock at his door. He opened it quickly, expectant.

Kate stood on his porch.

"May I come in?" she asked quietly.

"Of course," he said, disguising a deep disappointment. He pulled forward a chair.

She looked around the room. "So many books," she said. "When do you read them all?"

He was silent. She turned to face him. "You expected Bridget, didn't you? Am I not welcome?" There was danger in her voice.

"Of course you are."

Her voice was flat, definite. "I told you I cannot be your friend."

"I don't see you as an enemy."

Her tone became brusque. "No, you see a blackness, as you said. I don't think I'm your enemy. Yet there will come a day when many hands will be raised against me." She raised her head to look directly at him. "Will yours be among them, Aengus? No, don't answer. I don't think you will be one of them."

"Why should I turn my hand against you?"

She seemed to address herself. "It will not be long, in any case."

He waited, tired of her riddles.

"Never mind that now," she said, brusque once more, as though she had read his thoughts. "You wonder why I'm here tonight. You have put Bridget in danger."

His face went rigid. "What do you mean?"

"Seth was waiting for her when she came back from being with you," she said, looking at him evenly.

"What did he do?"

"He beat her, Aengus."

"Beat her!"

"She's not hurt. Not seriously."

"What did he *do*?"

Seth's sudden appearance had shocked Bridget, but she told him she had gone for a walk. "He shook her and asked her if she'd been with someone. She said she'd gone alone. Finally he believed her, but he was still in a great rage. He took a broom and snapped off the handle and beat her with it, hips, shoulders, legs, but not, thank God, her face. I stopped him from that, Aengus. It would be a tragedy to damage such beauty."

His legs suddenly went weak. "Where is she now?"

"At the house, terrified, but not for herself."

"Who, then?"

"Seth told her that if she strayed again he would carry out a threat he once made to her."

He lost self-control. "How can you live with him, Kate?"

She straightened in her chair, her long body rigid. "Don't ever ask me that! How dare you say *that* to me!"

He retreated. "I'm sorry."

"Never say that again, Aengus! My life is my business. Not yours. Nor anyone else's."

"I accept that."

She went on as if he had not spoken. "I came here tonight because Bridget asked me to bring you a message. I don't like being a messenger, but she's very definite that she means every word." She paused. "You won't like this."

"Tell me!"

"Stay away. She never wants to see you again."

She watched his expression change to something approaching despair. "Stay away – from her?"

"Yes, Aengus."

His voice was husky. "Did she say anything else?"

"Just this. She said: 'Tell him to stay away. I'm sorry for him, but I don't want to see him again. Whatever there was between us is finished. I'd face him and tell him that in person if I could. Tell him that, Kate.'"

"That's all?"

"Yes, that's all. Do as she says. I warned you before, and I do so again for the last time. I can smell death, Aengus, and I smell it now. Someone will die unless you do as she says. Go away from here."

He rose. "Is that all?"

"Yes. That's all." She rose and made for the door.

He stopped her. "Tell her I accept what she says, but God help Seth."

"Aengus!" Her green eyes glittered.

"Tell her that. Please. I will stay away from her, but Seth – Seth is another matter. There I make no promise. Goodbye, Kate."

Her eyes glittered again as she turned to him. "Aengus – "

"Goodbye, Kate."

The Book of Aengus

She or another might have died because of me. Instead he beat her. He beat a defenceless girl whose only crime is that she is related to him. I find it unbearable.

I am at my lowest ebb. I have lost her, just when I had begun to hope.

Narrative

The river was in its full beauty a week later. Little clouds of mayflies flew their mating dance above the banks, settling on the branches of the willows and alders, a dance of life and death, the spinners flitting on the light breeze, touching the water for an instant, rising into the air then settling again, the female's body jerking in spasms as she laid her eggs and died, spent.

The wagtails and swallows and flycatchers and wildfowl chased them in the air and on water, the comical ducklings and moorhen chicks joining in, and the trout took them with abandon. The faster glides sometimes resembled a miniature dinghy race, with the mayflies in full sail, wings up. He watched a dun flit on the surface and rise into the air again, then a great brown trout in perfect condition take it, the fish's body leaping clearly out of the water for a moment as its pale mouth opened. The trout sank back towards the waving weed and safety. One of the fishermen noted the rise and moved into position to cast. Aengus moved on.

Before dawn on the following morning Seth awoke to hear a din in his yard, so loud that he thought at first it came from inside his house. He pulled on trousers and shirt and boots, picked up his knife in its sheath, and hurried downstairs. The noise grew louder, a mixture of banging and bawling. He opened the back door of the cottage to see a faint light in the eastern sky. The noise came from his shed across the yard. His hair prickled as he approached the shed door. Something was kicking it from the inside. He unsheathed his knife, tiptoed to the door, and put his other hand on the bolt. He drew it suddenly and opened the door, the knife held high. A heavy stick knocked the weapon from his hand, sending it flying across the yard. A foot in the small of his back propelled him, off balance, into the shed, a dark void, and the door slammed behind him, the bolt clanging shut.

He began to rise from the floor, breathing heavily, and something kicked him in the face, shattering his jaw, then lashed out again and he felt his ribs crack. He fell to the concrete floor again while his attacker rushed around the shed, bawling like a wounded bull. The door opened and he saw the antlers of the stag against the dawn light as it rushed from the shed. The door closed again and Seth fainted.

The Greek

The siege continued, as did the talks outside the walls with Marcellus and the tribunes. I went again to Epikydes, who admitted me, perhaps because he no longer saw me as a threat. In the time before my visit I had walked to Hexapylon and seen the sentries sleeping, and on a tour of the walls I had seen the entire garrison at Euryalos watching a *pankration*, a contest they had staged for themselves when they should have been drilling. I saw drunkenness among the signallers at Tykhe who should have been watching for a fresh Roman attack. I told him this, and reminded him that Marcellus was the general whom Hannibal most wished to remove from the ranks of his enemies, not just for his bravery in battle but for the artifices he used to fool his opponents. He had even outwitted Hannibal himself.

– *What should we do, old one?* he asked from his couch. Among those present I saw the boy I had seen with Damippos, but I continued: – *Make one mistake, leave a single tower unguarded or let their navy slip into the harbour quietly by night, and Syracuse will fall and the city be given to the Roman soldiers who will massacre the citizens and rape and sell the remainder as slaves.*

– *We hear you, old one*, they said as I prepared to leave, telling me they had sent again for help to Carthage. Reinforcements would surely come, said one, and what did I, an old philosopher who built deadly machines but did not understand wars and alliances, know of the best course for Syracuse?

– *Go home and celebrate the feast*, they said. As I left I heard them laugh. I remembered then the warning of Kallimakhos, and knew the city was lost.

The Book of Aengus

Marcellus broke into Syracuse soon after. His men had been allowed so close to the walls while he pretended to bargain over the return of Damippus that one saw that the wall close to the Galleagra tower near Hexapylon was lower than he had expected, and could be scaled using an assault ladder. As the festival to Artemis was under way and the Syracusan sentries revelled, then slept off their wine, Marcellus sent a tribune to lead a maniple of handpicked soldiers over the wall in the darkness, to kill the sleeping guards on the other side. Other maniples followed, until a thousand Roman soldiers were inside the walls. This Roman force continued to Epipolae, sounding trumpets from all sides in the darkness to confuse the Syracusans garrisoned there. The garrison fled, believing the full force of the Roman army to be inside the walls, and the invading force paused, as ordered, on the plateau in the darkness to wait for Marcellus to join them. At dawn the Consul took one of the towers while the guards slumbered, sent his men along the walls until they reached one of the gates of the Hexapylon, battered it open, and the moment the Consul had awaited for almost three years had come. The army of Marcellus, the Consul to the fore, began to pour through into Syracuse. Within hours they held the plateau of Epipolae and approached Tyche and Neapolis, killing as they went.

The Greek

I heard shouts from the citizens, and went outside. Deserters ran through the gates into Akhradina, shouting that the Romans were in the city. I found my sword and hastened as fast as I could across the causeway to Ortygia, where I saw Epikydes calling everyone to join him in repulsing the enemy. At first all was confusion. I told Epikydes to stand on the steps of the temple, where I joined him, calling loudly to the citizens to be calm, to gather their arms quickly, and to join us in repulsing the barbarians. A few slunk away, but most recovered their dignity when they saw a familiar old man shouting at them and said they would fight with us. After a time we had gathered a force of some size, and manned the walls of Akhradina, stopping the deserters as they ran in and calling on them to join us. Some ran on, heads bowed in shame while the soldiers in our band jeered them, but most heeded us. One told us that Marcellus had tried to take the fort at Euryalos, but the garrison had repulsed the Romans and its leader had sent for assistance from Himilco. The Roman Consul had taken up his position between Neapolis and Tykhe, and his soldiers were plundering the houses of the citizens in both quarters. A little later a runner came in to say that Himilco was bringing up a large Carthaginian force.

We had a chance then. I told Epikydes that we must try to relieve the fort, that if the Carthaginians came into Euryalos from the west they could take the Romans when they were most vulnerable, splitting them in two, hemmed in by the walls. A surprise attack from Euryalos would trap them like fish in a net and might turn the opportunity into a decisive victory, but the Syracusans might surrender the fort at any moment, I told him, so we must act at once. He hesitated, then said he would return into the city to gather more men. I insisted that there was no time, that there were enough brave hearts among us to make the attempt when the Romans did not expect us, but he left and when he returned a few hours later the commander at Euryalos, despairing of reinforcement, had surrendered in return for the garrison's safe conduct to Akhradina. Several days later, when Himilco arrived with Hippokrates and the Carthaginian army set up camp near the harbour, Marcellus was in position, ready to receive them, and prepared to starve Akhradina into surrendering.

At length Epikydes and Hippokrates decided on a simultaneous attack, Hippokrates against one of three Roman camps, Epikydes against Marcellus himself. I wished then for a return of my youth. I would have liked to go with them, knowing the odds were that

I would perish, that Marcellus would expect us as we had thrown away the advantage of surprise, but I was eager still to deal the Romans one last blow. Instead I was left behind to remain on the walls, to watch as Marcellus routed Epikydes and his men. Hippokrates, too, failed, so badly that the Roman general Crispinus chased him until he ran for his life.

Stranger, we draw close to the end. The Carthaginian admiral Bomilcar slipped away with part of his fleet that night to seek reinforcements from Carthage, while Epikydes sailed out to join him, and soon after the Goddess, angry with the crimes of men, brought down a plague on Syracuse.

The Book of Aengus

It was autumn, an unusually hot autumn according to Livy. The plague swept through both sides, Roman and Carthaginian. It killed relatively fewer Syracusans who were inured to their climate, but the Carthaginians, less acclimatised and more exposed to the fetid marshes on the edge of the city where their camp lay, died like fish left high on a beach. The army of Carthage in Sicily perished to a man outside the walls of Syracuse, Himilco and Hippocrates among them, while Marcellus moved his men up from the swampy ground, into Tyche and Neapolis, and saved enough of them to keep his force largely intact.

The war was almost over, yet Carthage made a final attempt to win Sicily. Bomilcar sailed from Carthage with a reinforced fleet, Epicydes on board. The east wind forced him to stay out to sea, and when it changed a Roman fleet, smaller than his, confronted him, sent by Marcellus who feared being pent up in Syracuse. Bomilcar's reaction still puzzles the historians. Perhaps because the wind did not suit, perhaps remembering a naval disaster from the first Punic War, perhaps saving his fleet until the odds were even more in his favour, the Carthaginian admiral did not engage the Romans, but sailed away. The Syracusans under siege in Achradina and Ortygia saw all was lost and sent envoys to Marcellus to ask him to spare their lives if they surrendered. While the talks went on Marcellus bribed one of the three garrison commanders in Syracuse, a Spanish mercenary, to open a gate in the walls near the fountain of Arethusa. After a siege of three years, the Romans finally entered the inner city. That was the day that Archimedes died.

Syracuse surrendered, and Marcellus gave it to his soldiers for a day, a tradition the Romans enjoyed after the long siege. The Syracusan treasury was seized on behalf of the Republic, its riches to be unmatched even when the Romans took Carthage itself. The wealth of the individual citizens fell to the soldiers who ran through the streets, breaking into houses, killing and raping and taking slaves. The temples were ransacked and Marcellus, even as he publicly lamented Archimedes' death and protested that he had instructed his soldiers to spare him, ordered the portable sculptures and altars and treasures of Syracuse to be collected and shipped to Rome to allow the citizens of the Republic to gaze, for the first time, upon the glories and culture of Greece. Among them was a mechanical orrery representing celestial motion, possibly driven by water power, that the descendants of Marcellus were to display to their friends. Another was a solid celestial globe. Both were made by Archimedes. The globe, a wonder of science that Marcellus placed in the Temple of Vesta, was to inspire Ovid:

> *There stands a globe hung by Syracusan art*
> *In closed air, a small image of the vast vault of heaven…*

The citizens of Rome did not give the returning Consul a triumph for his victory, but a lesser reward, an ovation, as Syracuse was deemed to have been taken by artifice rather than by the sword. The rules were strict on this point. The *mobile vulgus* of Rome gazed upon the spoil from Syracuse. Its beauty left them unmoved at first, while many of them accused Marcellus of defiling the gods of the Greeks by removing them from their natural places. Later, a delegation from Syracuse who came before the Senate to complain of the Romans' uncivilised treatment of the city was given its hearing and turned away. Marcellus explained in person that he had merely acted according to custom.

Perhaps he had, but Syracuse would be avenged. When Marcellus returned to the fight against Hannibal in Italy, the soldiers of Carthage ambushed him in a wood and killed him. Hannibal, acting according to custom, honoured him by burning his body.

Seth is back.

He had returned from hospital, his jaw heavily wired and his ribs bandaged. Aengus had not seen Bridget.

"She never leaves the house," Kate told him angrily when he stopped her on the path to the main road. "Do you realise the damage you've done?"

"How?"

"How, he says! How! You nearly killed Seth, but he's alive, and full of hate, so full of hate he seems to have gathered all the hate in the world and swallowed it whole, without leaving any for others." Her voice grew intense: "You couldn't imagine there was that much hate in the world. He radiates it! He sits there, brooding, growling to himself, willing his body to recover from the wounds you dealt him. He hasn't spoken a single word to Bridget or me since I found him howling in the shed that morning – howling like a wounded beast! And his eyes! You should see his eyes. They're fixed, Aengus, fixed on something in the distance, almost all the time. Can you guess what he sees?"

"Me, I suppose."

"You suppose! He will not rest until he kills you, Aengus. I wouldn't give a moonbeam for your life. You should have left him alone, or killed him, but you did the worst thing possible – you humiliated him, but left him alive."

"For what he did."

"Yes, but don't you see!" Her voice grew exasperated. "He thinks she's his property, Aengus. He always has."

"What does he intend for her?" His voice seemed frozen. He could not read her expression.

"To follow a custom."

He felt a cold hand grip his innards, and for a moment he saw Seth as he had dreamed of him. He forced himself back to reality.

"Do you know when?"

She shrugged. "Soon."

"What about Bridget, Kate?"

"She's wasting away. She eats nothing, and says nothing. I cook for them, and Seth eats but says nothing. Bridget says almost as little and eats nothing. Once I spoke of you, when Seth was out of earshot, and she told me she didn't want to hear your name again.

She's fading, and it's terrible to watch. Go before he kills you, too."

She saw how drawn his face was as he spoke: "I can't leave before August."

"That will be too late, Aengus."

"I must stay until then."

He looked at her, the breeze ruffling her untidy mass of hair. Her head was turned to one side, her strong jawbone prominent, her lips moving. She seemed to mutter something to herself before she turned back to him, with an air of finality, and said: "Then the tragedy must be acted to the finish. Goodbye."

Weeks passed and the countryside blazed with colour and blossom. The mayfly hatched and died, and the trout became lazy and choosy, sated by the yearly feast. The river settled down to its summer mood, broody and quiet but proud of its finery, chuckling past the willow branches that dipped into the current, rushing through the narrows, spreading over the shallows, slowing to a stately flow in the deeper reaches. In these quieter stretches, in and out of the reedbeds, rode the young ducklings, miniature coots and the odd solitary cygnet, guarded by proud parents. Once, at dusk on one of the carrier streams, Aengus glimpsed a strange series of little bobbing backs and drew back because the shape resembled that of a water serpent, then saw it was the otter cubs following their parents.

Dawn and dusk were the least difficult times for him as he replayed in his mind what Kate had said. The calls of the hedgerow birds, woodpigeons and collared doves brought him from his cottage when the sun rose and he had completed many of his daily chores before Sid and Bill appeared. When dusk fell he took up his post above Seth's cottage, seeking a tortured consolation in her closeness.

The beauty of June passed into the sultriness of July, when the air grew listless and heavy and the night sky frequently flashed with lightning, the thunder answering from across the river. After such a night the dawn air seemed light and cool, a relief after the feverish hours that he spent in his cottage, burdened by doubts and despair, torturing himself with the recollection that Bridget did not want to hear his name. Many times he considered rising from his bed, shouldering his pack and taking the road to the north, north as far as he could go to where the colder winds would blow away the terrible feelings of frustration and guilt. Only the images of the mother and daughter yet to be reunited, and of the old Greek in a bloodstained *chiton*, stopped him before he put his foot on the floor of his bedroom. Many times during the nights he asked himself why he had been chosen for either labour, why even the Greek and the raven seemed to have forsaken him, and heard only the young owls and the river respond. It was on one such night, when his thoughts were at their most agonising, that the Greek, long absent, returned.

The Greek

The clean east wind had blown through the city as if to cleanse it from the plague, then the hot weather returned, bringing a storm so loud that it woke me during my last night alive on this earth, a storm that clapped and thundered like an angry god as it brought the great purple clouds in from the sea.

I had slept in fits, still feverish from a touch of the plague that had killed so many. When a thunderclap woke me I donned a *khlamys* and climbed to the top of the house.

Thunder spoke while the spectacle before me weighed heavily on my spirits. Soldier and citizen alike wandered the streets, some of them drunk on black wine, some looting the houses of their fellow citizens while below me the slaves had to stand guard, ready to defend the house like heroes even though I had freed them all before the siege began.

I thought of the men who had led Syracuse in the past, of Gelo who made everyone quake before him, of Agathokles the terrible, of Dionysios the mighty Tyrant who put the fear of death into Carthage, and of cunning Hiero, my kinsman. I would have given much to have any one of them lead the city that night.

I saw the glare of a fire from Ortygia, and wondered whether the citizens, in frustration, were setting fire to the city buildings. Eventually the glow subsided. I turned away. There was a mighty bolt from Zeus, a peal of thunder that shook the city itself, and in the flash I saw my own shade dressed in a burial robe. All was darkness once more, and when the next flash came that place was empty. I knew then that I was about to die.

The Book of Aengus

He was probably hallucinating, standing in the rain, still feverish, watching his *polis* crumbling around him, feeling the end was near.

My own spirits sink also as I begin to think we will not find her in time.

Narrative

The wheat waved in the fields on the downs and the young cuckoo had fledged, leaving the meadow pipits proud but tired. The fox cubs had been taught to hunt and been pushed away by their parents to hunt for themselves. The earth turned its northern face towards late summer and the browns and golds of autumn, and the chalkstream country began to look overblown, the colours of the flowers in the water meadows beginning to peak as the year passed into middle age and the summer temperatures steadied before the annual decline. The harvest moon would fill within a few days, and still he did not know to where the woman had been moved.

It was at that critical time that his hopes sank into despair and it was at that critical time – a particularly oppressive morning, listless and muggy – that he made a desperate telephone call and heard the news that she had been found.

The Greek

The time of your visit to the Goddess is at hand, yet I fear for you and sense death close by. Be wary. Look for enemies. You are young and have much to complete. I would the Goddess had granted me but one more year. I would have accomplished much.

They gave me a monument after they had killed me at Syracuse, Stranger, and they sang the paean for the safe passage of my shade, yet they did not understand the soul of the Greek, that it could not rest until the work was finished.

I would like to say to you that I chose to be a philosopher

because I sought the beauty of truth. It would be truer to say that I chose that life to satisfy a restless curiosity of spirit that constantly needed to be fed, as fire needs wood and the body needs water. I chose mathematics because I could prove the truth of what I found. It was my path. It was a life in which there was always something new.

At the end of the circle of my life I drew what I saw to be the rough order of the cosmos. There were many gaps, and my guesses at distances and speeds would need years of observation to prove them, yet I saw its proportions and regularity, the planets not as wanderers of the heavens but as everlasting sentries of the sun, keeping to a rhythm that we, blind as we were, had not seen, the earth another planet with its own orbiting sentinel, the whole in proportion with the sun, the cosmos like a temple where all is balanced in mutual attraction, a syntax, but so large that it brought a strange sense of exhilaration to know that, in spite of its size, I was part of it. Even as I waited for Akhradina to fall I began to think of what lay beneath the cosmos I saw, the smallest matter of which everything is made, the *atomos* of Demokritos perhaps, smaller perhaps even than a grain of sand, with a geometry of its own of which we knew nothing, except that every proportion in it, irrational or whole, was as natural as the cosmos, that it had to be for the world around us to continue as it had, obeying the laws that were with us from the beginning, if there was one.

Narrative

He held the telephone close to his ear while his heart thumped and his brow glistened with sweat, his tone disbelieving as he rattled questions at the lawyer in London, demanding proofs and reassurance beyond reason, the dam of frustration breached at last.

He spoke to the detective next, writing the details awkwardly while he held pen in one hand, phone in the other as he steadied his notebook against the scratched Perspex wall of the phone booth, checking the information more than once, elation finally overcoming doubt. When he replaced the receiver and stepped from the booth he looked up at the sweating sky and breathed deeply.

At his cottage he studied a map, part of him relieved beyond description that the waiting would soon end, while something elsewhere in his being pained him with an acuteness that he could not escape. It was an effort to take up his journal and record the words of the Greek.

The Greek

I arose on the last morning of my life to begin work at first light, knowing the end was close. The air was wonderfully fresh and pure after the rain. When the sun came up I began drawing in the wax, then stopped. The earth seemed to clamour and I heard the sounds of trumpets from the direction of the causeway. I resumed work. Soon the Romans entered my home.

I have told you what happened then, but they were not plane circles in my tablets, Stranger. They were spheres, a plan of the cosmos. I have come to you to tell you of this, and of the events leading up to my death because, Stranger, I know you to have the vision of a god. Tell me, then, what you see when you meet the Goddess, the nature of the cosmos that we philosophers sought.

The Book of Aengus

First I must act, and act quickly. Seth will be like a mad beast when he finds her gone.

He'll drive to the house and find it empty, then come here to choke the truth from me, probably to kill me. He plans to do that in any case, but at a time of his choosing. I have a plan to delay him, but it depends on timing and luck.

We approach the final act also in our tragedy, as Kate said, but one to be played at the chalk of Silbury Hill rather than at the limestone theatre of Syracuse, and one where I act on my own. If my luck holds as it has I will reunite the two who were torn apart because of a primordial lust that has survived through many generations of what we term civilisation. Mother and daughter will be together once more, an achievement that I could not even hope for a short while ago. It will bring the peace I seek, if peace is possible without her, and then I will go to Silbury to see little but the harvest moon and perhaps experience some sense of the

Stone Age people and their festival. That will be the finish of it all, and I will leave here, alone again. Yet I have a feeling of psychic intuition, almost a conviction, that I will be given a revelation of some kind, a moment – probably not more than that – when I will see a truth. Perhaps he says I have the vision of a god because he thinks I have a gift of seeing, an Orphic sense of knowing, or *nous* as the Greeks called it.

Part of me dreads such a revelation, and part of me welcomes it with a wild anticipation, even though I'm warned of danger. Who knows how to account for our feelings? The search for our inner self, for the deepest secrets and inherited memories of the psyche, is more challenging than the search for the truth about the universe, and yet they are the same search.

Narrative

He slept badly, his mind a vortex of conflicting thoughts, but woke resolute. During the evening before he had made his arrangements, gone through his plans several times, checked all the eventualities his brain could assemble and begun to pack his things, leaving a note for his lawyer in case he did not return. Then he had left the cottage in the darkness and cut through the woods to the main road, crossed it and found his old spying post under a sheltering oak. A slight breeze came from the south-west and the moon, almost full, shone dully from a misty sky. He caught several glimpses of Seth against the lighted windows, glimpses that reassured him and hardened his resolve. He glimpsed another figure and his resolve wavered for a moment, but he shook his head to clear it and left for his cottage, to take what rest he could.

He waited until the middle of the morning before he left in the keeper's van, driving east before turning north for the Thames which he crossed at Lechlade, the air lighter, his mood alternating between a feeling of dread that he would fail, and one of relief that the waiting would at least be over. As the miles passed these mood swings settled to a sense of inevitability that sat uneasily alongside a growing nervousness of what he might find when he reached his destination, and what his reception might be.

He began to rehearse his opening explanation, discarded it and attempted a second that sounded even lamer. So preoccupied was he on the third that he missed the turning off the main road and had to reverse. His subsequent irritation with himself brought a return of concentration.

He found the next turning successfully, the map then firmly fixed in his mind, the old van rattling and shaking as it passed narrow farm gateways and tall hedgerows that hid the fields from his view. Several times he had to pull onto the verge to allow a tractor or another farm vehicle to pass, then the road opened slightly as he reached the outskirts of the village. He stopped for a moment to check his notes, and drove up the single street, past the shops and low houses of grimed Cotswold stone that had once been the colour of honey. On the pavement was a woman – a stocky, cheerful-looking lady in her forties – whom he recognised from his notes as the detective. He parked and went to meet her.

"Aengus?" she said.

He nodded. She led him down a side street to a row of small, terraced houses, and pointed.

"Do you want me to wait?"

He nodded again, then walked up the front path and knocked.

As he waited it seemed to him that all background noise ceased. A car went soundlessly past. Two women with shopping bags walked by the gate, their mouths opening and closing in silent conversation. One of them looked at him strangely and said something inaudible to the other. A mist seemed to descend over his eyes, shutting him from the outside world. It was a warm summer's day, yet he felt a chill.

He did not hear the light footsteps in the hallway, or see the door open and a figure emerge. He was detached, weightless, floating alone in a void, feeling without feeling, being without being, all in suspension, helpless in his weakness.

A female voice, grave, with a trace of an old authority and in some way familiar, penetrated to him. The mist cleared, and he saw a tall woman dressed in grey looking directly at him.

He stared at the head that was held high like a goddess and instinctively took a step back, overwhelmed by a presence that seemed wildly out of place in this banal house with its rickety little porch of glass and gaudy yellow tiles, its neglected garden. He lowered his eyes, feeling a ridiculous urge to bow to the regal woman whose dark hair was tinged with silver, and who was smiling gently, a look of inquiry changing to concern on a face full of compassion and grief, the high cheekbones and great eyes so like Bridget's that he stepped back again, ashamed of his worn tweed coat, shabby trousers, and scuffed brown shoes.

She surveyed him for what seemed an age. "I don't need anything if you're trying to sell me something," she said, but kindly, as if she felt sorry for him.

He found that he still owned a voice. "I'm – ah – a friend of Bridget. Bridget, your daughter," he managed, the words almost a mumble.

There was a silence. The woman paled and drew back. "I have no daughter," she said, almost in a whisper. "Please go."

He cursed his clumsiness. "Bridget is alive," he said. "Please listen. I've come to bring you to her."

Her face filled with anguish. "You are mistaken, whoever you are. I have no daughter. She is dead – or at least dead to me. Please go."

He heard her voice as the echo of the cry in the night. "No, she's not dead, and nor is she dead to you," he said, some of his courage returning. "That was a terrible trick of Seth's. She loves you still – more than ever – and waits for you."

He saw different waves of emotion – desperation, hope, relief, disbelief, then hope again – cross her face as she struggled with them, and underlying these emotions he detected the remains of a great dignity that he recognised. He stepped forward and led her into the porch and sat her on a broken basketwork chair. He went back to close the door, glimpsing the detective on the opposite side of the road.

The woman sat up, the hope in her expression mixed with doubt. "Who *are* you?"

"I'm a friend of Bridget's. I live and work near her. I met her by accident, and gradually discovered her secret."

She hesitated, then her eyes blazed suddenly. "Seth says she became an addict, that she was dead to me – didn't want ever to see me again – but that he would kill her if I tried to find her."

Her eyes were full of questions. "She's not an addict, " he said gently, "and she wants to see you more than she wants anything in the world."

She looked directly at him, and he saw where Bridget's courage originated. "How do I know this is not another trick of Seth's? You're not – " She gestured at his person.

"Not dressed like a gentleman? No, but I've brought you a card of a solicitor in London whom you can ring. He'll tell you I speak the truth."

She took the card, looked at it, searched his face, his eyes, and made her own decision. "I'll come with you."

He breathed deeply, relief flooding him. "Pack now. Take only what you need. Hurry! Seth could arrive at any time."

They left the house fifteen minutes later, Aengus carrying her suitcase. The detective waited on the corner. "Excuse me one moment," said Aengus, putting down the suitcase, "I must have a word with this lady."

The detective grinned. "Well done," she said. "We did it."

"Yes. Will you call the others? Tell them I'm on my way with a passenger."

"Gladly," she said.

"I've seen that woman before," said Bridget's mother as they walked to Sid's van.

"You have," said Aengus. "She's been looking for you for months."

He glanced frequently at the rear-view mirrors as he drove, feeling the woman's gaze fix on him, gauging his character from his head, looking into his soul. Evidently she approved, as there was a warmth in her voice when she spoke, asking the question she had not dared to put.

"How is she?"

He was frank. "She seems healthy, but she's not eating." She lowered her head at that and was silent, her hands clasping and unclasping. He took a deep breath and told her where her daughter lived, her circumstances, of Kate, and of the aboriginal rage of the captor who still held her. He spoke of the terrible house, and of how the local people shunned it. Then he told of how Seth had confessed to murdering his mother. The woman gave a sharp intake of breath at that, and after a pause he saw her nod. Perhaps it was not a surprise.

He turned onto a main road and accelerated, the noise level increasing as the van bowled along. It was hot inside, but neither noticed as she began to question him again.

"Why are you doing this? You're the one in danger now. Seth can have terrible rages. I saw them. Even as a youth he had them."

She was silent while she studied his profile again, then she spoke of the day that Seth took Bridget from her, of the promises he had made, the lies and deceptions he had used to turn mother against daughter, and finally the threats that he had issued to both. The time of parting was like a death: "I wept all that night before she left. Her room was next to mine. Once I lifted my head and heard her sobbing, but when I went to her she pushed me away, telling me it was her decision and hers alone. She lied to me to save me."

He squinted at the road in front, giving her time to recover. The sun was almost directly ahead, dazzling him.

"That was the worst night of my life," she said. "The next morning she was outwardly calm, but she broke down when he came to take her. We clung to each other. He swore at us and pulled us apart. Then he took her away. He came back a few hours later when I was still in shock and moved me to a house he had rented."

They passed under the motorway, only a few miles from safety or calamity. Parkland opened out on both sides of the bypass. They were close to the Kennet. He began to breathe more easily.

Bridget's mother spoke again. Seth had moved her abruptly, arriving late one evening without warning. He had thrown her things into a van and taken her to another village. She would be safer there, he told her.

On her first night in the new house she had had a dream in which she heard her daughter crying quietly, and had cried out to her in return, waking at the dead of night, alone and helpless.

She was silent again before asking: "What will become of us?"

He would take her and Bridget to a safe place in London: "He will try to find you, even as we lay charges against him. We'll make sure he doesn't."

There was a note of approval in her voice: "You seem very certain."

"I don't know why I should be, but I am," he said. "Some sense tells me he will be the cause of his own destruction, that he'll die before he goes to jail. His violence may be the weakness that will kill him."

She looked at his profile again as he drove, his head almost touching the roof of the van.

With the instinctive curiosity of a mother, she asked: "Are you and Bridget close?"

"We were," said Aengus after a pause, the words coming with difficulty, "we were for a short time – a very short time – but then it ended. In any case I leave in a few days' time, and won't be back."

She sounded surprised, almost hurt. "I'm sorry to hear that."

She was silent again then, absorbed in her thoughts, evidently refusing to allow herself to raise her hopes too high, and said little until they reached Sid's house where the little keeper and his wife awaited them. There he asked her to write a note to her daughter, dictating the outline. He left her then, clutching the envelope, feeling a curious sense of anti-climax as he reflected that rescuing this regal woman had been almost too easy.

He planned to watch Seth's house until Bridget was alone. He waited in the wood and after an hour saw Seth emerge, climb into his car, and drive towards Newbury. "That's a stroke of luck," he thought, "but where's Kate?"

He saw her, and the feeling of anti-climax vanished as he knew his luck had stayed with him. She was leaving the house with her dog. She looked around before she began to walk, and for a moment she seemed to have seen Aengus, who shrank behind a young oak when he felt her piercing gaze appear to rest on him. The mastiff followed her stare. She hesitated, spoke briefly to her dog who growled impatiently, then led him away.

When she was out of sight he moved quickly, keeping to cover where he could, but determined to seize the opportunity. He reached the house, pushed the note through the letterbox, knocked loudly on the door, and ran for cover again. He watched the door. It did not open. For a moment he was convinced he had blundered, that she would not answer or – worse still – that she was not at home. He felt cold as he thought of Seth returning and finding the note.

After an age the door was flung wide and he saw the girl, thinner than ever, with hollow cheeks and huge eyes, holding a note in her hand. She looked into the yard. He ducked, then raised his head again. Bridget still stood there, in a worn cotton dress, looking wildly around her. Then, as he watched, she ran inside, leaving the door open. He breathed again, and almost sagged with relief when he saw her emerge once more, look around her to check she was alone, then run across the main road and down the lane towards the estate cottages.

He followed her, keeping his distance, but she did not look behind her, running at full tilt then, with light and very rapid footfalls on the lane, running and running, sensing the moment of freedom was at hand, her skirts flying, knees pumping, arms swinging, hair streaming on the wind, and he ran too, but discreetly, so discreetly that he lost her when she rounded a bend in the lane, running faster than ever.

Aengus stopped then, and waited. He heard a cry, then another in answer, and entered a willow thicket by Sid's cottage. Another cry sounded. When he reached the edge of the trees and could watch without being seen, he saw two figures in a close embrace. On instinct he bowed his head.

He was back in his hiding place when Kate returned with her mastiff, entered the cottage, and re-emerged, calling for Bridget. He felt her piercing gaze again as she slowly scanned the landscape. Then she shrugged and went back in the house.

It was late when Seth returned, parked his van in the yard and entered his home. Aengus heard raised voices, Kate's high and shrill, Seth's a bellow of rage. Then the door of the cottage opened and Seth stood in the yard, the nearly full moon outlining the bullet head and the burly figure. He stood there for an age as Aengus waited. The silence was shattered by a voice like an angry bull, an unearthly call full of rage and agony: "*BRIDGET!*"

That cry of pain and loss echoed in his mind throughout the evening, and the clear night that followed, as Aengus determined to watch the man closely, to attack him if he stepped on the estate. Seth climbed the slope behind his own house, calling as he went, but more quietly. At one point he came so close to Aengus' hiding place that his breathing was audible. Aengus sat as quietly as a fox, tensed, ready for Seth to spring on him, but the man walked by, head bent as if with grief. Seth returned to the house, and he heard raised voices once more, Kate's taking on a threatening tone, Seth's bellows gradually subsiding. Aengus waited for an hour after the light went out in the house, then went to his cottage for a few hours' sleep. Before dawn he was back in the wood.

When his stomach called for breakfast he saw Seth leave the house, climb into his car, and drive away. "He's going to check on Bridget's mother," Aengus murmured. "I wish I could be there to see it." He watched the departing car and stretched his cramped limbs while his stomach sent a further appeal. He went home.

He was sitting on the porch after breakfast when Bridget and her mother, flanked by the two keepers, appeared on the path. He stood, feeling strangely awkward, in awe of the tall woman and afraid of what her daughter's reaction might be. Bridget did not greet him, or meet his eyes, but kept her place behind her mother. The air felt heavy suddenly.

It was the tall woman who spoke. "Do we disturb you?" Her voice was kind, solicitous, filled with her own form of gratitude. Bridget's big eyes fixed upon him for a moment, then looked away, her expression unfathomable. She seemed to keep as great a distance from Aengus as she could. Whatever sense of achievement he had felt drained from him then.

"No, not at all. Please sit down," he said. He had placed only one chair on his porch. After some hesitation, Bridget's mother took it, looking around her, at the cottage, the river, the bird perched on the willow whose branches swept the porch roof, and then at Aengus who leant against the porch. The others stood by, mutely.

"I came to thank you," said the lady in a halting voice, "but the right words won't come. Perhaps our debt to you is too great." She glanced at Bridget, who remained silent. "Perhaps we don't realise yet how much we owe you, or what you've delivered us from." She paused, looking a little lost, then asked: "Is there nothing we can do in return?"

He hesitated, then said: "Only that the two of you leave as soon as possible. You must disappear."

The lady reached to put her hand on his arm. "Your friend will soon be here to take us away, Aengus," she said softly, her eyes full of compassion. "Will you come and see us when we're settled?"

He hesitated, feeling Bridget's eyes upon him. "No, I think not."

"Where will you go?"

"Possibly to Iceland."

Bridget spoke for the first time. "His mother came from there, Mummy." Her voice sounded tense.

"I see. Aengus, is there nothing I can do for you?"

"Thank you, but I've everything I need."

She gathered her things, a little unsteadily, then said: "Come along, you lovely men! Bridget, we had better leave or we'll be late."

The lady kissed Aengus and embraced him as she would a son. She held him again for a moment, then turned away, her hand going to her eye for an instant before she pushed the two men to the path.

Bridget did not follow immediately, but turned to him, her face lacking any expression. "Goodbye."

He reached for the outstretched hand and pressed it gently. His heart felt numb. "Goodbye, Bridget."

She hesitated, her eyes suddenly moist. Then she stood on her toes and kissed him on the cheek, as a sister might. "I'm sorry." He noticed the huskiness in her voice, even as he felt through his numbness the certain finality of his dismissal. A mist seemed to cover his eyes. Through it he saw her walk quickly away, without looking back.

The Book of Aengus

Until then I must have allowed myself to hope without realising it, perhaps because it was the first time we'd spoken since she sent Kate to me. It's strange how the ego clings to hope, no matter how fragile the reason, until truth intrudes with a peculiar violence of its own. It's strange also to feel so terribly alone, more alone than I've ever felt. I'd grown used to solitariness. I must grow used to it again, however hard it will be.

The numbness had turned to a dull pain when he saw Seth return and heard his rage as he shouted at Kate. Then at lunchtime the cars began to arrive. By mid-afternoon there were six of them. Seth had called in his friends. "Too late!" murmured Aengus, with grim satisfaction. "They've flown."

He waited and watched, fighting the feeling of hopelessness that crept through his guard. Seth and his men had been indoors for an hour before Aengus stirred himself and went to the phone box on the main road. He called the emergency number and told the police that there would be a drugs shipment that day from Seth's house. He did not give his name.

When the police cars arrived he went to his cottage and sat on the porch on the edge of despair, listening to the moorhens squabble. The river flowed quietly past him and the willows whispered and gradually he fell into a merciful doze. He woke an hour later and realised he had missed lunch. He made a sandwich that he could not eat, then, his mind in a daze, he watched the river until it was time to go.

The police cars had left when he reached the main road. He turned into the woodland paths, walking without his customary springy pace, then arrived on the main road at the far end of the estate to wait for a bus.

He went first to Avebury, where he found a festival of sorts preparing, groups of young and middle-aged evidently readying for a torchlit procession after the earlier ceremonies, chattering and calling in loud voices. He moved among them, feeling very alone and out of place, watching an ageing hippy with long white wispy hair smoking a strange cigarette, leaning against the great Barber's Stone, almost certainly unaware, Aengus thought, that this stone had once crushed a man to death, and that his skeleton had lain beneath it for six hundred years before it was discovered. A youth with bad acne was playing a guitar by the Blacksmith's Stone while his friends danced in a circle and sang, a strange, discordant song that meant nothing to Aengus, who tried to recall the magic of his visit with Bridget to this spot, but Avebury was different that night, the sarsens surrounded by smells of frying fat and burgers and noise. He saw several furtive men darting from group to group, exchanging money for something in plastic bags.

He left with a sense of escape and started on the path from the car park that would take him to Silbury, a mile away, glad to breathe the clean air, reminding himself that however unhappy he might feel his tasks were almost done, unaware that several men had left the throng at Avebury and were following him. Dusk was falling when the conical shape began to loom against the sky.

To his left rose the upper edge of the full moon, behind the beech stands at the top of the far downland. The sky was clear, the air colder than usual, but the moon soon lit patches of cloud and he guessed that visibility would fluctuate as the night went on. There were a few visitors walking around the base of Silbury Hill, but they soon left, taking the footpath to Avebury and the festivities.

Aengus laid his old waxed coat on the ground and sat on it, his back propped by a grassy mound that was already wet with dew. He looked at the shadow of the hill above him, craned his neck to look at the constellation of grieving Cygnus above his head, then at Draco which lay a little west of north, south of the Little Bear. Cassiopeia, a vain queen, had swung around in her chair in her endless, futile quest to cradle the Pole Star in her lap. He picked out that north star and reflected that he looked at the past, that its light had travelled for more than four hundred years to reach him, that the pinprick that met his eye had left the star while Shakespeare was writing his plays and Elizabeth Tudor sat on the throne of England, just as the light that contemporary astronomers saw in deepest space had travelled for nearly thirteen billion years from the galaxies near the furthest part of the universe from him, enabling man to look back directly almost to the beginning of time and space, an inseparable unity. The stars were points of silver in the lightening sky, while the moon was slowly dragging its body from the edge of the earth.

Silbury Hill seemed to glow gently in the growing moonlight, its flank flecked with a silvery tinge. Above it shone the Milky Way, a wave of starlight that the Celts had called the Track of the White Cow. He knew that what he saw was the galaxy from its side. From the front it must be a terrific sight, a great spiral wheel made up of billions of stars, each a massive nuclear furnace, unimaginably hot, many of them much greater than the sun in size. Its centre was an enormous black hole, its gravity so intense that the light of the stars it swallowed could not escape. The immensity of it comforted him strangely as he reflected that that single galaxy contained perhaps four hundred billion stars, and there were up to 150 billion galaxies beyond it again.

He looked at the hill again and thought of the people who had built it and who had certainly gazed up at much the same night sky. As he gazed he shivered, sensing that danger was near. He looked around him, lying flat to improve visibility at ground level, but saw nothing. He stared across towards Avebury and saw flickering torches. The festival of sorts had evidently begun. He settled down to wait, trying to concentrate.

A little later he saw the lights of several electric torches approach from the car park at the foot of the hill, powerful torches that swept their beams along the paths, then on the ground around its perimeter. Rough voices sounded. One of the beams caught him, dazzling him, and he put up his hands in anger. The light remained on him. He rose to his feet, nerves tingling and temper rising, but the light swung away again and a voice called: "Sorry!" The torches continued to move, away from the hill and back towards the car park.

He settled once more, but uneasily, a feeling of premonition growing. The moon was then clear of the downland, a majestic silvery-yellow orb beginning its journey across the sky, rising imperceptibly, the dark places of its craters and ashen seas visible to the naked eye. Wisps of cloud obscured its face from time to time, then the moon sailed through them, as if in triumph, showing its face proudly to the watchers on earth. Aengus, still in a daze, stood to ease his limbs, and a few moments later a raven croaked from the hill.

He whirled, and the movement saved him from immediate death. He saw Seth, arm raised, saw the flash of moonlight on the blade of the big knife, heard the scream of rage and revenge, and threw himself at the man, but too late. He felt a hot, searing pain as the knife plunged into his side, heard the roar of triumph, launched himself at Seth and felt the knife plunge again. The light of the moon dimmed as his body hit the ground, and he lay on his back, the pitiless galaxy above him, the pain too much to bear. He heard the baying of a dog, and a shrill call, a woman's shout, imperious and immediate and somehow familiar, and heard Seth shouting in return. Consciousness left him and he lay still, at the foot of Silbury Hill, his life's blood draining from him.

The Vision of Aengus

He was kneeling at the edge of a wood, looking down a valley. A Doric temple stood in the distance, a small gem of a temple, its raking cornice and pediment in harmony with the valley, a plain architrave carrying the entablature of frieze and cornice of blue triglyphs and yellow metopae with delicate sculptured reliefs of the huntress, the shafts supporting the top fluted and drummed, tapering towards each capital. As he watched, a centaur crossed in front of an altar close to the temple, joining another at the right hand side. Both cantered slowly away from him, towards the head of the valley. Aengus looked down.

Below him was a spring from which a winding stream flowed. A beautiful young woman, naked as the white marble statue of a goddess, was emerging from it, her handmaidens, their faces a startling white, advancing with towels towards her. A delicate silver bow and quiver lay on the grass by the water's edge.

The sunlight caught the lustre of her hair and rested on her face and bosom. He tried to avert his eyes, but they would not obey. Instead they feasted on her beauty, and he knew that he saw what no mortal man or god had seen before. He felt a command to kneel and the movement evidently caught the eye of the goddess. She turned to look directly at him, and he saw she had the face of Bridget. He groaned aloud.

The face changed to that of a beautiful stranger, became convulsed with outrage, and he, with a sense of shock, saw that he had committed the worst of sins.

He turned to run and heard the baying of the hounds in pursuit, gasping for breath as he ran through a grove of holm-oaks, then out into a clearing. He heard the voice of the goddess calling to her hounds, and knew he would die, to be torn apart for outraging the modesty of the virgin huntress.

His body seemed to float towards the face of the moon, which grew larger, so enveloping that he felt he could reach out and touch it. Soon he stood in a great stone circle, dwarfed by the sarsens. Around him was a sea of lumpen faces and flaming torches, the faces looking at him curiously with a mixture of adulation and pity. He felt them push him forward to where an old man in a long tunic of rough leather stood. The toothless ancient was speaking, but Aengus could not hear his voice, nor the noise of the crowd whose expectant looks were focused on him. He felt a weight on his head and lifted his arm to feel a crown of antlers. The people bowed to him, their mouths working in a noiseless chant as he was led forward to where the old man held his arm aloft, a knife of flint in his hand, its handle a carved snake, and he knew that the end of the year had arrived for the stag-king.

He approached the face of the moon again and saw its shape change and Bridget's face appear once more, but this time the face was full of compassion for him, compassion and pity and love for a lost one. Beyond her face the background was empty, utterly empty, totally void, and he realised the universe did not yet exist. He turned to Bridget's face in the moon and saw that she wept for him.

He reached for her and felt the warmth and closeness of her body as she embraced him, but at that moment he saw a tiny egg, a pinprick of light, a singularity, and as he looked it burst into a mighty fireworks of shooting flames, with fireballs hurtling in all directions, a mass of flame and explosions, waves of fire obliterating a black sky, enormous Catherine wheels of flame forming into spirals of gas and dust. He tried to close his eyes against the dazzling brilliance of the Creation but could not. The effects of the explosion continued, then stopped as abruptly as they had begun. When he looked again he saw the sun, its light a strange white. New stars appeared around him as the spirals became glowing balls of fire, then nebulae and stars and planets floated serenely, a universe of clockwork, Jupiter with its moons, Saturn with its rings, but when he looked again he saw that the universe, impelled by a strange force, was in motion, as the stars in the Andromeda galaxy were swiftly growing brighter, while the distant stars were fading to tiny points of light as they raced away from him. He ran after them, but felt his body grow heavier, felt himself sag under his own weight, forcing him to halt and to watch in horror as some of the stars disappeared down into a great spiralling pit that whirled like a black millstream. A strange conviction gripped him, then passed.

When he looked down at the earth he saw a plain of rock, pitted and fissured, with gas and smoke issuing from vents in its surface. He floated above it and saw parts of it dissolve as water seeped through the fissures. His vision seemed to have the power of a telescope as he saw an egg at the bottom of a hollow where there was a shallow pool of yellow liquid, and from it the tiniest insect fluttered from the water and took wing.

A cloud covered the moon, a black cloud. The light grew dimmer. The ground beneath him shook. He saw the face of Bridget again, felt her hands pulled from his neck by someone unseen, heard her cry to him in anguish. A Roman legion appeared, eagles high, marching through the Parthenon, then through the Library of Alexandria, tramp, tramp, tramp with the rhythm of a metronome, the people walking like slaves behind them until all of Europe and much of Asia marched at their heels. The Romans gave way to a procession of churchmen with crosses, emperors, kings and barons and vassals riding or marching behind them with swords and battle-axes, followed by an Inquisitor in his robes, all heading heedlessly into the black cloud until he could see them no longer.

The moon appeared to him once more, weeping for him, closer until he could touch it. He felt her tears wetting his face, but he was drifting again, the pain beginning to ease as he felt death draw near, and he saw Seth with his throat cut, a great gash of red, a dark woman wielding a long knife standing grimly over him. A golden-haired young man with a lyre, a strikingly beautiful youth, appeared, while from a blinding sunburst came a golden chariot in which rode a splendid god holding a white raven. They were followed by a tall, mystical figure that he recognised from a dream. As that image faded, the form of an old Greek with a long beard appeared on the sea wall of Syracuse and Aengus saw him bow to a goddess with a silver bow, saw her smile down at him, lovingly, but this time her face was different, a beautiful Minoan mask. The orb of the moon crowned her head like a halo.

He drifted again, searching for the moon, but found only a

waning lunar image which slowly dissolved into a pregnant woman with eyes of black ellipses, then into the face of a stone figure with an eye carved on its forehead. That merged with the face of Kate and she, too, looked down at him with compassion, knowing that he was near death, or perhaps beyond it.

He saw Silbury Hill with the moon riding above it, saw the moon stop in its path and the hill rise to meet it, then the orb came down to him again, great and luminous, and he felt its embrace, then its kisses, heard her calling to him with Bridget's voice and felt her kiss him again with Bridget's lips. He tried to rise, to respond to her love, and sank into darkness.

Narrative

The world was a sea of pain from which he tried to swim away. He lay helpless, floating, surprised because he knew he was dead, and that the dead could not feel. He considered this while the waves of pain came and went, and wondered what would happen if he tried to open his eyes. Sometimes he heard a rustling noise, and light footsteps, and felt something sharp inserted in his arm before his mind drifted again as the pain receded.

Sometimes he heard voices, hushed voices, whispers, and knew he was hallucinating when he recognised Bridget's soft tones. He was content to lie there when the pain left him from time to time, listening to her, knowing her presence was an illusion, slipping again into a pleasant dream where she held and kissed him, deciding that he would not open his eyes, that if he did his temporary, peaceful world would shatter and he would fall into a void of despair once more. Sometimes he left the sea of pain to crawl into a warm womb of comfort and drowsiness, but agony returned intermittently and he left the shelter and groaned as he felt arrows pierce his body. From time to time the voices grew louder, authoritative voices that called urgently for a consultant to be summoned or his drip to be refilled, then the pain would recede and he would drift into his pleasant dream once more.

The hot August sun that streamed through his window one morning, when the blinds in the room were partially drawn, surprised him into opening one eye. When he saw Bridget asleep in a chair by his bed he opened the other, gazing at her in astonishment, convinced he had passed into the other world for a moment, yet he noted the drips in his arm, the swathes of bandages across his chest and the lingering pain in his body. He lay quietly for a time, looking at her, increasingly aware that he was alive, yet not trusting his senses.

She stirred, and he asked her for the second time since he had met her, in a voice he did not recognise as his own: "Are you real?"

She rose to her feet, eyes wide. She smiled. "You've come back."

He stared at her. "I suppose I have."

"You have," she said, a strange look crossing her face. He saw that her eyes were hollower than ever. She looked very ill.

"I dreamt that you cried for me, Bridget, that you tried to kiss me back to life."

"We thought you were dead."

"I see," he said, feeling a sharp pain in his side.

"Your wounds are terrible," she said, the strange look returning. "You must sleep."

He slept, and this time he did not dream. When he woke, Bridget was gone, but he smelled her perfume and went back to sleep. When he woke again, she was by his bedside.

His voice was hoarse, almost a croak. "Can I ask you a terrible question?"

"If you must. Then you must rest."

"Is Seth dead?"

She drew back, her face in shock. "How did you know?"

"I saw him in a dream. His throat was cut, wasn't it?"

She nodded, mutely.

"Kate?"

She nodded again. "It was terrible. She cut him again and again."

He sat up, the pain gripping him. She tried to push him back on his pillows, but he resisted. "What's happened to her?"

"She disappeared. The police look for her everywhere. I dread them finding her."

He sank back on to his pillows and said faintly: "They won't. She's gone where no man can find her. And her dog?"

"Is gone, too."

He drifted for another day, down into various layers of unconsciousness, and hovered there, his mind in confusion, the pain increasing until the drugs drove it away. He was intensely aware that Bridget had abruptly left his bedside.

When he awoke he was not surprised to find that the room was empty. His spirits sank until all was blackness. He drifted in and out of sleep, his mind recoiling from the horror of Seth's death, Kate's sudden flight, and the last moments by Silbury Hill. Presently a nurse entered with a bowl of soup and he turned his face to the wall. Sid and Bill arrived to see him. He sent them away, ignoring the hurt he caused them. Bridget's mother and Simon came with flowers and he turned his face to the wall again, refusing to speak. The nurse remonstrated with him. He sent her away, shouting that he did not want visitors.

He slept fitfully for a week, his wounds a nagging pain that sank and rose, his spirits lower than they had ever been. Hope drained from him when he saw each day that Bridget was not by his bedside. His recovery halted and he began to sink. The surgeon who had saved him shook his head and said he had done what he could, that he needed the will to live if he was to recover. His patient, who ate nothing from the hospital kitchen and drank water sparingly, turned a haggard face to the wall once more.

His pulse weakened further and the doctors began to feed him intravenously, trying to revive him with different drugs, applying every test, knowing their patient was dying. Outside the hospital the country lay in an August heatwave. Inside the darkened room the man slowly gave up the will to live.

The doctors saw this happening, but did not give up their fight to save him. The day came when they said that the next twenty-four hours would be critical, yet shook their heads when they discussed it in private. That night, when the duty doctor stepped quietly from the room of the dying man, she signalled to the nurses to be prepared for the worst.

Aengus woke on the night they expected to be his last, hearing the distant hospital noises. A thin beam of moonlight cast a small wedge of light in the room. He lifted his head and looked around, the pain from his wounds subdued, and saw he was alone. When the door opened and a nurse entered, he lifted his head briefly. Life flickered in his eyes for a moment, then dimmed when he saw the face was not the one he hoped to see. His eyelids fell. While the nurse finished her tasks and left the room with a downcast head, he lay back and drifted, the thread of life barely pulsing, drowsiness overcoming him, all willpower gone, sensing that his next sleep would be a permanent one, and heard a voice that he had thought he would not hear again.

The Greek

Stranger, I asked your help and you responded, but do not sacrifice yourself. Atropos does not cut your life now, and you do not have that right. You have much to tell me. You must live that I may die. Tell me what you saw.

Narrative

The breeze had a hint of autumn, but the day was sunny and warm, the last of a seasonal hatch of daddy-longlegs was building on some of the pools, and the trout were active again after the heat of August when they lay dazed in the shade of the crowfoot. The season would end in a few weeks.

A covey of French partridge flew across the meadows to his left, chattering to him as they passed. Autumn was at hand. The hedges were full of blackberries and sloes. The swifts had left. When he had left hospital they had been plentiful, darting and wheeling in the heights until it was too dark to see. The swallows still swept the grasses of the water meadows, swooping and dipping, gathering the insects that would sustain them on their long flights over water and desert to another continent. Soon they would mass on the telephone wires, ready to leave. The milder winters would keep some of the chiffchaff and blackcap at home, but the other migrants would leave and the riverbank would wait for the equinoctial gales and for the leaves to fall.

He walked slowly down the river path, gingerly because his wounds had not fully healed, and saw a fisherman with dark wrap-around glasses, hat pulled low over his forehead, staring at something under Bull Bridge.

The fisherman saw him and beckoned. “There’s a big trout there. D’you see him?”

He had answered the questions the police had put to him, relating as little as possible of Kate, who was not to be found. On the previous evening he had walked past the place where Bridget had been held captive for two years. Seth's house was deserted, a place of horror, viewed by the locals with a mixture of dread and morbid curiosity. Rumour said it would be demolished and replaced. Weeds grew around its doorways and yard, most of the windows had been broken by the local youths, and the front door still hung drunkenly on broken hinges when workers from the estate boarded them up. A charm of bullfinches fed on the seeding thistles which had taken over the beds that Bridget had tended in her exile, and the rooks quarrelled in the wood above the abandoned house, long his nightly hiding place.

A big brown trout in perfect condition – a trout of five pounds or more, a wild Kennet greenback – swayed from side to side in the current, tail swinging gently, feeding on the nymphs that the stream brought down to him, occasionally darting to either side to take his food, never breaking the surface under the bridge.

"I can't get a fly up to him, to go over his nose," the fisherman grumbled, "and when I get one near him the current in the middle drags the fly."

"That's how he grew so large," grinned Aengus. "He's a wily old chap. He knows he's safe under the bridge. Or thinks he is."

"You think you can catch him? Have a go," said the fisherman, confident that the other would fail. Aengus hesitated, then took the rod, stripped line from the reel, shot a length of it using several false casts, and sent it arcing through the air once more, flicking the rod tip sharply up and back when he saw the leader turning over, forcing the artificial nymph to land with a tiny but definite splash, a foot downstream from the fish's tail. The trout heard the fall of food behind it, turned and seized the nymph. Aengus played the fish until he could bring it to the bank where he slipped the hook from its mouth. The trout, feelings ruffled, hid in the weedbed. "He'll be more careful next time," said Aengus.

He had moved back to his old cottage when he left hospital, his friends waiting for him in some force at the entrance, persuading him in his weakened state that he must be helped. His obstinacy had waned but he insisted on looking after himself. Bridget's mother, her face so drawn with worry and suffering that he was touched by it, had been among those at reception. He did not ask for her daughter and she did not mention her. He kept any emotion from his voice as he thanked her, refusing politely her offers of help. Sid's wife fed him for the first few days and would have done so indefinitely, but he hugged her and said he would cook for himself from then on.

He slept poorly, beginning to recall the events of the fateful night, glimpsing stray fragments of what he thought he had seen, the light of the Creation flashing to his brain while he winced at its ferocity and totality. Fragments of memories came to him in chaotic order in his weakened state, tumbling from his subconscious, the Orphic Egg of Creation, the Minoan figure of the goddess with the moon in a halo behind her head, the great march of history, and the recurring image of Bridget's face merging with the moon. He recalled the sensations of her light hands holding him, the cool touch of her lips, and sometimes he groaned aloud at his loss while the river flowed past his door and the willow sighed of remorseless change and impermanence.

When the sense of duty weighed too heavily he rose, remembering not to move too quickly because of his wounds, and tried to reassemble the fragments for his journal. It was late when he began to write.

The Statement of Aengus

Greek, I saw Creation. I saw that in the beginning there came matter, matter first, then life, and with that life the primitive Soul of Man was born. The first cell was a spontaneous creation of life from matter and energy, life in its simplest form, born directly of Nature, a germ or parasite, probably created in the primordial waters that sheltered such delicate atoms from the worst of the sun's unsheltered glare. It was our common ancestor. Everything that has lived or died has descended from it, a hundred million species in all, of which only a tenth have survived and changed to evolve down the Tree of Life, and it seems possible that the earth has its own Darwinian instinct to survive and evolve, to shelter its Life-child down the aeons from the cosmic forces that have destroyed the chances of life on its sister planets.

Matter itself was created at the beginning of time, from an infinite density, a monstrous explosion after the collapse of gravity, leaving an echo to be discovered more than thirteen billion years later, an echo captured as the hiss of radio waves from the edge of the universe. This was the echo of Creation, the missing evidence the scientists sought before they could prove by contradiction how the universe began. Darwin, a century or so before, had not the echo of Creation to guide him, only the life forms he saw around him or those preserved in rock, the fossils that suggested the age of the earth, incredulous at first as he realised how old life had to be for the process of selection to run its natural course down the ages. In his time the philosopher-churchmen said the earth was not more than five thousand years old.

Mendel's gene with its replication and mutation, its chains of nucleotides and codes that Crick and Watson brought to the light, gave us the chemistry that Darwin's natural philosophy could not.

The physicists have assembled their own Creation myth, piece by piece, retracing their steps frequently when the hypotheses crumpled. Most agree, however, that before that tiny point of tortured matter exploded, nothing existed, neither time, nor space, nor life of any kind. History began in that unimaginably short moment when the universe, unbounded yet finite, was created.

Your fellow philosophers Leucippus and Democritus of Abdera said, as you remarked, that everything is composed of atoms. They viewed these as the smallest items of matter, guessing at or speculating about their existence even though they could not see them. More than two millennia later Einstein looked into a cup and through the eye of his brain he saw them, billions of atoms in a single swallow. Scientists subsequently proved that all matter is composed of atoms, in almost unimaginable quantities, and that each is made up of a nucleus of protons and neutrons around which the electrons orbit. These atoms are so empty of matter that the human body in its essence has a volume smaller than a grain of sand. All is proportion, you said, and you were startlingly correct. All atoms of whatever element, from light to heavy, from helium to plutonium, carry the same number of electrons as they do protons. Matter seems as balanced as a lever in equilibrium, but the paradox is that inside the atom the behaviour of the tiniest particles is as wild and as wilful as a child-goddess, and man has had to turn to mathematics to model it.

Nothing seems final in physics. It is an infinite series of peaks and valleys. Climb one peak and another appears. Probably a new school of thinking will appear that says you have climbed the wrong peak. We have seen it all, and we will see it again – Thales, Plato, Aristotle, Ptolemy, Copernicus, Kepler, Newton, Einstein, Bohr, and Hawking – all great men but many of them humbled by a succeeding great mind that is humbled in turn – and each time that we progress, when we know more than we did, another peak looms across the valley. Illusions are shattered once more. A peak of science may be called Newtonian gravity, or relativity, quantum mechanics, the uncertainty principle, string theory, or many other names. Someone with a strange sense of humour picks an ugly word from Joyce to give us the quark as the smallest particle of matter that exists, while the scientists press on towards quantum gravity and a unified theory of everything, attempting to reconcile the physics of the tiniest particles with the behaviour and forces of the universe – the smallest with the largest – because only when that is achieved will we have something that approaches complete knowledge.

The geniuses among them found some years ago, when all seemed settled, particles smaller again than the atom, that the protons and neutrons of the atom could split into quarks, and that these particles with the ugly name were unpredictable and demonic with energy. Yet, again, that proportion that you saw in everything exists even in these indivisible particles, the very grains of matter, as every proton and neutron contains an equal number of them, proving that nature at its most fundamental, fizzing with packets of energy though it is, is not only proportional, but equally proportional, as the atom is.

These were the particles, the physicists say, that broke away from their mother atoms after the explosion of Creation and began to annihilate each other, filling the universe with radiation, a heat so terrible that it created fresh pairs of quarks, matter and antimatter, equal and opposite, identical twins entering the fresh cycle of destruction, transforming mass into energy until they finally returned to their mother atoms and the infant universe pressed on with its expansion and began to cool. A mere two hundred million years later the first stars were born, massed energy producing light, and three billion years on from there the stars clustered into the galaxies we recognise today because we see their light as we look back in time, not metaphorically, but literally.

The physicists continue with their search for a theory that will unite the largest with the smallest. Perhaps they will gain that knowledge, and perhaps then they will find that nature has baffled them again because another peak will appear to tantalise the next school and contradict the last. Light bends, time is not absolute but in unity with space, the universe is like a stretched sheet, warped or distorted by any object in it, the cosmos exploded from a pinprick of matter, the behaviour of an electron cannot be predicted, yet it seems that the more we know, the more peaks we find.

Yet you would sing to the scientists to keep climbing because we have a daemon inside called the unconscious that needs to know. That daemon will live until our sun burns out and Apollo dies, when the universe will live on without us, because we seek a kind of immortality through the discovery of eternal truths, as you did.

The scientists say our planet was born four thousand six hundred million years ago. It was born of whirling gas and dust and gravity, to become a boiling hell of rock and metal bombarded by meteors. A theory has it that one struck it, bounced, was attracted by the earth's gravity and slipped into orbit to become the moon, the bringer of time and the bringer of death, the shining light that died each month to be reborn, the life force of early mankind. It is also, as it happens, the gravitational consort of the earth. Without its steadying pull, say the scientists, our planet would roll like a ball at sea.

They say life began when the earth had spun on its axis for around seven hundred million years and the energy of the unfiltered sun probed the different types of matter, the proteins and nucleic acids and the water, like a great bird sitting on an egg to incubate it. Perhaps the meteors brought more essential chemicals from distant space to complete the mixture needed for life on our planet. In any case these and other matter fused in a unique chemistry to produce a phenomenon I think of as *Little Bang*, the creation of Life, the first cell, our common ancestor that would replicate into the earliest living beings on earth, the first to breathe, spontaneous life from non-life in a moment of creation that was grander than any biblical miracle, life that evolved to think about itself and wonder where it came from, to be aware of itself, to look through the circle of consciousness to what is beyond.

A profound irony is that the reality of the discoveries of today matches many of the myths of the ancients, and I find it particularly striking that science tells us that the chemistry of our bodies is identical to that of the earth three billion years ago. Somehow, perhaps because our chemical composition has not changed by as much as an atom, in spite of the evolution that has taken place since, inwardly man remembered that he came from earth, that she was his mother, and made the Great Goddess her symbol.

If the Pythagorean brothers associated Creation with a goddess, as I suspect you also did, that is probably the reason. Societies that are regarded as primitive, such as the Stone Age peoples, knew we came from the earth, and acknowledged it by quarrying from the earth's body the great stones that symbolised their ancestry and by placing them in a sacred circle that would bring Man into a communion with Nature and time. They worshipped the Great Goddess as the earth itself, a great womb, the mother and bringer of light and fertility, the bearer of life, and they reserved their worship for her into later times, leaving us without a reference to a father figure, retaining the mythical image of a goddess emerging from the early waters of the earth from whence Life came. Many of the Great Goddesses, whatever name they bore, seemed to have been born from that sea, Isis, Aphrodite, and Nammu of Sumer, among others, while Mary's name is the word for the sea itself.

Later, mankind seems to have realised that the sun impregnated the earth and that the earth brought forth the Tree of Life. We may have one such allegory of the marriage of sun and earth from our own, more recent mythology, after your time. In the Christian story of the virgin birth of Jesus, Mary, a figure in the tradition of the Great Goddess, including a chosen consort, conceives a son from a distant deity in the heavens, a parallel with the ancient vision of the distant union of earth and sun, and gives new life to the world, as earth itself gave birth to life from the sun.

The sun is our father, as the Egyptian priest shouted to you, and as mad Pharaoh Ikhnaton sang:

Thou shinest so beautifully on the horizon of heaven,
Thou living Sun, who created life.

The creation of physical life is as simple, and as complex, as that. It is simple because all great mysteries have simple explanations, like that for natural selection, and it is complex because the proportions – the combinations of numbers of different forms of matter and the amount of energy from the unfiltered sun that went into the creation of the first cell of life – were almost infinite in terms of possibilities, including the conditions of the time, which do not exist now. Such natural, spontaneous life could not happen today. It needed the conditions of a young earthly biosphere that lacked oxygen.

Life evolved much as Darwin said, but life also remembered what had gone before. Here is a proof. Our bodies, when under stress, unconsciously remember when oxygen was scarce, as it was when life began, and instinctively fall back on a metabolism developed by early bacteria, a memory programmed into all of us of the earth's early biosphere. If one such memory has lain within us since the Creation of life, it seems very probable there are many more.

Some of them, as I said, seem apparent through our mythologies. I am wary of any hypothesis that takes bites from this or that holy scripture because there is always a sentence or a phrase there that will support or destroy a point, but I think of a passage from that oldest of holy books, the *Rigveda*, written by an unknown poet – probably a seer or hermit in the deep northern forests of India, living centuries before Homer – who sang of the beginning, when

There was no death there, nor immortality,
No sun was there, dividing day from night

and of how wise men knew that the germ of *being* was in *not being*. I took little notice of this when I read it first, idly scanning Griffith's translation as I rested in the shade above the burning-ghats of the Ganges, but it resonates with me now, as it would have appealed to Darwin and Wallace and Mendel because of its startling similarity to the modern scientific explanation of how we began:

At first within the darkness veiled in darkness,
Chaos unknowable, the All lay hid.

And then:

Till straightway from the formless void made manifest
By the great power of heat was born that germ.

By the great power of heat was born that germ, the hermit-poet of the *Rigveda* chanted, so uniting the natural with the spiritual world, disdaining the dogma of later religions to sing of what the wise men knew in their hearts, that the heat from the fire of the sun fathered the first life and gave us the light of consciousness.

In all peoples and all religions, consciousness appears as the creation of light. Light, says Neumann, signals the birth of the conscious when man discovers a subjective reality, the ego is formed and the individual emerges, the unconscious still in darkness.

All light comes ultimately from heat or fire, and perhaps that is why fire is such an old divinity, worshipped by man while he was still part-ape, manifesting itself later as a fire goddess in many societies, as a sun god in others, a pyramid to the Greeks, a universal image retained by the evolving human spirit which clutched it for its psychic imagery as much as for its vitality.

Does our collective unconscious go further and contain the memory of our own evolution into different species, from that simple germ that was our common ancestor, and could this be an explanation for the theory of rebirth, the *metempsychosis* of Orpheus and Pythagoras, the *anamnesis* or soul-memory of Plato? Perhaps we carry the history of the universe in our innermost selves.

Narrative

The Indian summer continued to help his recovery. His walks grew longer. He returned from one of them to his cottage one evening to find Bridget's mother sitting on his porch. She rose as he stopped in mid-stride. "I have something to tell you, Aengus," she said quietly. Her face was gaunt and strained.

He sat heavily on the other chair, his wounds suddenly troubling him again. "You needn't have come, though I'm grateful," he said, keeping his voice even. She lifted her hand as he spoke, but he continued: "She's gone from me. I accept it."

She lowered her hand, a graceful mother figure still, and said: "That's not why I am here. That's very far from being the reason I came."

His legs felt weak suddenly. He sat on the other chair, his heart filled with dread. "Please tell me."

"She's been very ill, Aengus. Just like you."

Each word struck like an arrow. His voice was a croak. "Does she live?"

"Yes. She's better. She's very weak, but she'll recover."

Relief made him weak. "What happened?"

"She collapsed when she was told you would live. She came straight from the hospital to me and fell in my arms. She had a terrible fever. Her face was hot, burning. She was as weak as a baby." Her shoulders shook. She put her hands to her eyes, then resumed, her voice muffled. "I rushed her to the doctor who had her admitted to hospital straight away. She had viral pneumonia, with complications, not the least of which was the fact that she had no strength left. She had no energy left at all."

"She'd been to hell and back," he said, his voice shaking. "She hadn't eaten for weeks – months – and the strain of the last few weeks must have been terrible. Then she nursed me. She did everything to save me." He turned to her, guilt and remorse making him angry: "Why didn't you tell me?"

"She made me promise that I wouldn't. She thought you might have a relapse."

"I did, as it happens," he said grimly. "I thought she had shut me from her life."

"I know," she said. "But I did not tell her how sick you were. I thought it might finish her. I make no apology for that."

"I understand. May I see her?"

"She's in Sid's cottage. Come and see her tomorrow. Don't be too shocked at how she looks."

The Statement of Aengus

You were at peace with your Goddess and you will be at rest when I tell you all that I saw. I saw her light, and the meaning of what you saw in your image. Through the infinity of the circle you saw the mystery of Nature symbolised by the Goddess.

This was a mystery that troubled you as a geometer, one that had to be squared in time, and it was one very personal to you, although I think Callimachus saw much the same mythic image, but as a poet, using a different language to yours. You heard him sing of it and address her intimately as Nature herself, while you used your imagination as a mathematician to look through that mystery of Nature until you had your first sight of the vast cosmos in motion. The image was essential to your wholeness as an individual, and it impelled your shade to continue its restless search for a truth until you found it.

I saw also the anger of your Goddess, as Actaeon did, and saw how Artemis was interchangeable with Hecate as a dual goddess and why she was the most feared in the Olympian pantheon. The stag was sacred to Artemis. Twice in my dream I was a stag, or stag-king, once in the sacred grove of Artemis, and once at a Stone Age sacrifice, and I saw that I had become sacred to the Goddess so that I might understand the essential balance of the cosmos, that matter is not only mutually attracted, as you were the first to discover, but mutually dependent, as Nature is.

I saw you with the Goddess and by her side was a weapon that shone like a new moon. I understood then why you believed she had killed you.

You were correct. She had. You died from the silver bow of Artemis.

The explanation is in the *Odyssey*, where Homer describes Artemis and Apollo relieving older, sickening people 'with shafts that hurt not', releasing them from life before they begin to suffer. You were not killed for an act of *hubris*, as I suspect you feared you were, but from mercy. It was an act of kindness by the Goddess who told Atropos to cut your life line because she wished to shield you from what was to follow.

I saw Orpheus with his lyre, and saw what the seven strings symbolised to you, the power of man to magnify the forces of nature through knowledge, as you did through numbers to master the infinite, as Orpheus magnified the power of music, with its mathematical order, to avert destruction and death and to call on the Greeks to seek pure truths. Apollo rode beside him in his golden sun-chariot, with a raven the god had forgiven and made white again, the sacred bird he sent to protect me.

I saw Pythagoras, the mystic who attracted you in spite of yourself with his worship of numbers. Earlier, in a dream I had of him, I sensed that his real significance lay in his power to enchant others to follow him, though perhaps he, or those who built his myth, saw that numbers have divine powers in that they exist independently of us and they are eternal, and infinite, as is the number we now call *pi*. They symbolise order arising from the chaos of Creation. If we remove the characteristics of a group of objects their number will still remain, producing an objective order, as Jung saw. The scientists believe that number pre-dated man, and that it exists in the heredity of lower life (the crow family can count up to three). Perhaps the *tetractus* of Pythagoras was a primitive symbol of order that came to Greece at the time of Orpheus, and perhaps the Pythagoreans, unless we dismiss them as a meaningless cult, did not worship a triangle as such, but the order that lies within Nature, even as they failed to rationalise it.

Your instinct, and that of Plato before you, was that the cosmos has an order and that this order could be modelled by mathematical constructs. That has turned out to be startlingly correct. Without mathematics, there could be no physics. You introduced one into the other. Without physics we would know nothing of the universe, and would be ruled by superstition which is still present in my time, in even the most supposedly developed and civilised societies. You asked, if some numbers, however irrational or incommensurable or even transcendental they are, are indeed natural, what does this say about Nature? It says that Nature, however strangely it appears to behave, obeys physical laws that may only be described precisely through mathematics. A mathematical model of nature is therefore a natural model. The mathematician does not construct truths, any more than a physicist does. He discovers them, as you said, because they are there.

I saw you, too, at Syracuse and I thought of your death on the day it fell as the end of the Greek Heroic tradition. There was something of the spirit of Ulysses and Leonidas in you that would not have lived easily under Roman rule. The fall of the city was in itself a very important event in several different, sometimes unconnected ways. Amongst others, it was the beginning of the successful expansion of the Roman Empire into the great sea they called the Mediterranean, with Sicily becoming the first of the

Roman provinces.

When the cavalry of Scipio Africanus won the battle of Zama, Rome's rival was finished. Carthage had kept a balance of power with Rome and when it fell the Romans' conquests grew until they took Alexandria and the Egypt of the Ptolemies more than a hundred and fifty years later, to become more powerful until almost all of Europe and part of Asia lay at their feet. As this happened they professed a love of all things Greek, but they did not take up the greatest prize the Greeks possessed, the spirit of pure inquiry into the abstract for the sake of knowing.

The literature of the Greeks, and in particular the philosophies of the Stoic and Epicurean schools, appealed to the Roman mind, and influenced it strongly as a Graeco-Roman culture emerged, with its own philosophers – Epictetus the slave, Lucretius, Marcus Aurelius the Stoic Roman Emperor who wrote in Greek, Posidonius who taught Cicero, Plotinus who wrote a compelling interpretation of Plato's thoughts and founded what the scholars call Neoplatonism. Geometry, arithmetic, medicine and pure astronomy did not so appeal, and the Romans were generally content to leave the development of inquiry into the abstract to the mathematicians and the masters of other disciplines in Alexandria who continued to flourish under their rule. Perhaps they did not take these up because such disciplines had little tradition in Rome, or because they saw no use for them, or because Stoicism, the dominant philosophy of the Roman governing classes, was too rigid to provide the inspiration that surrounded you in Alexandria. Creative Greek mathematics, of course, did not die with you but continued to flourish for centuries, as did medicine and astronomy, but they did so in Alexandria rather than in Rome, the new world centre of influence and power to where the taxes and tributes of the expanding Republic, then the Empire, flowed from the provinces.

The cynical would say that Rome was to take its culture like a cloak from the Greeks, and that this began at Syracuse when Marcellus looted every altar and sculpture and took them to Rome where the citizens, seeing the works of Greece for themselves for the first time, decried them at first, then began to copy them, but the history of the world frequently consists of one civilisation absorbing some of the culture of another, and such a sweeping generalisation, popular with the more romantic historians at one time, does not hold. Rome absorbed much of Greek culture, but Greece also took much from the Mycenaeans, from Crete, from Babylonia and from Egypt, and was the richer for it.

The probing, independent curiosity of the Greek mind lasted well into the Roman era, particularly at Alexandria, while a young religion, to be chosen by Rome as one above all others to be that of the late empire, gradually encountered a body of Greek philosophy and was attracted by it. Persecuted Christians sought common philosophical ground with the works of the Classical thinkers to counter those who criticised them, and found it in successive schools of Platonism. They focused in particular on two of Plato's dialogues. One – *Timaeus* – dealt with Plato's cosmogony, his view of the relationship between the Creator and the Cosmos, another – *Parmenides* – with problems of Being and Identity. From these dialogues emerged approximately common beliefs with the followers of Christ. There were disagreements, too, of course, particularly over Plato's doctrine that the soul possesses an immortality independent of its creator, and reincarnation had to be sidestepped, but the early Christians were used to this, as they constantly argued over points of doctrine among themselves and knew how to search for compromise, as did the Platonists with the dynamics of their own philosophies. The interpretations of successive schools of much of Plato's thought on how the soul might be liberated to find a godlike state of perfection would enter Christianity, and a body of Greek philosophy fused with the teachings of the Gospels. Christianity had acquired a Classical tradition, and would do so again in the thirteenth century when St Thomas Aquinas adopted such parts of Aristotle as Christian doctrine could absorb.

The young Church seemed to pose little threat to independent thought. It struggled against persecution from without and with constant heresies and schisms from within, but it preached against capital punishment and torture, to some degree against slavery, and appealed for charity for the poor. Rome, finally attracted by its appeal to all and concerned to hold its Empire of the West against invaders, made it the state religion in AD 312 and later forbade all sacrifices to the old gods, officially shutting the pagan temples in 391, by which time Christianity had spread through the cities of the West under Roman rule and the Greek city-states finally vanished under a centralised bureaucracy. Christian doctrine continued to evolve through the break-up of the Western Empire as the churchmen debated whether war was ethical as a form of defence, an argument that we might contrast with that used centuries later for the Crusades against the Church's rising competitor, Islam. St Augustine, who reasoned that a just war was ethical on the grounds that those who desired peace must first love justice, went on to develop the doctrine of Original Sin some four hundred years after the death of Christ, without an obvious biblical foundation, and Western man from then on was told by his Church that his purpose in life was to redeem his soul through suffering, to have faith in the doctrines of the Church, hope in the next world, and to give charity to his fellow man. Augustine, the founder of Western Christianity and one of the most prolific writers ever on theology, believed the wisdom of Man to be worthless, as Man needed only God to illuminate his soul.

It seems easy to condemn him now, this towering theologian who took his doctrine of God from Plato and had such an influence on the West. He would not wish to see what I saw on that night, that his doctrines did not change the behaviour of man for the better. I watched the march of the Roman Empire and the rise of a proselytising church, the Christian crusades that sacked Christian Byzantium, traditional rival and enemy of the Latin Church, the wars that destroyed the tolerant and creative Moresque civilisation in Spain, the Inquisition in the name of a Church that in its youth had strongly condemned judicial torture and execution, yet perhaps Augustine, probably haunted by his own sins and deeply disturbed by the shocking violence of the disintegrating Roman Empire in the West and what he saw as the wretched state of mankind, genuinely thought, in his zeal to serve God, that man would lead a better life on this earth if he were to conduct it in fear of the next. Such knowledge that man would need to enrich him spiritually through his life in order that his soul might be redeemed lay in the Bible and the doctrines of the Church.

Perhaps it was as these doctrines permeated the West that the spirit of inquiry into the abstract, devoid of divine implications, diminished, or was viewed increasingly as a worthless currency when spirituality was meant to transcend all. Philosophy in the early mediaeval period in the West was to be mainly concerned with points of theology, strongly influenced by Augustine and Boethius and Christian Neoplatonism. The free spirit of the Greeks faded over successive centuries as the *polis* did, but the works of the moral philosophers, the poets, the medical men and the mathematicians, the works that survived outside Byzantium, were taken up and translated by those who had been viewed as being the fringe peoples of Hellenistic civilisation, the speakers of Syriac, Aramaic, Coptic, Hebrew, and Persian, and were embraced by the flourishing civilisation of Islam, particularly that of Baghdad in the ninth and tenth centuries when Arab and Persian and Jewish philosophers treated such knowledge not as history but as a living corpus of work that they would develop as philosophers in their own manner, possibly using the logic of Aristotle to demonstrate that Islam encouraged them to learn science and explore its meaning. The resulting body of knowledge, complete with the discovery of algebra and the works of the Islamic philosophers, was to return to the West and transform it through the Renaissance from the fourteenth century onwards when, once again, the quest for pure knowledge could co-exist with religion, and two centuries later Raphael would be commissioned by the Pope, seemingly without raising an eyebrow, to paint a fresco for his library in the sacred citadel of Western Christendom that depicted an Islamic philosopher in the same scene as Plato and Aristotle. Perhaps by then the Church felt secure in viewing the work of the great philosophers as something that culminated in its own theology.

Contrast the Augustinian relationship with the divine to your own. I think you belonged to a tradition in which the gods in the night sky, or the chthonic deities on earth or beneath it, were always present in a familiar sense, often close by, in groves and dells and valleys, on mountain tops, by springs and wells and in rivers, in the dwellings of mortals and in the houses of the gods themselves, the temples. The relationship of the Greek with his gods was therefore intimate, and in that way similar to his relationship with his city-state or *polis*. Provided he sacrificed and propitiated and honoured them, man lived with his gods with the ease he lived with his family, and if he forgot them during the day he was reminded of them at night when moon and stars emerged. Gods to you, in that sense, were part of nature, just as religion was natural, and man did not have to suffer in order to be redeemed because he did not need redemption.

Perhaps the easy relationship with the gods began to decline in the West when Aristotle split the cosmos, stating that earth and moon together were separate from the heavens, and were made of different stuff, corruptible matter below, above it the *aether* of the heavens, the fifth or quintessential element. As such this might be regarded as a typical Aristotelian hypothesis, worthy of dialogue with successor philosophers, but as time went on a philosophical barrier seemed to descend between the ideas of heaven and earth, and man's old intimate relationship with the divine changed its character. This probably had little effect by your time, but the division probably widened further when the pantheon of the old gods was replaced with the Trinity, to enter the doctrines of the Christian Church and become a theological division, with the Christian God assumed by some Church thinkers into the role of Aristotle's Unmoved Mover, the force that made the cosmos revolve around the earth, with heaven and earth artificially separated by a wall of religious doctrine. Such thinking did not long survive the arrival of the telescope in Galileo's time, but its spiritual offshoot did, and Western man has yet to regain what he has lost.

Narrative

She was shockingly thin. He saw her wrists first as she held out her arms to him, slim bones thinly coated in flesh. He hugged her, emotion flooding him as the barriers fell and he sensed her gladness. He kissed the great hollow eyes, then the high, fine cheekbones that stood out even more strongly than before. He pulled her head to his shoulder and held her, then lifted his head back to look at her. He thought that she was more beautiful than ever.

"Come with me," he said.

The Statement of Aengus

I saw a tiny item of matter, a singularity as today's scientists call it, saw it compressed into an unbearable density and knew I witnessed the birth of the universe when it abruptly expanded and exploded. That was the moment of Creation fourteen billion years ago, and before it nothing existed, even time, as I said.

It was the first fire festival – fire everywhere, massive units of matter forming from spirals of gas and dust as gravity began its work and matter attracted other matter. The stars were born, great nuclear furnaces like our sun, many of them far larger, hundreds of billions of them as the universe began to form. One or more of them, supernovae, at least ten time the size of our sun, exploded, scattering the matter that gathered into the suns and planets of the second generation that gave us birth. From those supernovae came the stellar atoms of which we are made.

Man looks through the telescopes in space beyond the haze of our atmosphere, the telescopes that probe the galaxies of deep space, and sees the most distant stars as they were billions of years ago because that is how long their light has taken to reach us. It was on that night at Silbury Hill that I began to appreciate the proportions of the universe, how many grains of sand it would take to fill it, that it takes the sun two hundred and fifty million years to orbit our own galaxy, and that our galaxy is one of many billions. I saw our own little solar system, with our earth below me, perched in an obscure corner of our galaxy, and thought how small we were, and how insignificant, until I saw an egg, the symbol of life on earth, and began to realise our real significance, that we survive to live, that we are sentient beings that seek to know, to reach out again into the cosmos, and know it as we would know ourselves.

The gods have left Olympus and we search for the thunder of Zeus in the distant galaxies, among the fiery spirals and the gas clouds. There, five thousand and more new stars are born every hour, every day, turning matter into heat and light, while others die in the expanding progression of the universe which has its own life force, its own natural selection, its own invisible hand, its own mysteries.

I saw the stars racing away from me into the distance and pursued them but I grew heavier as I approached the speed of light, as Einstein said would happen, and I saw the force of gravity pulling brilliant stars into great black pits and extinguishing them as the sea would snuff a candle. As I watched the most distant stars accelerating away from me, propelled by a force the scientists call dark energy which they do not understand and cannot explain, I saw that the universe was still expanding even though it had then existed for fourteen billion years or so, and may expand forever. The answer to your unspoken question about Creation is that it has not ended, but continues. The universe is still in creation, and so are we.

As the stars raced away from me that night a conviction gripped me that I touched for a moment the outer influence of a truth that lies so deeply within our unconscious that it may never emerge, something that is beyond the power of the science of today to absorb and explain, a truth beyond our intelligence. It left me with the conviction that we and our universe are almost infinitely more complex than we can imagine.

Narrative

A soft autumn breeze ruffled the willows as they walked by the river.

"I failed you," she said.

He stopped. "No. You saved me."

"I returned to you in time," she said, "but when he beat and threatened me I abandoned you. Don't mistake me – I wasn't afraid for myself. My fear was that he would kill you both."

She held him away. "Please let me finish. You have to know this."

Her face, pale as parchment, filled with pain. "I did something terrible then. I told myself I despised you."

She panted a little as she hurried on: "I tried to expel you from my life, to put you beyond Seth, but also beyond me. I tried very hard, and for a time I succeeded. When I sent Kate with that message, I believed that I meant every word."

She paused, then resumed before he could interrupt: "I rejected your help, and when I did so I tried to reject you, too. I did so to survive, to keep my faith with her, and to drive you away. I forced myself to think of you as a useless dreamer who lived through his books, an escapist, a failure in everything, even in his marriage."

She lowered her eyes, then raised them again to look directly into his. "I can't hide that, particularly from myself. It fills me with shame. When I found it didn't work, that I kept thinking of you, that in my heart I felt very deeply for you, I was torn apart. I saw only your goodness then, every tenderness, how true you were, and the realisation almost killed me. I stopped eating or sleeping. I gave up hope, but the shame stayed. I could barely face you when you brought my mother back to me. She had to force me to see you."

"You were very ill." His voice was hoarse.

"Yes, because I was crushed by guilt. Even in the hospital I couldn't find the courage to tell you."

"You told me once to blame *him*," he said, unable to speak Seth's name. "I say the same to you now." He paused: "I say also what I've wanted to say to you many times. I live for you."

She looked at him, read the truth, and touched his face. "And I for you," she said. The breeze shivered the willows and the past had a lighter hue, draining each of them of the sense of dread that had hung over them like a perpetual winter, to leave the only question for him that remained.

"I have to know what happened that night," he said.

"At Silbury?"

"Yes. I couldn't bring myself to ask the others. My mind screamed when I began to think of it. Now we must speak of it, to finish it." He paused. "All I see is you and Kate."

"It was she who saved us."

"Are you strong enough to tell me?"

A coot came quietly out of the reeds on the opposite bank. It eyed them, then paddled upstream.

"She went to your cottage first, and found it empty. Then she went to Sid's," said Bridget.

"But you had left by then."

"No, Aengus, I had not." She faced him, and reached up to his face again. "I had already abandoned you once. I kept seeing the look of hurt on your face when I left you, when you looked so haggard and vulnerable, so alone. I couldn't leave here until I had told you everything."

"Bridget!"

"My mother was safe. Simon took her to London. I told her I would join her when I knew you'd left. They didn't like it, but I forced them."

She stopped him before he could speak, and went on: "They

left. Later, when I had finally gathered the courage to go to you, Kate arrived, banging on the door, her hair all over the place. There was a green blaze in her eyes. Wild! She was shouting: 'Hurry! Hurry, or he will die!' You're crushing me, Aengus!"

"I'm sorry," he said, relaxing his hold.

"We have time now." She kissed him gently, and pleasanter memories of that night flooded him. "Let me finish. We asked her to explain, but she shouted: 'Never mind that! Get your car! I'll explain as we go.' Sid thought it was a trick, but I knew she was trying to save you from Seth. All we had was Sid's van. Kate sat in the front shouting: "Left! Right! Now faster! Hurry!" Bill and I were in the back with the dog which growled at him throughout. He thought his end had come. That was a terrible journey."

She told him how Kate had heard Seth ordering his men to search everywhere, after the police had left. "One of his men looked for you on the road and drove past you when you were getting on the bus. He rang back on his mobile phone, and Kate heard Seth shouting at him to follow you. He asked the man if there was a girl with you, and howled with rage when he was told you were alone. Then he heard that you were walking from Marlborough. He told his men to go straight there. They lost you for a while, and he went into another rage. Then they saw you going in the direction of Avebury, but lost you again. Seth left with his mobile phone, shouting into it for someone to meet him at Avebury. Kate came to us as soon as he left. She said you'd be at Silbury. We went straight there, and ran from the car park. Kate was the first to see you and Seth."

"What did she do?" He found himself shaking.

She had unleashed the dog, pointing to Seth. It ran at him, straight for his throat. "Sid saw it and told me. Seth threw up his arm. The dog seized it and wouldn't let go. Seth was roaring with fear or rage, or both. Kate came up to him and told him to go, that she would deal with him later for killing you. We got there as Seth left. He was certain you were dead." She faltered, panting a little.

"Stop now," he said.

"No, I'll finish."

"Did he see you?"

"No, I'm sure he didn't. Bill and Sid were in front, shielding me."

"Good men."

"I found you soaking in blood. Terrible moment! Kate took your pulse and said you were alive, but only just. We ripped bits from our clothes to stop the blood. Kate told Bill to run down to the main road and call an ambulance, but Sid had a mobile phone and rang them. I held you and wept."

"I thought it was a dream," he said.

"Then the ambulance came. It was probably very quick, but it seemed to take forever. Three of us got in with you, but Kate said she wanted Sid's van. He gave her the keys." She paused. "I never saw her again."

Bridget looked at him and finished: "Next day the police received an anonymous call telling them that Seth was at his house, dead. The call was from a woman."

He gripped her hand and thought of Kate, of an unearthly dignity in the depths of her green eyes, of the darkness about her that seemed to belong to another world, and of a power that had sent an aboriginal soul into the blackness. The nature of man, he thought, however civilised he felt he had become, had not changed through the ages, as capable of unselfish love or of brutal acts still as he had been since he first stood.

The Book of Aengus

This is my last night by the river, and I write the last entry in my journal. One day I may show this book to her, but not yet. She's still very weak. I go to her tomorrow. Then after a time perhaps we will go away.

I have only a little to add. We know that we have a purpose, ignoring the philosophers and putting the divine to one side without trying to dismiss or distort it. All life has a basic code written into our cells, a memory that instructs us to survive, to evolve and to replicate or reproduce, to think and therefore to act as individuals. This last power lies deep, suppressed by many of us in our desire to seek comfort from an inherited commonalty of customs and the wafer of civilisation, but it is there nonetheless, unquenchable, and it will surface whenever it can. That is what I think of as the Soul of Man, which is born of matter and yet carries an independent, eternal spirit. It is the essential, irreducible part of each of us that survives, to be passed down the genetic chain, and it is part of our very identity as individuals, to make each of us unique. It is what Hardy called

The eternal thing in man,
That heeds no call to die.

Everything I saw or dreamt on that night makes me suspect that our unconscious is as deep and as mysterious as the universe itself. If *pi* says something about Nature, perhaps that is it. Its innate randomness may be a glimpse into the immense complexity of ourselves and of the universe. We are physically part of that universe, not apart *from* it, and in that sense we *are* the cosmos itself, something the ancients instinctively knew and which became more opaque to us until we turned away from it, to reject the truth because it appeared so primitive, and embrace in its place the doctrines and superstitions developed by Man. I know also that part of our fate is bound up in that remorseless progression of change and impermanence that has existed since its beginning when the first particle of matter was created, constant inconstant change, perpetual mysteries that we must unravel as we go, the solutions to some buried deeply within us. The rest of our fate lies with us. The future is not an immutable thing, as the past is, something already decided, waiting for us to flow into it. Anything can happen. I find that a glorious truth.

We take the strands of our life that we cannot control and give them to the Fates to spin and measure and cut. How they do so is out of our hands, but the freedom to choose how we act lies within us, to take our own paths, to believe in what we choose to believe, to possess an indestructible spirit. Even as Man burned witches and heretics and books, that spirit survived.

One other thing I know. Imperfect as we are, we carry no sin with us into this world or into any other, except those we commit that diminish us as beings. Instead we carry a purpose, to think. That I learned from the Greek.

Narrative

He continued to sit when he had finished, listening to the sounds of his last night by the riverbank. A great doubt gradually entered his soul. Had he built his own myth of the Greek and allowed it to dominate his unconscious self, to the extent that the entire episode was an elaborate hallucination? For a time he sat while he agonised, until the memory of the Mediterranean voice, with its strong, musical timbre, came back to him, as on the first night when the dog fox had barked as it guided the shade of the Greek, the wind had dropped to nothing, frost had bound the ground like rock and he had sought his bed.

He thought of the visits, always when there was a moon, always when he lay between sleeping and waking, when the resonance of the introduction brought him to life, all attention – or so he had thought until then. Perhaps, he thought after consideration, he had been overwrought, susceptible to visions and fantasies, having a dream he dared not share with anyone in case they thought him to be deranged, and so created a mythology of his own.

Yet he had always considered himself to be well balanced, even at the worst of times. He recalled other tales of strange phenomena, of people who heard voices from the past and poets who saw visions, of the belief in a parallel universe. He thought of his own vision of Seth lying with his throat cut, of Kate who had seemed to read his thoughts as easily as her own, and of holy men he had listened to in India and the Middle East, civilised and cultured minds who believed devoutly in reincarnation and rebirth and who communicated easily with djinns and spirits and spoke of their beliefs in the most matter-of-fact way.

It was the voice of the Greek that he remembered when he was most troubled by doubt. Even as he told himself that it mattered only to him, and to no other, whether the visits were real, the voice returned to the aural memory as if it still spoke to him, and he rose with an easier mind and went to bed, to sleep until the autumn sun woke him at dawn. When he stepped outside the old moon still lingered faintly in the morning sky. He saw fresh marks in the earth beside the porch in the shape of a circle, and he knew that his visitor would not return.

THE END